Born in the UK, **Becky Wicks**  wanderlust from an early age. S all over the world, from London to Dubai, Sydney, Bali, NYC and Amsterdam. She's written for the likes of *GQ*, *Hello!*, *Fabulous* and *Time Out*, a host of YA romance, plus three travel memoirs—*Burqalicious, Balilicious* and *Latinalicious* (HarperCollins, Australia). Now she blends travel with romance for Mills & Boon and loves every minute! Tweet her @bex_wicks and subscribe at beckywicks.com.

Louisa Heaton lives on Hayling Island, Hampshire, with her husband, four children and a small zoo. She has worked in various roles in the health industry—most recently four years as a Community First Responder, answering 999 calls. When not writing Louisa enjoys other creative pursuits, including reading, quilting and patchwork—usually instead of the things she *ought* to be doing!

WHITE CHRISTMAS WITH HER MILLIONAIRE DOC

BECKY WICKS

A GP WORTH STAYING FOR

LOUISA HEATON

MILLS & BOON

First Published in Great Britain 2021
by Mills & Boon, an imprint of HarperCollins*Publishers* Ltd,
1 London Bridge Street, London, SE1 9GF

www.harpercollins.co.uk

HarperCollins*Publishers*
1st Floor, Watermarque Building,
Ringsend Road, Dublin 4, Ireland

White Christmas with Her Millionaire Doc © 2021 by Becky Wicks

A GP Worth Staying For © 2021 by Louisa Heaton

ISBN: 978-0-263-29783-6

11/21

MIX
Paper from
responsible sources
FSC® C007454

WHITE CHRISTMAS WITH HER MILLIONAIRE DOC

BECKY WICKS

MILLS & BOON

Dedicated to my parents, Liz and Ray,
who always gave me magical Christmases as a child.
Much love, xxx

CHAPTER ONE

JAX CLAYBORN DROPPED to the wooden bench in the ski lodge and pulled off his mask. Balancing the phone on his shoulder, he slid out of his boots. 'Talk to me.'

'The report came in from Gallatin County twenty minutes ago. A male in his fifties was riding his mountain bike alone when he was attacked.'

Dr Fenway's voice was grave from the medical clinic at Base. 'You sure it was a grizzly?' Jax tossed the boots into the locker with his jacket and mask. 'It's only just the start of November—they're supposed to be hibernating.'

'Something must have happened to lure it out. Mike found the victim by the side of the road.'

'How big was it?' Jax knew Mike, one of the rangers. They sometimes skied together. He knew every local within fifty miles of their small Montana town.

'The bear? The guy said it was damn near eight feet tall, and it almost clawed his arm off. I know you have to get to the airport, but we thought you should hear it from us first.'

Jax snapped the padlock shut on his well-used locker and made for the door. He was running late for the airport already, but flights never arrived on time around here anyway.

He contemplated a grizzly on the rampage as the chair-lift juddered with him down the mountainside. The crisp winter air had been cleansing his lungs on a rare morning off. He'd been making a mental note of all the things he'd have to do for the Christmas season's locum—a certain Ophelia Lavelle. A fitting name for an ER doctor arriving so close to the festive holidays, he thought. His son, Cody, had been the one to inform him that the name had Greek origins and meant 'helper'.

His new helper was thirty-three, so ten years his junior—not that it mattered. She was board-certified in family medicine, came from a line of doctors with a trusted family practice to their name in Brooklyn Heights, and her enthusiasm for the two-month role had been welcome in her interview a month ago. It was near-on impossible to get talented doctors to come and work all the way out here in winter.

Still, she'd probably never dealt with a grizzly bear attack in the concrete jungle she called home. He sincerely hoped she wouldn't have to here either.

His father, Abe, was calling. Right away his mind went to Cody...something happening to Cody. *Please, no.*

'A grizzly bear, Jax? At this time of year?' Abe sounded flummoxed. News travelled fast in these parts.

'It was probably confused and hungry,' he said in relief. His son was clearly safe, as he always was in his grandfather's care. 'I'm sure it's a one-off attack, but we can't be too careful. Mike will let the school know if he hasn't already. Did Cody get to class OK?'

'He's fine. He even asked if he could have a coffee for the ride.'

Jax snorted. 'Coffee? He's nine!'

'Anything to be just like his dad, you know that. Are you on your way to the airport for this new...what's her name?'

'Ophelia.' Jax shook his head at the thought of Cody asking for coffee. 'Almost. The powder was too good this morning, and I lost track of time.'

'My offer still stands to collect her myself.'

'I know, and I appreciate it, but I always pick the staff up, you know that.'

'It's your call.'

The ski base swept into view at the bottom of the slopes. Jax was grateful beyond words for how his father had chosen to spend his retirement years, sharing the care of his grandson. Jax wouldn't have coped with Cody on his own after Juno died, not with his duties piling up like snowdrifts on top of his mountain of grief.

It was five years ago he'd started as Chief of Ski Patrol at the only on-mountain resource for residents and vacationers for miles around. He was a qualified physician and the role was something that had seemed to evolve naturally, born from his love and knowledge of the mountain. This would be the third year running he'd brought people in for the Mountain Medicine Programme. Training the rescue volunteers for their Outdoor Emergency Care certificates out in the field in the run-up to Christmas helped channel his experience and always gave him a new sense of purpose. It helped to fill the long dark weeks, and made him feel as if he was at least doing *something* to ensure that what happened to Juno wouldn't ever happen to anyone else.

A new lot of students would be here soon, which gave himself and the team a week to show Ophelia the ropes before they arrived.

He thought of the luxury cabin the staff had picked out for her. She'd like the view, for sure. They had more than enough space at Clayborn Creek to house everyone. Better to fill the place with action and laughter over the

Christmas period than sink back into grief again over the missing piece—his late wife, Juno. Juno had loved Christmas more than anyone. He celebrated it for Cody now. Everything here was for Cody.

'Thanks for doing the school run, Dad,' he said as his toes hit the snow at the ski base. 'I'll take over soon as I get back, let you hit the Christmas store in peace.'

'Did you tell Ophelia about the full-time role yet?' Abe sounded hopeful, and Jax sighed. His father, a retired orthopaedic surgeon, was looking forward to Carson, their oldest physician's impending retirement next spring. Probably more than Carson was. The two men had been friends for decades. Abe was already planning their summer fishing trips, and new animal-tracking routes for the kids to explore with them next winter.

'I haven't told her that, Dad. You know I don't advertise full-time positions right off the bat. It scares them off. It would probably scare Carson too. He doesn't like to think about retiring, it makes him feel old.'

'He should feel lucky to be old. Some people don't get that far.'

They were both silent for a moment, thinking of Juno, no doubt. Abe had adored Juno, everyone had. No one had seen it coming, the sudden end to 'Jax and Juno', least of all him. They'd been the enviable couple others aspired to be like, he a medic, she an artist, different in every way but somehow aligned in everything that mattered. They'd been married almost eight blissful years before Juno's accident. He'd lost his mother, Kay, to colon cancer three years before that; it was just the men left now, from three generations. Himself, his father and Cody.

This woman, Ophelia, might be a tough-as-nails New Yorker, with or without any grizzly bear experience, he thought, watching the snow build in the distant clouds, but in order for him to offer anyone a full-time position on his mountain, they would have to prove their worth. They would ultimately become part of their family out here.

'Small-town life isn't for everyone, Dad, you know that. How many locums have we had in the past who've just disappeared as soon as they could? Anyone can take a full-time position and then hate it here and leave us in the lurch. We don't need someone like that around here. We're a team. We're a family.'

He could almost hear his father roll his eyes. 'You need to at least try and let new people in, son.'

Jax jumped from the ski lift and raised a hand at Melanie on the snowplough as he headed for the parking lot, keeping mute in the face of antagonism. He was doing just fine, now. At least that was what he told himself most days when the loneliness crept in.

'Stay indoors, Dad. Keep an eye out for that bear, OK?' He sighed, then hung up. For some reason, he felt a little nervous about picking up Ophelia. Her pretty, angular face and sleek, ebony-black hair had stuck with him ever since her video interview, but there had been something else about her, lingering in the silent moments during their call. Something he hadn't been able to put his finger on. Something intriguing. He hoped she'd enjoy the little welcome gift, already waiting for her in the truck.

The direct flight to Bozeman from New York was only four and a half hours. Ophelia Lavelle had distracted herself from the rattling windows and seat-back trays by counting thirteen men with snap-button Western shirts and blue jeans.

It was already glaringly apparent that people from

Montana, and *in* Montana, dressed nothing like they did in New York. A glacial lake appeared below, aqua, white and blue. It took her breath away. There were icebergs too—melted jagged chunks like ice cubes in a blue martini. A steady white waterfall frozen in motion, a giant herd of deer, or antelope. Something was cantering zigzags along a snowy trail. Wow.

The sheer scale and dazzling beauty were like an art museum, created by nature, she thought. Ponderosa pine cover, prairies and snowy peaks were all part of her new home, at least until the end of the year. Dr Jax Clayborn had said his land had been in the family for five generations—some thirty thousand acres of rivers, forests and open grassy plains. On that land, his staff manned almost six thousand acres of skiable terrain, and she'd be working at the medical clinic at Base, out on the snow for the first time without her brother, Ant.

She focused on the cantering herd below them, tracing the silver arrow on the cord around her neck with her fingers. Ant was everywhere, still, even after more than a year.

'It's been fifteen months, you need a change of scene,' her father, Dr Marvin Lavelle, had told her this morning outside Terminal One at JFK. 'We can discuss the partnership properly when you're back. Just make sure you come back, OK?'

Her father had been teasing her, of course, but she could tell he was less enthusiastic about her departure than he was letting on. Deep down, he was probably afraid she wouldn't come back. Things hadn't exactly been the same, since Ant died.

But here she was, the epitome of fake it till you make it. Taking on a job somewhere crazy before life got less than adventurous. Her future was already set at the family practice, Health Dimensions, in Brooklyn Heights, and she was determined to build up a sense of excitement for it while she was away. It was a great opportunity, a full-time position in the close-knit community she and Ant had grown up in. Some of the kids she'd seen in the waiting room with their parents back then would be *her* patients soon. The salary was impressive, at last she'd be striking out on her own, and she'd be extending a line of legendary physicians...

She sighed at the window, staring at the mountainous peaks. It sounded so good on paper but, somehow, it just didn't feel right for her any more.

Health Dimensions had been her grandfather's practice and he had been the top recommended physician in their zip code. Then her dad took over, changed the name to something more snazzy and promised that some day she and her younger brother, Ant, would join him. *'Captains at the helm of the family ship,'* he'd said.

Marvin had made it sound like such a grand dream. For years she had ploughed through med school, a fellowship, seventeen-hour night shifts and worse, working to achieve that dream, working to be good enough to impress her father. She'd spent years believing that taking the role with Ant and her father was her dream, and not his.

Still, she wouldn't let him down, not now Ant was gone. In her father's eyes she was the only remaining heir to the practice, and he'd lost his only son.

So did you, she thought suddenly. *You lost your only son too, along with your brother.*

The reminders always came when she wasn't expecting them. She'd thought about the baby she'd miscarried shortly after Ant's death for almost the whole flight, maybe because this was the furthest she'd been from the wreath of candles she'd added to her brother's grave as a memorial to her lost baby. She was further than she'd ever been from either of them now.

Her hand went to her belly. How would he have looked by now, if he'd made it to full term? She'd always imagined it had been a *he*. She'd called him Little Bean.

The nightmares used to make her howl, all of it at once. She'd lost both Ant and the baby a thousand times over in her dreams. She'd drifted through her days back then like a ghost around her fiancé, Sanjay, thinking if she'd paid more attention to Ant's ever-growing anti-social habits she might have noticed sooner that he liked a little more than a drink at the end of a long day. Her younger brother had always been more prone to wild nights out than her, but she'd thought he'd stopped all that to focus on med school. She should have checked up on him more frequently, asked him who he was with when he stopped picking up his phone at night. Maybe if she had, he wouldn't have OD'd in a drunken haze, and she wouldn't have been such a bad host for a baby.

What was Sanjay doing now? Did he even know she'd left New York? Gazing out of the window, she swore she saw his face in a cloud.

Sanjay had blamed their sudden split on her needing 'proper care' after losing the baby, but Ophelia knew he'd been looking for a way out of their engagement long before Ant's death and the pregnancy. They were just too different, he a jazz musician in three different bands, she a medical professional. Their schedules had never aligned and neither had their priorities. The day he'd broken off the engagement she'd felt a strange kind of relief, as if losing the baby had saved them both somehow from compounding their mistakes.

She had never told anyone that, though. It would have

sounded as though she hadn't wanted to be a mother. She *had* wanted to be a mother, more than anything. Not like Sanjay. She'd always known his religious father had pressed him into proposing to her when she fell pregnant, but she'd still said yes. And he'd definitely been relieved when the miscarriage let him off the hook. No more Little Bean. No more engagement. No more Sanjay.

'Just go clear your head, find your peace,' her sweet, enduring mother, Cecelia, had said only this morning. *'And come back rested and ready. Your father can't wait for you to start this new chapter of our lives together. Ant would have been so proud of you.'*

Ophelia couldn't help but wonder if things would really be so peaceful where she was headed. She would still be surrounded by emergencies after all. She tried to picture the Clayborns. She knew from her research they were doctors and environmentalists, and local heroes.

She forgot her worries, suddenly, recalling Jax's low, gravelly Montana drawl. It had come to her unsummoned from time to time since her interview with him and Dr Carson Fenway. Before that she'd never had a conversation with anyone who had a set of vintage skis mounted on the wall behind him, but it wasn't just the décor of their million-dollar ski lodge that had stuck with her.

Jax was undeniably handsome. She recalled the way her words had caught in her throat, in spite of her cool demeanour, when she'd first logged on to the call and seen his piercing eyes, the slight dimple in his stubbled chin, the way his broad shoulders and big, strong arms filled out his sweater. He'd been consummately professional, and so had she, but there had been a moment at the end of their conversation, she swore, when they'd met each other's eyes for a handful of long, silent seconds, seemingly just taking one another in, acknowledging a sudden shared shift in normality. It had left her feeling quite flustered for the rest of the day.

Thinking twice about the real-life Jax waiting for her at the airport, she hastily checked her mascara hadn't streaked mid-flight. They were almost at Bozeman.

CHAPTER TWO

THE TEENAGE GIRL at the coffee cart in the airport took seven minutes to make her latte. It was almost amusing, watching how she did it with such pride, at a pace that wouldn't much rival a snail's. She'd be fired for being that slow in Brooklyn.

'Dr Lavelle?'

Ophelia spun around at the voice, and promptly had her words snatched away by her sudden intake of breath. He was much taller than she'd expected.

'Jax Clayborn,' she managed, adjusting her hat and matching scarf. His dark almond eyes studied her with the same depth and intensity that had stirred her up in their video call, but it reached inside her now on a whole different level. Jax was as striking as she remembered, but he was all about presence too, commanding the attention of everyone who passed, especially the women.

'It's so nice of you to come pick me up.' She watched him remove one glove, then took his bare outstretched hand. *Big,* she noted, *like my father's hands.*

Tufts of his dark hair flicked outwards from his beanie hat, and when he clamped his palm firmly to hers, something told her she should wake up now and pay attention. It was the strangest feeling. It totally caught her off guard as he studied her eyes up close.

'Shall we?' he said. He pushed a stuffed bear into her hands and then bent to pick up her suitcase.

'What's this?' she asked, turning it over in amusement.

'A welcome gift. Everyone gets one.'

The air was freezing outside. A dark cloud promised more snow. Craggy white-peaked mountains framed Jax like a moving painting as he carried her case towards a huge white truck in the parking lot. Damn, he looked good in those jeans, she thought. He was even seriously pulling off a flannel shirt under his ski jacket—not an easy task for any man.

He caught her eye as he flipped the trunk on the shiny four-wheel drive. 'Again, my apologies for being late, Doctor. I was out on the slopes, then I got the call about the bear attack…'

'A bear attack?' she echoed.

Jax lifted her suitcase into the back as if it were nothing but a feather and flicked the red scarf she'd tied around the suitcase handles. 'I wouldn't go waving this colour around here. Unless you want to attract that bear right into your room.'

She swallowed. 'I'll remember that.'

The first step up into the truck was almost knee height. Ophelia placed the stuffed bear on the seat first and tried to climb in gracefully. Jax hovered behind her to make sure she wouldn't fall—he was probably fighting the instinct to make a comment about her rather impractical high-heeled boots, she thought.

'I like the heated seats, nice touch,' she told him, self-awareness making her hot.

'I liked them too, last time I broke down in a minus-thirty snowstorm,' he remarked.

When he dropped to the leather seat behind the wheel

and closed the door, she still hadn't managed to fasten her seat belt.

'Need help with that?'

She stopped breathing as the smooth sleeve of his padded winter coat slid a millimetre above her lap. His fingers made a split-second job of clinking the chunky seat belt into place, and there it was. His wedding ring. Disappointment surprised her, but there was something in Jax's expression as he spotted her clocking the ring that stunned her into looking away.

She knew that kind of emotional pain very well indeed. A bad divorce?

No, he'd likely have taken the ring off if that was it. It was more than that, something worse.

Something had happened to his wife.

'So, where did you say this bear attack took place?' she asked when the silence during the drive got too heavy. He didn't seem too chatty. She was aware of his every slight movement in the driver's seat, the way his eyes scanned the mirrors and the roadsides intently, as if he was expecting a grizzly to pounce at any moment.

'Guy got unlucky out on the Trout Camp Trail… Eagle Peaks Mountain Club community, slightly northwest of Sunset Range.'

The geographical information meant nothing to her. She was still thrown from seeing that look in his eyes, the same one she'd seen all too often in the mirror… She'd know the face of grief on anyone. What had happened to his wife? Jax was older than her, maybe by a decade, but being widowed at his age would be grossly unfair, not to mention tough.

'Seems like it was a pretty surprise encounter,' Jax continued. 'Pretty is probably the wrong word for it. Poor guy had to crawl up to the road after the bear left him for dead.'

She winced. 'That's…terrible.'

'The ranger up there found him. He thought it was weird that some guy was taking a break, just sitting in the snow. Then he saw the blood everywhere. Guy couldn't speak but he scratched out "BEAR" in the snow with a stick.'

Ophelia put a hand to her mouth. 'God, I can't even…'

'The fire department brought him to us, but we sent him to Willow Crest Trauma. The lacerations were beyond our team's capabilities to fix on-site. He had puncture wounds on his face and all down his back. Slashes all up his arms and stomach, and you don't want to know what those claws can do to a man's—'

'I'm pretty sure I can imagine.' Ophelia hoped she didn't look as horrified as she felt. She thought she'd seen it all in New York, but never a bear attack. 'I can't imagine it, actually,' she admitted. 'It's just too horrendous.' What sort of job had she walked into?

'Don't worry, this kind of thing is very rare. I didn't mean to scare you. I'll give you a tour if you like, show you where *not* to go. Are you going to open that, by the way?'

Ophelia held the stuffed bear up to face her. 'This?'

'Open it.'

Obediently she dug inside the bear's belly to find a clasp. Pulling out the aerosol container inside, she held it up over the dash. 'Bear spray. Are you serious?'

'If you need it, start from the feet, right up to the head. And if that doesn't work…' He reached across her knees again, and she caught a whiff of his scent, no cologne, something primal and musky that was all his. It left her breathing in expectantly, wanting more. Pulling the glove compartment open, he revealed loose rags, a few sticks of gum…and a gun.

Ophelia froze. 'Have you ever actually used that?'

He seemed to contemplate her question. 'I wouldn't carry it if I didn't need it.'

'So, you have, then.'

He snapped the compartment shut, and his almond eyes narrowed behind the wheel. 'We're not at the top of the food chain out here, Ophelia. No matter what happens, we all respect that. But we always shoot as a warning, never to kill. I can teach you how to use a gun for protection.'

'I probably won't take you up on that.'

'As you wish.'

When she looked at him, he was smiling faintly, as if she amused him. He'd probably laugh out loud if she mentioned her own attempts at self-defence, the taekwondo classes in an old gym hall in Brooklyn that she'd given up on after only three weeks. She shuffled in her seat. How was he affecting her like this?

'So, Dr Lavelle, you must love the winter, huh, coming all the way out here?'

'I like this new opportunity you're all giving me,' she said carefully. 'Call me Ophelia. Or Ophie. Or…' She trailed off. The name Fia still got stuck in her throat.

Jax flicked a lever that made his windshield wipers work overtime. Thick snowflakes were fluttering on the edge of a blizzard that had come out of nowhere. 'How many names do you have?' he asked.

'My brother was the only one who called me Fia,' she told him as her hand went to the silver arrow—Ant's Celtic talisman. It hadn't left her neck since the day of the funeral.

'*Was?*'

'He died.'

Jax drew one side of his lip between his teeth. He stared at the road and his next words were heavy, as if he'd had to drag them from the bottom of a deep well. 'It never goes away, does it? The feeling, like you've lost a part of yourself too. It's always there deep down. You can't run from it, Ophelia. It follows you.'

The baritone of his voice seemed to reverberate through her bones, and she felt trapped suddenly. She dug her nails into the bear. It wouldn't do to get emotional.

'How long ago did he pass?' he asked.

'Fifteen months,' she managed, shifting her gaze to the window. She couldn't even mention losing Little Bean too; it was too much to think about right now.

'I'm sorry that happened, Ophelia.' He paused, eyes still fixed on the road. 'I lost my wife, Juno, four years ago.'

Her next breath stuck in her throat. So she'd been right. 'I'm sorry to hear that, Jax,' she heard herself saying.

In the next instant she was scolding herself for being glad that he was single. That was a terrible thing to think, and besides, not all single men were available, especially not after losing a wife. Would he tell her how it happened, if she asked? she wondered, before deciding that it definitely was not the right time to be baring all their secrets. They drove the rest of the way in silence.

CHAPTER THREE

It had taken all of twenty minutes to cross the snow-fields from the grand entrance to Clayborn Creek to the inlet of guest cabins in a snowy enclave, next to a forest of Douglas fir. Lamps lined the pathways. At night, closer to Christmas, they'd illuminate the towering trees and several outhouses with fairy lights in rainbow colours—she'd seen it in photos already and the thought sent a flash of excitement straight through her.

In the distance Ophelia could see the ski lifts juddering up the mountain of Sunset Slopes. The medical centre Jax called Base would be somewhere over there. Her breath caught as she glimpsed the main house, where Jax lived. It was more like a mansion built from red timber and giant logs. The roof sloped to six or seven feet above the ground, like a fairy-story house on a grander scale. The snow clung to the tiles and windowsills, and lights flickered in the windows.

She longed to know suddenly who else lived there, how many rooms it had…whether Jax kept the memories of his wife alive inside. He hadn't mentioned her again. But she hadn't mentioned Ant either. It made her feel anxious getting that close to the very topics she'd come here to avoid.

The bed in her cosy cabin was a beautiful four-poster

with pillars constructed from thin, full-sized tree trunks. A couple of hours after arriving, as she sat gazing out at the snowflakes, she couldn't help thinking how her home for the next two months would be perfect, if she hadn't been warned about the grizzly bear on the prowl.

It was a world away from her childhood bedroom anyway.

Moving back to her parents' place from Chinatown after her break-up with Sanjay had been a blur. The whole of the last year had been a blur, slowly crawling out of the hole of grief and resuming her regular existence. Except it had never gone back to normal. People had tiptoed around her at work. She'd focused on the bullet wounds and the car-crushed limbs in the ER, but the whispers had been constant in the background: *'She lost her brother, and a baby, and then her fiancé left her...just imagine, the poor thing.'*

She'd adjusted to a new kind of isolation in crowds, until it had started following her home. Alone she'd felt like a failure on every front. The miscarriage had brought her and her mother much closer, though. She really should call her, she thought, and let her know she'd arrived safely...

A knock on the door.

Ophelia hopped from the bed to the sheepskin rug on the floor. 'Who is it?' she cried, making a grab for the bear spray on the way to the door.

'It's just me. Jax.'

The sight of the handsome, broad-shouldered Jax against the backdrop of Montana winter pines was enough to make her blink, as though she were waking from a dream.

'If you think a grizzly will knock on your door before

it goes for the jugular, you're mistaken.' He smirked from the doorway, gesturing to the can.

'Very funny,' she said, tossing it to the bed, flustered and embarrassed that he probably thought she was out of her depth. She tried to imagine Jax in New York and couldn't. Already he seemed to belong right here, and only here, like a vital element of the wild she'd stumbled into unprepared.

Jax was wearing a puffed sleeveless vest over a thick-knit burgundy sweater, and the same jeans tucked into black boots with red laces. 'You left this in my truck.'

'Oh, thanks, I hadn't noticed.' She took the red scarf that had been tied to her suitcase handle.

Jostling the snow from his hat with one hand, he peered around her slightly. In a shaft of sunlight she noticed the salt and pepper flecks across his shadowed jaw that only made him look sexier. 'How's the unpacking going?'

Ophelia stepped aside, allowing him to see the open suitcase on the bed, still full. 'I guess I got distracted by the view,' she said truthfully, cursing the underwear she now realised was on full display, along with a pile of cables and charging equipment. Several of the items she'd packed screamed 'city' rather than 'wilderness', she thought with an internal groan, spotting a cropped jogging top and wondering again if he thought her amusing, if he regretted offering her the job.

'I don't seem to have Wi-Fi in here,' she told him quickly.

'No Wi-Fi in the rooms, I'm afraid. 4G should work?' Jax seemed more than a little distracted now. He kept glancing round the side of the wrap-around porch behind the door and she seized the chance to sweep her clothing into a pile that hid her bras and lacy knickers, and a black bikini she'd last worn at a fancy spa in the Catskills.

'Most people like to connect with nature instead, while they're here. If you do need the other kind of connection, we provide that over in the lodge.'

'OK… Well, I guess I can connect my laptop to my phone…'

'Such a city girl,' he quipped. 'Cody, what are you *doing*?'

'Cody?' Ophelia stepped past him barefoot in the doorway, then found herself letting out a laugh. A little boy, no more than eight or nine, was standing at ground level below her porch decking, placing a row of snowballs on the deck, one after the other.

'These are for you, in case you need to throw them at the wolves,' he announced, gesturing to his handiwork in huge blue padded gloves.

'Cody, don't scare her by mentioning the wolves.' Jax snickered. Ophelia crossed her arms, amused by them both.

'Well, thank you very much. It's good to know you've got my back,' she told the kid with a smile. She was aware of Jax close beside her, watching Cody roll another snowball in his gloves. This was his son. She knew it without Jax saying a word. Cody's soft features were those of a younger Jax: he had the same almond eyes, the same high cheekbones and the same slight dimple in the cleft of his chin.

Her heart went out to him suddenly. Cody had lost his mother. She didn't know how, but now Jax's loss took on a whole other meaning. This family must have been devastated.

'I'm Ophelia,' she said, holding up a hand at the boy. 'And I should probably warn you, I'm a snowball-fighting champion from New York. That's mostly why I came here, you know.'

Jax raised an eyebrow under his hat. A smile played on his lips just for her, and as their gazes met she felt the same jolt of adrenaline she'd felt in the truck on the way here.

'Do New Yorkers wear high heels when they engage in these snowball-fighting activities? Or *any* kind of shoes?' he teased, motioning with his chin to her bare feet.

'You're on fire today, Doctor,' she shot back, and this time his eyes smiled along with his mouth.

Thud.

A snowball hit the porch just by her bare toes. Jax stepped in front of her and took another hit to the front of his denimed thigh. 'Cody, that's enough!'

'It's OK.' She laughed as Cody made to dart off into the trees. Jax was careful to shake the wet snow off away from her doorway, and she felt flushed, feeling his eyes on her painted toes and all the way up to the neckline of her cashmere sweater.

'I should put some boots on and get outside, you're right,' she said quickly. 'Do you guys want to walk me to the lodge?'

'Dad usually watches Cody after school, but he didn't want any distractions in the Christmas store today,' Jax explained, putting her coffee down in front of her. He took the stool next to hers, careful not to brush her leg with his knees. Already her sophisticated perfume and subtle make-up had him all riled up, though he'd never show it. 'He's gone to get the lights already. He likes to jack this place up like Disneyland at this time of year.'

'That's what I came here for. New York City does nothing for Christmas,' Ophelia deadpanned, and he watched the lights catch in her sleek black hair as she took in the lodge. The look on her face had him rippling with pride. It was as if she'd never seen anything like it before.

The twenty-foot-high river-rock wood-burning fireplace, the vaulted ceiling with bulging log-truss beams, the antique bar and rustic willow furniture draped with sheepskin—he'd sourced it all himself. A few stragglers were playing cards, reading books, nursing beers or gazing idly out over the snow that blanketed the slopes.

'Wait till the Christmas Eve party. It's the talk of the town,' he said. 'Last year, Abe—that's my dad—had the great idea of making up one of the horses to look like Rudolph. He set up a little stall in that corner. Cody rode it out around the tables, throwing candy canes at everyone.'

'That sounds amazing!'

'It was pretty impressive, till the fake red nose fell off on the floor and Mirabel Freeman—that's one of Cody's teachers—slipped on it and broke her glasses.'

Ophelia chuckled. 'Never a dull moment. And Cody is great.' She turned to look at the child who was dropping coins into the pinball machine over by the kitchen door. 'He looks so much like you.'

'He's my world,' Jax heard himself saying, almost under his breath. Ophelia didn't know it, but his son had Juno's smile. He was all he had left of her…except the music room, still locked up with all her stuff in it.

Ophelia's features hovered on sympathy for a moment and he straightened up. He didn't need that. Not from anyone, especially not this woman, who he'd be working with very closely for the next two months. She had come here knowing nothing about Juno's existence, let alone her tragic death. It was refreshing, having someone new around, someone who didn't know how he'd fallen, broken, and clawed his way back up in the aftermath like an injured mountain lion clinging to a cliff edge. It never got easier, acting the part of happy Jax in a crowd, while somehow still feeling completely alone.

He watched as Ophelia lowered her face to the level of the glass on the bar, as if she were studying a science experiment. She was strangely bewitching. She'd probably been a man magnet in New York with a smile like that, and hair like…that. They didn't get glamorous women like her around here too often. He wondered absently if she'd brought her hair straighteners with her. They didn't have much occasion for styled hair round here, not when you had to live in a hat.

'This smells different,' she observed.

'I'll bet you've never had a cold-smoked coffee before.'

'You're right about that.'

'Dad makes it right here. We smoke the beans in a closed room off the basement for up to fourteen hours. It infuses the flavour of the firewood right into the beans—there's nothing else like it outside of Montana.'

'I can tell you're very proud of it.' She was teasing him.

'Damn right.'

'I could get into this.' She closed her eyes and breathed in what he knew was twenty years of the Creek's love and labour. The perfect blend of coffee bean. 'It's unique,' he said, noting the heart shape of her glossy top lip. 'People miss this when they leave. You don't know it yet, but so will you.'

'Your father lives here too?' she asked.

'Up in the main house with me and Cody. Just the three of us now.'

She gave me that look again over her drink—the one that was jarring in the way it unsettled him. His hands went to adjust his hat. 'Cody will inherit this place one day,' he explained. 'He deserves a childhood here at the Creek like I had, even after what happened to his mother. He's been through a lot, but he's a tough kid. This place will make him a man.'

'Like it did you?' Ophelia's intelligent green eyes surveyed him over her coffee, causing a stir somewhere inside him he hurried to try and ignore.

'My father too.' He signalled to Hunter for peanuts. 'Abe Clayborn was the best orthopaedic surgeon in Bozeman. He still sticks his nose in more than he should now he's retired, but so does everyone around here. They love to talk.'

'Is that right?' Ophelia swished the ice in her cup as if she were judging it for melting. Would she keep up the make-up? Her perfume and fancy sweaters? No, Jax would bet a year's earnings she'd be bare-faced with ice-frozen eyelashes soon, too busy to look in the mirror. But she'd still be the most beautiful woman for miles. Her eyes were the kind of green he'd only seen in spring, the colour of creeping juniper first thing in the morning.

She was definitely an exotic fish out of water here, he thought.

'So…all of this is yours? This place must have quite a history.' She gestured around them and he noticed her necklace now—a Celtic pendant in the shape of an arrow. He'd spent some time studying Scottish history. Cody was fascinated by tribes from all over the world; they had books of them in the music room Jax never went into.

'My great-great-grandfather rolled up here without a dime in his pocket,' he said, resisting the urge to touch the arrow at her throat. 'He earned his keep on a cattle farm and bought two thousand acres. Grew the rest out himself to thirty thousand acres and made himself a legend and a fortune, but that wasn't enough for him. He was also the first around here to train as a medical doctor, and one of the first to work with the tribes on sustainable agriculture. He started the Clayborn Trust, buying up the ranches, kicking out the cattle and opening up the land to bison, wolves and even grizzly bears.'

'You still do that now?'

'Of course.' He caught another whiff of her enticing perfume as she crossed her legs his way in her too-new jeans.

'Sounds a little different from how our family practice got started in Brooklyn Heights,' she said, and he noticed her demeanour immediately change, as though just mentioning home or her family made her uncomfortable. Now that he knew about her brother's passing, he couldn't help wondering if she was trying to escape those haunting memories back home. Was there anything else she was running away from, all the way out here?

'I can't imagine growing out twenty-eight thousand acres anywhere these days,' she continued. 'There isn't any room left. Sanjay and I were saving for an apartment to buy together on the Lower East Side, in Manhattan, but they were pretty much all the size of that pinball machine over there.'

'Sanjay?' Jax tried to ignore the twinge of discomfort at hearing her mention the name of another guy.

'My fiancé.'

'You're engaged to a guy in New York?' He was irritated suddenly. Jealousy? It couldn't be jealousy. He hadn't felt anything for anyone since Juno; he hadn't even entertained the thought.

'I *was* engaged.' She pushed her glass away slowly. 'Our relationship kind of fell apart after Ant died. It was a number of things, really.'

'Dad, look!' Cody was ramming his hands against the whirring pinball machine, shrieking over the coins dropping. The moment for asking more about Ophelia's brother, and her ex, and the other things he was tempted to ask her about, was gone.

It wasn't the time or place anyway, he thought. Hunter was slicing lemons at the bar, glancing between them. Jax introduced them and told Hunter with his eyes not to push it. Hunter had known him when he was with Juno; he'd been working here almost six years.

He listened to their small talk, and Juno seemed to fade more and more in his head until she was gone and he was thinking about Ophelia's past in New York instead.

So, she'd been engaged. That wasn't so hard to believe. Ophelia was smart. She was also a very attractive and educated woman. He recognised the hole she was trying to get out of, the grief that probably still consumed her underneath her aura of confidence. He could see that in her like looking in a mirror.

He'd seen the black bikini with her underwear on her bed too. She'd probably enjoy the hot tub here. Why could he not stop thinking about that?

'This coffee is…wow,' she enthused, breaking into his thoughts as Hunter left to take a restaurant reservation. 'And this whole place… Jax…it's incredible.'

'Well, I'm glad you like it,' he said. 'Is the Wi-Fi here to your satisfaction?'

She nodded. 'I was able to contact my parents. They worry, you know.'

'You're thirty-three,' he reminded her, pulling his vibrating phone from his pocket. Then he kicked himself. They were probably worried about her because they'd already lost a son.

'New York isn't too far away,' he added quickly. 'I have a plane, in case of emergencies.'

'So you said at my interview. I just told them I'd arrived safely. I didn't even tell them about the bear.'

'Probably for the best,' he said, swiping the phone screen to accept the call and putting it to his ear. He listened intently for a few seconds, feeling her watching him.

'We need to go,' he announced abruptly. 'Emergency.' He pulled a pile of loose change for Cody from his pocket. 'Cody, stay right here with Hunter.'

Jax helped Ophelia with her scarf as Cody scooped the loose change up and darted back to the pinball machine. 'Ever ridden a snowmobile before?'

'Snowmobile?'

'Yes, it's an all-terrain utility vehicle that actually requires a lot of physical strength to operate, given its inherent manoeuvrability, acceleration and—'

'Yes, thank you, I know what it is,' she said from the folds of her scarf. Her voice held a hint of impertinence that made him smile. 'I've just never ridden one for work.'

'Looks like your job on the mountain starts now, city girl,' he said, ushering her out into the snow.

CHAPTER FOUR

'It's a pretty tight squeeze, but I've done it before.' Jax veered sharply left on the uphill slope and her hands went to clutch his middle on impulse. 'You're OK, I do this every day.' His gloved hand landed like a steel protective device over her thigh behind him, but he didn't realise she was laughing.

'This is amazing,' she gushed. 'I've actually never ridden a snowmobile before at all!'

Ophelia hoped the woman who'd taken a tumble on the icy slope wasn't too badly hurt as they drove, with Jax not taking his eyes off the horizon. 'This is nothing. I'll have to show you what this thing can really do another time. If you trust me.'

'I trust you,' she yelled over the engine, pressing a hand to the top of her hat to stop it flying away. She did trust him, at least she wanted to; there was probably no one better to be out on this mountain with than a man like him.

'Hold on to my sides more tightly, if it's too bumpy,' he called back, and she obliged, aware of the closeness and her heartbeat that hadn't stopped thudding too quickly since the journey from the airport. 'Loop them fully around my waist, if it's easier,' he instructed. 'I don't bite.'

At that she wrapped her arms fully around his middle, pressing her cheek to his back over his thick winter jacket as he gathered speed and the snow churned beneath them. *Who the hell is this man?* she thought to herself, feeling every nerve in her body set on fire.

Jax was making a circle around their patient now at the scene of the accident, his boots three inches deep in the snow. He was holding the woman's pink ski helmet between his hands. Ophelia fought the vicious wind from using her lashing hair to blind her. The top of the mountain was clouding over and they had to assess the situation quickly.

The twenty-seven-year-old female snowboarder was hunched over in a neon pink-and-purple ski suit, and she looked as if she was having trouble standing up. The instructor was holding her up to the left, and another guy was on her right with his mouth to his radio. Ophelia was at her side in two seconds. 'I'm Ophelia. I'm here to help you. What's your name?'

'Amanda. My tail bone hurts the worst.' Amanda pressed a hand to her lower back and Ophelia pulled it away gently.

'We'll get you checked out, don't worry.'

Jax had signalled for someone to clear the crowds. 'Your tail bone or your hip?' he said to Amanda now. Ophelia felt his hand on her own back to steady her as another gust of wind blew in from nowhere. She appreciated how he was looking after her too, in the simplest ways—not that she hadn't been trained for emergencies, but this was a whole different world.

'No, it's right on my tail bone. I didn't have the strength to go on. So I stopped right here.'

'You did the right thing. Stay as still as you can.'

Jax urged Ophelia back with him to the snowmobile. He was careful to stand in front of her at all times, she noticed now, to protect her from the direct wind. 'Her spinal cord could be damaged,' he said, and she nodded. Of course, she knew that.

'What can I do?'

'Help me,' he said. He was already unstrapping a spinal board from the back of the snowmobile.

Adrenaline, cold and excitement overrode the fact that it was much harder to move in bulky cold-weather wear, at high altitude, than in a hospital at ground level. People had started to stare and some were even taking photos, which Jax blocked whenever he caught a prying lens. 'Give us some room, please! Ophelia, the board looks good, let's get her on to the snowmobile...'

He was orderly and authoritative and she felt a strange sense of calm at his side, in spite of the hostile environment. This was Jax's land after all. Together they strapped Amanda to the spinal board for transport.

'Where are we going?' Amanda looked panicked as the snow picked up around them.

'We're taking you to Base, but we need to keep you as still as possible,' Jax said, and Ophelia wondered if he could feel his cheeks at all, because she couldn't feel hers. 'Ophelia and Dr Carson will check you out properly at the medical centre, OK? It isn't far.'

'My legs are tingling.' Amanda was clutching Ophelia's hand now. Ophelia met Jax's narrowed eyes over the board. He knew as well as she did that this was a sign of possible neurological damage. They had to get to Base as fast as possible.

'Isn't it faster to go down that way?' She pointed, calling out to him. They were speeding downwards now, but she'd seen another path they could have taken. It had fewer trees, fewer people, and with Amanda strapped tightly to the back on a sledge, it had looked a lot safer too.

'We don't go that way.' Jax navigated carefully around two kids on snowboards and hit the horn to clear the skiers in front of him. She gripped the dash as he worked the accelerator and brakes simultaneously, appreciating how he was being careful not to judder too much with Amanda on the back.

'Why not?'

'We just don't,' he said, and his tone was as cold as the snow. 'It's dangerous. Off limits, didn't you see the sign?'

'No, we were going too fast...'

'Well, there's a sign. I make sure there's *always* a sign.'

Ophelia bit her tongue until Base came into view. He sounded almost angry and she couldn't think why. Maybe he was worried for Amanda. This was perilous work, and she admired the team and Jax even more now, though she suspected he'd taken her out here with him as some kind of test, to see what she could handle. Her role was supposed to be based in the medical centre, while up here was *his* terrain.

After they'd unloaded her, Amanda took her full attention for the next hour, but Ophelia was aware of Jax as he moved around her, left and came back inside, everywhere at once. He was careful not to meet her eyes... so she couldn't ask him anything else, perhaps?

It seemed as though she'd affected him with her questions, and she had the distinct impression that there was something about that other path that had really darkened his mood.

'The X-rays are clear, vitals are normal, there's no permanent damage, but her tail bone is badly bruised. Amanda will probably find walking painful tomorrow. Better tell her to stay off the snowboard.' Ophelia handed the file to Dr Carson Fenway, pleased that her first case had been nothing too serious.

'You can tell her yourself, if you like,' Carson said. 'It's good to have you on board, Dr Lavelle.'

'Well, I can't say it's anything like what I'm used to, Doctor. But that's not necessarily a bad thing. And it's Ophelia.'

Carson was a sturdily built, thoughtful-looking six-tyish man with deep crow's feet around kind eyes and a calm half-smile. He was certainly older than any medical professional she'd seen still working in Manhattan, but she didn't doubt he was capable of doing the job—in fact, he looked like part of the furniture. The way Jax had issued a brotherly pat to his shoulder when they'd walked in suggested he'd been on the team a long time, and that they were friends.

But she couldn't exactly see him racing up a mountain with Jax, if duty called. Then again, what did she know? People in Montana seemed to be made of stronger stuff even than New Yorkers, if Jax was anything to go by.

She issued Amanda with some meds to ease the pain, and, once she'd helped her outside where a friend was waiting, she took a moment to familiarise herself with the layout of the medical centre, located at the base of Sunset Slopes.

It was small, constructed of timber like most of the buildings on the mountain, but well equipped. She wouldn't do it an injustice by saying it was cosy, it was still a medical facility, but it had a distinct positive vibe, thanks to the posters of cheery skiers around the walls.

She noticed Jax was chatting to the ski instructor who'd followed them back to Base, and she caught his gaze momentarily. Something churned in her belly at the eye contact, finally.

'So I guess you heard there's a grizzly roaming around?' Carson handed her a lanyard with her name on it. 'I told Jax while you were with Amanda, the guy they choppered out this morning is stable. He has more stitches than skin in some places, but he'll live. Next person might not be so lucky. Be careful out there, will you?'

Ophelia slipped the lanyard over her head with a sense of pride she hadn't expected to feel so soon, and adjusted Ant's necklace around it, so it wouldn't be tangled. Was Carson testing her too? To see how she'd react to danger? 'I'm sure everyone here is on the lookout, and prepared,' she said coolly. 'As am I.'

'There's no way to prepare for a bear that decides it wants a hug,' Jax interjected, stepping to her side. The mood shifted. The faint scent of his musky manliness mingled with the snow and disinfected floors and set her nerves on edge as much as his words.

There was something about him that could easily have had her visibly flustered if she hadn't been well-trained to keep her cool in challenging situations. She couldn't stop thinking about how he'd avoided that other, much faster path down the mountain. She wouldn't have thought much of it had he not acted so strangely.

'I have my bear spray, I'll be fine,' she said now, although in truth she'd been so distracted by Jax and Cody that she'd left it in her cabin.

'Sure you don't want to join me for a shooting lesson?' Jax cocked an eyebrow, and she shook her head.

'Quite sure.' What was with the folks in these parts? If a guy mentioned guns this often in New York he'd be on a suspect list for a murder within minutes.

'I'll give you that tour I promised tomorrow, show you where's safe to go and where isn't.'

'Like that other path, down the mountain?' She faced Jax head-on now. 'Why wasn't *that* safe? It's just off the beginner's hill, medium level, right, not even a black diamond run? Do you think the bear might be hiding out there?'

Silence.

Jax's jaw seemed to shift this way and that. He pulled his damp hat back down over his head and she watched as tufts sprang defiantly from the sides again, as if his hair had its own idea about how it wanted to arrange itself. Carson eyed the floor tiles for a split second too long, before the men exchanged a look she couldn't read.

'What?' She narrowed her eyes between them. 'If I've said something wrong, you need to tell me. Is there something not safe about that slope that I should know about?'

Silence.

'Guys? If I'm going to be working here it's imperative you tell me…'

'I don't know where the bear is. It's probably long gone by now. But there's no real trail on that run for snowmobiles or skiers, not for anything or anyone. It's a no-go zone. People know to stay away, and so should you.'

Jax's tone held the same gruff warning note as before. Ophelia almost challenged him anyway, but he pulled his phone from his shirt pocket to signal the end of the conversation. 'I'll tell Hunter we're on the way back for Cody. We should go while we still have some daylight.'

Ophelia crossed her arms. 'I'd like to stay a while longer with Dr Fenway, if that's OK, Carson? I have a few questions before my shift tomorrow.'

She locked eyes with Jax. For a second Carson disappeared and it was just the two of them, embroiled in a kind of silent battle. An icy chill seemed to rush in out of nowhere and envelop them. 'As you wish,' Jax grunted, eventually. 'Carson, make sure she gets safely back to the cabin.'

'I don't need anyone's help,' she said quickly. She knew she probably sounded affronted, but she was, so why hide it? 'You don't have to worry about me, Jax.'

Something like irritation and helplessness flared around his almond irises. His jaw did that thing again, as if he was grinding his teeth, but he bowed his head almost submissively and made his exit out into the snow without another word.

She turned to Carson as the sound of the snowmobile faded into the twilight. Her heart was pounding in her throat. 'What was all that about?'

Carson looked awkward to say the least. She felt bad for putting him on the spot, but she had a right to know about any potential danger, didn't she? 'There was another path down the mountain. He wouldn't take it on the snowmobile...'

'He doesn't let anyone take it, Ophelia,' Carson said stiffly. 'It's where his wife was killed.'

Ophelia closed her eyes, feeling sick on the spot. She'd pressed him, argued with him, pushed all his buttons. Talk about putting her foot in it.

CHAPTER FIVE

JAX STOOD CLOSE to Cody, circling him from behind with both gloved hands on the axe over his. 'Ready, son? Just like we practised. After three. One...two...'

'Three!' They brought the axe down hard into the birchwood log together, splintering a satisfying dent in the side. Jax watched the Cheshire-cat grin spread across his son's face, and Jax's heart spilled as he ruffled Cody's hair. 'Good work, couple more hits and we'll have our first pieces of firewood. Let's go again.'

They were high-fiving the first splits of the season going into the firewood buckets for the guest rooms when Ophelia walked into the woodshed. She took off her hat and shook off the snow, and he saw a touch of sheepishness etched on her face as she nodded a silent greeting. He had left a note on her cabin door late last night and told her to meet him here before sunset.

'How was your first day at Base?' he asked her now, a spark plug stuttering deep inside his chest at seeing her. He still couldn't place why he was so drawn to her; she was so polished, so glamorous...and totally different to Juno.

Out of the corner of his eye, he spotted Cody about to raise the axe again. Quick as a flash Jax snatched it from his hands. 'Not without me, *ever*, you know that.'

Cody rolled his eyes to the ceiling.

'Go find Grandpa, help him get a start on supper,' he said, annoyed with himself more than Cody. He'd been distracted.

'OK, Dad. Hey, Ophelia, I like your boots.' To Jax's surprise Cody high-fived Ophelia on his way past and ran out into the snow.

'My day was great. Carson showed me the ropes,' Ophelia said when Cody was gone, looking around the woodshed. She was wearing the too-new jeans again, he noted, and designer snow boots that looked more fashionable than anything he'd seen in the thrift store in Bozeman, where most women resorted to buying their clothes around here. It wasn't exactly New York, when it came to shopping. He wondered how long it would be before she got homesick.

Her breath left faint clouds in the light from the open door behind her, and she looked kind of awkward now, as if she didn't know what else to say while he finished up with the wood. He knew they'd got off on the wrong foot before. It wasn't her fault she'd questioned him about the slope. How was she to know why he'd had it cordoned off for the last four years? She'd just caught him off guard, that was all.

'Carson's a good guy, an asset to this community. He's been on the team a long time,' he said eventually.

'He told me. He was very informative actually.'

Jax frowned to himself. What did Carson tell her? Did he tell her how Juno had died out there? That she'd steered around what she'd assumed was a small bush that turned out to be a twenty-foot buried tree with just its tip showing? How she was smothered instantly as the hollows sucked her deep between the drifts? How they couldn't get her out? How Cody was forced to watch it all?

'We had a sprained ankle, an incident with a hung-over Austrian who fell off the ski lift, luckily right at the bottom,' Ophelia said to his back. 'No bears, thank God.' When he turned around he met the full force of her emerald stare.

'Good to hear Carson filled you in,' he said, clearing his throat.

'On the job, yes,' she said carefully. 'He's very professional.'

He threw the gloves down with the axe; the rest of the chopping could wait. Of course, he should have trusted that his friend wouldn't tell a new recruit more than necessary. Carson would leave that up to *him* to do, if and when he was ready. Which he wasn't. Ophelia jumped out of his way as he went to roll an unchopped log back to the pile with one foot.

He wasn't used to talking about how Juno died, especially not with strangers. Not even ones with eyes like hers…as if they were seeing right through him. Ophelia knew all about grief, he remembered. She'd lost someone close to her too.

'So, Cody chops wood. Does he help you fell the trees every season too?'

'Of course.' He shrugged into his favourite jacket, wishing he didn't feel so unaccountably magnetised to her. 'Why wouldn't he? He's strong, he's smart.'

She was half smiling now. 'Where I'm from, kids mostly play video games.'

'Well, here, they have to learn how to deal with reality,' he said, reaching for his scarf. 'It'll be getting even colder soon. We have enough wood to last the guest cabins all season.'

Her eyes on him, wrapping his scarf around his neck, made him fumble slightly and get it caught in his jacket zipper as she trailed him to the exit. Her lashes were blacker with mascara again, but the lip gloss was gone. He scowled. Why was he even noticing these things?

This was the kind of attraction that could make a man weak. He wondered briefly what her ex had been like. It felt kind of uncomfortable to think about, especially when Juno seemed to hover on the edge of every conversation.

He bolted the woodshed shut behind them as a gust of wind whipped up a drift by the door. 'So, city girl, are you ready for your tour?'

The sun had started its descent towards the mountains, leaving peach and salmon streaks across the blue sky. On the back of the snowmobile, Ophelia alternated between holding the side handles and gripping Jax around his middle like before. The latter felt weird, as if she was getting too close to him, but she was undeniably mesmerised by Clayborn Creek. 'You can never see this much of the sky at once in New York,' she heard herself saying in awe.

Jax took another turn and slowed the snowmobile along the edge of a babbling stream. 'We can build you a skyscraper if you like,' he joked in his low, gravelly voice, and she contemplated that he actually could if he wanted to. The man was rich enough. She still couldn't get her head around the size of the property.

'I'm enjoying all this space. It reminds me of what I picture when I'm doing my meditations. You know how they make you picture a snowy mountain, or somewhere else that makes you feel calm?' She closed her eyes, took a deep breath. '"*The present moment is bliss. This is all that matters now."*'

Jax smirked. 'You don't think it will drive you crazy?'

Ophelia frowned into her scarf. Was this another one of his tests?

'It's just that most people start out loving the space. Then they get tired of it, seeing only the same places, the same people. It's not a meditation class. Most people...'

'I'm not most people,' she interjected sharply.

Jax dragged a gloved hand across his jaw and his hat as if he hadn't been expecting that. She knew she would rise with confidence to his every test, but it didn't stop the tension between them swirling, or the tiniest leap of her heart in her chest whenever she remembered yesterday.

Ophelia had maintained her professional stance so far, introducing herself to the staff they came across, complimenting the state-of-the-art facilities on the runs, questioning him on the difficulty levels of the hiking trails up the mountain. She'd asked him more about the wildlife, the students due to arrive soon to train with him for their Outdoor Emergency Care certificates. But the stretches of silence in between, she took as a sign that he didn't want to mention the way their time together on her first day had ended. He probably didn't want to bring it all up again, she thought. Talking about that closed-off ski run would mean talking about what had happened to his wife.

Carson hadn't told her anything else and she hadn't asked. Obviously Juno must have got into trouble on the disused slope and Jax had kept it closed down ever since. It was unbearable, feeling forced to relive difficult memories in front of strangers, she knew that from back home. So she'd been forcing herself to ask Jax about other things, like why he chose to chop the wood himself at Clayborn Creek when he had all these staff members.

Not that she was complaining.

His strong olive-skinned forearms on full display with his sleeves rolled up, wielding an axe with sin-

BECKY WICKS 47

ews straining…it had almost been impossible to walk in a straight line towards him in the woodshed. The coarse black hair that trailed a tempting line up from his jeans to his navel, and the shadow of abs when his shirt rose… Jax had the kind of body that was pure muscle and power, proof he'd found the time to overcome adversity and channel his time and strengths into something worthwhile—himself. He was dangerously attractive, no matter how troubled, she couldn't deny it, and now he was hurtling them both across another ski field.

'Ready for the best bit?' Jax had slowed the snowmobile to a stop by a snow-covered gate but her heart was still pounding with adrenaline. Thick fir trees parted for a tiny path that looked as if it might be about to get steep. He grabbed up a backpack from a hook between his thighs and helped her down from the seat into the snow.

'Where are we going?'

'We have to walk from here. It's worth it, trust me.'

'Even with a bear on the loose?'

'You have your spray, don't you?' He slung the backpack over his broad shoulders and tucked his thick scarf further into the top of his puffer jacket.

'I was hoping you'd have your gun,' she confided, then she paused in her tracks. 'I didn't think I'd ever hear myself say that.'

Jax laughed. It was the kind of laugh that came from his soul, a burst of joy that vanished almost instantly, as if he was surprised by it, or felt he shouldn't have let it come out. Something about it made her want to hear it again.

The forest seemed to whisper more secrets she couldn't quite untangle from the breeze as she followed him through the thickening forest. He explained a distant sound was a coyote, and told her how he'd saved a wolverine kit once, all tangled up in some fencing wire. Every now and then he'd stop and hold a chivalrous hand out to help her up a rock or steady her.

Ophelia's skin tingled as if someone were injecting champagne into her veins every time they made contact. But the unspoken subject matter lingered like a cloud on the horizon. One of them was going to have to mention Juno, or that slope, eventually.

'It's beautiful out here,' she breathed. They'd finally arrived at a lookout point in a clearing on a clifftop with views out to infinity. Jax pulled out a flask of hot chocolate from the backpack and she wondered if his gun was in there too as he poured them both a steaming cup.

'You should see it in the spring,' he said. 'I'll bet you've never seen greens like the greens we get here.' He handed her a steaming cup of chocolate, meeting her eyes as if he was memorising their colour. It made her feel unsettled in a good way. As if she was alive and being seen. 'So, do you like to ski?'

'I prefer snowboarding,' she answered, crossing with him to the wooden railings and soaking up the endless sky. 'But I bet I'm a long way off being as good as you probably are at both.'

In the distance the tiny ski lifts crawled up the mountain, taking skiers on a sunset ride. Birds he said were nightjars and swifts circled the vast space in between. They probably had thirty minutes before it got dark and they'd have to wind their way back down to the snowmobile, but Jax didn't seem fazed.

'Sanjay was the skier. He did it mostly on business trips to Dubai. They have a huge indoor ski place there.'

'Skiing in Dubai?' Jax almost laughed again, but he

seemed to think better of it. 'Give me the clouds above me any day. You can't replicate this indoors.'

'That's what Ant would have said. He spent a lot of his vacation time in Boulder before...' She trailed off, lost in her own thoughts.

Silence enveloped them.

Should I say something about the disused slope? Just to let him know it's OK to talk about it?

Jax hadn't taken her anywhere near it on the tour. He probably hated it if that was where his wife had died, she thought. She could relate to that feeling. 'You know, Jax, I am sorry if I upset you yesterday,' she started tentatively. 'Carson said—'

'So, he did tell you, huh?'

'He said the slope you keep closed was where your wife died. Nothing else.'

Jax nodded slowly, bringing the steaming cup of chocolate to his mouth and staring at the sky ahead of them. Ophelia's heart was drumming like a tribal instrument, so loudly she was sure he could hear it.

'When my brother Ant died, it was impossible for me to even visit his neighbourhood,' she started, watching their breaths meeting in the frigid air. 'I couldn't go past Tony's, where we used to order whisky sours for half price in happy hour. Or the farmers' market, where we bought ourselves this overpriced ten-dollar cheese with cranberries every time we had a movie night, in case the cheese guy asked where Ant was. It would have hurt too much to talk about it.'

Jax's shoulders were hunched, his jaw almost locked. 'It sounds like you were close.'

'We were very close,' she managed. She watched another bird circling the valley below. Her throat was dry, and she didn't tell him the other reason she couldn't go to the bar she used to drink at with Ant. Tony had tracked their father down one night while she'd been on a late shift at the hospital, unable to get to the phone. Ant had gone into the bar alone, drunk, and started a fight. It hadn't been like him at all. Looking back now, it had been a red flag.

Yet he'd been a master at hiding his issues, sweeping them under the carpet, till she'd been certain her worries had all been for nothing. *'I'm just living my life, Fia! One drink...that's all! Have a gin and tonic with me?'*

Jax was looking at her sideways, seemingly trying to read her thoughts. 'How did your brother die, if you don't mind me asking?'

Suddenly she was too cold. She rubbed her palms together through her gloves, feeling his eyes searching her face. 'It was a heroin overdose,' she said quietly. 'Dad was the one who found him.'

Jax shook his head and she felt another twinge of guilt for being such an ignorant sister. She'd had no clue that things had got so bad for Ant. A bar fight had been alarming enough, but doctors didn't mess around with drugs, did they? Then again, he'd complained of being bored more than once, feeling trapped. Maybe Ant hadn't particularly wanted the life their father had planned for them either, though he'd never said it out loud.

'I still remember Dad walking through the door and falling apart on the kitchen floor. He'd found Ant alone in his apartment, sprawled across the bed still wearing his shirt and his shoes. Dr Marvin Lavelle, the happiest physician in the Heights, had to pull that needle from his son's veins, hand Ant's stash to the cops then wait around for the coroner. He and my mom are still in the thick of grief... Sometimes I don't even know why I took this time out here when they need me so badly.'

Jax exhaled long and hard through his nose. 'I'm so sorry to hear that, Ophelia. Your family must be devastated.'

His face blurred through her tears. She hadn't meant to get emotional but now she couldn't help it. She had desperately needed some time out, but her mom and dad still needed *her*. Her father needed her to take the position she'd been training for her entire life, so he could retire with peace of mind that his legacy would live on, with or without her brother. And here she was, running away and having second thoughts. Was she being selfish, hiding out here?

Jax was linking and unlinking his fingers as if he was looking for something to do with his hands. 'Like I said to you before, it doesn't matter where you go. This stuff follows you,' he said gruffly.

She squeezed her eyes closed, swallowing her emotions. 'I know.'

'It changes something in your DNA, I think, when you're dragged through hell and back,' he said. 'But I'm pretty sure your parents would be rooting for you to make the best life you can for yourself after what you've been through.'

She dabbed her eyes with a finger—her mascara must be a mess. She almost mentioned her responsibility to take the partnership at Health Dimensions, but she didn't want Jax thinking she already had one eye on leaving. She'd only just got here. 'Jax, I'm sorry if all my questions brought up anything you don't want to be thinking about…'

'You were only trying to do your job.'

'I know, but I also know what it's like to avoid the things and places that remind you of people you've lost.'

His lips were a thin line before he spoke. 'I'm moving

on from Juno,' he said, though his tone implied to Ophelia that he was saying it more to convince himself than her. 'In fact I've already moved on… I had no choice. People here need me. They need my full attention. Cody only gets the best of me. I made that promise to myself a long time ago.'

He glanced her way, putting his cup down in the snow. 'But, yeah. I think about the accident every time I ride past that run. Like you seeing that bar and the farmers' market. I think about it every time I look at Cody.'

'I know, I mean, I understand.'

She held his eyes. She was opening up so much, and so was he, when they barely knew each other, but they'd experienced so much grief between them, it was impossible not to acknowledge it, not to feel comforted that someone else knew how they felt.

Still, she shouldn't have said that—how could she really understand what that was like? *That*, specifically. To lose your spouse and the mother of your child? To see her resembled every day in a living, breathing human being you'd both created?

Poor, sweet Cody. He'd been so young when he'd learned his mother would never hug him after school again, never whip him up a sandwich in the kitchen or call him for a bath. He would always be different after losing her like that. 'You've both been through so much,' she heard herself saying.

'I keep my wedding ring on for Cody, so he knows I won't forget his mom.'

Suddenly, she couldn't say a word past the lump in her throat. Otherwise, maybe she would've said something about Little Bean. She would have done anything for her baby, even when he'd been too small to see. Feeling him blossoming inside her like a flower, then watching him wilt away in a pool of blood in a shower stall at work, still regularly haunted her dreams.

Motherhood was a terrifying prospect to her now. Even hoping for it set the fear in motion: What if she fell pregnant and dared to feel excited, and safe, and then had another late miscarriage? She would never recover from the loss a second time. She'd probably never be a parent, let alone a good one as Jax was to Cody.

Jax must have seen the look on her face again. He took her cup, then her hand, and she stopped thinking. It was slow motion and lightning bolts at the same time. 'You know, we don't have to talk,' he said calmly.

She watched his big fingers curl around her palm even tighter, then link with hers. 'Isn't all this silence why you came here, really? I can't imagine you get a lot of it in New York.'

For one…two…three long seconds the world seemed to crumble into fragments and reassemble itself. They stood there together quietly, hand in hand, until the sun dripped below the mountain peak and disappeared.

CHAPTER SIX

'WHERE DOES IT HURT?'

'Obviously, my nose,' Nils from Norway snapped at Ophelia. Jax put a firm hand on the writhing sixteen-year-old boy's arm.

'Answer her questions, son. She's trying to help you.'

'I didn't want to come here… Wherever we are…'

'The ski patrol follows strict procedures in these cases,' Jax said. 'Dr Lavelle needs to take a look at you.'

Ophelia shot him a thankful glance from under her eyelashes that Jax felt like an ocean wave washing over him. 'So, what happened exactly?' she asked.

'He was knocked unconscious,' he said, noticing her pale pink lipstick in the morning sun, which she'd worn in the medical centre every day this week. Ever the glamorous New Yorker, ever more impossible to look away from. 'Had a bad landing after a jump. His father was first on the scene.'

He led her eyes to the stocky, short man in a heavyweight snow jacket loitering ten feet away by the Christmas tree. Carson's questions would soon clarify, but Jax suspected the guy had enjoyed a little too many après-ski shots before hitting the slopes and taken his son along for the ride.

Bringing his mouth to Ophelia's ear, Jax lowered his

voice to a whisper. 'The guy smells like he had a case of tequila for lunch.'

He heard her sharp intake of breath. They both seemed to freeze for a fraction of a second before she stepped away from him, as if they'd got a whisper too close. 'Nils doesn't smell like he's had too many beers,' she said with her voice still lowered. 'I know what that smells like.'

Ophelia seemed to fumble slightly getting her antiseptics and cloths from the cupboard, and Jax watched her work, wishing her presence weren't so all-consuming. 'His heart rate's been about eighty to one hundred, a little variable, but respirations are good...'

Over the past week or so since Ophelia's arrival, he'd processed many things they'd touched on up on the lookout. He was glad he'd suggested silence to appreciate the view, but only because Ophelia had seemed to need it. If she was anything like him, talking with someone new about her brother's death wouldn't have been easy. He suspected that she'd opened up the way she had as a way of comforting him for his loss, confirming that she understood the agony he'd experienced first-hand. Her transparency, and the common ground, had cemented a brand-new respect for her, but with it had bloomed an even stronger attraction.

'Where am I, again?' Nils sounded panicked. His eyes darted around at the newly decorated medical centre with its silver-tinsel drapes and snowman-shaped lights.

'You're at Sunset Slopes Medical Centre, Nils. Do you remember how you got here?'

Jax placed a hand to his shoulder reassuringly as the teenager tried to wriggle free. Ophelia took off her gloves, asked him to tell her how many fingers she was holding up. She still had painted fingernails the colour of blueberries, and Nils failed the task spectacularly.

'Tell me, Nils, what's your home address?'

'I can't… I don't know.'

Ophelia's voice was patience personified. 'Do you know what year it is?'

Nils spouted a series of completely inaccurate dates before deciding on the year 2005, and Ophelia started a series of quick neurological tests to try and rule out serious brain injury.

Their eyes locked throughout several of the youth's answers and Jax lost his train of thought every time, damn her. What was he supposed to do with this woman?

He'd managed Team Christmas Lights after hours all week and the delivery crew had been late bringing the flame torches for the hot-tub area, which came new every Christmas season. All that had ruled out any free evenings after patrol. He'd had to help Cody with his homework too, and finish preparing the coursework for the students. He'd also created all those excuses to stay away from Ophelia and now he was reconfirming to himself why.

She's going back to New York in a few weeks. Forget about this attraction to her. What is it you always tell people about focus, man?

The last five nights without talking to her, he'd gone about his duties imagining what she might be doing in her cabin, or out in Bozeman with the other staff. It wasn't like him at all. Why was he feeling like this? Maybe it was *because* she was leaving. He couldn't have her, because he didn't do flings. He'd never insult Juno's memory with a casual affair that might hurt Cody—the kid had been through enough. But Jax wanted something for himself, for the first time in a long time, and damn if denying it wasn't frustrating as hell.

'We need a transfer to Willow Crest Trauma,' she murmured to him.

'I'll call Dan to send the ride.' He headed for the desk just as his radio demanded attention from run one. The call was urgent. He took Ophelia's arm gently as they crossed paths on his way out. 'I'll take care of the transfer. Are you coming tonight?'

'Tonight?' Her eyes lowered to his hand, still gripping her sleeve.

'The welcome dinner for the rescue patrol, at the lodge?' He scanned her eyes for recognition. He knew she'd seen the invite. They could talk again properly with people around. Because then he wouldn't be tempted to kiss her.

'Oh, I think Carson mentioned that. I'll try and make it,' she told him casually as she was called away by Carson. 'No promises.'

Christmas was a while away still, but they'd gone to town with it all in the lodge already. The season to be jolly was extended in Montana, apparently. Ophelia's eyes went straight to Jax. He cut an even more handsome figure than ever, standing by the roaring fire, surrounded by five or six of the rescue patrol, volunteers he'd be training out in the field. She noticed his almond eyes appraising her, lingering on her tight velvet dress just as she was noticing him and the way he was stealing the room.

Of course, she'd said no promises, but that was probably the worst attempt at being cool she'd ever displayed in front of a man.

He looked different tonight. She took a steaming glass of mulled wine from Hunter on her way past the holly-laced bar and watched Jax straighten up slightly as she approached him. Was she making him nervous too, after she'd been careful to keep her distance the last few days?

The strange connection between them had brought a dormant part of her soul back to life since she'd arrived, but she had to be realistic. She wasn't here to have an affair, and even a mild crush could distract her from her responsibilities. What would happen then? Distractions could prove fatal in a place like this. Besides she wasn't staying here long, she had responsibilities back in New York. Again, the thought of setting up her office at Health Dimensions without Ant made her queasy.

'Ophelia, I'm glad you could make it. You look… great.' Jax was scanning her outfit now in a way that made her feel empowered. His eyes went from her heeled black boots, up to the maroon fabric widely scooped at her neck, leaving bare shoulders. She felt the cool zing of the swooping gold earrings on her cheek as she tilted her head to meet his eyes again up close.

Boom.

She had wanted to test herself tonight, she realised now, to see if the spark with Jax was still there. A kind of mental torture, she supposed. The spark was definitely still there, she thought wryly, struggling to suppress a shiver. He was introducing her to the students now.

'These guys have flown in from as far as Florida and Iowa…and Michelle here has come all the way from the UK…'

She contributed as articulately as she could to the conversation that flowed, overly aware of Jax, his every laugh, the glimmer of his Rolex watch from the sleeve of his pine-needle-green sweater. It looked soft and expensive, in a heavy knitted wool that conjured thoughts of safety, snuggling on a firelit couch, talking about wolves and chopping wood and…

Is this what happens if you stay away from New York too long?

Jax's exterior was showing off his wealth in a way that, thus far, he'd seemed to keep pretty much hidden. Tonight there was no beanie hat. His dark hair was the kind that you could lose your fingers in, along with all track of time, she thought with an internal groan.

He placed a hand to the base of her spine, shooting her pulse straight up. 'Hey, Ted, it's good of you to come tonight. Have you met Dr Lavelle?'

She tried her best to be social. Working at altitude was already proving an energy drain, and with all this... Jax...on top, she wasn't used to it. Jax was being the front man, she noted, mirroring his manners in front of strangers.

He was being the man everyone loved, who wouldn't burden the world with his worries. She respected that, but the Jax she'd seen at the lookout was a different Jax. That was the one she most wanted to know.

'What do you think of the rescue group so far?' he asked her, when they'd inched their way together under the guise of getting pre-dinner snacks from the dining table. The three-course meal ahead was a surprise. Jax would be giving a speech after it to formally welcome the students.

'Well...' She looked around the group, who were chatting excitedly amongst themselves. A girl called Marni kept watching them. 'They seem like a very smart, very considerate crew to me. I'm looking forward to joining you out there in the field sometime.' She stopped short of plucking a cheese cube on a cocktail stick to add to her plate. 'If you'll have me, one day?'

'I'll have you one day...out in the field.' Jax's mouth

twitched with a contagious smile. He studied her lips as a guy might study a textbook about sex for the first time, as if he wanted it, badly, and she met his smile, embarrassed suddenly. The moment lasted less than a second. She swore he could have kissed her then, in front of a room full of people who would certainly all have disappeared, but after that it felt as if everyone in the room conspired to keep them apart.

Every time she felt Jax's eyes on her she was thankful for her choice of dress, but less thankful that she was starting to care too much about what Jax Clayborn was thinking, and what he thought of her.

They hadn't had the chance to speak away from the medical centre, not since their tour. He'd been busy and she'd been glad—it had given her some time to soak up the silence and drown out the noise…until she realised there was a new noise. Him. Jax was like some catchy new Christmas jingle, driving her crazy. He would not leave her head.

She diverted her eyes from his again, annoyed with herself. To him she was probably just another doctor passing through, nothing more. He had hundreds of women passing through here, all the skiers, the students and locums. She was hardly any different.

At least, that was what she'd thought, until this morning, when he'd pulled her in close and whispered about Nils's drunk dad.

She should have been thinking about Nils, she thought now, watching Jax talking to Marni. But she'd been swallowed whole in that thing he did, when it felt as if he'd reassembled her soul just by placing a hand on her elbow. Ridiculous. She had simply been starved of affection and attention so long that the slightest bit now made her giddy.

Half an hour later, Jax had cornered her under the

guise of finding out about their disoriented skier, Nils. She watched him watching her, over her mulled wine. 'A broken nose wouldn't stop Nils,' she commented, noticing his cologne again, realising that in spite of its pleasant woody tones she still preferred his natural scent. 'Luckily, he has no neurological damage. But we told his father not to let him ski and Carson told him not to drink.'

Jax snorted. 'Sounds like Carson. People do stupid things out there sometimes.' He drummed the side of his near-empty glass with neat fingernails, and she sensed he was thinking about Juno again.

'Accidents can happen anywhere,' she reminded him quietly. She hoped whenever he thought about his late wife, it was mostly good memories, and not whatever happened on the last day he saw her alive. She wouldn't wish *those* thoughts on anyone. She could still see Ant the last time she'd left his apartment. He'd waved her off from his fire escape while she'd carried his bag of beer bottles down to recycling.

'So, did she love Christmas, as much as you, your wife?' she heard herself asking.

Jax raked a hand through his hair, making his Rolex sparkle. 'Juno had three parties every year, one when the decorations went up, one on Christmas Eve and one when they came down. Any excuse.'

She smiled when Jax did, wondering what Juno had looked like. She felt a stab of envy, then empathy. Why should he not think about her? Cody was a part of her, after all.

'We only have the one on Christmas Eve now,' he continued, glancing off towards his son. 'Cody wishes we still had more, I'm sure.'

Her hand slid to his arm over his soft green sweater. It felt as good as it looked on him. She almost asked why they didn't have the other parties any more, when Cody loved them so much, especially in the Christmassy lodge with its roaring fire that reminded her of extravagant homes in Hollywood movies. But his attention had shifted back to her again and her mind went blank.

He leaned in closer to her shoulder then reached out and swept her newly straightened hair behind her ear. He tilted her chin slightly to the left. She held her breath as his eyes grazed her collarbone.

'So, tell me, which ex-boyfriend gave you the Celtic pendant you never take off? Was it the guy you almost married?'

'What?' Her fingers went to the necklace. 'It…it was Ant's,' she stuttered, thrown by the physical contact. How could he change the subject that fast? *How on earth did he know it was a Celtic pendant?* 'I took it from his apartment after the funeral.'

'Damn, I'm sorry, Ophelia.' He stood back. His Rolex dimmed like a fading star as he ran a hand across his jaw. 'I can't seem to stop putting my foot in it with you.'

'No need to walk on eggshells around me.' She closed the gap between them again, feeling her thrumming heart in her throat. 'We've both lost people we love, Jax, and that's not going to change. Like you said, it follows you. But I'm not made of glass and I get the distinct impression from tonight that neither are you.'

She didn't know why exactly she'd felt the need to drum that into him, but he looked as surprised as she was to have said it. She continued, 'He got this somewhere in Scotland on a school trip when he was eighteen. He said he was drawn to it…'

Jax was watching her lips again. A couple of the students were starting to bob heads their way and whisper; Marni looked annoyed that all his attention was on her.

Still, she couldn't seem to step away from him. Would it always make things weird here, knowing they were clearly attracted to each other? She continued, determined not to make things awkward.

'So, the secrets of the Picts are supposedly inside this pendant. They were known as "the painted people", one of the Celtic tribes who inhabited Scotland.'

'I know.'

'How?'

'Cody has books.'

She was impressed. 'Ant said that one day I'd be wise enough to hear their wisdom. He was just joking. It was only a tourist thing.'

Jax picked up the arrow. 'Or maybe you're not ready to hear it yet?'

She almost gasped as his fingers grazed the sensitive skin at the hollow of her throat and prickles broke out down her spine. What was he doing to her? He continued his examination of the sharpened arrow tip, studying it closely, as though he was feeling its importance for himself. The heat from his touch was like fire against her flesh, but she stood, allowing the heat to seep in, feeling something inside her start to thaw.

'Maybe you'll hear more, now you've left all that noise behind in New York,' he murmured.

A cough made her turn around. An older guy in a suit jacket and jeans, with a tie that had the slogan *Welcome to Clayborn Creek* embroidered into the knot, was beckoning Jax towards the kitchen.

'Dad, hey, come and meet our new physician, Ophelia Lavelle…'

'Nice to meet you finally. Jax, a quick word?'

The two men stepped away, but his father's crackly, brash whisper was loud enough for her to hear. 'Jax, I don't want to alarm anyone, but there's a commotion downstairs in the basement. We think it might be the bear.'

'It was my fault.' Hunter was there now with his apron all undone, hurriedly wiping his hands on a cloth. 'I meant to take the garbage all the way out to the bins, but the delivery arrived before I could do it, then someone called me back up here. I must have left the outside door open.' He clenched his fists to his head and cursed himself as more people turned to look.

'Stay here,' Jax hissed as Cody ran up between them. 'Everyone, stay here. Don't draw attention. Cody, stay with Ophelia, please.'

Ophelia froze as Jax started backing off towards the kitchen. His hand reached around his shirt for the slick silver weight of the gun in its holster on the back of his belt. Then he darted through the swinging doors.

The bear's in the basement and Jax is going down there?

Paralysed, her mind went blank, then wild as a tornado as Cody suddenly slipped away from the crowd and followed after Jax. Every cog inside her that had ground to a halt blasted back to life with a force she'd never felt before.

CHAPTER SEVEN

'CODY! CODY, GET back here, it's not safe!'

The basement smelled like state-of-the-art equipment and beer. The sleek wooden spiral stairs felt eerily unsafe as she made her way down. 'Cody, where are you?'

The darkness and the steady hum of generators blinded her and muffled her footsteps. Cody was definitely here. He'd raced right down from the kitchen. He couldn't have just disappeared. Fear coiled her insides like a snake.

'Cody?'

His voice came from the shadows below. 'Be quiet. Bears don't like noise when they're trying to eat.'

As quickly and as quietly as she could she made her way down to the bottom step and caught his forearm. 'We have to go, you shouldn't have come down here.' She made to usher him back up the stairs in relief that something unimaginable had just been avoided, but then she saw Jax. And the grizzly bear.

The bear was huge, she could see that much, even though it was scuffling on all fours, less than three feet away. It seemed to be rummaging through what looked like black sacks of garbage. Jax, in the shadows of beer barrels and crates, was too close to it for comfort. A scream bubbled up in her throat, but Cody pulled her down to a crouch with a strength that defied his size.

'He's herding the bear,' he whispered.

'What? Cody, we need to go.'

'He's herding the bear towards the exit with the firewood kindle. Otherwise when he shoots, she'll run the other way back up to the party. No one wants that.'

She stared at him in horror, then almost laughed. Who *was* this kid?

'They can't see very well,' Cody continued in a whisper. 'Also, they don't really want to harm us humans, they just see us as a threat to their food source. She can probably smell my dad, but the garbage in the bags over there smells better.'

Jax was striding over to them now, silhouetted by the open doors. A blizzard threw snow in from outside around his towering frame, and she realised she was barefoot and freezing. She'd kicked off her heels to run down here. 'I told you to stay where you were. *Both* of you.'

She almost put up her defences. He couldn't bark orders at her like that, the world didn't work like this outside Montana…but he was right to be disappointed in her, she realised. She should have watched Cody closer, the second she knew what was going on. Instead she'd been watching Jax.

'I'm sorry,' she started, urging Cody back to the stairs, but Cody was gripping her hand now, refusing to move.

'It's not her fault. Ophelia followed *me*, Dad.'

Jax found her eyes in the low light and time stopped. 'Is that right?'

A noise behind him. In a second Jax was blocking the staircase with his body. The bear was plodding towards them, its breath hitting the floor in raspy, ragged snuffles like a dying vacuum cleaner. 'Jax,' she heard herself gasp, but it didn't sound like her voice.

It happened in a second. The giant bear lunged towards them from Jax's left. Her arms went around Cody as she spun to make a shield. The gun fired, sending the world white, and she sucked in a lungful of Cody's child-scented hair.

She couldn't turn around. She couldn't let her mind go there. There was no way in hell she would sleep tonight if she had to witness a dying grizzly on the floor, especially as it would be her fault if he'd killed it. She should have been looking after Cody upstairs instead of panicking over Jax and freezing.

'It's OK, she made it out. She's somewhere in the forest by now. That would have scared her.' Jax slammed the door to the snowy lot outside, plunging them into darkness. She heard him cross the basement and take the stairs two at a time, before he ushered them both up to the kitchen.

'I thought you'd killed it,' she breathed, holding Cody close. Jax was bolting the basement shut now, pushing two huge, heavy wooden blocks across the door. Straw clung to one arm of his green sweater. Abe called Cody over and she released him with another pang. She couldn't bear to think of what might have just happened to them all.

'I told you, we don't shoot to kill,' Jax reminded her. 'I was herding it, that's all.'

Just like Cody said.

Ophelia felt the velvet dress slipping further down her shoulder. Abe and Hunter were fussing around the boy, along with some other people.

Jax slid the gun back into its holster at the back of his jeans with one hand and fixed her dress strap with the other. 'You followed after Cody?' he said, glancing at him over her shoulder.

'Of course, Jax, I couldn't let him be hurt. But I should have stopped him sooner.'

There was more in the silence that followed than he could have said out loud, or maybe she was just being paranoid. She felt like a terrible mother figure all over again, and worse, so much worse because she'd let Jax down, just when he'd started to open up to her.

She watched him cross over to Cody and crouch to his level. 'What did I tell you about disobeying me? Do you think I need to lose you to some stupid grizzly bear?'

'I just did what you would do and you know it,' Cody said defiantly. He crossed his arms. 'I told Ophelia you were herding the bear!'

Ophelia felt stuck in the middle. Cody was like a miniature Jax; he was probably always getting into trouble, like this. But she'd put him in danger; she'd put them all in danger.

Suddenly, she felt nauseous. She slipped away back to her room unnoticed, but in what little sleep she snatched that night, she dreamed a grizzly bear was stalking her, trying to break into her cabin.

Jax slid his skis to a stop at the peak and dug them into the snow. The sun was coming up, throwing wispy red clouds over the valley. It might snow again later but the morning would be busy. He wondered what medical emergency would happen first to take him back to Base, where Ophelia would be.

He crouched to the snow, pulling out his coffee, picturing her in that velvet dress.

She'd left pretty quickly the night the bear got into the basement. Three days now and the most they'd spoken was to discuss a German guy, Klaus, who'd sustained tears to his anterior cruciate, as well as a lateral tibial plateau fracture in his right leg. Nasty stuff but pretty standard for overenthusiastic skiers in these parts.

He'd felt the tension in the air every time he'd seen her at Base, spilling over from the party, when he'd thought far too long and hard about kissing her. He'd stewed ever since on how to thank her for what she'd done for Cody. Every time he decided how to do it, though, it led him right on to wanting to *be* with her. He wasn't sure what to make of the thoughts and feelings Ophelia seemed to bring to the surface, and it wouldn't do much good to indulge his desires anyway, not when she'd be gone by the end of December.

He took a swig of the steaming coffee from the flask and let his mind whir. They all left eventually, all the locum doctors who thought they could see themselves here permanently, then changed their minds. They all went back to their tick-tock lives and forgot how time stood still out here.

Cody had slept fine that night the bear had broken in, but he'd sat there by his son's bed, watching him as a wolf might guard her pup. He didn't know what might take Cody from him or when, but he was damned if he would leave him in anyone else's hands again.

So he wouldn't get addicted to Ophelia's scent or her smile, or her eyes, the way she looked at him, not when it meant he was off his guard around her. Definitely not if a mutual attraction to him meant she was also off guard around him too. He needed her focused on her work.

But then…he couldn't unsee it. Her face on the stairs, her bare feet, the way she'd run to protect his son. Ophelia had taken off her heels to go after Cody, knowing she'd be faster that way. She'd run into a basement with a bear because of something else, some *new* focus that was overwhelming both of them, it seemed. Not just because she was a doctor. What was he supposed to make of that?

The radio hummed and buzzed against his thigh, telling him something had happened. Swigging his coffee and flicking the drips to the snow, he got back to his feet, told Dan he was on his way and skied in the direction of the accident.

There were so many things he didn't know about her, and wouldn't get to know about her in the short time she'd be here. If only she could be here for longer...so they could unravel whatever this was between them slowly, carefully. That was his style now; it had to be, for Cody's sake.

Still, though, there was no excuse for making her feel on edge around him. He owed her an apology at least.

'I need to talk to you.'

Jax's hand on her arm sent the goosebumps prickling her skin, as if a snowdrift had blown in with him and the twenty-six-year-old Canadian female who'd sprained and bloodied her wrist landing backwards on glass from a bar stool.

Jax had brought their patient in on the snowmobile. He'd walked in the door, shaking off snow, and sent her heart bucking as it always did whenever he walked in with someone else he'd rescued from the mountain's various hazards.

She reached for the gauze, but he handed it to her first, moving slowly around the bed, observing her in action. When he walked away to talk to someone else, her sensors were primed to Jax's location every time, without fail. It was getting very disconcerting.

'Did anyone else see the bear yet?' she whispered

when they'd sent the woman off gratefully with her boy-friend and some painkillers.

Her bear spray had sat like a bored weapon by her bed every night since she'd left Jax and Abe and Cody in the kitchen, with the party still going on obliviously in the lodge.

Jax motioned her to follow him to the corner of the room. The mistletoe was pinned up there, she thought suddenly, wondering what on earth he was thinking in a room full of people.

Her heart started an anxious thrum again. It filled her ears as she realised how serious he looked. Was he going to say something about the bear, or about how disappointed he was that she hadn't stopped Cody going down the basement stairs? Did he even know how the various, gut-wrenching outcomes had spun in her dreams like a horror show ever since?

'I just wanted to say thank you for what you did. Going in after Cody like that. I'm sorry it took me so long to say that.'

She blinked at him in surprise. 'I thought you were angry at me for not looking after him better.'

'That wasn't your responsibility, not really. I shouldn't have even asked him to stay with you…you were just… there.'

'I was watching *you* instead of Cody, Jax.'

'I know,' he said, stepping closer. His jawline was starting to sprout a beard again, framing his lips with an extra layer of intensity. He paused just short of reaching for her hands and then balled his own at his sides against his bulky snowsuit. He hadn't even noticed the mistletoe, but she was even more on edge now, at the way he was looking at her after what she'd just admitted.

'My mind was pretty much all on you too, all night,

Ophelia,' he said next. 'And I don't know what I think about that, yet.'

He held her eyes.

'I know how much Cody means to you, Jax,' she said quietly as her insides leapt like circus performers. 'Trust me on that—you can trust me with Cody from now on.'

She looked to him to tell her it was fine, that he trusted her, but he didn't, and she couldn't read him. He'd admitted she'd distracted him—all night—but instead of filling her with excitement it felt as though she had failed some kind of test. There was always some kind of test here.

Carson was calling her away now. 'Ophelia, we have a suspected fractured rib over here. Can you run the X-ray?'

'You go. I have to get back to the slopes. It's time for field training.' Jax touched a hand to her shoulder that took her breath away and magnetised her closer in one swift motion. 'Come by the house…six p.m.,' he whispered into her ear.

She took a step back, aware of her racing heart amongst all these people, aware of the mistletoe above them. How did he do that time and again: walk in here and throw her emotions out completely? 'OK…'

His eyes rose to the mistletoe. Before she knew what was happening, Jax bent forward and grazed her cheek with the softest of kisses. 'I mean it, thank you for what you did for Cody.' His voice was low and husky against her cheekbone. 'It didn't go unnoticed, not by me, not by anyone.'

His stubbled jaw left a trail of tingles on her skin. He was about to step away but her hand found its way to his somehow, as if it needed some further contact. She stood there caught in the connection as he clasped her fingers tightly in response and traced her mouth again with his eyes, all along her lower lip, as if he were looking at a map, making a plan. Her cheeks burned even more when she caught Carson watching them. What was going on here?

In a beat Jax dropped her hand and hurried back outside into the snow.

CHAPTER EIGHT

OPHELIA WATCHED JAX pull on his ski boots one by one. Cody was swinging on the porch swing with Kit, the housekeeper, both of them swathed in thick blankets, engrossed in a huge book called *Amazing Animals of Montana*.

Jax had left a note on her door, told her to dress for a hike, and she felt excited but nervous in his company after he'd kissed her cheek like that earlier on. The action had made Carson throw her knowing looks, all day. She'd contemplated not coming, she was far too invested in Jax for her own good already, but intrigue had won her over and she liked how Jax kept all her other thoughts away—the ones she'd come here to avoid.

'Where are we going?' she asked. The sun would be setting soon. As usual, Jax didn't seem fazed at the prospect of being out there after dark with a bear on the prowl.

'Just some place I did a frostbite and cold injury seminar today, with the students.'

'I hope everyone survived,' she joked as he led her to the snowmobile again. It was parked in the tree-lined driveway between two huge snowdrifts. He handed her a helmet, and her breath caught as he fastened the clasp under her chin then helped her up to the seat.

'We covered the latest research that's informed the

most up-to-date medical practices, the stuff that's reducing the need for early surgery,' he said, motioning her forwards in the seat and swinging his leg over behind her. In a second he was straddling her from behind. Her heart skidded as his thighs locked around her legs.

'What…?'

'I think it's time you drove us, don't you?'

'Really? You trust me?'

'I think it's time you trusted yourself.'

Ophelia did her best to let his instructions sink in as she steered them away from the house on the path carved out in the snow for the snowmobile. All she could think was that if his legs weren't locking her in place she might have floated away.

'You're doing great,' he enthused as she took a turn on a snowy corner lit by a blinking reindeer light and shrieked with the thrill of it. It wasn't as difficult as it looked. They were headed for the base of the mountain, where the trails began. Her feet were warm in her boots, for now, with his own wedging hers protectively into the foot treads either side. She felt safe with him, or rather she wanted to. It was her heart that was the problem.

Jax was far too attractive and emotionally unavailable to consider her as anything more than a locum, a temporary presence that kept him distracted from missing his dead wife. And she didn't belong here anyway, she had to keep reminding herself. No matter the undeniable attraction between them, she was a future partner at the prestigious Health Dimensions over two thousand miles away…though she hadn't quite committed to her father's plans for her yet. Not in writing anyway.

She wondered absently as she drove what he'd do if he knew she was having serious second thoughts, and had been for a while already.

* * *

The path through the forest was thick with heavy branches. Ophelia hadn't walked this way before, but Jax was storming through it as if he had an agenda, moving the branches to clear her path whenever it got too narrow. Every now and then a clearing revealed how high they were climbing into the sunset-streaked sky.

'How are you handling it, city girl?' he asked her, stopping to offer her a hand over a huge fallen log. She almost slipped on some icy snow, but his grip was firm and she found her feet.

'Is this another test or something?' she asked him, and he laughed, forging ahead.

She flung some branches out of her direct eyeline, ducking to avoid their vengeful swipe. 'You keep calling me city girl, like you think I can't handle myself out here.'

He stopped short in front of her. 'Well, can you?'

Jax was smiling now. At least, the top row of his teeth was on display and there was a faint curve to his lips. No crease below his eyes, no twitch of the cheeks. He was vaguely amused by her, she realised, feeling her cheeks grow hot.

'You just haven't said exactly where we're going,' she said, narrowing her eyes.

He smirked. 'And you seem to be a person who doesn't much like surprises. Come, we should be quiet till we get there.'

She followed him, keeping her mouth shut, watching the way he manoeuvred himself and scanned the forest around them with some kind of sixth sense. He was giving her the benefit of the doubt, letting her drive the snowmobile and having her hike with him out here after a long, tiring day at Base, but if he really didn't think she could handle his outdoor 'surprises', she was going to keep proving him wrong. Even if the bear showed up.

Ophelia shivered involuntarily, staying close to Jax. Was he thinking about the bear at all, as she was? Or did he think of Juno on long walks out here, where he'd probably hiked with her and Cody loads of times? Had he honestly thought nothing of the fact she'd almost put Cody in danger? She wished she could switch off her thoughts and embrace the silence as he'd suggested, that time on the lookout, but it wasn't always easy.

She felt an ice-cold lash of dread, knowing she'd do anything to protect a child, but would probably never have another. She'd wanted Little Bean so much, and look what had happened there. The thought that she might be an unsuitable childminder, let alone host for another baby, added to her weariness.

'Here we are,' Jax said suddenly, stopping at the entrance to another clearing. Giant trees towered over a rocky archway, its entrance obscured by low-hanging branches. Her knees ached from the long hike, and her damp scarf was starting to make her shiver, but she wouldn't show it. She might have grown up a city girl, but she'd never had adventures like this in New York.

Jax swept aside a curtain of fir, sending snowflakes swirling around them. The sight that revealed itself was breathtaking. A waterfall, seemingly frozen in motion, was making icicle white teeth around the mouth of a yawning cave, almost ten feet wide. What was left of a river swirled a few feet below. 'Stay close,' he told her, inching along the rocky precipice towards the entrance.

Icicles hung like upside-down towers from the ceiling, shimmering in the late sunshine, and Jax ventured on, carving a path for her with his footprints, looking over his shoulder with the excitement of a child wanting to share his magical findings.

'I don't bring everyone here,' he said, and his words echoed around the wet rugged walls, adding a whole new dimension to their adventure as he led her inside.

'Memories like this will keep me going, when I'm back home,' Ophelia announced, coming up to stand alongside him. 'How long does it stay like this?'

She was spinning around now on the rocks at his side, gazing up at the icicles that lined the mouth of the cave. 'It's like this from early October till March,' he told her, bewitched for a moment by the sight of her. Her bright red scarf was dazzling against the pale shades of winter. Her cheeks were rosy from the cold, and he knew he had to get the fire going. She was more fragile than she let on.

He felt her eyes on him as he pulled a warm blanket from his bag. 'Thank you for bringing me here, and showing me this,' she said as he draped it over her shoulders. He could see she was tired after a long day at Base, but he hadn't forced her into anything. Maybe he *was* testing her. Or testing himself, to see if that look she gave him sometimes still made him want to kiss her. He took the firewood from his bag, arranged it on the dirt inside where no icicles could melt and fall.

Her shadow fell over him as he lit the fire, as it had every time he'd put her first, to walk ahead of him on their hike. He'd watched her in shafts of orange sunlight through the branches, the way she hugged her arms to herself, or held her shoulders rigid when she was struggling with not saying something. She'd been enduring every minute for him and, judging from the way she'd been walking at times, trying not to take hold of his arm or hand to steady herself. She was probably as confused by this…thing…between them as he was.

Carson had come by after his shift, pretending to need to talk to Abe. Instead, both older men had questioned him together about Ophelia: *'We've seen the way you look at her…what's happening?'*

He didn't even know the answer to that himself, not that he would have shared if he did. She was different, so different from Juno, and not his usual type, a city girl. But, for all their differences, at her core she was the same, a fighter, a survivor like him, who'd wandered a wilderness of her own to get this far. And she seemed to really see him, in a way he hadn't felt seen in a while. 'I come here when I need to think,' he said, pulling out the food he'd brought and offering her the package in tin foil. 'I had Hunter make us these.'

Ophelia crossed her legs. Her snow boots scuffed the ground and the blanket fell from one shoulder as she unwrapped the sandwich. He watched her mouth in the firelight as she took a bite. Those lips…not glossy or pink any more. She'd abandoned the make-up along with her hair straighteners, it seemed. He liked her even more like this, all natural.

He'd wanted to kiss her since the night of the dinner, and every time it had come to a perfect moment for it, he'd backed off, or made an excuse as to why it was a bad idea. He knew he was running out of excuses.

They ate in silence, which was normally fine for him, except he wanted to know more about Ophelia. 'Cody really likes you, you know,' he said.

She turned to him, wiping her lips slowly, smiling into her napkin. 'I like him a lot too. He's so in tune with this place, and he's learning an incredible amount about the world through you, the real world. It's not the kind of education we're used to where I grew up, but it's different out here. You have a whole other set of rules.'

The way she spoke made him swell with pride and desire, two things he hadn't felt for a woman in a long time. 'I'm glad you see it that way,' he said. 'He wants to work with the eight tribal nations in Montana, you know, to promote tourism to Native American territories. He's more in touch with this land than I am. He gets it, how it is, how it used to be. You should see him in the summer on the horses.'

'I'd like to see that.' She smiled, watching him over the ruffled edges of the blanket. 'It's clear you're doing a great job with him, Jax. You make me wonder what kind of mother I would have been if I hadn't lost my...'

Ophelia stopped talking and flinched as if she'd said something out loud that she'd meant to keep inside. His heart was thudding hard.

'You had a child?' Something made him reach for her hands, but she pulled the blanket around her more tightly, blocking him. Her eyes fell to the floor.

'I was safely past the twelve-week point, but I miscarried not long after Dad came home and told us how he'd found Ant. I had never seen him cry before that day... Everything just fell apart after that.'

The vulnerable hunch of her shoulders ignited some primitive urge to shelter her.

'Sanjay never wanted the baby from the start. He wasn't ready to be a father.' She scrunched up her nose. 'Gosh, I'm sorry, Jax. I didn't mean for that emotional outpouring...'

'It's OK,' he said. He didn't know how to tell her that what she'd said had made him respect her even more. To think she'd lost a child and come out the other side as she had was a miracle. If anything ever happened to Cody he would crawl into a hole and never come out, which was pretty much the same as dying.

'And what about you, Jax? Do you truly feel a sense of peace about what's happened to you?' she asked him, still dabbing her eyes. 'I've seen you work the crowds, everyone thinks you're moving on just fine, and you say you are too, but you won't reopen that disused ski slope.'

Damn.

He dropped his eyes to the fire. What was he supposed to say to that?

She continued gently. 'All I'm saying is, I've noticed we could help a lot of people get to Base much faster if it was open. So you must have a very good reason for keeping it closed.'

'Cody was out there with us, when it happened,' he said eventually, watching a twig crackle and spark against the icy ceiling instead of her eyes.

'We were a few months off the start of the new season. Juno and I...we thought we knew the mountain well enough to go off-piste while we still could. This time I had Cody on a toboggan. Juno was ahead of us on skis.'

Ophelia looked speechless. 'Jax...'

'I will never forgive myself for letting them go out there when it *wasn't* safe, Ophelia. Cody had to watch the accident. He watched his mother die.'

He lowered his gaze and searched her eyes, looking for the judgement he knew he deserved, preparing himself for the disbelief that he could be such a careless father and husband, taking his wife and kid out off-piste on skis and a toboggan. He expected her to ask for details about the accident, but she didn't. He thought for a second that he'd said too much, but at the same time he knew he could talk to her about it. He wanted to.

'You keep it closed for Cody?' She was studying him closely, quizzically. 'How does he feel about that?'

'He doesn't need to be up there. He doesn't need to see that every day.'

'Or maybe *you* just don't want to see it, because it reminds *you* of that day,' she said gently.

He frowned, contemplating her observation. There was no judgement in her eyes, but no one else had ever said that to him before. He felt his wedding ring burning like a hot gold reminder that he was verging on falling hard for someone he could never really have. But he hadn't counted on making a connection like this with anyone in such a short amount of time; he couldn't have seen it coming. He felt paralysed, glued to her eyes. Talking like this, about all this personal stuff—it made him want to shut down, but at the same time *she was driving him crazy*.

'I think we could write a book about grief together,' he told her. 'Or...'

He didn't finish, instead he pressed a kiss softly to her upper lip, testing her, tasting her, silently asking if she wanted more.

She did.

CHAPTER NINE

JAX TASTED LIKE salt and snow, and their crashing kisses sent hot electricity pulsing from her lips to everywhere else.

Jax seemed to kiss her as if she were his lifeblood, then the next second had her dangling in the abyss as his lips left hers to focus on another part of her aching body—aching from the hike, aching inside to feel more of him.

In every split second before his lips kissed a different part of her, every nerve in her body and brain was electrified. The anticipation of being with him in a brand-new way was almost as good as feeling it happen. It felt as though hours passed as she caved into her carnal desires and he worshipped her as if he'd been storing up all the different ways he might please her, ever since they'd met.

She was in an ice cave by a fire, Jax was the hottest man she'd ever been this close to, and this was nothing like she'd ever experienced...what if the bear came in?

Jax didn't seem concerned. He was only focused on the areas of her body that were being exposed as he undressed her. Strangely she wasn't shy, she wasn't embarrassed, she only felt hot, flaming desire and the urge to satisfy him too, however she could. It surprised her how quickly and how easily they surrendered to each other, and how much she loved it.

He could dominate her, and then submit to her himself—both made her desire him more. Naked on the soft blanket, they moved as one, and it was the most exhilarating sexual encounter of her entire life so far…even if she might regret it later. As time passed in sighs, and moans, and kisses, and strokes, she felt as if she were watching the scene from outside herself somehow.

'You are something different,' she whispered into his chest at one point. She couldn't help it.

'I knew you were something different too,' he groaned, pressing his hips to hers, drawing her closer against a backdrop of icicles. 'The second I saw you on that video call.'

'We might regret this,' she breathed, but it was too late to stop. His body was one thing, but the way he moved with her went beyond the carve of his muscles. She couldn't recall how long they spent like that, discovering each other in the silence, but as they were curled up together in the afterglow a voice from somewhere outside made Jax turn rigid in a shield around her.

'Help! Is anyone here?'

She could barely make the words out. Jax was on his feet in a second, snatching his gun back up from the floor. She scrambled into her jeans and watched him stamp out the fire in heavy boots.

He fetched a heavy bag from the moss at the back of the cave. 'Hurry, we need to go.'

'I'm coming, hold on.'

Shivering at the shift in atmosphere and urgency, she shoved the blanket back into his backpack with shaking hands. The voice called out again: 'Help me, please!'

The pathway from the frozen waterfall felt dangerous at night. Uneven snowdrifts seemed to block their path on purpose, but she had to trust Jax. His flashlight lit the way around the trees, and Jax bent the branches ahead, forging a path as if he'd done it a thousand times before. 'Where's the voice coming from?' she hissed, feeling the cold creep back into her bones.

'Over here!'

The look on Jax's face was pure determination now as he made off in another direction, and she trailed him as if she were under a trance, still tasting him on her tongue. She'd just slept with him in a cave! This was getting out of control. She wasn't here to be his winter distraction... if that was even what he was doing with her.

But, oh, God, that had been the hottest, most unforgettable encounter of her life. She wanted to go back and relive it all over again. She'd said they might regret it, and he hadn't replied. Maybe he was regretting it already?

Jax took her hand at a rocky outcrop. 'Stay close. There's a steep edge here,' he warned her. She could barely see a thing around his flashlight. Her throat dried up as he inched her closer with him through the trees, then a rustling behind her froze her rigid. Jax seemed to hear it too.

'The bear,' she squeaked.

'It's probably not the bear—it sounded too small,' he assured her, but she saw his hand move to the back of his belt, where he kept the gun.

'Is anyone there?' The voice again.

Jax pulled her through the gap in the branches and the wind lashed at her instantly. They were on an open cliff edge, nothing but the moonlit valleys ahead. Jax made a shield of his body, holding the flashlight high. 'Stay behind me,' he ordered. Her defences rose instantly—she could handle a bit of wind—but a gust almost took her hat, and she remembered, he knew this place, this land... her body.

His flashlight froze on a hand slipping from a branch, just over the jagged edge of the snowy cliff. Jax inched closer, still shielding her. Any closer could be suicide, and she knew he knew it. He didn't seem fazed, however.

'I think my leg is broken. I can't stand up...'

'Hold on.' Jax was holding her back behind him, stopping her getting any closer. 'Call Mountain Rescue,' he told her, pushing the radio into her hand.

Stay calm, this must happen a lot, she told herself, fighting for calm as Jax got to his stomach in the snow, flat against the driving wind. 'There's a ledge below,' he yelled back. 'He's fallen on to that, but he's in danger of being blown over.'

She crouched behind him, signalling for help on the radio. The young guy's voice came again, agonised, terrified. 'They can't get a snowmobile up here, Jax. They have to hike the way we did,' she told him.

'They'll send the chopper,' he said, and her stomach lurched. It was getting colder by the second. He motioned for the backpack. 'Get the rope out.'

Heart pounding, she clenched her fists around his belt with one hand so he couldn't topple over himself and rummaged in the bag for the rope. He looped it around one arm and started lowering it over the edge. His hat blew off and away, and she swallowed back a shriek.

'What are you doing? Jax, you're too close...' She was colder than she'd ever been; the fire seemed like a distant memory now. And Jax seemed like a different man. 'Jax, this is critical, we need to wait for emergency rescue...'

'I've got you,' he called down to their patient, before he turned to her, hair flailing. His voice was calm, authoritative, his eyes were laser focused and it flicked a switch in her back to the doctor she was. This was the ER and they were the only rescue here. 'Ophelia, we can't wait for them. Sit on my legs if you have to. I'm bringing him up.'

The helicopter's basket spun perilously in the wind as it lowered the stretcher to the clearing. 'It's OK, help is coming.' Ophelia was trying to soothe the patient, Trevor, over the sound of the blades. The whirring steel was shooting up snow showers like sparks off the cliff edge, and she could hardly feel her face.

Jax had taken off his jacket. He held it like a tent over them while she cut away Trevor's jeans and cleaned the blood. His leg was definitely broken. It looked like a stable fracture, but he'd bruised and bloodied his right arm too on the rocks. Her fingers and the ends of her sleeves were covered in blood.

'I went out to take photos at sunset,' Trevor told her. His voice was shaking. She pulled his hat down gently further over his ears and fixed her scarf around him. 'Then I heard the bear... I think.'

'Did you see it?' She tucked the blanket around him, blinded by the chopper's lights.

'No, I didn't.'

'They're coming in, let's get you ready.' Jax fixed his jacket over Trevor's blankets. The stretcher whirled above them like a spinning top in the sky, then dropped to the ground with another blast of snow. It took them less than five minutes to get the young man strapped in the basket, and five minutes later Jax had his arm around her shoulders in the back of the chopper. She felt as if she'd just endured hours on that mountain edge when it must have only been minutes.

'Are you OK?' Jax looped his scarf around her too, even though he'd already donated his jacket, and she burrowed into him, just for a second, breathing in his calm. She hadn't realised she was shaking till now.

'I'm here,' he said, taking her hand on her knee. The two words touched her deeper than any of his kisses had, or anything else they'd done in the cave.

Now you've started something, and you can't just push it away.

She felt his arm slide out from around her shoulders as the lights from Willow Crest grew brighter ahead. Right before landing, he cupped her face in his palm. The look in his eyes made her suck in a breath. 'I should never have put you in danger like that,' he said. 'Can you forgive me?'

'*Forgive* you?'

A voice from the pilot. 'Let's go, guys, help us get him out the back.'

They were offered a room in Willow Crest but Jax refused, because he had to get back to Cody. He held her hand across the back seat of the car, and back at Base they were surrounded by other people asking about their night. Cody, Abe, Carson, the sheriff.

She had to admit that it had shaken her. Darkness turned this place on a dime into something she had *not* been ready for. But then again, nothing in New York had made her come alive like this. No one had ever made her come alive like this…not even Sanjay.

She kept her eyes on Jax the whole time they were apart. She had to fill in a bunch of forms, and her fingers felt like rigid blocks against her pen. It was still hard to get warm. She and Jax had gone through a lot tonight…

No one here knows how much, she thought, glancing at Carson. He was definitely suspicious.

'As you can see, something like this is a community affair.' Jax's deep drawl made her jump. He handed her a cup of hot chocolate over her shoulder. The whirl of action around them was finally dying down. His presence drew her closer, but Cody snaked an arm between them and stole some change from Jax's pocket.

'I'm getting a candy bar!' he called back, and Jax stepped away to watch him go, the way he always did now, tracking his direction.

The rest of the room melted away suddenly. 'Let me take you back to your cabin,' he said. His eyes searched hers, and she knew he was implying so much more. Her legs felt suddenly unstable.

'I think I need some time alone,' she told him honestly. She was falling too fast after just one...whatever that had been, life-changing, soul-shattering. His whispers and primal moans had been the kind of intoxicating she'd only imagined before, but she wouldn't sleep with him again, not tonight.

'Can I at least drive you back?' He looked concerned for her, she realised, more than disappointed. It only made her want him more. 'You know, I don't want to scare you, Ophelia, but that bear...'

'It would never come back here after you fired your gun at it,' she told him coolly. 'You know that.' She crossed her arms across her coat, knowing he could see right through her, knowing he was also fighting the need to feel her lips on him again.

'I fired *around* it,' Jax reminded her, looking directly into her eyes. 'But tonight I did put you in danger on the edge of that cliff, and I shouldn't have done that.'

'I was with you, Jax. I *chose* to go with you,' she said. His eyes burned into hers, making her hot, then cold as she saw his mind churn with something he wasn't going to say. She needed space to process what had happened, and she was too close to it all as it was. Carson was here watching them again from the desk. She didn't want to be a rumour around this place. She already had enough on her plate.

She lowered her voice, studying his face, reliving the sensation of his tongue snaking around her navel, his fingers working her in places that had never been touched like that, ever. He wasn't thinking about that now, though; he was still somewhere else. The realisation struck her like a thunderbolt.

'This isn't about you putting me in danger tonight, Jax, is it? I chose to go with you and I'm a doctor,' she heard herself say. 'Is this really about something else? Is this about what happened to Juno?'

Silence. She bit on her cheeks, cursing herself for saying it out loud, but she could see him drifting right away in front of her. 'I'm sorry,' she whispered quickly. 'You don't have to tell me any more...'

'Like you said, I'm not made of glass. I can talk about the details if you want, somewhere else. But right now, all I seem to want to talk about is you, and me, and this. So, you see my dilemma?'

He was brushing the topic of Juno off, and she stood stock-still, willing her limbs not to long for him. She had willingly surrendered her body, and they barely even knew each other. Maybe he wasn't over his wife, but he was hardly going to admit that now.

She shouldered back into her bloodied jacket, turning to Carson. She was too exhausted for this mountain drama. This was all getting too much. She told everyone she needed to go and answer an email—one from her father she'd forgotten to open till now—and left without looking back.

In her cabin she forgot to check the email from her dad, and in bed she regretted the tiredness that had made her seem as though she'd indignantly walked away from Jax. She knew she hadn't meant it like that. She'd felt her walls come up, hearing what else he'd said...which was 'you, and me, and this'.

This, whatever it was he meant by *'this'*, was too good to be true.

This was tracing the lines of Jax's face up close in the firelight, imprinting the look in his eyes in her mind, kissing the hairs from his navel down, down, down to where she'd never expected to go when she'd set off on that hike. She'd felt powerful with him inside her. It was different from what she'd had with Sanjay. With Jax, it was as if all of it was refitting, refinding some forgotten groove, beyond their control.

This was her liking him too much, getting all caught up in his world instead of facing her responsibilities in New York. Why get invested when she was leaving? She had to take the partnership, didn't she? Sure, it wasn't her wildest dream any more, but she had disappointed herself and her parents enough, failing at her engagement, failing as a sister, failing to make them grandparents...

Still, maybe she could help Jax somehow while she was still here, she thought. He had to do something to stop himself equating that closed-off slope to Juno's accident whenever he went past it, or dwelling on the fact that he'd somehow put Juno, and now her, in danger on his mountain. Jax had to make the disused slope the beating heart of the resort, she realised now. So many more rescues would run smoother if it was open and Jax knew it.

Still high on adrenaline, she reached for her phone to type the idea as it formed. With some architectural twists it could be a snowmobile path with another clinic situated halfway along it, for emergencies. It would be a memorial to Juno that saved lives. She started to feel excited—maybe this could *be* something, even if *they* couldn't be.

A wolf howled somewhere outside and on instinct she clutched the bear spray to her chest over the covers. Her mind flickered back to Jax, pushing deep inside her for the first time, filling her up…

She tore off her shirt, hot and frustrated, wanting him now. Knowing she shouldn't.

A knock on the door. She bolted upright. 'It's me,' Jax whispered from outside.

Oh, my God. Jumping from the bed, she almost forgot she'd taken off her shirt, and she pulled it back on, en route to the door.

'Can I come in?' He looked slightly sheepish in the doorway. She motioned to the bed and sat back down on the edge, but he perched on the chair by the dressing table, tapping one boot to the floor, twisting his mouth as if he was looking for the right words.

'What happened…in the cave,' he said slowly, eyes on the floor. 'I can tell it's made you uncomfortable around me. Maybe we should chalk it up to a mistake? Start again, as of now? We shouldn't be blurring the lines of our professional relationship anyway, Ophelia.'

'We're colleagues…right. You're right.' Gripping the mattress either side of her, she struggled with what else to say. She knew he was right, she'd been telling herself basically the same thing before he showed up, so why did her hands itch to pull him back to her, the second he was pulling away?

She let out a sigh. She had to be strong, even though seeing him so close, in her room, was driving her imagination into a fresh frenzy. 'I mean, it's not just that we're colleagues, Jax. We're from entirely different worlds.'

'Exactly,' he agreed, standing up. 'You're only here

for two months, and I could never leave Cody, or our life here...'

'Of course,' she hurried, wishing he would go so she could breathe again.

'It won't happen again,' he affirmed, but he hadn't moved back towards the door. Instead he was hovering on the hardwood floor, hands in his pockets as if he didn't trust them to be free in front of her.

Seconds ticked past. They felt like minutes. She stood and met him in the middle of the floor, folding her arms to match his posture, all defence, all pent-up desire. 'I guess that's it, then,' she said. 'No more ice caves. Unless...' She couldn't help it, his scent, his eyes, his presence were all man, weakening her resolve by the second. 'Unless we both agree to one more mistake, in a regular bed, before we never touch each other again?'

He reached for her at the exact same moment she reached for him, and before she knew it they were locked in another passionate embrace, tearing off each other's clothes for the second time. 'Or maybe if we just decide that we both deserve some fun, in secret, while I'm here,' she tested, and Jax groaned into her mouth, urging her on to the bed.

'You speak such sense,' he murmured, arching over her and gripping her hair at the back of her neck and kissing her as though his life depended on it. 'I don't know if just one more time would be enough anyway. I seem to find you completely irresistible.'

Ophelia melted into him. This time he was pure animal, claiming her in all the positions the cave wouldn't have allowed for. Her body reacted as if she'd known him for years, blowing her mind again, but she wouldn't dwell on that—this was fun. This was the new agreement. It didn't have to be a dilemma if she looked at it another way.

Luckily Jax was very good at making her see things from new positions. Neither of them came up for air between their orgasms, and she knew that once he left, back to his own house, they'd be powerless to stop this happening again. Resistance was clearly futile, for both of them.

CHAPTER TEN

JAX STUDIED THE group standing around the fire ten feet from the door of the shack. The snow was coming down heavier now, twilight had a grip on the mountains and a coyote howled somewhere in the distance through the trees.

The evening tutorial was set to cover scene safety, triage and management of injured casualties in the remote environment. It was the second time Ophelia had been out with them since they'd started sleeping together, three weeks ago, which added an element of discomfort, as it always did when she was anywhere in danger. But as the weeks had passed, he'd enjoyed seeing her learn from her own mistakes, and light up over her own personal achievements.

When she'd fired a bullet straight into the centre of his target the other day on the practice range, it had struck him that maybe she wasn't such a city girl after all, not that he'd told her so. Things were complicated enough already.

'Tonight, we'll be delving into the physiology of trauma and the effect of the cold on the human body,' he said, his eyes finding hers across the fire. 'Later in the hot tub...which I'm sure you'll all need...we'll discuss the techniques for mitigation best practice pre-hospital and in hospital…amongst other things.'

'Really? Is that what you want to talk about in the hot tub?' Marni was grinning around the group, and a couple of them snickered. Ophelia just looked redder in the cheeks, though she kept her head high. He knew, and she knew, that people were whispering about them, and it bothered him that she felt embarrassed. Most of the ladies seemed excited about the Suds 'n' Santa night later on, but there was no secret smile from Ophelia. His heart felt chipped. He always seemed to be crossing some line with her that was blurred or undetermined to begin with.

What did you expect, signing up for a temporary affair?

He'd been trying not to have any regrets—they were both adults, enjoying the time they had while she was here—but he was more than aware of the clock ticking… of losing her now that he'd found something good again, of getting his heart smashed to pieces and taking Cody down with him.

'Does anyone have any questions, before we start with our first patient?' he pressed on, gesturing to the dummy they'd brought up to the mountain on the snowmobile. No one spoke, they were all just huddled into themselves against the snow as if they couldn't wait to be anywhere else. This was endurance, more than education.

'We have suspected amnesia, the cause is unknown, and he says he can't move his head. Marni, you're first on the scene, what are you going to do?'

Marni was a petite Indonesian American doctor taking his course. He'd felt her eyes on him for weeks, and now her knowing looks and sly comments were starting to grate on his nerves. 'I'll check him for obvious breakages,' Marni said, running to him in her purple ski suit and helmet. She got to her knees at his feet by the dummy and, for a moment, pretended she was going in for a kiss.

'We need to focus here,' he reminded Marni gently as his own hypocrisy burned at his neck under his scarf. He'd been distracted by Ophelia ever since she arrived, and they'd done a lot more than kissing. And even though reminders of Juno were everywhere, the more he looked at Ophelia, the more he was noticing them less and less. Cody had caught him coming out of the music room the other day and asked why he'd gone in there. He'd avoided it for years. Without him saying a word, Cody had asked if he could help move some of Juno's stuff out.

Hunter's eyebrows had shot up when he'd told him that, but he'd offered to help too. 'We can all do it. I'll drive the van. I know a great charity in Bozeman if you want to offload some stuff...'

Jax had shrugged it off, masking the deep discomfort that always came with the guilt at knowing he was letting Juno go. Faster every day. Some days he didn't think of her at all, not even walking past the music room.

He'd piled all her stuff in there, boxed up around her piano, but he hadn't got rid of it then, because what if Cody wanted it some day? It had sat there untouched for years, like the ski slope, taking him backwards every time he tried to move forwards. He didn't even know what had propelled him to walk in there the other night, before Cody caught him. Maybe he'd been testing himself, to see if it hurt as it had before Ophelia had exploded into his life.

Usually he would have dismissed Hunter's offer of help altogether, but instead he was starting to think that maybe it *was* time to make some changes around here.

Ophelia pressed her back to the delicious massage of the outdoor hot tub's jets, looking down at her own breasts bulging in the bubbles. She was glad she'd packed the black bikini, and now she was even more glad that she'd stayed behind after the others had left. The party was over. Having the Christmas lights and bubbling hot tub all to herself was bliss beneath the stars. She liked having the time to think out here in the open. This was the kind of opportunity she would never have at home, where privacy and space were unheard of.

Of course, her thoughts drifted off back to Jax.

Jax didn't know her life was already laid out for her in New York, regardless of whether she wanted it, not that he had asked her to stay beyond her contract. They'd agreed on a temporary bit of fun, so why was it getting harder just to live in the moment? Even Marni's harmless flirtations with him annoyed her. She was trying to enjoy their time together while it lasted but, deep down, she knew she was getting in way too deep.

Speak of the devil…

Jax appeared on the fir-lined pathway. He'd gone to put Cody to bed, but he'd come back to her. She watched him kick off his snow boots and peel off his shirt against the backdrop of snow-covered mountains in the moonlight, fighting an audible whimper of desire. His muscles and taut, toned abs and arms had been drawing attention from every female student around the hot tub before, not just Marni.

'How's the water?' he asked, crouching down to her, eyes grazing her breasts, making her feel wicked.

'Why don't you find out?'

Jax lowered himself into the bubbling froth slowly, right in front of her. Snowflakes hovered on his eyelashes as he tossed his woollen hat to the side, pushed his hands through his hair then ducked his head under the water.

Then… Jax's hand around her ankle under the water made her gasp.

She felt his lips on her inner thigh, and her legs parted as he trailed two, maybe three explorative, promising fingers around the lines of her bikini bottoms, then he re-emerged from the bubbles as if nothing had happened, right in front of her. 'I can confirm, this water is *hot*,' he announced with a grin meant just for her.

Ophelia was breathless as she found herself swept into his possessive embrace. She'd never had sex in a hot tub before, but she was getting used to firsts with Jax Clayborn. She had to stop thinking of each encounter like a ticking clock. She was pretty sure *he* wasn't.

They were deep into the most erotic and literally the hottest sexual experience she'd ever had in the great snow-covered outdoors when, on the side of the hot tub, her phone started buzzing. Reaching for it, she saw it was home and gathered her thoughts, extracting herself from Jax's limbs, trying hard to regulate her ragged breathing.

'What's wrong?' Jax gasped. He was trying to pull her back by her waist, but she was already climbing out.

'It's my mom,' she said, realising how late it was. Something must be very wrong.

CHAPTER ELEVEN

'DO YOU NEED to go and see him?'

Ophelia looked helpless for a second and Jax already knew the answer. Her father had suffered a mild heart attack. They'd got him to the ER pretty fast and now he was waiting on a non-invasive echocardiogram at St Maxwell's Infirmary.

'He's with the best there is in Brooklyn, but my mom got a shock, finding him like that. God, Jax, he's only sixty-two.'

She fiddled with the belt on her robe anxiously and he tightened it for her; it was freezing out. His own arms were steaming with residual heat from where he'd hauled himself out of the hot tub. Quickly he ushered her into the sauna and shut the door behind them.

'I can fly you straight out tomorrow. Or, there's a four-day window coming up,' he told her, sitting her down as his thoughts started to churn with the idea that had sprung from nowhere. He dropped to his haunches in front of her, rubbing her hands between his. The bench was hot, but Ophelia was shivering.

'We send the students out to Yellowstone with the rangers. I usually take Cody out of town while they're gone—we go see a different place each Christmas. If you can wait just a few days, we'll come to New York with you.'

Ophelia looked as if he'd stunned her. 'You want to come home with me? You and Cody?'

He tried not to look as if it were a big deal, though they both knew it was. Still, he couldn't stand the thought of her leaving sooner than planned, and not coming back. 'As long as we're…I'm…back here for the Christmas Eve party. Abe has some surprise planned. I don't even know what it is myself.'

She wound her fingers around the cuffs of her robe. Her face told him he had crossed another unidentified line between them, but Hunter and Cody had both got him thinking. 'Whatever this is, Jax, it could get complicated for lots of reasons,' she said, pulling her hands from his. 'It's already keeping me from what's important, so I should probably go alone.'

'As you wish,' he said quickly, masking his disappointment by reaching for the wooden bucket and launching the water on to the coals. Steam filled the sauna and Ophelia disappeared. 'But just for the record,' he said quietly, 'I think Cody would get a kick out of seeing New York at Christmas.'

The steam cleared. Ophelia was staring right at him and he knew what she was thinking: he was finally bringing Cody into this, whatever it was.

She went to leave the sauna, but he put out a hand to keep her where she was, tilting her chin up to meet her eyes. The truth was, he couldn't put into words how he felt any more. All he knew was the admiration, respect and the burning, mentally debilitating primal urge to keep this woman close were all making him think about doing things he'd never done. Crazy things. Like follow her to another state with his son in tow.

He lifted the robe, ran a hand along her inner thigh and slid a knee between her legs. Ophelia made a moaning sound at the back of her throat as she curled a fist around his hair and brought her mouth to his.

A knock on the door. She sprang from him a second before she could kiss him. Hunter's voice was right outside.

'Jax, we have an incident out on run three. I know it's late but we need you—'

'Think about my offer,' he told her, straightening his shorts. 'You can fly out tomorrow and we can come meet you later. If you don't want us there with you at all, you only have to tell me.'

'I want you there,' she said after a moment, but she was staring at the floor now, as if she still wasn't really sure. 'I do, and I appreciate your offer, really.'

'Then I'll be there,' he confirmed, but he didn't miss the flicker of trepidation in her eyes as he said it.

The clinic was a whir of activity as usual, and even the tinsel around the windows was swooshing in the frenzy. Ophelia's father had been released from hospital in Brooklyn, and now he was resting at home under strict supervision to watch his diet. She felt a little better about things, and he'd insisted she not rush to see him. So with things being crazy busy at Base in the run-up to Christmas anyway, she'd agreed to wait a week for Jax and Cody.

Still, between patients and after her shifts, she'd declined the offer to go skiing with Jax. She knew the subject of her partnership would have to come up sooner or later. She needed to tell Jax about it herself, so he knew where he stood. So they both knew where they stood. She was taking the partnership.

She felt sick, just thinking about it. Why did it feel so wrong now? It wasn't just because of Jax—it hadn't felt right in a long time. She'd just never truly admitted it.

Ophelia fixed the IV for Louisa Holton, a netball coach from Boston who'd limped in with her girlfriend after knocking herself unconscious in the batting cage. Carson took over as Ophelia's phone started ringing. He put a reassuring hand to her arm that told her it was OK, she could breathe.

'The scans are on the way,' Ophelia told him gratefully. 'I'll be right outside.'

'Why are you still working?' Jordi, her friend in New York, sounded horrified on the phone. 'You poor thing, take a break!'

'I am now,' she said. 'I'm just putting my coat on.'

'It's not flannel, is it?'

'No,' she lied, lowering her voice and shrugging on the thick checked jacket Jax had bought for her to put over her white coat. She slid the radio into her pocket. It was snowing again outside and as usual she hadn't taken much of a break till now. 'I owe it to the team to carry on, especially as I'm leaving my responsibilities here to fly to New York with Jax and Cody. Can you believe Dad had a *heart* attack, Jordi?'

'It was a mild one, and his heart came through unscathed. He's going to be fine,' Jordi reminded her. 'Last I heard, he was even insisting you shouldn't take time off to see him. Flights are so expensive around Christmas.'

'Jax has a plane,' she reasoned, but she wasn't really thinking about that. 'I should never have taken a job so far away.'

The mountain air felt good in her lungs. The skiers were weaving colourful lines through the fresh white snow and the Christmas lights twinkled around the confectionery stall up ahead. She was lying to herself and Jordi, voicing any regrets about being here, she realised. She just felt guilty that she loved it. All of it. She'd let herself drift so far away into Jax and Cody's world that she'd left more than one of her father's emails unopened over the past few weeks. The truth was she'd been dreading him asking her whether he should line the documents and the lawyers up, ahead of her taking the partnership. Or asking anything about it, really. She was a terrible daughter, keeping quiet instead of facing up to his inevitable wrath. He needed to know where he stood, after all.

'Ophie, losing Ant changed everything for you. You're entitled to do whatever you want that will make you happy. Life is short, remember.'

'I know,' she replied, because it was what Jordi wanted to hear. She had a feeling Jordi hadn't ever imagined the extent of her guilt, maybe no one had. She would always feel like a failure for not noticing her little brother had issues beyond liking a few drinks at the pub, and his flat… and any other place he could crack open a can, or a bottle of vodka. She should have seen he was messing with drugs sooner. What kind of sister had she been, spending all that time with him, thinking they were close, only to realise she never really knew him at all?

'Well, I called to say that if you do decide to bring this mountain-man-shaped dilemma home, I can reserve us all a table at that nice Thai restaurant we like, near your old place. I'll bring the surgeon, Damian—he's a little square, but I'm giving him a chance.'

'I don't know if Jax is actually coming yet. I'm giving him space to change his mind,' she answered. The thought of him there, at the restaurant around the block from where she'd lived with Sanjay, was completely surreal.

'Jax doesn't know about the partnership,' she admitted

next, resting her arms on the safety barrier hugging the base of the kid's slope. 'It wasn't something I explained in the interview, because I didn't want them to think I was distracted by preparing for something else while I was here. But then things escalated with Jax, and there just hasn't been a good time to tell him my life is all planned out for me, back home.'

Jordi sounded surprised. 'Planned out? Ophie, you don't *have* to take this partnership. I mean, I know Marvin would be disappointed…'

'He'd be more than disappointed, Jordi. You know my dad, he'd be furious. He'd say I'd been wasting his time all these years, as well as mine. I would never hear the end of it.'

'OK, maybe you're right,' Jordi said with a huff. 'But he'd come around eventually.'

'I don't know about that,' Ophelia murmured, just as she spotted Cody in a yellow-and-turquoise ski suit, helping a little girl called Aubrey she'd seen around the place get her snowboard on. He waved enthusiastically when he saw her. So did Abe, standing with a blonde woman who looked in her thirties who must be Aubrey's mother.

For a second she felt a smile cross her lips, watching Cody boarding demonstratively slowly with his knees bent. She was quite sure Cody knew about his dad and her, otherwise Jax would never have suggested bringing him to New York. She'd been careful not to involve Cody herself, and so far Jax hadn't touched her in front of him either. She'd assumed he didn't want Cody seeing his casual affairs with the women who happened to cross his path briefly in the absence of Juno.

But the kid was smart, and observant. What was more, he really seemed to like her. If they came to New York, she'd be sharing her world, inviting them both in further.

It would ultimately be harder for all of them to say good-bye if…when…she left for good. Maybe she should tell them not to come?

Suddenly a shriek from Cody made her drop the phone, sending it tumbling to the snow. Someone—an adult—had hurtled down the slope at full force on skis, lost control and crashed into Cody on his snowboard. Right in front of her eyes, the pair of them flew three metres into the fence and landed twisted up in a powder puff of falling snow.

She was beside them in less than a second.

CHAPTER TWELVE

MEANWHILE, ON THE mountain the snow was coming down so thick that Jax could hardly see the rest of the group, but Marni had taken his hand, insisting she needed assistance. He wasn't about to deny anyone that in weather like this.

'Almost there,' he called behind him, where all eight students were on his trail. 'Just keep your eyes out for branches, and bears.'

The wind kicked up snowdrifts as they followed him onwards around near-invisible boulders and fallen branches towards the shack. The map of the hand-built shacks was clear in his head. Over time he'd memorised the pathways, so at times like this he could make his way to the closest one, wherever he was on the property.

'The snow's getting heavier,' Marni moaned, yanking her hood down with her padded hand. He caught her sleeve as she slid and she batted her snowflake-covered eyelashes at him in thanks, but it was Ophelia's face he saw. Was she safe at Base, and not stuck out in this storm? Was she somewhere thinking about their trip to New York tomorrow?

Cody had been asking him where they were going on their annual trip this year. *It's a surprise this time,* was all he'd said so far. He'd been giving Ophelia space to process what had happened with her father, and sort out her affairs, but her silence and noticeable trepidation also gave him reason to think she might still change her mind about them coming for some reason. Hunter had asked him why he hadn't offered Ophelia Carson's role yet, following their trusted doctor's impending retirement next spring. The truth was, already he didn't really know how his heart would handle it if she said no. Or how Cody would handle it if she said yes and stuck around. He knew Cody liked her, but was he ready to see his dad in another relationship?

Then again…four years was a long time, he supposed. Long enough for Jax to know he didn't want to be alone for ever.

'I knew we were doing an altitude seminar, but no one mentioned it would be in a literal snowstorm,' Marni said, breaking into his thoughts. 'We're so high up…'

'It'll pass,' he told her, guiding them left at a fork in the snowy road. He would already have radioed Base to see if they should close the slopes, if Marni weren't slipping more than she was walking, glued to his arm. He'd been about to delve into the pathophysiology of acute mountain sickness when Mother Nature decided to show them the extent of her ill-mannered mood swings. The irony wasn't lost on him.

He'd just unbolted the thick steel lock from the wooden shack and ushered the group inside when his radio blipped.

'It's Ophelia. Jax, where are you?'

Pulling his arm from Marni's, he turned his back to the group. 'I'm on slope nine, almost fifteen hundred metres up. It's pretty bleak but we found shelter till it clears. Are you OK down there?'

'It's Cody. Jax, there's been an accident.'

Jax's vision went white. His fist landed hard against the door, and he heard the whispers start up behind him. 'Start the fire,' he called out, hearing anger and fear escape in his voice. He swallowed his heart from his throat.

Was this it? The call he'd always dreaded would come.

'Is he...?'

'A skier lost control and hit Cody pretty hard. I thought you should know. He's with us at Base. I was there, Jax. I saw it happen. Abe too.'

'I'm on my way.'

'It's OK, he's safe, and you need to stay where it's safe too...'

Jax didn't even hear what else Ophelia said. He shoved the radio into his belt under layers of clothing he was even more grateful for now. 'I have to leave you. I'll be back as soon as the storm clears.'

Marni looked horrified as the door rattled and shook behind him in the wind. 'You're going out there, in that?'

'Yes, ma'am, I am. You're safe in here, I promise, and I'll be back for you.'

There was no time to explain, and he had to think straight. This storm was set to last another hour at least and he had to get back the fastest way possible, from all the way out here. Cody needed him.

Jax just made out the sound of Marni's gasp as he half pulled, half surrendered to the strength of the door. The blizzard swept in like a dragon and blew out their fire.

Ophelia had seen it happen.

He hadn't had the time to ask why, how or where this accident had occurred exactly, or why Abe hadn't been watching Cody closer—not that he could ask Abe to watch him twenty-four seven, of course, but thankfully Ophelia had been there. A doctor, someone Cody knew and trusted. Still, he was failing his son, and failing Ophelia too, every second he wasn't down there with them.

The snowmobile was working overtime, sliding on imperturbably, bumping over rocks he wouldn't be risking if anyone else was with him. The wind was harsh, freezing slaps on his face around his mask, but his GPS and all five senses had always kept him safe. They'd guard him now, while Ophelia kept Cody safe.

Thank God for Ophelia, in so many ways, he thought to himself, making a right turn some five metres from the mountain ledge. He could just make out the hazard ropes, and the black and yellow flags that marked the start of the closed slope. Something deep in his belly rose hot as he edged closer.

It was the fastest way down. The only way now. The other slopes would be too dangerous with all the skiers being blinded by this snow. The weather could change in a heartbeat out here. It could clear up, or it could come at him harder, costing him more time.

The snow churned up when his engine revved in blunt refusal against some ice. Someone else would have seen that as a warning, he thought, someone else whose injured son wasn't in pain at the bottom of that slope.

Jax made swift work of clearing the ropes aside, edging the snowmobile closer. He ran ahead on foot and checked the run was still as it used to be. A memory hit as he stood there, straining his eyes for the pathway, he and Juno closing the entrance with orange cones, so no one else could interrupt them. They'd had this side of the mountain all to themselves for years; it was host to some of the property's best views, and some of the best sunsets too.

They'd had it to themselves on the day she'd died,

which was why it had taken longer for help to arrive after she skidded into the tree and disappeared—he hadn't told anyone where they were going, and he'd turned his radio off. The signal had always been bad out here, so far from the radio mast.

It had meant Cody had to watch her die. It had kept him away from here, all of it, the pain, the guilt, but being out here now reminded him that he and Juno had made some of their most beautiful memories out here too, in all kinds of weather.

How could he have forgotten that?

Jax drove the snowmobile down carefully, but as fast as he could around the path they should have been on, on that day…before they'd gone off-piste. He saw the boulders in the distance, the start of the danger zone. He wouldn't go that far, but getting to this point was a huge personal achievement after so long.

In spite of the snowstorm and Cody's accident, he was surprised how being here no longer filled him with dread. All he felt now was regret that he'd kept this slope closed off, when it was the fastest way to Base, and when it had been one of Juno's most cherished places.

The pictures on the walls in the private room at Base were lined with tinsel, and Ophelia could hear carols being played across the speakers outside. Beyond that, though, the wind was still howling. 'Will I still be able to take my trip, with Dad?' Cody said as he buttoned up his shirt. His vitals were fine and the shock was wearing off, though he still looked pale and was complaining of a sore wrist.

'Which trip is that?' she asked him, distracted. Abe was here too, talking to Carson in the corner, who was preparing to take some X-rays. She got Cody to bend his wrist and tell her where it hurt, and her heart broke a little when he winced and made an ouch sound.

'Last year we saw Chicago's Christkindlmarket. Did you know it's one of the longest-running Christmas markets in the US? People go just for the sausages. This year I don't know where we're going yet. Dad says it's a surprise.'

Her pulse quickened as she continued with her ice bath, keeping as much of Cody's pain away as possible. 'A surprise, huh. Well, that sounds like fun. And yes, I'm pretty sure you will still be able to go. As long as you don't do anything too crazy.'

'Maybe you can come with us,' Cody said now. His eyes grew wide, as if he'd had the best idea ever. 'I know my dad likes you a lot.'

'Does he now?' Ophelia felt her face flush bright red as she heard Abe bark out a laugh, right as Jax walked into the room. He was still in his winter coat, dusted with snow from the storm outside.

'I got here as fast as I could,' he said, crossing to Cody's bed. She watched him take his son gently by the shoulders and start inspecting him for signs of visible damage. 'What happened?'

'I'm OK, Dad. I still want to take our trip,' Cody said quickly.

'I'm sure you do.' Jax put a hand to his face, then ruffled his hair. His mask was pushed up on to his hat, and Ophelia could see the worry in his eyes. She explained properly what had happened, and how the other guy on the skis was thankfully unhurt, and she was glad all over again that she had been there to help. At least she hadn't frozen this time—she had brought Cody straight back here.

'It's either a sprain or a fracture in his wrist. We'll

know soon enough,' she told Jax, aware that her palms were sweating now that he was back in her orbit and she was seeing him care for his son. Did he trust her yet? Or was it mistrust that had propelled him back here so fast in a snowstorm?

To her shock he put his arms around her, pulling her close in a tight embrace. The cold dampness of his clothing made her shiver, but her arms looped automatically around his shoulders. 'Thank you for being there, for helping him,' he said sincerely. 'I'm so grateful it was you.'

She was so touched that her eyes started watering on the spot. Abe and Carson were still watching but he didn't seem to mind.

'How did you get here so fast?' she whispered into his neck. 'I thought you took the group out at high altitude.'

'I did,' he said, releasing her. But not before squeezing her hand. Then he turned his attention back to Cody, as if he didn't want to say any more about it. Suddenly she knew exactly how he'd got back here so fast. He had taken the slope he usually kept closed—it was the only explanation. He had faced his fear to get back here for Cody. Everything Jax did was for Cody...which was perfectly understandable. In fact it melted her heart. But she was getting in the middle of a family unit, getting involved, when she was only going to have to leave soon.

When Carson was busy with the X-ray machine she heard Abe telling Jax, 'Lucky Ophelia was out there when it happened. She knew what to do. I heard Cody say your trip was a surprise, by the way—is this something you're *both* still planning, you and Ophelia?'

Jax replied in a whisper that was so low she couldn't hear his words, but Ophelia felt her temperature rise again just thinking about how selfish it was for her to be stalling. If she told him about the partnership, there was a chance he wouldn't want to come to New York and, dear God, she wanted him there. She wanted his arms around her and his chest behind her. She wanted both of them there more than anything, but it had to be *Jax's* decision, based on all the facts. Time was running out. She had to tell him as soon as possible.

CHAPTER THIRTEEN

JAX WASN'T HOME when Abe welcomed her into the main house the same night. 'He brought Cody back here, then he went back to the students,' he explained. 'I guess he'll be home soon. Sherry, while you wait?'

'I'll have one, Grandpa!' Cody called, and Ophelia smiled, unbuttoning her coat as Abe closed the door behind her. Thankfully, the storm had subsided.

'I don't think you will, and neither will I, thanks, Abe,' she said as he took her coat. She didn't want her thoughts muddled any more than they already were.

'How is our patient now? Is that wrist support sling working out OK for you, sir?' Cody was lying horizontal on the giant squishy couch, wearing a red Christmas sweater, and she picked up his hand as she examined his support bandage. 'You were lucky it was just a sprain.'

'It feels OK, thank you, Ophelia,' he said over the Christmas movie on the TV, and her heart fluttered as Cody put down his book and moved up the couch to make room for her.

'What are you reading?' She picked up the book as she sat down. It was a heavy, thick, hardbound book called *Six Hundred Generations*.

'It's about the archaeological evidence of Montana's Indigenous human history,' he explained. 'I like the part about the first people who followed mammoths here, into this landscape. There were probably mammoths hanging out where the ski base is now twenty thousand years ago.'

'Is that right?' She felt her eyebrows rise. God, this kid was smart. She couldn't place the feeling amongst the warmth and comfort of the rugs, and timber beams and Christmas lights, but something about being here filled a hole inside her that she hadn't known was still there.

Anxiety quickly followed. She was getting too strongly attached to this place, to these people. It wasn't a good idea. She was here to tell Jax what she needed to tell him.

'Shoot, the firewood is almost out,' Abe grumbled, tossing the last log from the bucket into the fire, making it crackle and spit in the hearth. 'Would you mind watching Cody while I go get some more from the shed?'

'Of course.' Ophelia helped herself to a chocolate from a silver bowl on the coffee table. Cody copied her and threw her a conspicuous wink. Seconds later, they were alone in the big house, eating all the chocolates.

'So, I think my dad is planning to take me to New York,' he said from out of nowhere, over a chocolate cherry. Her stomach wound into so many knots that she stopped mid-reach for another candy.

'He was looking at hotels in New York on his laptop the other morning. I always wanted to go there at Christmas. My mom has a programme for The Rockettes with all her other theatre stuff. Do you want to see it?'

Before she could answer, Cody was on his feet, heading down the hallway. Ophelia followed him, unsure what else to do, till he disappeared into a room that she'd only ever seen closed.

In the wide, darkened room lined with bookshelves, Cody vanished behind a tower of stacked-up boxes, flicking on a light. An orange glow came over a huge mahogany-brown piano, and even more boxes. She had a feeling she wasn't supposed to be in here. 'What is all this…?'

'Here it is!' Cody held up a bunch of white and yellow playbill booklets, bound with an elastic band. 'She has the ticket stubs too. Hey, look, I found the chess set as well. Do you want to play before Dad throws it away?'

Ophelia was staring at the piano again. She'd missed playing the piano. She was sure she'd told Jax that during one of their private moments in the last few weeks, so why had Jax not told her he had one here? Tentatively she walked to the red velvet stool and flipped up the lid. Memories flooded in and Cody was on the stool beside her like lightning as she sat, as if on autopilot.

'Can you play?' he asked her.

'Yes, can you?'

'A little, but not with one hand.'

'Good point.' She smiled.

'I could never play this one right anyway,' Cody said, turning to a page on the piano stand with his good hand. It was a composition she didn't recognise. As her fingers started to dance with the notes, Cody hummed a tune she'd never heard. It was beautiful and she caught herself drifting off, back into the good times.

She and Ant used to play The Beatles together, often changing the words, and almost killing themselves laughing. She'd written a song for her baby too. It had made her mother cry. Cecelia Lavelle had been so looking forward to being a grandmother.

Those memories had conjured up so much pain, she'd stayed away from the piano. Now for some reason, with Cody at her side, the thoughts flew in and then out again like the melody without getting stuck. She felt nothing but peace.

'This is a beautiful song,' she told him, just as the piano lid slammed shut, narrowly missing her fingers.

'Dad!' Cody leapt from the stool.

'What are you doing in here?' Jax was silhouetted by the light from the hallway. He looked angrier than she'd ever seen him. He jerked his arm back from her instinctive touch and marched Cody to the door. Ophelia sat there, frozen.

What was happening?

'I just wanted her to play Mom's song,' Cody protested.

What? Ophelia felt ill. *That was Juno's song?*

'I'm s-so sorry,' she stuttered, but Jax wasn't looking at her.

'Dad, she didn't know. It's my fault we were in here…'

It was all falling into place. This was Juno's stuff. Jax was keeping all of it locked up in this room in boxes with her piano?

'Jax, I'm so sorry,' she heard herself say again as she followed them from the room, but her blood was heating up in horror and mortification as he ignored her and ordered Cody up the stairs. Cody refused, and Jax followed him up this time. Abe was still nowhere to be seen.

Ophelia wrapped her arms around herself in the hallway, head spinning. As soon as she heard them reach the landing, she hurried for her coat and left the house.

Outside, the melodic strains of 'Hark the Herald Angels Sing' almost drew her to the lodge, but she couldn't trust her emotions not to make her well up again in front of all those people. Jax's face just now…she couldn't unsee it.

She'd overstepped a mark just by being in Juno's room with all her belongings. But by playing Juno's song on the piano… Perhaps Jax had walked in and for a split second against all credibility thought she was Juno.

He'd been angry because she wasn't Juno...

The night was still and dark, a sharp contrast to this afternoon when she'd raced to Cody and bundled him up to her against the wind. She'd led him back limping to the clinic, hearing Jax in his distorted cries, seeing him in his eyes. She'd have given anything in that moment to just have Cody be OK.

She'd been on tenterhooks checking for damages, then overcome with relief to hear him talk and even laugh. *That kid*, she thought, picturing Cody's face at the piano. He had come to mean as much to her as Jax, somehow, despite both adults trying to hide their attachment to one another. Kids saw everything, they knew everything, they were like little sponges, she realised. They were a package deal and she'd been feeling like a part of the family, as if maybe she *could* somehow make things work between here and a life and career in New York, if that was what Jax wanted too.

But now she was an outsider again.

Whatever had made Jax look at her like that, she never wanted to see it from him again. It was a good thing she hadn't mentioned her idea about turning the disused slope into a rescue route—who knew what he would have done? It was clear that, for all his words about healing and moving on, he didn't want to change a thing that reminded him of Juno.

Her boots stopped her at the lift. She raised her eyes to the snowy peaks above and something made her sit down. The chair started up automatically and she buried her cheeks further into her scarf as it juddered upwards, feeling the wind try and turn her tears into icicles.

This time tomorrow she'd be at home in New York. Ant, or his voice in her head, would be chasing her through Brooklyn, urging her to tell her father she would do what she promised she would. She would not let them down. It was time to admit she'd just been escaping into a winter fantasy world out here because reality just made her even colder.

Reality was leaving all this behind and focusing on the partnership. She had to tell Jax their affair was over, if he hadn't just decided that himself.

A lower level of the disused slope was just a short walk from the lifts. Looking around, she waved at Melanie, the on-shift patroller, and motioned that she was taking a photo. Curiosity took over and Ophelia found herself walking towards the *No Entry* signs.

Her scarf caught in a gust of wind. Things could change out here so fast, but she wouldn't be long. She'd just come for the air, and the silence, and…maybe she should just have a little look at whatever it was that made this slope so dangerous?

How did Juno die, exactly? She shuddered thinking about it, but intrigue propelled her forwards, almost to the edge of a line of boulders. They seemed to be a barrier of sorts and something told her not to step any closer. She'd never asked Jax for the details from that day, and no one had provided them, almost as if the incident itself had been too awful to speak of. He'd asked her about Ant, though. He'd helped her heal in some ways just by being at her side. Maybe *he* wasn't as ready to heal as he thought he was.

Where had they all been that day? Cody had been here somewhere, when his mother died right in front of him. Cody…

Her flailing scarf blinded her momentarily again. She wrestled with it and tied it more tightly around her neck.

'Ophelia! Get back here!'

She spun around. Jax was ten feet away, taking giant strides through the snow as if she might tumble backwards and fall before he could reach her. 'Are you OK? You shouldn't—'

'I'm fine,' she snapped, putting a palm to his chest as he reached her. 'I know, I know, I shouldn't be here either, Jax. Is there anywhere here I *should* be any more, or should I just stay in New York when I fly home?'

He looked traumatised for a second and shame stabbed at her like a knife. 'I'm sorry,' she said quickly. 'If hearing me play that piano reminded you of her...'

'I shouldn't have reacted like that. Can you just come back up here with me, please?' He led her urgently over a drift back to the *No Entry* signs and gestured to them dramatically with his gloved hands, as if she could have possibly missed them.

'I know, I know,' she huffed, but it was only then she saw the pure relief in his eyes.

'You caught me off guard back at the house,' he told her, taking her shoulders. 'You sounded so beautiful playing that song. I wasn't expecting...you, this. Ophelia, I want you to know that I was planning to donate it. All of that stuff in the music room.'

'It's OK, Jax...' Something was coming back to her now. Cody had found the chess set in the room of Juno's stuff. He'd asked her: *'Do you want to play before Dad throws it away?'*

It didn't matter now. She had to tell him. 'I went to you tonight to tell you something, Jax. There's something at home you don't know about.'

She paused for him to ask who or what it might be, but he didn't, he just folded his arms, pulled down his hat and waited. Her heart was in her throat. The air was still, as if the wind were holding its breath. 'Go on.'

'It's a partnership at my father's practice. I'm bound to it, Jax. I've all but committed to taking it. I wanted to think about everything out here, with no distractions. Then I met you. I want you in New York, but I know that's selfish of me. I promised my parents I'd come here to clear my head, prepare for the role. It's going to be full-on and I already took more than a year out after Ant died.'

'Wait,' he said suddenly, uncrossing his arms, 'you're bound to it? What does that mean, exactly?'

She couldn't read his expression now and she swallowed the rising lump in her throat. 'I mean, it's been my plan for ever. Ant and I were both supposed to take over the practice so our dad could eventually retire. Now it's only me left, so...'

Jax looked more confused than annoyed and she watched him bend to scoop a handful of snow in his fist and ball it purposefully in his hands. 'Plans change,' he said simply.

'Not this one,' she replied, hugging her arms around herself, picturing her father's stern face if she threatened to throw a stick in the wheel of his plans for Health Dimensions after all this time. After everything they'd all been through.

Jax launched the snowball at the *No Entry* sign. He was mad now, she could tell. He had every right to be. 'You're angry I didn't tell you before.'

'I guess I should be, seeing as how we've been sleeping together for the last few weeks, but technically I hired you for two months. What you do after that is up to you, Ophelia. I'm not about to come between your plans, or you and your family, when I have my own to think about. Come on, let's get out of here.'

His last words stung like a rogue wasp, but she followed him closely as the snow started to swirl. She wanted to tell him how she hadn't planned for this, on meeting him, on falling for him, but he wasn't offering any alternative solutions. In fact, he was putting up walls, making it quite clear he had priorities that didn't concern her. Maybe she was just a temporary distraction after all…one he'd been enjoying, that she'd just sucked all the joy from.

On the ride down the mountain, the breeze rocked them both as she apologised again, and wished she'd just told him sooner. Jax kept his hands to himself the whole way. She knew he probably wouldn't want to come to New York with her now, but somehow neither of them went home alone. Jax came with her to the cabin. She went to close the door on him, aware of how closely he'd been guarding himself till now, but he barged inside at the last second, all man, all power, and took her in his arms, and kissed her as if he was afraid of losing her. She felt exactly the same. How could she resist?

On the warm cotton sheets of her bed a while later he stroked a hand along her side, leaving tingles in the trail of her last orgasm. They'd just made love in silence, each dominating the action in turn as if trying to reclaim something the other was taking away.

'Ophelia, you do know that the past should not determine your future, right? God knows, enough people have told *me* that, before now.'

She studied his eyes and almost broke in two. Didn't he see how she couldn't let her father down, not when he'd already lost Ant?

'It sounds a lot to me like you just don't want the same things you wanted before,' he said. Then he turned on to his back, staring up at the ceiling. 'You're making me contemplate a few changes in my life too. Things I never thought I'd want to do.'

She thought of the stuff in the music room. Was he really planning to get rid of it all now? What did that mean, exactly? He still hadn't asked her to stay beyond the two months. This was all just turning into one big, complicated mess, though her heart thrummed in protest and her pulse zinged at his proximity.

Suddenly his fingers swept her hair aside and the look in his eyes turned her cold. 'Where did your arrow go?'

Her hand went for her necklace. *Oh, no.* The leather chain and arrow had disappeared. She bolted upright in the bed. 'It must have fallen off.'

Jax got on his knees with her on the floor, searched the bathroom, even the snowy porch in his bare feet, but it was nowhere to be seen. 'You could have lost it outside in the snow,' he said, and she suddenly remembered wrestling with her scarf in the wind out on the slope. It could have come off then, which meant it would almost certainly be buried by now. She was shaking.

'We'll look for it at first light,' he told her. 'Before we get on the plane—together.'

'You still want to come with me to New York?'

'I do,' he said, pulling her astride him on the bed. 'I've always wanted to go.'

She raised an eyebrow. 'But, what if I end up taking this partnership?'

He paused a second. 'I guess that's up to you. You have options, you know. A woman like you could take herself anywhere and find success. You can do whatever you want, as long as you believe it.'

She half expected him to ask her to stay here at the end of her contract—that would be another option he'd have thought about, if he liked her being around—but again, he didn't say anything of the sort and her heart ached for him, even with her leg draped across his under the sheets.

At first she'd assumed he was protecting himself after what he'd been through with Juno, and Cody, but what if this was purely a temporary arrangement to him, and he really did just want to see New York at Christmas?

Ophelia sighed heavily against his chest, trailing her fingers up and down his arms. Deciding the future was too painful to think about, so she let her limbs and lust take control as they picked up where they'd left off. But by the time Jax finally fell asleep with one arm curved protectively around her, she was wide awake, and feeling even more torn.

CHAPTER FOURTEEN

THE MARBLE KITCHEN, radiant slate bathroom and all-white adjoining surgery at the Lavelle residence was a world away from his log house in Montana, Jax thought from his seat between Ophelia and Cody at the glass dining table. Amusingly, they even had a remote-control fireplace.

'Dr Clayborn, it was good of you to come back here with my daughter,' Marvin said now, arms folded on the table in a navy V-neck sweater. He lowered his glasses to peer over his nose at him as he'd been doing since they arrived, with some element of mistrust. 'I can assure you it wasn't necessary. I'm fine.'

'We came to see the museums, actually,' Cody interjected, and Marvin offered a small smile over his glass of water, much to Jax's relief. He was getting the distinct impression that Ophelia's father considered his presence here to be a little threatening.

'Have you been to the Intrepid Sea, Air & Space Museum yet, son? You can see a real space shuttle there.'

'I think I want to see the Museum of Natural History next. Did you know they found the first baby dinosaur bones in Montana, at Egg Mountain?'

Cody, in his new Knicks shirt, launched into a full rundown of what he'd read about the museum's tyrannosaur superfamily exhibition, and thankfully Marvin's full attention moved to Jax's son.

'My dad loves him,' Ophelia mouthed, bobbing her head at Cody, and he let the warmth of the fake fire and her family embrace him momentarily.

Cody loved his room at the Renaissance hotel in Times Square. They'd both been away from Ophelia yesterday, touring the sights while Ophelia had been hanging out with her father. Had they talked about this partnership then? Jax hadn't had a chance to talk to her in private today and he was itching to find out if she was as tied to it as she said she was.

'Honey, I'm so sorry you lost your necklace. I know that was Ant's favourite,' her mother, Cecelia, said now. Cecelia Lavelle had Ophelia's wide smile, and the exact same shade of nail polish.

Ophelia pressed her hands to where the pendant used to be. Jax felt his jaw tic just thinking how they'd looked everywhere for it before they left, and hadn't found it. He'd told the staff. They were all keeping their eyes peeled but nobody was hopeful.

'It's just a shame I never heard the voices he was talking about, from the Celtic tribe. I never found out what they had to tell me,' Ophelia said as his eyes caught something huge and wild outside the window behind her, priming his senses, before he realised with mortification that it was just a bus rolling past.

'You've learned a lot in Montana,' he said to her now, shifting in his chair, feeling Marvin's gaze practically lasering his cheek. 'More than I bet you realise.'

'She ran after me when I was with Dad and the bear,' Cody effused, twirling his glass of juice.

'You did what?' Cecelia, in a vivid blue shirt with printed peacocks on it, looked horrified.

Jax sat back in his chair. 'Damn right she did, Cody. Legend has it, Cecelia, when you face a bear, you inherit their courage and strength. The tribes see them as protectors and healers. Ophelia's always been one of those anyway. Now she just has a little more Montana tribe in her, and a little less Celtic.'

Cecelia's mouth was agape. 'Maybe the tribes led her to you, then, Jax,' she said after a small pause.

'Maybe that's right, Dad,' Cody followed, grinning, and he almost felt a weight lift from his shoulders, till he saw that Marvin was eyeing him over his glasses again, in a way he could only call disapproving.

'The practice has been busy. Everyone is looking forward to you joining us soon, Ophelia. You know, Ant would be so proud of you. You both worked so hard for this,' Marvin said deliberately.

Jax watched Ophelia close her eyes and inhale softly, as if something was on the tip of her tongue. She couldn't look at him now. Was she realising how much this partnership really meant to her, now that she was back home, and didn't want to say so in front of him and Cody?

Marvin spoke again, this time putting a hand over Ophelia's. 'I'm sure you'll be sad to leave all these tribal affairs behind, and these two fine gentlemen,' he said pointedly. 'But all good things must come to an end, right?'

Cody dropped his spoon. 'Ophelia doesn't have to leave us, does she, Dad?'

'I'll be with you for a while yet,' Ophelia cut in quickly. She shot him a look full of apology then scowled at her dad, and Jax took a swig of his own juice to clear the words he wanted to say but knew he would regret.

He'd already revealed a side of himself to Ophelia that he wasn't proud of. He'd overreacted, seeing her at the piano the other night, and he was ashamed of it. After Juno he'd been desperately lonely and when his grief had subsided, a cold kind of nothingness had kicked in, like turning the page of a good book to find it blank, with no ending in sight.

The last thing he'd wanted was for Ophelia to know how he'd been holding on to what little he had left of Juno, not when he was finally ready to let his wife go. He'd packed up the last of those boxes himself, before he'd packed his bags to come here.

Only now, he felt stuck in quicksand again. This partnership news had come as a total surprise, and he was still figuring out how he felt about it. Maybe he should have mentioned Carson's role to her, giving a reason for her to stay in Montana instead of returning here to all the ghosts of her past…but he still hadn't said anything about that. He knew why. Deep down he didn't want to hear her say no. He would take it too personally. He was still protecting his heart.

Cecelia stood with their stack of empty plates. 'Come, Cody, help me get this cake served up.'

Tension swirled as soon as they'd gone; he could feel it like a thunderstorm coming.

'What exactly is going on here?' Marvin kept his voice low, glancing to the door.

Jax stood up from the table, moving to stand behind her chair. 'Dr Lavelle, we're very much enjoying having Ophelia at Sunset Slopes, and Clayborn Creek. I think you'd be proud to see what an asset she is to the family.'

'Family?' Marvin raised an eyebrow.

'We tend to think of our team more as a family,' Jax replied, refusing to move his eyes from Marvin's disapproving stare. Ophelia's shoulders tensed under his hands. Why did this feel like more of a battle than a casual conversation?

'Well, I thought having a mild heart attack was… interesting, but this is even more interesting. Ophelia, does this new so-called family in Montana mean I might have to find another partner?'

'Dad, please. I told you we would talk about this later.'

'But you haven't been answering my emails about lining up the contract.'

Jax frowned. She hadn't? This was news to him. Ophelia cleared her throat, awkwardly, and crossed her arms on the table.

'Dad, you're being kind of pushy. Is this really the right time for this conversation?'

'OK, OK, we'll talk later.' Marvin threw his hands in the air in defeat. Jax felt a frown darken his face as he crossed to the arched window facing the street. She clearly just didn't want to confirm her future plans with her father again in front of him, when he and Cody had come here for a nice time.

'When was the last time you played that piano?' he asked her, gesturing to the instrument bathed in light from the windows. For the first time in his life he couldn't stand the silence.

'She hasn't played in a long time,' Marvin said distractedly, just as Cody and Cecelia came back in with a chocolate cake, complete with a holly-covered top made of icing. It reminded him of Kit their housekeeper's Christmas offerings, which in turn reminded him they had to get back soon for the lodge's Christmas Eve party. He was far enough away from his duties here as it was. Coming to New York had probably been a huge mistake.

'Want to play something with me, now your hand is a little better? Can you manage?' Ophelia asked Cody, taking a seat at the piano stool, much to his surprise. He was more surprised to see how enthusiastically Cody got up to join her.

As they played a cheerful Christmas tune he tried to focus on Marvin and Cecelia watching Cody as if the sun were radiating from his belly button, rather than the fact that with every passing second he was wading deeper into a potential mess that he knew wasn't going to turn out in his favour.

The following afternoon Ophelia was fiddling with the satin of her red skirt in the car on the way to Radio City Music Hall. Jax had bought them all tickets to The Rockettes matinee and her parents were sitting with Cody in the back row behind them, chattering excitedly. Cody was loving it here, which filled her with the deepest joy. But Marvin had treated Jax with the utmost suspicion ever since they'd arrived and she could hardly blame him. Her father knew something was going on between them, even if she wasn't saying so.

'Too loud and crazy for you yet?' she asked Jax now. He'd been quiet ever since lunch the previous day, and now he was staring out of the window, lost in thoughts of his own. Behind him the streets were jammed like sardines, a moving blur of shoppers wielding bulging bags, yellow cabs and flashing lights. He probably couldn't wait to get back to the silence, she thought despondently.

'I won't deny, I was thinking how I'd never get used to this,' he confirmed, running a hand through his hair. 'But home is home, I guess. For both of us.'

'I guess so,' she heard herself whisper. She reached for his fingers on the seat, but he moved his hand to his lap away from her and her stomach contracted as if he'd just produced a knife.

Cody started tapping them on the shoulder excitedly from behind. 'Dad, Ophelia, look, it's the Empire State Building! We're nearly there.'

She tried to enjoy The Rockettes—it was Cody's day and she should have been ecstatic that Jax was here with them all, making such a huge effort in spite of her announcement about the partnership. Her mother was certainly charmed already. But her heart was a stone where it should have been butterflies—he was literally pulling away from her now. Maybe he was realising her future really was all lined up, and that he shouldn't have got involved with her or brought Cody along for the ride.

She stared at the shoppers, and a guy in a Santa's hat who reminded her of Hunter. Going back to this life, after throwing herself so fully into life in Montana, was going to be tough, but she had always known that. Jax and Cody's home was in Montana, and hers was here. She'd seen the look on her father's face earlier on; his reaction went deeper than just his desire for her to take the role he'd always planned for her. He was also worried that he might lose her to Montana, after losing Ant. She simply couldn't let him down.

CHAPTER FIFTEEN

THE THAI RESTAURANT was like a busy Christmas cave of Buddha statues, somewhere on the Lower East Side. Marvin and Cecelia had been kind enough to offer Cody a bed for the night after the matinee, and Cody had been entranced by the promise of ice cream and New York history books instead of the hotel. So here they were, he and Ophelia, sitting around another table with two more people he'd never met before.

He would have preferred for him and Ophelia to do something on their own, like find the stars through the smog in Central Park and talk about this partnership. It had crossed his mind that maybe she regretted letting him and Cody come here. The resentment he felt was tough to ignore. He knew he should have been stronger and not brought his son into this at all, but he'd done it anyway. This was all on him.

'So is it true that everyone carries guns in Montana?' Damian asked him. Damian was Ophelia's friend Jordi's boyfriend, a plastic surgeon with far too much gel in his hair.

'That is not true,' Jax answered, stabbing a chopstick into a dim sum. He wasn't quite sure how to eat such fancy food.

'But Montana *does* permit people to carry firearms in

public without a permit or licence,' Ophelia said beside him, eyes on his chopstick error.

Jordi smirked. 'Are you planning on heading out there, shooting up some cowboys in a bar brawl, Damian?'

'The cowboys rent out a percentage of my land in the summer,' Jax cut in. He saw Jordi mouth *my land* at Ophelia from behind her hand, as if she was impressed, but he wasn't trying to brag. 'They staff our working ranch vacations. Horse riding and cattle drives are a big summer draw when the skiing stops. Maybe you'd like to learn something from those cowboys, Damian, before you shoot them.'

He wasn't in the mood for this guy's stereotypes, or the fancy food. Ophelia was looking at her hands on her lap under the table. 'I didn't know you hosted cattle drives in the summer,' she said quietly.

'There's a lot you won't get to see at Clayborn Creek, I guess,' he told her.

Jordi put a hand on Ophelia's. 'We're running out of time to visit you there. You don't have long left, do you? Unless you're thinking of staying? I'm sure Jax would have you, for as long as you wanted.'

'Ophelia has other plans,' he announced curtly, catching Jordi's eyes as she reached for the bottle of wine.

'Well, it's always good to have options. Right, Ophie?'

'Does this wine smell off to you guys?' Ophelia asked suddenly, swirling the Sauvignon Blanc in her glass.

He took it from her and sniffed it himself. 'No.'

Jordi was still glowering over her plate, tapping her fork in irritation against a fishcake. He got the distinct impression this long-time friend of Ophelia's knew she didn't particularly want this partnership and was encouraging her to consider alternatives. Ophelia was still pulling a face over the wine.

'Let *me* smell it.' Jordi reached for the glass, just as a commotion behind them made her spill it right into the dish of prawn crackers.

'Help, he's choking! Someone do something!' The cry from across the restaurant made them all turn to the couple at the table in the corner. Jax was off his chair like lightning. Ophelia followed, leaving Jordi and Damian behind. She still felt queasy from the single sip of wine she'd had and the mess her heart was in, but an Asian guy in a smart blue suit jacket was spluttering and banging his chest, gasping for air in his seat.

'Zhang, you're choking!' His date had sprung from the chair opposite him.

'I'm not choking,' Zhang managed to say when they reached him. 'Nuts,' he spluttered, putting his hands to his pockets, patting himself down.

'You have a nut allergy?' Jax started rifling through his pockets for him.

'Do you have an EpiPen?' Ophelia asked, but Zhang's reddening face told her no.

Someone had called 911. Jax pulled a cushion from a chair and together they lowered Zhang to the floor before he had a chance to fall. Balancing on her heels wasn't easy, she noted, realising she actually missed her flat shoes, back in Montana. She noticed white wine splashes on her red satin skirt as she helped elevate Zhang's legs over another pile of cushions. Somewhere, someone was snapping photos of the emergency on their phone. Why did people have to do that?

'Oh, my God, what's happening?' The woman Zhang had been dining with was dressed in a Christmas patterned blouse and headband, tottering awkwardly on high-heeled boots beside them in a panic.

'He must have eaten nuts by accident,' Jax said. 'Why did he come out without his EpiPen?'

'This is only our first date, so I don't know,' she answered, grabbing up her purse. She was clearly mortified. 'I have antihistamines—will those work?'

'No,' Ophelia and Jax answered together. She met his eyes, finding the calm place only he could take her to, wherever they were. Everyone in the restaurant was looking, and the man seemed to breathe one last laboured breath before his body went limp on the floor. 'Looks like full-blown anaphylaxis,' she cried, as rapid heat built up at her collar.

'Help is coming,' someone said. She was trying to stay calm, but the woman's crying was going straight to her heart, and her stomach was still in knots. There was no substitute for epinephrine, which she and Jax both knew was the only first-line treatment for anaphylaxis.

She crouched beside him as he started CPR, keeping count as sirens wailed somewhere outside. Jax was all dressed up for a night out in Manhattan. His Rolex flashed from the sleeve of her favourite soft green sweater as his hands pumped for life at Zhang's heart. The sight filled her with the most harrowing helplessness, until he ordered her to take over.

Her palms were sweating. Zhang still wasn't breathing. The blue lights from the ambulance flooded through the restaurant door and out of the corner of her eye she saw Jordi and Damian watching the scene in shock, their meal and wine forgotten.

Her palms worked Zhang's heart, and silently she begged it to start. She'd helped dozens of people out of trouble in the wilds of Montana over the last few weeks, she was not about to lose a patient now, in a Thai restaurant in New York.

Jax had gone to fill the paramedics in and now he was back, putting a firm hand to her arm. 'Ophelia, let them take over,' he said gently, just as Zhang drew a huge, agonised breath under her hands. He was conscious again, barely, his face and lips all swollen. She could hardly believe it. His date emitted a giant sob and some mumbled relieved profanities, and Jax helped Ophelia up from the floor as the stretcher appeared beside them. They watched from the sidelines as a male paramedic administered the epinephrine.

'You both saved his life,' Jordi announced in awe behind them.

Breathless, Ophelia almost stumbled on her heels as she folded into Jax's arms in relief.

'I guess that was their first and last date,' Jordi lamented outside as the ambulance blared its siren again somewhere along Orchard Street.

'He'll be OK now.' Ophelia hugged her coat around her as Damian approached from the restaurant.

'He wouldn't let me pay,' he murmured about Jax, who was still inside. 'Then the manager wouldn't let *him* pay. They're calling you both heroes. Jax is in there answering some journo's questions, by the way. She was sitting at another table watching the whole thing. I think she wanted to get your man alone.'

'I'm not surprised. Jax is so hot,' Jordi whispered to her, flashing her a secret smile above her thick winter scarf. The New York night was almost as cold as Montana was now. 'You were amazing in there, both of you. Whatever's going on between you, you do make an impressive team.'

Ophelia winced, dragging a hand through her hair

before pulling her hat back on. 'Whatever's going on? Is it that obvious?'

'I sensed a little tension before that episode. The way he said, *"Ophelia has other plans"*... Sounds like you finally told him about the partnership?'

'I did,' she said, eyeing the door for Jax. 'I shouldn't have brought him and Cody here. It's just made everything more complicated.'

Jordi's eyes narrowed. 'Love is complicated, though, isn't it?'

'I don't know if it's love...it's way too soon...'

Jordi made a disbelieving sound, then laughed, lowering her voice. 'Ophelia, this is so romantic, a whirlwind!'

Ophelia put a hand to her own stomach. She still felt nauseous and her friend saw to the core of her, which had always meant so much. Still, she couldn't speak the truth out loud—it would make it real and so much harder to ignore.

'It doesn't matter if I am in love with him,' she said tightly. 'Dad needs me here and Jax will never be with someone who isn't *there*—that place is a part of him. With Ant gone it's up to me...'

'Ophelia, please listen to yourself. If Ant was here he would tell you to do what makes you happy. I knew him too, don't forget. I think you're just scared to fall in love again, because it means putting your heart on the line. Your heart has already been through a lot, and it sounds like his has too.'

She closed her eyes as the cold, wet snow fell on her cheeks. 'You're right about that.'

When Jordi and her man left in a taxi, the snow fell in slow motion around her while her head spun. Jordi was right about Ant, Ophelia realised, staring at the blinking Santas lining the door of the bar across the street. He would just want her to be happy. If only he were here to give her some direct advice, but Ant was harder to hear on these streets than he used to be for some reason.

Where was Jax?

'Hey, excuse me, miss, do you know what just happened here? I live around the block, and I heard the sirens.'

Ophelia recognised the voice before she even turned around.

'Hello, Sanjay.'

Her past life in the poky apartment flashed before her eyes, along with all the nights she'd waited up after sixteen-hour shifts in the ER just to be awake when he came home, only to discover he'd avoided her and slept somewhere else again. Even before Ant had died. Wait, why hadn't he recognised her? She put a hand to her hair and realised it wasn't exactly as sleek as it had been when she'd lived here.

'Ophelia? How long have you been back?' His surprised brown eyes scanned her outfit up and down, as though he really were seeing her for the first time. His winter coat was the same grey duffel he'd bought five years ago in the Macy's sale, and his trouser legs still didn't meet his shoes. He thought it made him look like more of a creative, more of a musician.

She told him about the incident inside and he tapped the toe of his sneaker to the toe of her boot and smirked. 'I always had a feeling you were Superwoman,' he said. She didn't respond. In fact she stepped back impulsively, feeling nothing. Where was Jax?

'My date will be out any second,' she said. 'It was nice to see you again. Merry Christmas.'

Sanjay shifted awkwardly and the blue pulls from the hood of a sweater she recognised fell from the top of his open coat. She'd pulled him closer by them once after dinner in this same restaurant, but the memory was vague and almost not her own. It was only Jax's face she saw now.

Sanjay must have seen something else in the dead air between them. The second she went to turn away he caught her hand and pulled her in close for a hug.

'God, you look so...*you*,' he breathed into her hair, inhaling her scent like a drug. 'How could I forget how the sight of you used to make me—'

'No, Sanjay. I'm here with someone else.' She disentangled herself quickly, only to see Jax exiting the restaurant, wrapping his scarf around his neck, looking straight at them.

'Who was that?' he asked her when she reached him. He was following Sanjay up the street with his eyes now, like a hawk.

'Just someone I used to know,' she told him, flustered, trying not to look back at her ex. Jax knew Sanjay had all but abandoned her after losing her brother and her baby—any interaction between them would be awkward at best. These were two separate worlds, and two very different men that she did not need to witness colliding in front of her. Sanjay had made a hurried exit too, after seeing Jax approach her. Maybe he felt the same way?

Her heart skidded all over the place, the whole way back to Brooklyn.

CHAPTER SIXTEEN

'ARE YOU OK?' Jax slid cautiously into the seat next to Ophelia's. Cody had opted for an empty row behind them in the plane and was lost in a book her dad had given him. 'Your silence is kind of loud.'

'I'm OK, just...thinking.' She was still staring at the sky outside and he frowned at the seat back in front of him. Thanks to the event coordinators being promised Jax's plane for the Christmas party supplies, they were on the commercial flight back to Bozeman together. And he still had no idea where they stood. Instead of spending the last day in New York with them, Ophelia had just met them at the airport.

If she didn't want to talk he couldn't force her, but he hadn't seen her alone since he and Cody had left her parents' place this morning, after the Thai restaurant incident the evening before.

'Are you thinking about this partnership?' he asked. 'I guess your father's keen to get everything set up before you're due to start working there...not long to go now.'

He was testing her and he knew it, asking indirectly if she'd changed her mind, but Ophelia simply nodded, pulling the edge of her lip between her teeth. He couldn't help thinking she was stewing over how to remind him that she'd warned him coming home with her would be a bad idea. He'd been going over the ways she might end this whole thing.

'Can I get you a drink, Mr Clayborn?' The hostess was far too cheery for his mood.

'No, thanks. Ophelia, do you want anything else? Did you eat earlier?' Again she shook her head and went back to assessing the clouds through the window.

The hostess wheeled her cart on and he pressed buttons at random on the in-flight entertainment system, waiting for Ophelia to speak, his own mind going round in circles. Who was that guy he'd seen with his arms around her last night? The way she'd answered his question had made it sound like an ex, and hadn't she said her ex-fiancé was called Sanjay? Asian perhaps, like the guy he'd seen. If that had been him, why hadn't she just admitted it? Did Sanjay have anything to do with Ophelia's silence now?

Damn this. The quieter she was, the more questions reared up to torture him. He'd already messed up big time, letting Cody bond with her, and her family too, for that matter. Why was he even waiting for her to tell *him* that they were over?

'I guess this is where we end things,' he heard himself say, suddenly.

'What?' Pain shimmered in her green eyes as she turned to him in surprise, but the words were out and he knew he had to hold his ground. He had to do it first, now, or it would be worse when she left after Christmas. She was getting to him more than was good for anyone. It would just drag on, and this could affect Cody even more if Jax wasn't careful.

'I know you think your life is in New York, and I accept that, but it means this…you and me, we can't continue, for all our sakes. You know that, right, Ophelia?'

* * *

Ophelia swallowed the lump in her throat and pulled herself together. Jax was breaking her heart, but she hadn't exactly given him any concrete answers about her future plans. Or told him how she felt about him. The words *I think I might be pregnant* just wouldn't leave her mouth.

'Maybe we were both a little hasty, taking Cody to New York with us,' Jax ventured next, when she didn't speak.

'I thought he had a great time,' she followed quietly, but she knew that was exactly Jax's point. Cody was getting attached to her, and her parents too. Marvin and Cecelia had treated him like some surrogate grandson the whole time. They'd invited him to stay with them whenever he liked, and Marvin's offer to be his official museum tour guide had filled her with joy and left her with an equal sense of foreboding.

She searched Jax's eyes, wishing she knew how to tell him exactly why she was being so quiet and distant.

Alone at Ant's grave early this morning, she had told her brother she'd always love him, but it was time to make some of her own life choices, instead of following what had once been their dream of working together with their dad. She'd prepared to tell her father she would help him find another partner for the practice, how great it would be to admit to Jax that she was finally free. She'd thought that maybe Jax would have some other ideas for her that involved him and Cody, so at least they could spend more time together going forward. Fresh hope and optimism had consumed her the whole way back to her parents' house.

Then her mother had sat a smoked salmon bagel in front of her, and just the smell of it…

She'd made her excuses and gone straight to the pharmacy. Against the cool tiles of a hotel bathroom she'd unwrapped the pregnancy test and spent at least half an hour preparing herself to pee on the stick. Every time she'd gone into the stall, though, she'd chickened out, frozen in fear over what it might reveal. Time had ticked past in the hotel bathroom, until she'd realised she needed to be at the airport ASAP, so she'd left without taking it. The test was still waiting like a harbinger of doom at the bottom of her purse. She would have to wait till she got to Montana, but the fear was growing inside her by the minute, rendering her silent. She could hardly look Jax in the eye as it was. And now he was breaking things off? Now he really didn't want to be with her at all.

'I was about to talk to my father,' she managed as the panic swelled in her gut and threatened to make her sick again. 'But something came up.'

'What came up?'

She swallowed and looked at her nails. Counting back, she realised she was over two weeks late for her period. She'd failed to see the signs because she'd been so caught up in everything going on with Jax, and the job and Montana, but the more she thought about it, the more she knew she'd been here before—the aversion to regular tastes and smells, the swollen breasts, the nausea. This had happened before and she'd been proven right; the first test she'd taken in the apartment she'd shared with Sanjay had been positive. Then she'd got way too excited. She'd gone and told everybody far too soon.

And in a cruel twist of fate, she'd lost the baby when she'd assumed she was safe.

'Maybe it's best if we cool things down for now,' she said reluctantly, forcing her hands to stay on her lap and not reach for him, trying not to get emotional. Not only was he pulling away from her, Jax had been through enough grief in his life already, and so had she. If she *was* carrying his baby and anything happened to it…

She needed time to think. If she was pregnant, it warranted a conversation—hell, it would warrant more than that, her whole life would be turned upside down again, but she wouldn't know for sure until she took the test. There was a chance she was reading the signs wrong anyway, she thought suddenly, wracking her brains again as to when exactly this could have happened. They'd been careful, hadn't they?

Apart from that very first time, in the ice cave…

'You're a hero in New York.' Marni swooned a week later, shoving the phone into Jax's hand. 'Or maybe you're just a hero everywhere, huh?'

Jax scanned the article on the *New York Post* website, dated the day after they'd brought Zhang back from the brink of what had almost been a fatal anaphylactic shock in the Thai restaurant.

> *Montana native Dr Jax Clayborn was enjoying dinner with New Yorker Dr Ophelia Lavelle and friends when a ruckus at a nearby table caught their attention. Abandoning their meal, the brave pair were first on the scene, clearing the path for emergency services and administering CPR…*

'Sounds like the guy's only alive because of you,' Marni continued, taking the phone back.

'It was actually Dr Lavelle who brought him back from the brink,' he said, registering the tightness of his stomach at the sound of her name on his lips.

'So…what were you guys doing in New York at the same time anyway? Was that planned, or just a coincidence?'

'How about we focus on the hypothermia seminar notes?' he replied, tapping a finger to the book, which was open on a page about extracorporeal membrane oxygenation.

Marni chattered on about the seminar, and he answered her questions as best he could, though his mind insisted on raking over everything that had happened in New York, and on the plane home, when Ophelia told him something had come up. She'd failed to elaborate. Jax had taken no pleasure in admitting to his father that he'd ended his affair with Ophelia.

'You did what? Why? I think she's good for you, and Cody too.'

Abe had looked more angry at his decision than surprised.

'She has other obligations in New York at the end of this contract, with her father.'

'Are you sure you're not making excuses, after what happened to Juno? Give her a chance, son. I know you've been through hell, but it's been four years. You deserve to be happy.'

He knew Abe was right about him making excuses. It had been a snap judgement, telling her it was over, a voice born from fear and pride. He was still testing Ophelia's affections for both him and Montana, which was not entirely fair, but he couldn't shake the thought that something else was going on with her, something other than the partnership in New York. Something to do with that guy he'd seen with his arms around her, outside the restaurant, perhaps. Her ex. Was that the *something* that had come up?

The upcoming Christmas Eve party was a big deal to everyone, especially Cody. Now he couldn't even think about dancing with her under the damn mistletoe without bristling.

Don't think about her. Focus.

Marni looked up from her book as the wooden door swung open in a bluster of wind and snow. Ophelia was here, as if he'd summoned her just by deciding not to think about her. He watched her scan the lodge in her woollen hat and coat. His heart betrayed him as it kicked at his ribs in desire to go to her...right before she made a beeline straight for him.

CHAPTER SEVENTEEN

MARNI EYED HER up and down as Ophelia approached their booth, as if she was interrupting something personal. Jealousy flared into irritation as she realised Jax might be responding encouragingly to Marni's flirtations, now that their little fling was over.

You would only have yourself to blame if he were, she thought ruefully.

She'd called her father and admitted that, yes, Jax was important—or had been—and, yes, she'd been having second thoughts about the partnership. She'd asked him for more time, and surprisingly he'd given it to her, albeit with a warning not to take too long. Christmas was only a matter of days away, and she'd be gone soon after that. But she still hadn't summoned the strength to take the pregnancy test.

Every time she took it from the drawer in her cabin and went to the bathroom, telling herself to face the music, the thought of it showing up positive was so terrifying and raw...and a painful reminder of what had happened to her before...she put it straight back again. Consequently she'd been avoiding Jax and the opportunity to blurt out what she knew. Or didn't know, for sure.

'Aubrey Jenson and her mother are missing,' she told

him now, forcing her reeling mind to focus on why she'd come to find him.

Jax's handsome face darkened in concern as he stood and took her aside. 'Cody's friend Aubrey, who he was teaching to snowboard?'

Ophelia nodded, going to touch the arrow pendant on her necklace, which still wasn't there.

'Carson just called me,' she explained. 'He said Mr Jenson left the slopes early to shower. He expected them back in their cabin shortly after, but they never came back, and now Mrs Jenson isn't answering her phone. We think they're still somewhere out there on the mountain.'

Jax put a hand to her arm over her coat, and the heat of him pulled at her heartstrings. This was the first time he'd spoken to her properly about anything since they'd been back, and she suspected he'd been avoiding her too.

'How long has it been?'

'At least forty minutes.'

'Do Search and Rescue know?'

'Carson was calling them…'

'We'll take the snowmobile to Base. If no one's brought them back yet, I know places they might not have thought to cover.'

Jax grabbed up his scarf from the back of the booth and made his apologies to Marni. 'I'm afraid that's it for the extra tutorial.'

'I can come, help you guys look for them,' Marni said, closing her textbook.

'It's safer if you stay here,' Jax told Marni, pulling on his heavy jacket.

'But this is what we've been training for.'

'Not today,' he said.

'How come Ophelia gets to go? Is it because you're not so secretly dating?'

'No, it's because this is my job,' Ophelia answered her coolly. She kept her head held high as she followed him outside, in spite of her racing heart.

'It's been almost an hour now,' Carson said to him in concern when Jax swung through the doors at Base with Ophelia.

'Ophelia can come with me.' Jax snatched up his radio from where he'd left it and Carson made to pull his coat on, signalling to Nurse May to take over.

'I could take the other snowmobile...'

'No. Stay here, please.'

'Will do. Search and Rescue went to slopes two and three, that's where they were last seen,' Carson said, just as Jax's radio echoed with one of the guys out on patrol.

'No sign of them yet.'

Ophelia was shoving items into her medical kit: a flashlight, stethoscope, blood-pressure cuff and a bag valve mask. This would be interesting, the two of them together out there, he thought, catching her eye as she swung a backpack over her shoulders. Her own apprehension met his from across the room but he forged ahead with a deep frown. He couldn't get distracted.

Outside he strapped a board to the snowmobile, praying the Jensons hadn't gone far and that nothing bad had surprised them out there. No one had seen the bear in a while, but they couldn't afford to get too complacent.

Jax sped them towards the mountain, feeling her arms tighten more around his waist from behind with every bump. Absently he wondered whether moments like this were the only times they'd make physical contact from now on. It seemed as if she'd made her decision, whether she was saying so or not. Soon she'd be home in New York and she wouldn't be coming back.

At least there was always plenty here to distract him from the distraction of Ophelia, he thought to himself wistfully.

Minutes passed in silence. There was still no sign of Aubrey or Mrs Jenson and his radio had gone eerily quiet. 'Hold on tight,' he called back, making a U-turn off the slope into the forest. Ophelia gasped and for one horrifying second he thought she was about to slide off the seat and wind up in a heap against a tree.

In a blur of snowy branches he clamped a hand to her calf and skidded to a stop. 'I said hold on tight,' he said gruffly. 'I'd like to send you back to New York alive.'

Jax's eyes were boring into hers over his shoulder and she read only anger in them. Whether he was angry at her or himself for going too fast, she couldn't tell, but Ophelia hadn't missed the real meaning in his words. Jax was already preparing for her imminent, permanent departure, the week after Christmas.

'I'll be going back alive, don't worry,' she retorted, as her pride spoke over her real feelings. Even if she did want to refuse the partnership now, she could hardly stay here, seeing as Jax was backing off faster than a bullet in reverse.

Jax started the motor again, but he didn't move the snowmobile. She could almost feel him breathing in the calm of the mountain and the quiet of the snowy fir trees, trying to regain composure.

She heard the words in her head: *Jax, I think I'm pregnant.* She could say it out loud right now if she wanted to, right against the back of his jacket; the man had every right to know. But the thought of what she might see when he turned around stopped her yet again. Would he reject her outright? He'd already broken up with her. Fear and anxiety grabbed her by the tongue and dried out her mouth even as she pressed a cheek to his back and held on tighter. What would she do if she *was* able to carry his baby to full term, and he didn't want it, as Sanjay hadn't?

Now they were on a trail she hadn't seen before. It was colder than she'd ever felt it outside, and she was already bundled so hard into her scarf she could barely blink without it getting in her eyes. 'Jax, where are we?'

'Cody told me he and Abe took Aubrey to the ringing rocks once. I thought maybe she took her mom there.'

'Ringing rocks?'

'It's kind of a secret place on the property. The tourists don't usually go there, it's off a pretty perilous path—no phone signal either.'

Jax was whipping up the snow, making fresh tracks. She prayed he knew the kind of terrain that was hidden under the snow, but she trusted him as much to guide her out here as he'd trusted her with the recommended itinerary she'd made for Cody in New York. Still, he had another secret place out here that he hadn't shown her yet…

He probably has a million of them that he'll never get to show you if you keep on pushing him away.

She was still protecting her heart from Jax, she realised, as much as from the potential pain of losing another baby. It was getting her nowhere. Tonight, she decided, she would take the damn pregnancy test and let the truth decide her fate.

Suddenly Jax's hand was on her thigh again, yanking her from her reverie. Then he pulled the snowmobile to a skidding halt. 'I think I just saw something.'

Hitting reverse, they slid back on the track and Ophelia saw it too, a flash of pink up ahead on a smaller walking trail. 'A ski suit,' they said at the exact same time.

Quick as a flash, she was off the back before Jax had

even removed his helmet, wading through knee-deep snow towards some trees.

'Aubrey!'

Ophelia could see the child's long blonde ponytail dangling in a wet mess down the back of her hot-pink ski suit. The frightened girl was crouched in front of Mrs Jenson, lying lifeless on the snow. 'What happened, sweetie?'

'She's not moving. Please, help my mom!' Poor Aubrey's lips were blue and she was quivering with the cold.

Jax put an ear to the woman's mouth, then checked her wrist for a pulse. 'Her pulse is weak but she's still breathing.'

After seeing there were no obvious injuries, they rolled her carefully to her back while Aubrey sobbed beside them, breaking Ophelia's heart. The woman's face was ghostly white; blonde hair like Aubrey's hung limp and wet from her hat. Ophelia checked her eyes for signs of a spark, while Jax radioed Search and Rescue and the team at Base, and raced back to the snowmobile for the spinal board.

Pulling blankets out of her backpack, Ophelia let Aubrey help her cover her mother against the harsh wind and snow. Whatever had happened, hypothermia on top would not be good. Then she and Jax eased her on to the board, soothing a crying Aubrey at the same time. 'We're here to help her, honey. Can you tell me what happened?'

'We were walking on the trail, then I led her off to see the secret place. Then she said her head hurt and she fell down.'

'What happened to make her head hurt? Did she have an accident when you were skiing earlier?' Ophelia helped Jax lift the spinal board. It was tougher in the thick, wet snow, like wading through quicksand, but she summoned a strength she didn't even know she had in her. Still, she noticed Jax eyeing her with caution, as if she might break. How would he treat her out here if he thought she was pregnant? she wondered suddenly. Would he stop her working altogether? He couldn't have just stopped caring about her, just like that, could he? He was nothing like Sanjay.

But he told you it was over, she reminded herself, feeling colder at the notion of going through a pregnancy alone.

Aubrey followed them, her words still blighted by heavy sobs.

'She fell over and hit her head before. On the slope, over an hour ago. She said she was OK, though. OK enough to come see the ringing rocks.'

'She came off her skis earlier?' Jax met Ophelia's eyes now over his radio and she knew what he was thinking.

'Was she complaining of anything after she fell?' she asked the little girl. 'Headaches, nausea, any vomiting?'

'I don't know…maybe…she said she had a headache.'

'Was she wearing a helmet?'

'Yes.' Aubrey hugged her arms around herself, watching her mother being strapped to the back of the snowmobile.

Jax lowered his voice in her ear. 'She could have a subdural haematoma, or worse.'

'Should we send her straight to Willow Crest?'

'It'll be quicker to get her to Base right now through all these trees—a medevac won't be able to get to us fast enough.'

She held his eyes for the first time in days, wishing she could still be this close without wanting to grab him, and hold him. 'OK, it's your call,' she said.

She knew full well that all appropriate efforts had to be

explored and implemented before calling in outside help, and indeed the forest was too thick here for a helicopter rescue. But a haematoma was a slow-growing blood clot that could prove fatal, and Mrs Jenson's life was in their hands, at least two miles by snowmobile to Base.

Ophelia wrapped another blanket around the little girl's shoulders and let Jax lift her up to the seat. Her own worries faded into insignificance as they took off on the snowmobile with Aubrey sandwiched between them on the seat and Mrs Jenson on the spinal board behind them. Unlike back in New York when they'd had an ambulance around every corner, this was turning into a life-or-death situation in freezing temperatures, and they were losing daylight fast. The woman's suspected injury usually began with some slow bleeding, so sufferers tended to seem fine at first. Then, within an hour or two they usually complained of a headache...just as Aubrey had said.

'Jax, I think we should take the disused slope from here,' she told him suddenly, hoping he'd agree. 'I know there's no proper trail down but it's the fastest way.'

'You're right, and that's exactly where we're going,' Jax replied. To her surprise his voice had no hint of hesitation as he hit the accelerator.

CHAPTER EIGHTEEN

JAX LOOKED UP as Ophelia walked towards them with the CT scan results. Beside him Mr Jenson stood from his plastic seat. The poor guy had been wringing his hands for the entire last thirty minutes while Mrs Jenson had been hooked up to breathing assistance. Jax's heart was heavy, and Ophelia's face filled him with dread.

'Your wife is with Dr Fenway. You can see her in a moment. The scans show quite a lot of swelling in her brain, I'm afraid, Mr Jenson.'

'Oh, God.' The poor man looked as if he was about to fall over, and Jax put a firm hand to his arm, encouraging him to sit again.

Ophelia took the chair on the other side of him and Jax's stomach lurched as he noticed how unusually pale and tired she looked. 'I understand you were with her when she fell earlier, and she was definitely wearing a helmet?' she asked.

'Yes, of course, we always wear helmets.'

'Well, she should have sought medical help right after her fall, but maybe she didn't think anything was wrong.'

Jax drew a long deep breath. They should have reported the incident; there were signs up everywhere telling people to do so, but often people were so afraid of being taken off the slopes that they carried on skiing, even after accidents.

'Occasionally, a bleed of this kind is slow and the body is able to absorb the pooled blood,' she continued. 'We got her back here in time to ensure she's still breathing...'

'She's alive, because of you,' Mr Jenson croaked.

'We'd like to transfer her to Willow Crest Trauma where the neurosurgeon can better monitor her condition,' Ophelia interjected. Jax could tell she was trying not to infuse false hope in the man.

'You mean, she could have brain damage?' Mr Jenson's hands came up over his face. 'Oh, God, this is all my fault. I told her we should call the ski patrol to take her for a check-up after she hit her head, but she brushed me off, she insisted she was fine. I was so tired after skiing, but I should have made her go see someone...'

'It's not your fault,' Jax said quickly. 'Please don't blame yourself. That will get you nowhere fast.' He stood and paced the room a second, feeling Ophelia's eyes on him as she spoke to Mr Jenson calmly and gently, the way she did to every emotional relative. As a doctor he was practised at handling this stuff too, but this was all a little too close to home.

Taking a breath, he reminded himself he'd worked hard to battle his grief, and he'd moved on. He'd spent too many years beating himself up over what he could have done differently on the day Juno died. In the end, though, it had just been a terrible accident and nobody deserved to be blamed. Just like with Ophelia's brother.

Jax arranged for Aubrey to stay at the main house in his care while her parents were gone. Mr Jenson was in pieces and didn't want to upset his daughter even more, and Jax knew all too well what that felt like. He only hoped he could comfort the little girl if the hospital called with bad news... He hoped to God he wouldn't have to.

As if she were reading his mind, Ophelia offered to come back with him for a while. 'Only if you want me to,' she said with trepidation, as Carson approached. 'I'd like to be there for her.'

'That's going above and beyond, both of you,' Carson said with a tired smile. 'I can't tell you how grateful we are to have you on this team, Ophelia. In fact, I can think of no one else I would rather hand the reins over to next spring, when I retire.'

Jax's heart almost leapt to his throat as Ophelia's eyes narrowed.

'I'm sure Jax has discussed the possibility with you already,' Carson continued. 'While it's not my idea of heaven, sitting back and letting someone else take control, I suppose I'll be glad to know that someone like you might be on site permanently.'

Ophelia's weary smile had disappeared. 'Actually, Carson, Jax hasn't mentioned anything of the sort to me.'

'Oh...well, I'm sure he was planning to. Right, Jax?'

Jax shrugged. What could he say now?

Carson could see he'd put his foot in it. He made his excuses and moved swiftly to the consultation room, leaving them alone.

'You thought you'd test me out before you even mentioned Carson's role, am I right? Is that why you didn't tell me, Jax?'

Ophelia looked understandably defensive. They were standing under the mistletoe again, right where he'd first kissed her cheek. 'I was going to ask you, but you seemed pretty adamant you were going to take the partnership with your father and I didn't think it was right to stand in your way. What do we have here that's better than what he's offering you in New York?'

'Are you serious?'

'Serious as that bear that's still on the loose somewhere.' He couldn't help his tone—his own defences were out in force. She wouldn't have taken the job anyway, not with such prospects at home—this thing with them had only ever been a little fun for both of them, hadn't it?

Ophelia pursed her lips, and he was shocked to see her eyes flood with tears before she turned away and straightened up. 'You're right,' she said, head held high, arms still crossed. 'You're absolutely right, Jax. While I love it here, and I'm honoured Carson thought of me for the role, even if you didn't—'

'That's not entirely true,' he cut in.

'My obligations are with my family. They always have been.'

'And mine are with this team,' he followed, matching her stance. 'Making sure we have only the most dedicated people on board.'

Ophelia lowered her gaze. Already he was holding back the urge to pull her in, close the gap between them. 'I know your father needs you,' he said, his tone softer.

She let out a harried sigh and then looked him in the eyes. 'I spoke to him actually, and he gave me a little more time to think about the plan…our plan for the practice. You made me think, Jax, about the way I've been carrying all this blame over Ant. You made me think about how it's time I created my own path, whatever that means going forward.'

He nodded, watching her shift in her shoes a moment. He was glad Ophelia had come to this realisation on her own. Still…if creating her own path involved going back to Sanjay too, he would rather not hear about it.

He *had* to ask, though, else it would eat him up.

'Is there someone else, Ophelia, in New York? Someone waiting for you there. The whole package? Your ex, maybe?'

'What?'

He'd said it now, and he almost regretted it. Ophelia looked stunned, and horrified, as if he'd shot a moose in front of her and asked her to drag it down the mountain with him. 'Jax. Is that what you really think?'

He shifted in his boots, which felt heavier suddenly, like his shoulders. She didn't look at all as if she was lying, but what else could it be? His pride was telling him to walk away. How could this woman be affecting him like this, when he'd sworn not to let anyone shift his focus from the mountain and Cody? He didn't need the complications, and neither did his son, especially now.

'Jax, I know I've been distant lately, but...'

Her hand went to the missing pendant momentarily before she remembered it still wasn't there, and she dragged a hand through her hair nervously. 'There are some things I still need to deal with...'

There it was, he thought bitterly, that *look*. The *look* that told him she was hiding something.

'And I'm not going to stand in your way,' he said coolly. 'Now, if you'll excuse me, it's been a long day. I should probably handle Cody and Aubrey alone. Less complicated, I'm sure you'll agree.'

Before she could argue, he left the clinic and drove the snowmobile too fast back to the main house. As if the situation with Aubrey's mother weren't enough weight on his mind, all he could see now was that Sanjay guy with his arms around Ophelia outside the restaurant. Why had she not seen them on that last day in New York—had she been with him then too?

Maybe she just didn't want to hurt him by telling him the truth, but what difference did it make now anyway? They weren't together any more. But something didn't add up and he was not about to be taken for a fool.

Ophelia dropped to the bed in pure exhaustion. The events of the last couple of hours had almost broken her. Poor little Aubrey was sitting with Jax and Cody and Abe right now, wondering if her mother was going to make it. She should be there too, offering some kind of support… but Jax hadn't wanted her there.

It was most unfair of her to keep Jax in the dark because of her own inner turmoil. She couldn't blame him for leaping to the conclusion that she might have some deep, dark secret back home, but Sanjay? Did Jax really think she'd have feelings for her ex after everything that had happened? What a mess.

She couldn't put it off any longer. Reaching for the remote control, she summoned a Christmas movie to the TV for comfort, then pulled out the pregnancy test from the bedside drawer. Minutes felt like hours in the bathroom as she stared at the stick on the sink from the other side of the room.

Someone laughed on the TV and she took a deep breath. Everything *will* be OK, she reminded herself, though her mouth was dry and her mind was foggy. What if it came up positive, and she told Jax, and he was *happy* about it? What if she then lost this baby too? She almost couldn't look at the stick.

Leaving it sitting ominously on the sink, she paced the cabin, her thoughts whirring again. She didn't even really care that Jax had kept Carson's role a secret from her. He'd been right, she had been adamant that she'd take the partnership, right up to her realisation that the universe, or maybe even Ant from somewhere else, might be trying to sway her in another direction.

'I wish you were here, Ant,' she despaired at the mirror, putting a hand to her throat again where the arrow pendant should have been. 'Can't you give me some kind of sign that you're still with me, somehow? I wish so much we could talk about all this together.'

Hopefully she waited for something to happen, maybe a flicker of a light, or a gust of wind from nowhere. Nothing. Of course, nothing.

Picking up her phone in procrastination, she was surprised to see a message that she must have missed earlier. It was from Sanjay. Startled by the inappropriate and slightly eerie timing from her ex, she opened it. A photo. It was the two of them back in happier times, smiling side by side outside the same Thai restaurant where they'd bumped into each other before.

It was so good to see you. Thank you for the memories. X

She had to read it at least three times before the simple words sank in; her mind was still on the test, lying in wait for her on the sink.

'You're being ridiculous, Ophelia,' she scolded herself. 'Just look at the damn test!'

Tossing the phone down, she forgot the message instantly. Taking a deep breath, she picked up the stick, and almost fainted on the floor when she saw the result.

'Ophelia!' Jax watched his son get up from the floor by the Christmas tree and offer to take her coat. What was she doing here after their last conversation? he wondered, before thinking maybe he'd been a little harsh, telling her not to come with them. Of course she cared about Aubrey, and the kid was technically in both of their care till further notice.

'We have to be quiet. Aubrey is sleeping,' Cody whispered, taking her thick jacket and scarf, which probably weighed more than him. Jax watched half in amusement as he went to hang them up, stretching his arms valiantly to reach the hooks on the wall.

'Want some help, bud?'

'I'm good.'

'How is she?' Ophelia asked Jax. She was wearing a blue cashmere sweater, shaking off her boots by the door. Cody took her hat next and she smoothed down her hair, as if it mattered. He was used to seeing her less glamorous side by now, and he assumed she was more comfortable in her real skin out here too. Or had been.

'She's pretty shaken up, poor kid,' he said as she pulled a cushion to her lap on the opposite end of the couch to him—another barrier. She looked worried sick. 'I shouldn't have told you not to come back here with us,' he admitted quietly.

She shook off his words. 'I know why you said it. I came here to talk to you.'

'OK.' He glanced at Cody, struggling valiantly with the winter items behind the door. 'It's probably not the best time…'

'I know. Tell me about it.' She looked around the room anxiously, and he knew instinctively that whatever it was she wanted to tell him wasn't good. Was there anything good about today? he thought wearily, catching the invites for the Christmas Eve party on the table. Freshly printed reminders for tomorrow night. Tomorrow! It had come around so fast. So much had happened since he'd met Ophelia.

He was surprised at how differently he thought about Juno's accident now, compared to a few months ago, because of Ophelia. He'd got them all back to Base in half the time just now by taking the slope he'd closed off. He'd done it twice, in fact; it was clearly the best way back here. They should have made it a rescue route years before Juno's accident, instead of keeping those views for themselves. He owed his reformed way of thinking to Ophelia…even if they were no longer together.

'We just heard from Willow Crest,' he told her. 'They took Mrs Jenson in for emergency surgery. All we can do now is wait. They got her straight on to life support but the bleeding was intense. I'm guessing all we did was buy her a bit more time.'

Ophelia shook her head. 'We did everything we could,' she said softly. 'You took the disused slope back to Base. Short of airlifting her ourselves through the forest, which was impossible, there was nothing else we could have done.'

'You went out on the slope? Mom's slope?' Cody interjected. 'Are you going to open it back up now?'

'I think I might.' Jax waited for the onslaught of questions. Instead Cody studied them both at their opposite ends of the couch, like a one-person interview panel.

'I think Mom would have wanted it open,' he said after a moment. 'It was her favourite place to ski.'

Jax nodded slowly, letting it sink in. He'd been expecting this conversation to unnerve them both, but Cody seemed quite philosophical about the whole thing, just as he had about clearing out the music room. It was only Ophelia unnerving him now. She was a ball of angst, seeming too close and yet too far away at the same time. But she had been since New York. Because of her ex?

'Dad, do you think Aubrey will lose her mom too,

like I did?' Cody's question came completely out of the blue, shocking him.

'I really hope not, Cody,' Ophelia answered for him. She glanced his way and he knew she didn't want to give Cody false hope. 'But whatever happens, she has a wonderful father who's going to keep on doing everything he can to keep her safe and let her know she's loved, just like your dad does for you. You know, children are a parent's number one priority. Always.'

To Jax's surprise, Cody launched himself at them, wrapping his arms around Ophelia first, then him. Then he pulled them closer, till he was sandwiched between them, with an arm around each.

'We have to be strong for when Aubrey wakes up,' he urged them.

Time seemed to stop in their impromptu group hug until the phone rang in the kitchen. Abe answered and Jax held his breath. He knew it was Carson calling with news from Willow Crest.

'It's for you,' Abe said predictably, coming into the room with the phone.

Jax took the call. 'The surgery was a success,' he said on a relieved exhale when he'd hung up. 'Against all odds, they think she's going to be OK. It will take months of rehab and rest, but she's out of the woods...or forest, so to speak.'

'Oh, thank God.' Ophelia's hands came up over her mouth, just as Cody slumped back against the couch, hardly believing the news. Ophelia offered to wake Aubrey up and break the good news while Jax waited downstairs with Cody, who kept putting his hand over his, as if it was him giving his dad strength this time instead of the other way around. Neither of them were saying it but they'd been through this before, and it hadn't exactly ended up like this. They'd been expecting the worst.

'You see, Dad, you probably saved her life. You and Ophelia,' Cody said thoughtfully, and Jax ruffled the kid's hair affectionately. Whether or not it was true, and whether or not they could keep her, they'd all been lucky to have Ophelia here till now.

Ophelia lingered with Cody while Jax prepared to personally drive the shell-shocked girl to Willow Crest and Mr Jenson. 'Should I stay here?' she asked him, when Cody insisted on helping Aubrey get her coat on. 'We can talk when you get back.'

'As you wish,' he said, and Ophelia pulled his hat down over his head, keeping her hands to his cheeks a moment.

'Aubrey comes first,' she insisted.

He pulled her in closer, breathing her in, finding solace in the closeness of her lips, even if he couldn't read her eyes any more. 'You're one hell of a woman,' he muttered. 'And you drive me crazy.'

For the first time since they'd returned from New York Jax surrendered to his impulses and kissed her.

CHAPTER NINETEEN

WHEN OPHELIA AWOKE after 8:00 a.m., the body beside her in Jax's bed was decidedly less Jax-like than she was used to. Smiling to herself, she realised Cody had snuck in, no doubt to look after her in Jax's absence, being the sweetheart he was. She ran a finger gently across his sleeping forehead and he stirred on top of the blankets, making a clucking sound with his tongue before turning away from her on the pillow.

In that instant, she remembered her news. She'd come to tell Jax she was pregnant, but the events of the night before had delayed her, and now here she was in his bed on Christmas Eve with no sign of him.

Sneaking down the stairs, still in her clothes from last night, she scanned the living room, half expecting him to be asleep on the couch, booted out of his own bed by Cody, perhaps? But he wasn't there either.

'Don't worry, he's fine, everyone's fine. He hasn't got back yet. I didn't want to wake you or Cody.' Abe's voice made her jump. He was holding a cup of his famed cold-smoked coffee and she took it gratefully before remembering she probably shouldn't drink any caffeine.

She took a seat at the huge wooden dining table in the kitchen. The centre was obscured by a huge holly wreath dotted with red candles. Kit, the housekeeper, shot her a knowing smile as she rolled the dough for her gingerbread cookies on the countertop. Outside it was snowing again; she could even see elk prints in the snow. It was advent-calendar perfect, except for the lack of Jax.

'Did you hear from him?' she asked Abe over the carols blasting from the speaker. He was busy unloading the dishwasher, and a secret part of her enjoyed this cosy, homely vibe. It was much nicer than waking up alone, even without Jax here.

'The weather got pretty bad out there, so it was safer for him to stay over. Then he had to stop and collect some supplies for tonight.'

'The party, right...' It was only the talk of the whole town, but she was carrying too much weight on her shoulders to allow any excitement in yet.

'I guess we have more reason to celebrate now, huh?' Abe said, stoking the kitchen fire as she got up to help him with the dishwasher. She froze midway through putting the forks back in their drawer space. What did he mean?

'I imagine there will be a few toasts to Mrs Jenson's speedy recovery tonight, as well as far too much food and liquor,' he elaborated. 'There always is at these things. Are you OK, Ophelia? You went a little pale there.'

'No, no, I'm fine,' she said hastily, grabbing another handful of spoons.

'I hope you're not getting sick,' Abe said, frowning.

For a second she'd thought he knew about the baby... his future second grandson, or granddaughter.

How could he know? Calm down.

'Do you want some chokeberry tea?' he asked next. 'Kit made some the other day.' Kit was already pulling a bottle of dark purple liquid from the refrigerator.

'It's good for you. The Native Americans used it as a cold remedy.'

'Oh, no, thank you,' she replied, touched and also awed that a family of doctors would still reach for stuff like this over modern meds. 'I'm sure it's nothing. So, Abe, Jax says you have a surprise for tonight?'

'I think it will be even better than last year's Rudolph.' Abe chuckled and Ophelia wished she could tell them the truth.

They will know soon enough, she thought as another wave of nausea swept over her. She couldn't stop wondering how Jax would react when she told him he could be a dad for the second time. Would he want to celebrate?

Ophelia surprised herself by knowing where almost everything from the dishwasher lived, from Cody's dinosaur bowl to Jax's *Best Dad in Montana* mug, but when the doorbell rang she felt shaky, preparing herself for a snowy Jax to appear.

'That's just the guys who've come to move the piano,' Abe said.

'Move it where?'

'Jax wants it in the lodge tonight. I have a feeling you might have something to do with that decision.' She felt her cheeks flush as he hurried past her to the door.

So Jax really was clearing out that music room. What would he use it for instead? she wondered. Maybe he finally *was* over Juno and ready for something new. He'd even thought about opening the slope again too, before she'd told him about her idea.

Ophelia dared to allow a small flame of hope and excitement to burn the edge of her worry away, but when Jax didn't come back within the hour, she realised she'd be late for her shift if she stayed in this cosy and comforting house. There was no choice but to keep her news to herself a little longer.

'Over there, no, I asked for it over there.' The piano had been put in completely the wrong place. Jax had wanted it underneath the vintage skis, by the window overlooking the slopes, not by the fire. 'Don't worry, I'll move it myself. Hunter, can you help a second?'

Jax had been flat out all day. Christmas Eve was always crazy busy, even though the students' seminars were on hiatus again till after Christmas.

'Where were you this morning?' Hunter asked as they each took one end of the piano. Jax knew Hunter was frazzled too—he'd been in here since dawn stringing even more lights around the windows and making the cider punch.

'I stayed near Aubrey and her dad at Willow Crest most of the night—the snowstorm would have held up the US-191,' he explained. 'Then I had to stop by Eco Winery to go get all the booze you ordered.' He gestured around the piano to the boxes of organic wine for the guests, and Hunter grinned.

'You know you'll thank me later.'

Jax rolled his eyes. He knew he'd be watching Cody later, making sure he didn't try to ride any more horses dressed as reindeers around the place. He was also aware he and Ophelia still needed to talk. If it wasn't about her ex in New York, it was something else pretty serious, judging by the way she'd been acting. Maybe he hadn't been calling her on purpose, he realised, instinctively avoiding more bad news.

'Have you seen Ophelia?' He knew he had to find her, sooner rather than later. Christmas was no time for inviting added stress.

'Nope. I guess she's still working.' Hunter was strain-ing at the other end of the piano. It was on wheels, but it was still pretty heavy to move across the carpeted part of the floor. 'What did you want this in here for? Is it so Ophelia can play?'

'Not just so Ophelia can play—it's for everyone.'

Hunter snorted. 'You just keep on telling yourself that. Did you ask her to stay yet?'

Jax grunted. Hunter shook his head. 'I don't know what you're waiting for, man.'

They stood back and admired it in its new place. Its shiny mahogany flat top reflected the mistletoe hang-ing from the vintage skis for two seconds at the most, before Kit placed a wreath on top of it. 'Nothing goes un-Christmassed around here, huh, Kit?' Hunter teased.

'Not if I can help it.' Kit, dressed in a sweater with a snowman on the front, patted Jax's arm. 'I like Ophe-lia.' She winked. She had clearly been listening in. 'We all do.'

There was added meaning to her words, as they were standing around Juno's piano. Everyone knew it was a pretty big move for him, putting it here on display in-stead of keeping it locked up. Maybe Ophelia would play in front of everyone tonight, or maybe she wouldn't. It bothered him that he still didn't really know where they stood. They'd both agreed to end their affair, but last night had felt as though they'd built some kind of new imperishable family unit, a bubble with Cody at the cen-tre, and he'd liked that feeling a lot.

'I made Ophelia a box of cookies. They're on the bar,' Kit added.

Jax dropped a kiss to her cheek that made his house-keeper blush and bat him away. Abe had told him ear-lier that Ophelia had stayed the whole night, for Cody.

Cody had made his mind up that Ophelia was his friend, and it seemed as though she felt the same about his son. It was going to be very strange when she was gone, unless, of course, she'd changed her mind. Maybe that was what she'd wanted to discuss. It was possible she'd just been nervous about proposing it, after everything that had happened lately.

By the time the sun started to set, most things were ready for the party, and a few of the eager guests were starting to roll in, dressed in their Christmas best. He half expected Ophelia to show up after her shift, but she didn't. Swallowing his apprehension, he took the box of cookies from the bar, told Hunter he'd be back soon and made his way over to her cabin.

'It's me, Jax. Sorry I've missed you all day. I thought we could talk before the party.'

'I'll be out in a second,' Ophelia called from the bathroom. 'I got back so late—today was crazy again. And someone else saw the grizzly bear, did Carson tell you?'

'He did tell me,' he answered through the closed door. Jax perched on the end of the bed, holding the box of gingerbread cookies complete with a big red Christmas bow. She was in the shower. Just a short time ago he would have stepped right in there with her. 'He called on my way over here. He said they weren't one hundred per cent sure it was the grizzly...'

'It was a big brown animal, what else could it be?'

'Maybe it was Bigfoot,' he whispered to himself, wishing she would hurry up. He wasn't convinced it could be the grizzly in this amount of snow, and he was more concerned about what Ophelia was going to tell him. Whatever it was she had to say, he wanted to know now, before he had to be switched on in front of all the guests.

Jax put the cookies on the set of drawers beside the bed and was just about to turn some music on to soothe his nerves when her phone flickered to life. His eyes caught a message as it appeared on the screen.

Merry Christmas Eve, Ophie. This day was always extra fun with you. X

The sender was Sanjay. Blood boiled in his veins and his fingers itched to see what else he might have sent her. He knew he shouldn't, every bone in his body told him he shouldn't, it was violating her privacy, but if she had nothing to hide...

Picking up the phone, he clicked on to the message. The photo was of Ophelia in front of a giant Christmas tree—the one at Rockefeller Plaza. Sanjay was grinning next to her, like the cat that got the cream.

With rippling disdain he scrolled up in the thread, just a bit, only to find another photo and another message.

It was so good to see you. Thank you for the memories. X

Peering closer at the photo, he recognised the Thai restaurant in the background, the same one they'd been to on the Lower East Side. The same one he'd seen them outside. Jax swallowed the leaden ball choking his windpipe as the shower turned off in the bathroom. It *had* been Sanjay he'd seen hugging her out on the street. And he'd been right, they were back in touch.

He zoomed in, disgusted by the jealousy that consumed him. The two of them, side by side, looked beyond happy to be in each other's company. Ophelia was radiant, the arrow pendant sparkling at her throat.

Jax's knuckles were white. She had seemed so genuine before, so determined there was no one else. But she *had* been with Sanjay in New York, while he'd been following her itinerary for Cody in another part of Manhattan. She had lied to him. Unbelievable. Was this what she was planning to confess, now, before she left for good?

Seeing red, he put the phone back on the stand and stood from the bed on shaking legs. What a fool…he was such a fool, falling for her lies, her charms, bringing Cody into all of this, time after time, thinking he could trust her.

He almost stormed into the bathroom, but he didn't know what he might say. What could he do? She was leaving anyway, and he'd already broken things off. He had no claim over her. He had no right to requisition anything of hers at all. All he knew was that he couldn't be here in this room a second longer.

CHAPTER TWENTY

IN THE BATHROOM, Ophelia took a deep breath, pulling the belt tight on her robe. Her dress for the evening was benefiting from the steam on the outside of the shower cubicle. An A-line off-the-shoulder knee-length dress, pleated from the waist down, in a deep Christmas scarlet colour. She'd had no idea when she'd packed it that she'd be in this situation now...standing here on Christmas Eve, about to tell a man she was pregnant with his baby.

It was now or never. Opening the door in her robe, she closed her eyes. 'Jax, thank you for waiting...'

Silence.

She opened her eyes, expecting to see him in the cabin, maybe in a suit, or a Santa hat, dressed for the party. 'Jax?'

Where on earth had he gone? She opened the door, the freezing snow flurry threatening to blow inside as she scanned the deck and the trees beyond. 'Jax?' she called out. The only signs he'd been there were the snowmobile tracks in the snow. 'My God, it's freezing!'

Shutting the door again quickly before her toes froze, she dropped to the bed in dismay and confusion. Maybe he got called away again and she didn't hear.

A big red bow caught her attention on a box on the bedside drawers. She picked it up, and took off the bow, unwrapping the gingerbread cookies. He must have brought them over from Kit to surprise her, which was a really lovely gesture, but she'd been hoping he'd stay, so she could talk to him in private as she'd planned.

Sighing, she got up to get dressed, and noticed her phone was lit up. *Strange*, she thought. *It only stays like that if I've touched it.*

Her stomach sank as she saw what was on the screen. Another message and photo from Sanjay. This one was from a couple of Christmases ago, when they'd gone ice skating and taken photos by the tree at Rockefeller. What was Sanjay doing, dredging up all these memories now? If seeing her had made him miss her, tough luck. She'd done some moving on since then.

Oh, no. Ophelia froze. *Jax must have seen these photos.*

Anger and frustration made her clumsy as she raced to the bathroom, pulled on her dress and got the zip tangled in her wet hair. Then the hairdryer cord got tangled in itself. Jax had seen her with Sanjay outside the restaurant, and asked her about it too. He must have jumped to conclusions about the photos before she'd even had a chance to explain.

No, no, no…what a mess.

It took her at least thirty minutes to get to the party at the lodge. She had every intention of pulling him aside and setting things straight, once and for all. Only when she stepped into the cosy lodge where a five-piece band was already in full swing, and the smell of cider hung in the air, Jax wasn't there.

In the light of the moon, the mountains were the picture of Christmas perfection, and down in the lodge Jax knew the party would be going on without him. But he didn't trust his terrible mood not to ruin the night. Skidding to a halt by the barriers of the disused slope, he pulled the backpack from under the seat of the snowmobile, then took the skis off the back.

He didn't feel like dealing with other people. The empty slope was what he needed—space, air, speed. Strapping the skis on to his boots, he pulled at the straps a little too hard, taking out his anger on his own damn feet—this was his fault after all. He'd been given all the red flags since the start. Ophelia had never said she'd wanted him beyond a bit of fun. She had never said she wanted to stay here either.

Then again, Hunter had reminded him he hadn't asked her to. He'd spent so long testing her, to see if she belonged here, to see if she could live up to Juno, he'd forgotten to remind her how much he'd grown to need her, want her, himself.

Leaving the snowmobile behind the barriers, he took off on the route he remembered best. It wasn't marked out, it never had been, but he knew where the danger points were. How could he forget?

The fresh powder felt good to tear up. The still air chilled his cheeks around his goggles, numbing him in a way, but he still couldn't get those photos out of his head. All this time he'd felt as though they'd at least understood each other, as though they were somehow helping each other to heal. All these years he had prided himself on being a good judge of character, but how could he have been so wrong about Ophelia? He wouldn't believe this was happening with her ex now if he hadn't seen it with his own eyes.

A rustle in the trees towards the bottom of the slope made him skid to a sudden halt. Then he saw it.

'What the…?'

It was a figure, black as night, but recognisable in form. His heart leapt to his throat as he pushed up his goggles in disbelief. *Juno?* He could have sworn he just saw her. He must be going crazy…maybe his churning mind and the cold were making him crazy. Maybe his goggles were too scratched, distorting his view.

'Juno!' He called out her name now, feeling like a fool. But there was no one to hear him. The other slopes were out of earshot and everyone who knew him personally was at the party.

Edging forwards on the skis, he moved slowly towards the fir tree ridge, close to where the accident had happened four years ago. He hadn't been down here since he'd had the team lay the row of boulders, marking the start of the danger zone. He'd made a conscious effort not to even think about it, till Ophelia walked into his life.

He unclipped his skis, leant them against a tree and crunched in his boots to the heavy stones. Peering around them, he saw no one, nothing but snow-covered ponderosa and sky.

'You're imagining things,' he scolded himself, but just as he went to turn around something else caught his eye. Something solid and silver was shining up at him in the moonlight from a crack between two boulders, barely visible. The pine cover, oak brush and gnarly tangle of shrubbery had all kept the snow off.

It couldn't be…

He pulled off his glove, slid his bare fingers between the frozen stones and retrieved the silver arrow attached to the leather strap. Staring at it in disbelief, he turned Ophelia's necklace over in his hands. How on earth did it get all the way down here?

With a hammering heart Jax stumbled back against the boulder, clutching the arrow in his palm, scanning the slope around him. It was inconceivable that he'd been led here to find it by…no, he wouldn't even entertain the thought, it was too crazy.

Shaken, he shoved the necklace in his pocket and collected his skis, but as he dropped to the snow to strap them back on it struck him how he'd missed something about the photos on Ophelia's phone. She'd been wearing this necklace in them, he was sure of it now, which meant they had to have been taken at an earlier date. Ophelia had lost her necklace before they even went to New York.

'Idiot,' he said out loud. A lone bird swooped above him and seemed to carry his statement off into the sky.

Kicking himself, he skied to the bottom exit, thinking he would take the lifts back up to the snowmobile and then make his way to the party. Hopefully she'd be there and he could apologise properly—whatever it was she'd been keeping from him, at least it wasn't her ex. Sanjay was purely a man wrapped up in nostalgia over what he'd lost, what Jax had gained and then stupidly pushed away.

He was almost back where he'd parked when another shadowy figure crossed his path, blocking him completely. This time he knew exactly what it was.

'Hey, buddy, we meet again,' Jax whispered, reaching slowly around his shoulders for his backpack. 'Do you want to let me get past you? I kind of need to get back down this mountain to my girl.'

The grizzly bear stopped in its tracks in surprise, then rose to her full imposing height in the snow, assessing him with curious black, bright eyes. She swayed this way and that, not as big as some males he'd seen, but taller than any human man, assessing him with two wide feet planted firmly on the snowy ground. There was no doubt in Jax's mind that this bear was ready to club him into silence if he made any sudden movements. There was nowhere to go, no way Jax could get to safety unless he ran right towards her, to the snowmobile.

'I guess you're going to make this difficult, huh,' Jax said gruffly, looking the huge brown creature directly in the eyes.

Ophelia flinched on her bar stool as a gunshot cracked and broke the night outside. The guy announcing the next song on the mic paused. 'Don't panic, folks, it's probably nothing,' he assured the room, but her first thought was Jax.

'What if that was him?' she whispered to Hunter, who was pouring cider into glasses from a giant ladle.

He shrugged a little too nonchalantly for her liking. 'If it was, you can be sure he was the one firing the shot.'

She'd admitted to Hunter that they might have had a small disagreement. Hunter had said Jax just needed time to cool off, that he'd come back and that it was best not to worry anyone. But it had been over an hour already.

'He's not answering his phone, it still goes to voicemail,' she told him, and Hunter tried contacting him again on the radio. What must he be thinking of her out there after he'd seen those photos of her and Sanjay?

'Hello? Over… Can you read me? Over…' The voice from the radio was crackly at best, but her heart did a somersault. *Finally.*

'That's him! Hunter, that's him, where is he?'

Hunter leant over the bar, sharing the radio with her, just as Carson approached in an elf's outfit, looking for more cider. The radio was spluttering with white noise and broken words, but she'd recognise Jax's voice anywhere, and so did the others now.

'I'm…need help…bear…'

'*Bear*? Did he say bear?' Ophelia's heart was in her

throat. 'Someone saw it earlier. You don't think Jax is in danger?'

'He must be near the disused slope,' Carson interrupted, his elf's hat jingling at her side. 'The signal's not so great out there.'

Just then, the door of the lodge swung open in a blast of cold air, and Santa Claus appeared. Every kid in the room, including Cody, gave an excited shriek and descended on him like a whirlwind. She recognised Abe behind the fake beard, his wiry frame padded out with a fake round belly.

The radio was still blipping. Hunter lifted the bar hatch and strode towards Abe, and she followed and explained what they knew, all while Abe kept his face the picture of calm and control, doling out presents from a giant sack.

'Hunter, we have to go look for him at the slope,' she urged, imagining Jax out there somewhere in a face-off with a grizzly bear. She was the reason he was out there, angry and humiliated, having to confront a dangerous animal. Abe put a cool hand to her arm from the sleeve of his plush red Santa coat.

'We'll go together.'

'We'll all go,' Marni said now from behind her. When she turned, Jax's entire team of mountain-rescue students were pulling on their coats over their Christmas sparkles. One look at Marni's face told Ophelia she wouldn't be blown off this time.

'There aren't enough snowmobiles between us,' Hunter reminded them all.

'I have a better idea.' Abe thrust the sack of gifts at Carson. 'Take over here, Dr Elf? And watch Cody till we come back?'

'Of course.' Carson was engulfed immediately in a crowd of eager, oblivious children.

Abe returned from the basement with another huge bag that Ophelia knew contained emergency rescue equipment, and she felt more ill than ever as she bundled up again as fast as she could.

They followed Abe outside en masse, where his surprise was sitting in the snow. For a second she stopped short on the porch, blinking. She could hardly believe what she was looking at.

CHAPTER TWENTY-ONE

WAS THIS ANOTHER HALLUCINATION? Jax swore a sleigh full of people was jingling and sliding its way towards him, near the entrance to the disused slope. The sleigh was big enough to hold at least twenty people, and as it approached he saw Ophelia standing at the front with his father, dressed as Santa Claus.

'Jax!' Abe called out. 'Are you OK, son?'

Jax could barely answer; if he hadn't been so stunned he would have laughed. The sleigh was bulging with gift-wrapped items, sheepskin blankets and twinkling lights, and most of his students. The sight was overshadowed only by the pack of huskies, pulling them along in the snow.

'So, this is your surprise, huh?' he said as Abe clambered out of the sleigh in his red-and-white suit. His belly looked twice the usual size. Ophelia went to run towards him, but he held his hand up, stopping her.

He glanced up at the tree. The bear had gone still in the branches, frozen in fear no doubt. 'She's up there,' he told his new audience, pointing up with a gloved hand. Marni let out an audible gasp and Abe just nodded, dragging a bag Jax knew contained what they needed out of the back seat.

'Help him unpack the air pad,' Jax ordered his students. It would take at least five of them. 'Dad, I need the dart gun.'

'Soon as I heard "bear", that's exactly what I packed.' Abe was already pulling stuff out of the bag. They'd done this once before. Jax felt terrible for the grizzly. First he'd shot the gun into the sky to warn her off. Then the poor thing had run to the tree line and scrambled up high to escape.

Ophelia was by his side now. 'Jax, I was worried sick.'

'I'm all right. The bear's more scared than me.'

She followed his eyes to the sky and caught sight of the grizzly sitting right above them, watching with beady eyes. She froze in his arms. 'What the…?'

'At least we have her now, and we can help her.'

Ophelia shook her head in shock, then swallowed, seeming to remember what else was hovering over them. 'Listen, I'm sorry if you thought for one second I was lying to you about Sanjay. I should have just told you what was really going on with me, Jax.'

In the corner of his eye his father was loading the dart gun with a tranquilliser. The students were unfolding the zero-shock protection mat, designed to help people fall safely from impossible heights, and the grizzly, sensing something was up, let out a growl that shook the entire tree, sending a snow shower down over the group. 'Help them,' Jax told her quickly. 'We need everyone now.'

'You're going to try and catch that bear?' Ophelia asked as he backed away from her, directing the group to the patch of spotty snow by the tree line.

'We're *all* going to catch this bear,' he said, but Ophelia had frozen again. She wasn't moving to help the group, which wasn't like her.

'Stand back,' he ordered her instead. Abe was striding towards him with the dart gun, and some primal instinct had kicked in again, a need to protect her from whatever other beasts she was dealing with. The air around him seemed to fill with even more silence than when he'd been alone as he aimed the dart right at the bear's lower leg and fired.

For the second time in one night, Ophelia thought she'd never seen a sight like this in her life. The grizzly bear had taken the dart to its leg, and just a few long minutes later it emitted a deep guttural growl and tumbled from the branches. The creature must have weighed at least two hundred pounds.

She watched from her place a few feet away as the group, including Jax and Abe, hurried to soften the creature's fall with the giant air pad.

'It might take a few minutes for her to go completely under, so don't get too close,' Jax warned the students as several of them pulled out phones and started filming the ordeal. This was all so surreal.

Jax got on the radio, arranging for the tranquillised bear to be collected. 'There's a rescue centre halfway to Yellowstone. They're sending someone now to get her,' he told Ophelia. It was snowing again, and thick wet flakes clung to his hat and shoulders. 'It's an educational sanctuary too. She'll be safe there till spring, then they'll release her back into the wild.'

'Why is she not hibernating?' she asked him.

'I don't know. They'll check her out at the rescue centre. It's possible she's sick and disoriented. Or she might have lost a cub and gone looking for it.'

'You might have saved her life,' she said, accepting his embrace and burying her head into his jacket. 'That's you, Jax Clayborn, a lifesaver.'

Behind them, Abe was watching. 'Ophelia, come with us back to the party? Jax will stay and wait.'

'No, I'll stay with him,' she said.

'Are you sure? You're freezing.' Jax frowned.

'I'll stay,' she asserted. She needed him alone.

Abe hurried over with a thick blanket and Jax was quick to wrap it around her shoulders. 'Go put those husky dogs to work, Dad,' he said. 'Nice surprise, by the way, the kids will love it. Save a ride for us later, yeah?'

'Any time,' Abe said, pulling his fake beard back across his mouth and saluting them across his Santa hat. Ophelia couldn't help biting back a smile.

They watched the sleigh jingle off again into the horizon, until it was just the two of them and the sedated grizzly lying on her side on the soft air pad. Ophelia stepped closer to it, with Jax. She looked so peaceful and harmless now, like an oversized stuffed teddy bear, not unlike the one he'd given her on day one. She felt sorry for her; maybe she was a mother, as she would be soon.

'Jax,' she started, keeping her eyes on the bear as her heart started thudding heavily again. 'About what you saw. There is no one else, especially not Sanjay.'

'I know,' he said. He dug into his pocket and pulled something out. 'I realised that when I found this earlier. You were wearing it in those photos, but you lost it before we even went to New York together.'

He pressed Ant's necklace, complete with its silver arrow pendant, into her palm, and she stared at it in disbelief. 'Where did you…how did you…?'

'You wouldn't believe me even if I told you,' he said wearily.

'What do you mean?'

Jax frowned down at his feet, then let his eyes travel

over the bear into the forest. 'Do you believe in ghosts?' he asked her eventually, adjusting his hat on his head.

'Ghosts?'

She held the pendant to her heart, mind racing. Did he see Ant? she wondered. Did Ant answer her call to give her a sign, by leading Jax to the necklace out here? Did he see…Juno? He shook his head quickly, dismissing it before she could probe him and tilting her head up to meet his eyes.

'Ophelia, what is it? What have you been so afraid of telling me?'

She scanned his eyes in the moonlight, while the snow flurried around them. Taking a deep breath, she slid the necklace into her pocket and took both his hands. 'Jax, I'm pregnant.'

His eyes grew wide, and her stomach sank. She couldn't read him. 'Are you sure?'

'I had a feeling I was when we were in New York, but I was too chicken to take the test. It took me far too long to take it, Jax, then when I did, and it came up positive, I didn't know what to do. You'd already called things off… and I lost my baby before, Jax. What if it happens again?'

'Ophelia.' Jax pulled her into his shoulder and wrapped his arms around her tightly. She breathed him in, realising she was trembling. 'Can you forgive me for putting you through this?'

She pulled back a little to look at him.

'After everything you went through before, I'm not surprised you panicked,' he said. He leaned forward, pressing his warm lips to her cold forehead, which caused her heart to soar. 'Now I know why you didn't risk standing under that tree just now! But I would have gone through it all with you, Ophelia, whatever happened. I am not your ex.'

She said nothing, just gripped his collar at the back of his neck in her fists and took a huge, deep breath into his skin.

'You have nothing to be worried about,' he told her. 'I'm going to be here with you, for all of this, whatever happens.'

'Really?' She could hardly believe the expression in his eyes now—he almost looked…excited. Sure enough, his mouth broke into a huge grin, bigger than she'd ever seen on his handsome face.

'This is crazy,' he breathed. 'What are you doing to me, woman?'

'You're not angry?'

'Are you kidding me? I mean, I'm a little surprised, I wasn't exactly expecting it, but hell, Ophelia, I knew I was in trouble the second I met you.' A huge weight seemed to roll off her shoulders into the snow as he ran a hand across his chin. 'Cody's gonna get a brother or sister. Wow.'

'We don't know if… I mean, I can't tell anyone else yet. What if I can't have it?'

'Of course you can.' His face was straight again and she leaned into his hand as he swept her wet hair behind her ears. 'We'll keep it a secret for now, if that's what you want, but you are going to be an exceptional mother. We will work this out together, wherever you want to be. OK?'

Another bolt to her heart. Wherever she wanted to be? 'I want to be here, Jax. With you.'

'And what about the partnership?' he asked, as if she could possibly even contemplate that now.

'That was the plan for the old me. With or without this baby, Jax, I'm not that person any more. Everything changed when Ant died. *I* changed when Ant died. I want to be here with you, if you'll have me. If you think I'm ready for more of Montana?'

A noise in the distance caught their attention. Smiling, Jax took her face in his hands. 'You're about to hand over a tranquillised bear on Christmas Eve, I think you're ready for Montana. The question is, is Montana ready for us?'

'Us. I like the sound of that.' She sighed, feeling the tears prickle her eyes.

He kissed her again, then he lifted her high and swung her around in the falling snowflakes, till she couldn't help laughing at what they must look like to the approaching rescue-centre staff. They were here now, unloading a giant stretcher for the bear, which they'd pulled with three snowmobiles in tandem.

'I've been falling in love with you since I met you, city girl,' he whispered in her ear as they made their way over. 'Just in case you still have any doubts.'

'Same,' was all she could manage, holding tight to his hand. Ophelia's heart was so full, she thought she might burst. She still had to break it to her father, of course, that he'd have to find a different partner, but it was time to put her own needs and desires first for a change.

The rest of the night passed by in a happy, tired daze of eating, dancing with Cody and Carson, toasting to Aubrey's mother's recovery and, finally, making love to Jax in his bed, while Christmas music continued to ring from the lodge.

When she called her parents the next morning, to her surprise, her father informed her he already had someone in mind back home to take her place at Health Dimensions.

'Your mother told me I might have been pushing you too hard, and maybe she's right. I only want my baby girl to be happy. You're all I have left,' he told her, and she ached to see him again in person, to assure him he hadn't lost her. She was merely forging her own path from now on.

'I'm still your baby girl, Dad,' she replied, resisting the urge to tell him he would soon be a grandfather. She couldn't. Not yet anyway. She and Jax had agreed to wait at least a couple more months, just to be on the safe side.

For the first time in a long time, she felt completely at peace about what the future might bring, maybe because she felt blessed. Whatever had caused her necklace to reappear in the snow like that, it felt a lot as if Ant, or Juno, or maybe even the ancient tribes, had finally spoken. This was where she belonged now, heart and soul. For ever.

EPILOGUE

It was two years later on Christmas Eve when Jax found himself staring in awe at his wife of eighteen months, blossoming and radiant, pregnant for the second time. 'Let's play it again, Ophelia,' Cody ordered her from his seat beside her at the piano.

'Yes, play it again!' Hunter and Abe called out in unison, and in seconds the entire lodge erupted in a chorus of 'Play it again, play it again,' that made little Anthony grin and drum his hands on their table, from Jax's lap.

Ophelia laughed and rolled her eyes good-naturedly, and shot him a look meant only for him, with love, as she put a hand to her belly. This time, they were having a girl. It felt like only yesterday that she'd given birth to Anthony on that sweltering hot summer morning. Her parents, Marvin and Cecelia, had timed their visit to coincide with the due date, and Anthony had been so excited to meet them all, he'd come along four days early, when they'd all been out on the river observing the new clinic from a different angle.

He smiled remembering how Ophelia had produced her proposal for a rescue route on the disused slope. She'd been thinking about it for months before she'd suggested it, and, as it turned out, her plans had matched his own silent musings about how they might improve their rescue times, and honour Juno's memory at the same time. Ophelia Clayborn was now head of ER at the new clinic, at halfway point, while a second team staffed the base. The new helipad meant they could summon outside help even faster.

'Dad, come sing with us,' Cody called out now, and he shook his head vehemently, making everyone laugh.

'Your dad can do a lot of things, Cody,' Ophelia said, smiling over the piano top at him again, 'but he can't sing.'

'She's right about that,' Jax replied over the crowd, holding Anthony close and taking another spoon Hunter handed him, to replace the one the baby had thrown on the floor.

'You're a defiant little one already.' Hunter grinned from under his trusted Santa hat. 'I wonder where you get that from, huh?'

'I don't know what you're talking about,' Jax said, pulling off the hat with one swipe and putting it on his own head, making Anthony giggle around the spoon.

This baby, and Ophelia, had made him the happiest man on the planet. Cody was determined to teach his little brother to play the piano as soon as possible, as well as how to ski and snowboard, and chop up the firewood. Jax and Ophelia knew he'd be an amazing older brother to his sister too, when she came along.

A new baby was another new chance, he thought, humming along to their Christmas song, albeit out of tune. Another invitation for them both to be the best versions of themselves, against whatever obstacles were thrown in their path.

In Montana, there were always new obstacles to face,

from too much sun to too much snow, to rescuing lost bears and off-piste skiers. But with his family by his side, Jax knew he could handle anything life threw at him.

* * * * *

A GP WORTH STAYING FOR

LOUISA HEATON

MILLS & BOON

To Nick, David and Sean,
who have all been there for me
whenever I have needed support.
I could not have got through the last year
without you all.
And I will never forget all that you have done for me.
Love you loads, xxx

CHAPTER ONE

DR OWEN LEDGER cupped his mouth with his hands and blew a quick burst of air into them before rubbing them together. It was freezing, and standing in Sandpiper Bay Station in the middle of a blizzard, waiting for a train to arrive, was not his idea of fun. He turned up the collar of his jacket and stamped his feet as he saw the lights of the train in the distance through the thick flakes of snow, and he felt much better to know that soon the new doctor would be here and they could get back into the warmth of his car.

Dr Childs was going to be his ticket out of here and he couldn't wait to go. Make a fresh new start in a brand-new place where absolutely no one knew him. Where absolutely no one could judge him on his past and look at him with pitying eyes.

Okay, they might not actually be *pitying* eyes, but they certainly felt that way to him. The people of Morrow Island knew too much about him, and it was hard to create the professional distance that he needed as a doctor. He knew these people. He knew their families and their friends and what happened to them on a daily basis. Because the island grapevine never needed much time to get going and there were only a couple of hundred people here.

When it came to serious matters—when it came to having to deliver difficult news—it was hard to maintain the distance he needed to protect himself, as well as them, when they had all come to his wedding. When most of them had danced with his bride.

When all of them had attended her funeral.

The train pulled in and the doors slid open to allow an assortment of passengers to get off. He recognised Gerry Farmer, who gave him a wave, and then Peter Atkins, who said hello, shook his freezing hand and asked him if he needed a lift.

'I'm okay, thanks, Pete! Just waiting for the new doc,' he said, shivering in the snow.

'It's today? Gosh, I guess that means we don't have you for much longer?'

'Four weeks and I'm gone. End of January. Just enough time to get Dr Childs settled in and introduced to everyone.'

'I'll remind Josie. I think she's going to drop some scones round for you. She made a batch with ginger. Best things you've ever tasted!' Josie was Pete's daughter, who had aspirations to be on some baking show on the television.

He nodded and gave a brief wave. 'I'll look forward to it!'

'G'night!'

Owen watched as Pete hurried away, then turned back to look at the platform. There was only one passenger who remained. She was very small and dainty, wrapped in a calf-length coat with a multicoloured scarf and matching hat, and she was pulling behind her a suitcase that had to weigh more than she did.

He hoped she wasn't the doctor—because she was startlingly attractive and the two of them were going to have to live in the same house until he moved out. The property he lived in came with the job, and the surgery was connected to the main house.

She had large doe-like eyes, innocent and wide. Possibly brown, but it was hard to see in the dark and be sure. But she was pale from the cold and had a bright red nose—like Rudolph the reindeer.

Despite that, he very much liked what he saw.

'Dr Childs?' he said.

She smiled and nodded, snow hitting her face. 'Dr Ledger?'

'Owen. Can I take your case for you? I'm afraid the car is parked quite a distance away.'

'Thank you.' She passed him her case and he took it, surprised at its weight. What did she have in this thing? Solid oak units?

'How was your journey?' He turned so she could hear him over the strong wind that blew snow into their faces.

'Not bad.'

'That's great.'

'I appreciate you meeting me like this.'

He could barely hear her over the sound of the howling wind, and he kept checking to make sure she was keeping up with him as they walked against it. The tail end of this storm had brought them snow two days after Christmas, bathing the small island in white, frosting it like a cake. They didn't normally get snow there, so it was a novelty, but he was glad the off-roader was able to make it down most of the rural roads on the island, so that he could tend to his patients.

Dr Childs would have to get used to driving it, too. The car, like the house, came with the job.

When they reached the vehicle, he opened the passenger door for her, then took her suitcase and put it in the rear. He got into the driver's seat and closed his own door with a huge sense of relief, as if they'd just yomped miles over rough terrain.

'I'm sorry the weather's so bad. It's not normally like this at this time of year.'

She turned to smile at him, blinking those big doe eyes at him. A strange sensation hit him squarely in the stomach and he had to turn away, pretending he was struggling to get the key into the ignition. Dr Childs was very beautiful, but nothing was going to happen. He was very much single now, and Dr Childs could be Miss Fricking World and he wouldn't do anything about it.

He'd been burned once. Had his heart ripped from his chest, set fire to and stomped on. There was no way he was going to complicate matters before he left. She was here to work, and he was here to pack up and leave once she'd got orientated. That was all. That was going to be the extent of their relationship.

He started the engine. 'Ready to go home?'

She nodded. 'I am.'

The brightness in her dark eyes was hypnotic and he had to force himself to turn away once again, flicking on the headlights full beam. Turning on the windscreen wipers to remove a shield of snow.

What was going on here?

The sooner he could get out of here, the better.

Dr Lucy Childs sat in the passenger seat of the car, looking towards the old farmhouse that would be her new home. She couldn't see too much of it, because of the darkness and the blizzard, but it looked sizeable.

From the train station, Owen had driven them across the bridge that connected the mainland to the island and then down a myriad of winding country roads, until they'd reached a lane that was pitted with potholes.

The lane was bordered by drystone walls and ditches, but the farmhouse itself, from what she could see, looked nice. A curl of smoke issued from the chimney, indicating that a real fire was burning inside, and a solitary yellow light glowed like a beacon from one of its windows.

'I thought I'd have the place all warm for you when you arrived,' said Owen.

She turned to smile at him, grateful for his kind consideration. 'Thanks.'

Dr Owen Ledger was an astoundingly attractive man—which she'd not expected to find. When she'd come across the advert for a job here on Morrow Island she'd expected to find the outgoing doctor would be a silver-haired man, maybe a little portly. Someone ready for retirement, perhaps? With a penchant for reading a real newspaper and enjoying a pint down at the pub? And he'd have a nice wife—someone warm and welcoming, who wore a pinny and had her hair curled and set each weekend.

Not *him*. Not the thirty-something, handsome devil who sat beside her, with his raven-black hair and intense green eyes that were framed with enviable thick, dark lashes. The kind of lashes that women would pay lots of money for in extensions and expensive mascara.

And they were going to have to live in the same house for the next few weeks, before he moved on...

Hmm. I'll take one for the team, she thought with a smile. It would be a nice bonus, that was for sure.

'This place looks amazing,' she said.

'It is. It used to be a proper farm. They raised beef cattle here for many years, until the farmer sold off his land. The medical trust bought the property and moved the surgery here from its old place, which was in the middle of nowhere. At least here people can get to us quickly. We're on the outskirts of the village and the bus stops right at the end of the lane.'

'I understand it's just us?'

'Mostly. We have a nurse from the mainland who drives over once a month for our lumps and bumps clinic, and Helen is our receptionist. She works here every morning, and if she can't make it, her daughter steps in. I can give you a tour when we get inside. Ready to brave the snow again?'

Her stomach churned as the moment to step from the car grew closer. This was it. The start of her new life. She'd left everyone behind to do this. To come to the middle of nowhere, where no one knew her. That had been the whole point. A fresh start. A clean slate. The chance to start over without everyone watching her constantly and worrying over her, waiting for her to falter.

'Okay. I'm ready.'

They both got out of the car and Owen went to the rear of the vehicle and popped open the boot, pulling Lucy's suitcase from it and placing it on the road, before pulling up the long handle so that he could drag the case behind him.

The wind had dropped, and it was almost silent as she stood there in the road with the deepening dark and the soft, silent snow. She turned to look at the farmhouse, situated here on this small island just off the southern coast of Cornwall. It was meant to have the GP practice attached to it. Maybe it was in another building that she couldn't see?

That yellow light did look welcoming. And the smoke that hinted at a real fire made her want to get inside and be hypnotised by the warmth and pop and crackle of the flames, to stretch her toes out in front of it. All she had to do was take a step. And then another. And another.

She started forward, behind Owen. Her suitcase wheels were making more noise on the road than she was.

The farmhouse door was made of a modern uPVC, along with the windows, though the rest of the building looked as if it had stood for centuries. The stones were dark and covered in lichen or moss in parts, and when she reached out to touch this place that would soon be her for ever home she felt a soft furriness against the cold.

'Hello, house, I'm Lucy,' she whispered, staring up at the building around her and feeling incredibly stupid for having spoken to the house. But houses were easy to talk to. They didn't talk back, they didn't ask awkward questions she wasn't sure she'd ever be ready to answer and they didn't try and smother you or wrap you in cotton wool, as if you were a broken, fragile thing.

Owen looked at her with a quizzical smile. 'You say hello to houses?'

She smiled back, feeling her cheeks flush. 'You don't?'

He smiled again and turned to open the door, throwing it open wide, and the warm glow from within burst out to welcome her. He stood back, so she could go in first, and she stepped inside, brushing her feet on the mat and then pulling off her boots as she looked around the place.

A fire crackled away in a large inglenook fireplace, and above her head were old, black Elizabethan beams. The room was filled with soft, squishy chairs and the walls were lined with bookcases, stuffed to overflowing with books. In a corner, a guitar was propped up on a stand, and through a doorway, off to her left, she saw a sleek white kitchen.

'Wow.'

'Welcome home.'

Owen closed the door on the cold behind her and they both began to peel off their heavy overcoats. Owen took hers from her and hung it up next to his, which strangely seemed unbearably intimate, and then wheeled her suitcase over to the base of the wooden stairs behind them.

She couldn't help but notice, now that he was out of his coat, that Owen was rather delicious. He wore soft dark jeans and a black V-neck jumper with a white shirt over a nice flat stomach, and when he rolled his sleeves up she noted that he had very nice forearms and wore a chunky metal wristwatch.

Do. Not. Stare.

'Obviously you'll be free to decorate how you like once you've settled in,' he said.

'Are you kidding me? This place is perfect.'

She stepped forward to touch the back of one of the couches, running her fingers over the soft wool blanket that was draped over the back. Naturally, her gaze went to the books. As a bookworm herself, she could discover a lot about a person by the titles on their shelves. Owen had a mix of medical texts and science fiction stories and that made her smile. She'd always loved stories and films set in space, too.

'Fancy a hot drink?' he asked.

She nodded.

'Tea? Coffee? Hot chocolate?'

'Hot chocolate sounds perfect.'

He headed into the kitchen and after a moment or two she followed him in, watching him as he made his way around. It was quite a modern kitchen. Sleek and rounded, the cupboards had an automatic soft close that she liked, and Owen had filled the room with chrome equipment. There was a chrome toaster, a kettle and a large coffee machine in one corner. And yet on the windowsill were softer touches—hyacinth bulbs in pink and blue and a large red-leafed poinsettia.

Owen clearly knew his way around a kitchen, and she envied him that. She'd never been very good at cooking, and often became quickly acquainted with the microwave. But she was determined to learn. One day, anyway.

Coming here to Morrow was meant to give her that time. She'd not wanted a GP post that would take up her entire day, with all her evenings and most weekends on call. Morrow offered only a morning clinic, Monday to Friday, and though she would be on call after that, an island with two hundred people on it meant that her bleep would hardly ever go off, or so the trust had assured her during the interview process. Any real emergencies meant the island's residents driving themselves to the hospital a few miles away on the mainland, or calling an ambulance.

Owen had steamed the milk in some contraption she didn't recognise, and soon he was handing her a large mug of steaming hot chocolate. She sipped at it and it was delicious. He leaned back against one of the kitchen units and they faced one another in quiet for a moment.

'So what made you choose a job on a tiny Cornish island?' he asked. 'It's not the most obvious step in a career.'

She met his gaze, then looked away, blowing the steam from the top of her drink before taking another small sip. She didn't know him well enough to tell him everything—and what would be the point in that, anyway? The whole reason for coming here was so that she would have a clean slate and people would judge her on her ability, not her disability.

She smiled. 'I was just looking for a slower pace. Somewhere quieter than the inner city.'

'Where were you based before?'

'Wandsworth. London.'

'How many patients on your roll?'

'Two thousand.'

He raised his eyebrows. 'Wow.'

'What about you? When you leave here what are you going to do?'

'I'm going to a village practice just outside Tavistock.'

'What's made you choose to leave this place? It seems idyllic.'

Owen smiled and sipped from his mug. 'It is.'

But she could tell from the look on his face that there was something he wasn't telling her.

Fair enough.

What could he say? Tell her the truth and scare her off before she'd even unpacked? Tell her that the people here never let anything go and were happy to wallow in the past and never move forward?

He couldn't do it.

Not any more.

It had been two years, for crying out loud, and still they wouldn't let him forget. Two years of being a widower and still her name got mentioned with his. If he stayed here…? Well, he would never be allowed to find happiness. Never be allowed the future he had once dreamt of with Emily.

Marriage. Children. *Family.* Becoming the father he dreamed of being.

It had all died with her, and now that he'd announced his decision to leave, had put all the steps into motion, he wanted to get moving.

He'd found a new job. A GP surgery in a village just outside Tavistock. Two partners ran the place. Two other doctors were on staff. He'd be the third, along with an advanced nurse practitioner, two nurses and a senior-level healthcare assistant who, he had been reliably informed, was one of the best-trained HCAs he'd ever get to meet.

He'd driven over there a couple of times when he could. Put a deposit down on a rental property that was about a ten-minute drive from work. Just a two-bedroomed place—he didn't need anything bigger than that. He'd use one bedroom for sleeping and transform the other into a small office, where he planned to write the book he'd been scribbling notes for, on and off, for years.

It was finally time to move forward. To take the next steps. To shake off the shackles that tied him to this place and the haunting memory of Emily. Not that he would ever forget her—of course he wouldn't. She'd been his wife. His love. His very heart. They'd still been practically newlyweds when she'd died so unexpectedly, but he wanted to be able to move forward with his life without feeling as if the whole of Morrow was watching him. Judging him. Passing comment. Gossiping in The Boar and Bloodhound.

Though he suspected that they would gossip for some time *after* he'd gone.

Remember Owen? He left! Can you believe he did that? Walked away from everything that connected him with his wife. Almost like he couldn't wait to get away. Mind you...was he there for her when he was meant to be?

He couldn't stay on the island. Who could he find to be with? Who could he settle down with, knowing how much Emily had been loved by everyone there? They would think anyone he met was second-best. And she would feel it—of course she would. The eyes upon her. The gazes.

Emily had said to him when they were on their honeymoon in Dubai that if anything ever happened to her she'd want him to marry again. He'd told her not to be ridiculous, that nothing was going to happen to her—but what had he known? Look at how wrong he'd been proved. And now, feeling as incredibly lonely as he had been these last few months, he knew that if he was going to get the chance to start again, it could never be here. In this place.

Not here on the island that didn't forget.

Not here on the island where everything reminded him of his wife.

The church? They'd got married there.

That little cafe? That was where he'd spilt all that milk on her dress when they were first dating.

The harbour? That was where they'd shared their first kiss.

Carrigan's Cove? That was where they'd gone swimming together.

He couldn't turn round in this place without being reminded. And if the places didn't remind him, then the people did.

'You were such a sweet couple.'

'I remember you and Emily holding hands as you walked on the beach.'

'I've brought you some ginger cookies. They were Emily's favourites, weren't they?'

And now she was here. Dr Lucy Childs. His first step in unshackling the chains and being free. She was a tiny woman—like a little pixie, really. Slim. Well, it wouldn't take the islanders long to fatten her up. They liked to feed people and often set up meal drives. Broken leg? They brought you food. Recovering from an operation? They brought you food. Losing your new wife to a brain aneurysm? Food.

The people on this island looked after one another. He'd give them that. Sometimes he thought it was kind of smothering, but he knew they would spring into action to welcome the new doctor. Besides, bringing meals was a great way to introduce themselves and get to know her. Find out all the gossip to spread along the island grapevine. Because everyone here knew everyone else's business. That was what happened when you lived on an island with only a couple of hundred people. There was no privacy here. If Dr Childs thought she could keep any secrets... Well, good luck to her.

'I should show you your room...give you the tour.'

She nodded and smiled, and he put down his mug, glad of something to do. That smile of hers was really something. Warm. Inviting. Hypnotic. Those large eyes of hers...they drew you in.

He hefted her suitcase up the stairs and heard her softly padding after him. He'd taken the smallest bedroom after losing Emily. It hadn't seemed right to stay in the big one. He'd put most of Emily's things in the loft, save for a few special keepsakes that he kept in a box under his bed, and then he'd moved into the smaller room.

That had left two other bedrooms, and he'd chosen the one that looked out on to the woods for Dr Childs. Once he'd moved out she could take her pick, but for now it would have to do. He'd given it a clean, put fresh linen on the bed, polished, vacuumed. No doubt she would add her own touches to the place.

He flicked on the switch, that lit up the room. 'This is you.' He placed her suitcase by the large wardrobe and walked back towards the door. 'I'll leave you to settle in and we can catch up later. Then, when you're ready,

I'll fill you in on all the people you'll be living with for the foreseeable.'

He closed her bedroom door and let out a breath. The next few weeks were going to be hard in more ways than one.

The bedroom was lovely. A double bed sat in the centre of the room, covered with what looked like brand-new crisp white fresh linen. A pale rose counterpane matched the colour of the tiny flowers that adorned the curtains, held back by softly braided white ropes. The floor was exposed wood, with a fluffy white rug to put her feet on in the morning when she got out of bed.

Lucy noticed not only a wardrobe but a dresser, painted to look distressed, its handles made of leather loops the colour of warm caramel. To her left was a wooden door and, opening it, she found a small en-suite bathroom that comprised a toilet, a sink and a modern shower that not only had a large showerhead above, on the ceiling, but also showerheads that would squirt water from the sides, too.

She was surprised at the mix of modern and old-fashioned, but pleased by it. If this were to be her home she could do a lot to the place, if she wished. She had carte blanche to decorate however she wanted.

She went to her suitcase and unzipped it, throwing back the lid and placing her clothes on the bed, sorting them before placing them in the dresser and the wardrobe. It felt weird to be putting her things here, this far away from anyone she knew.

Her family had not been too impressed that she'd chosen somewhere so far away from them.

'But how will we know you're all right?' her mum had pleaded.

'Because I'll phone you at least once a week.'

'Once a *week*?'

It had been said as if she'd suggested only calling them once a decade, and then she'd received *the look*. Her sisters and her younger brother had all looked at her as if she was crazy.

'I'll be fine. I'm taking the meds.'

'But what if that's not enough? Look what happened to your father.'

She'd walked away then, needing a break from their intensity. They couldn't keep using what had happened to her dad as a weapon to punish her with. Was she to live her entire life under their watchful eye? Feeling enclosed? Trapped? Or did she have the right to live life as she pleased, enjoying every moment she could, as long as she was sensible?

Lucy preferred the latter option, and to do so had known she needed to move as far away as she possibly could, so that her family couldn't just drop in whenever they were passing by. Well, it was a long drive from London to Cornwall. She hoped it was enough. Plus, it also meant that she never stood the chance of running into Phillip again.

Her heart sank at the thought of him. Of how he'd abandoned her as soon as the results of her blood test had come through.

She tried to tell herself she'd had a lucky escape. Was glad that she'd found out what kind of man he was before it got too serious. But the truth of the matter was, it still hurt. He'd acted as if she was broken goods. Useless, with no future worth.

Who wanted to be with a man who treated a woman like that?

She wondered what kind of man Owen Ledger was.

He seemed nice. Calm. Welcoming. And a great deal more handsome than any man had a right to be. That dark, glossy hair. Those piercing green eyes, flecked with gold. Thank goodness he was only going to be here for a few more weeks, because he made her feel nervous. And not scary nervous, but excited nervous. Tingly nervous. Aware. Expectant.

He looks like he'd be a good kisser.

She blushed at the thought and laughed to herself. Owen had a fine mouth. A lower lip slightly larger than the top one. A manly smattering of stubble that made her want to run her fingertips over it…

Owen was the kind of man she felt attracted to—which might have been a problem if he were staying on here, but he was leaving.

It was a good thing he wouldn't be here long. A good thing that they wouldn't have to live together for more than a few weeks and then she'd be waving him goodbye.

It was safer that way. Staying alone was better for her emotional well-being. If she kept herself to herself, romantically, then she would never unwittingly put herself in danger of such horrible rejection again.

With her clothes put away, she took another steadying breath and headed downstairs.

Owen was in the kitchen, turned away from her, loading up the dishwasher, and for a brief moment she watched him unnoticed. He was rinsing off some bowls and plates under the tap first, before placing them inside. When he got to a large dessert spoon the water from the tap hit it at an angle and sprayed water all over his jumper. He jumped, and looked down at himself, and she couldn't help but smile.

'Need a hand?'

He turned to look at her and laughed, before grabbing

a tea towel and dabbing at his top. 'You'd think I'd know how to wash a spoon at my age.'

'They're difficult pieces of kitchen equipment.'

'You're telling me. I've put your hot chocolate over there. I can reheat it, if it's not warm enough.'

He indicated with his head and she saw her mug by the kettle.

Taking it in her hands, she sipped at it, grateful for the warmth of the hot drink. She noticed the dark water stains on Owen's jeans before looking away, trying not to think of how shapely his legs looked.

'Have you been here long?' she asked.

'As GP? Four years. But I've lived here half my life.'

'Long time…'

Owen placed a tablet in the dishwasher, closed it, pressed a few buttons on the front, switching it on, then leaned back against the kitchen counter, arms folded. 'It is. And it feels right to make the change now. Meet some new faces.'

'I guess you know everyone here really well?'

'Oh, yes! And they'll certainly get to know you, all right. It can be hard to keep your privacy in a place like this, so be warned.'

She sipped at her hot chocolate, trying to hide her anxiety at that. The last thing she needed was people prying into her personal life. Had it been a mistake to come here?

'A lot of them already know you were arriving today. In fact, I'm amazed they aren't lined up outside the front door already, come to introduce themselves. I was wondering if you fancied going to the local pub, to get it all over and done with?'

A pub? That wasn't really her thing. 'Would you mind if we didn't? It's been a long day, and I'm not sure I've got it in me to be sociable right now.'

'Okay. Want me to give you the full tour of the house and surgery instead?'

She smiled. That sounded more doable. 'Yes, please.'

Owen showed her around the house, room by room, and then walked her through the extension to the rear of the house, where the general surgery practice room was located.

'We run a morning clinic Monday to Friday, nine till twelve, have lunch and then make home visits, if needed. You'll get bleeped through your mobile phone, and generally you're on call all the time—but because there's only a couple of hundred people on the island, believe me, you'll hardly ever get called out for emergencies.'

'And if there is an emergency?'

'Then an ambulance gets sent from the mainland. But because it can't get here in less than seven minutes you'll act as first responder and keep people alive until the paramedics arrive and take over.'

She nodded. 'Okay.'

'We're equipped to do minor surgeries. And the last Friday of every month we run what I call the lumps and bumps clinic. Ingrown toenails, cysts…that kind of thing. A nurse comes over to assist from the main hospital. They usually send Ellen—she's very good and everyone knows her.'

Lucy looked around the room. It looked perfectly modern. Desk, computer, examination bed with lamp, scales, a cupboard full of blood-taking equipment and bandages. 'It all seems pretty hands-on.'

He nodded. 'It is. Work that at your old surgery you would normally have passed off to a nurse or HCA, here will be something you do yourself. It keeps things interesting. I've always liked that. You're not just sitting in this room and listening to people complain about colds and headaches, you really get to know them.'

'How often are blood and culture samples collected?'

'The large white box in the corridor we passed gets emptied at midday, Monday to Friday. The guy can access it himself—he has his own key.'

'Okay.'

It all seemed perfectly straightforward. But she felt nervous. It was one thing to talk about it in hypotheticals, but tomorrow she would actually start working here. Actually start meeting people who, Owen had suggested, might be quite nosy.

At that moment Owen's phone beeped, and he pulled it from his back pocket to look at it. 'I should never have said we hardly get called out.' He looked at her and smiled. 'I need to see a patient. You're tired. Why don't you stay here and rest?'

'No...' She smiled. 'I'd like to go. Best to start sometime, right?'

He smiled back at her. 'Right.'

CHAPTER TWO

'THE CAR COMES with the placement?'

Owen nodded. 'Yep.' He pointed the fob at the four-by-four and they both got in. 'You need a little off-roader for when the weather gets like this. You like snow?'

She smiled. 'I do. We often only get a little sprinkling in London, and then, within hours, it goes all slushy and grey, or the rain washes it away. I'm looking forward to living in a place that gets covered in a beautiful white blanket, thick enough to build snowmen and have snowball fights for days.'

'You sound wistful.'

'Do I? I guess it's just been a long time since I was able to enjoy anything like that.' The thought made her think of her family, and how she could imagine them standing there, watching her frolic in the snow, with stern looks on their faces, ordering her inside, where they'd promptly sit her down and check her pulse.

'Do you have family on the island?' she asked Owen.

'I do. My parents are here. They live in a small village called Southney, on the far side of the island. And I have a younger sister here, too.'

'Do you all get along?'

'We're good—though we have our moments, like most

families. How about you? What did your family think to you moving away?'

Hmm… Her mother's tears. Her siblings' anger. 'They were fine. We all have to live our own lives, don't we?'

'We certainly do.'

'What does your sister do? Does she work on the island?'

'She works in the post office, so she knows everyone. Knows everything. Just a heads-up: if you go in and a chirpy dark-haired girl with a tattoo of a bird on her right hand starts asking you personal questions, you'll know who's doing it.'

Lucy smiled. 'What's her name?'

'Bridget.'

She tried to take note of where they were going. Tried to notice landmarks. There was an old-style red telephone box at the junction of Hartness Road and Glencoe Road. A beautiful old church opposite an old World War II pillbox. The high street in the main village of Wytham was U-shaped, like a horseshoe, and ended at a school— Wytham Primary. She saw that one or two homes still had Christmas lights up, in trees outside, or along guttering, or in bushes.

'I noticed there weren't any Christmas decorations up in the house. Have you taken them down already?'

Owen shrugged. 'I didn't really bother. But there are some up in the loft, I believe. You'll have to have a rummage around.'

'Oh, okay.'

'You like Christmas?'

'I love it.'

'So does the gentleman we're going to see. I won't say too much. I don't want to spoil the surprise for you. But Mr Cushing is quite a fan of the festive season.'

She smiled. 'All right. Do we know what we're going to see him about?'

'Could be anything, of course, but Nige was in hospital recently, having surgery on his hand.'

'Oh?'

'He was in his garden and tripped over a stone. Fell headlong against his greenhouse and put his hand through a pane of glass. Severed a nerve.'

'How long ago?'

Owen thought for a moment. 'About ten days ago, I think. He's due to get his stitches out, but I don't think he will have called us out for that. He's a good patient. Not a time-waster. Considerate. Tries not to take up your time.'

'I'm looking forward to meeting him.'

'He'll enjoy meeting you.'

Owen continued to drive a little longer, taking them deeper into the countryside and away from Wytham. As they snaked along a dark and winding road Lucy began to notice a brightly coloured glow through the shadows of the trees, and before she knew it they were pulling up outside of a house that had every single inch decorated in festive design.

A life-size Santa on a sleigh being pulled by reindeer decorated the front lawn. Lights were draped over every window, door, bush and tree. There were snowmen and flashing red-and-white candy canes lining the path to the front door, and there was even a fake Santa clutching the house's chimney, high up on the roof.

Everything flashed and flickered, all the colours dazzling her eyes and making her smile at the visual delight. Then, as they stepped closer, she heard Christmas music begin to play—"Rudolph the Red-Nosed Reindeer". The front door opened and an elderly gentleman stood there, long white beard blowing in the evening breeze, pipe in hand, puffing out smoke. A modern-day Santa Claus.

'Nige! How are you? Can I introduce Dr Lucy Childs? She'll be taking over from me in a few weeks.' Owen stepped back so that she could shake Nigel's hand.

'Pleased to meet you, Mr Cushing.'

'Call me Nige. Everyone does. So, tell me, young miss, what do you think?' He spread his hands wide, indicating the house.

She could see beyond him that the inside of the house was just as much a grotto as it was out. 'It's fantastic— it really is.'

She must have said the right thing, because he beamed a broad smile.

'I do it every year. Try and raise money for the local lifeboat. Christmas Eve I do a big open house and everyone's welcome.' He leaned in and grinned. 'As long as they bring a Christmas present to be donated to the children's ward up at the hospital. So, you'll be very welcome next Christmas Eve. Don't forget.' He tapped the side of his nose.

'I won't.' She smiled, liking him immediately.

'So, what can we do for you, Nige? Is it the hand?'

'We'll go in and discuss it. Bit nippy out here. Come on—come on in.' Nige stepped back and ushered them through to a room that was so chockful of Christmas decor Lucy didn't know where to look first.

'I've been getting sweats and chills, and my hand hurts where they did the op. The missus is a bit worried that it might be infected.'

'Sally not in tonight?'

Nigel shook his head. 'Nah, she's gone round to Josie's to learn how to cook baklava. Whatever that is.'

Lucy smiled. 'I think it's some sort of pastry with nuts. It's very nice.'

'You should talk to my Sally. She'll let you join them next time.'

'I just might.' She smiled, knowing that she would. She'd love to learn to cook properly. Especially to bake. It was a skill that she'd never quite learned.

'How long have you been having chills and sweats?' Owen was slipping a small SATs monitor on to Nige's finger and pulling out the cuff to monitor his blood pressure.

'Two days.' He frowned. 'Thought the first day was just something and nothing, but when it went on through the night, and through today, Sally said I should give you a call. Get it checked. Told me not to wait until tomorrow. I do hope you don't mind me calling you out?'

'Not at all. Better to be safe than sorry. When are the stitches due out?'

'Tomorrow.'

Owen put on some gloves and began to unwrap the bandaging around Nige's hand and wrist. As more and more of the bandaging became removed they both noticed some yellow staining, and a bit of a smell was coming off it, indicating an infection of some kind.

The wound itself was Y-shaped. At least twenty stitches, so a sizeable injury. There was evidence of yellow-green exudate, and the wound itself looked quite red, showing that infection was stopping the healing process from proceeding as well as it should.

'Can you move your fingers and thumb?' Lucy asked.

Nige wiggled everything. 'It's sore, though.'

'It will be. Can you feel this? And this?' Owen stroked the sides of Nige's fingers and his thumb to check for sensation.

'Yes.'

'Good. But I think we need to get you on some antibiotics, and we might have to hold off taking those stitches out. Lucy, would you mind taking a swab for me?'

'Sure—no problem.'

'We'll get that sent off to the lab, and that should confirm we've got you on the right antibiotics.' Owen quickly wrote a prescription and signed it. 'Can you get this filled in the morning?'

'Can do, Doc.'

'Good. And start taking them straight away, all right?'

'I will.'

'Come and see us in a couple of days. We'll take a look at it and then see what we need to do with those stitches.'

Lucy swabbed the wound, labelled the swab and slipped it into a bag to send to Pathology. Then she helped rewrap the wound with a clean bandage, and they were soon heading towards the front door.

Owen headed out first, to put their bags in the boot of the car, and Lucy was just going to follow him when she heard Nige speak in a low voice. 'Er... Dr Childs?'

She turned, frowning. 'Is everything all right?'

'Dr Ledger...how's he doing?'

She turned to look at Owen, not quite understanding Mr Cushing's concern. 'Erm...he's fine...'

Nigel nodded. 'We're planning a bit of a send-off for him. A party,' he whispered. 'He says he doesn't want us planning anything, doesn't want anyone making a fuss, but we can't let him go without saying a proper goodbye.'

He pressed a finger to his lips to indicate that it was a secret.

Lucy liked it that Owen was so well liked by his patients that they wanted to say their goodbyes to him at a special party. It showed they cared. It showed they liked him and would miss him when he was gone.

Not only was he a handsome man, but one who seemed nice and kind, too. She could understand why they would miss him. Lucy wasn't used to nice and kind men, but she guessed that once you found one you'd kind of want to hang on to them.

She turned back to Mr Cushing. 'I'm sure he'll love it.'

'I hope so... He's seemed so different since...' He grimaced. 'Community Centre. January the thirty-first. Seven p.m. Can you get him there?'

'I'll try.'

He beamed at her and tapped the side of his nose. 'Mum's the word.'

She said goodbye and headed down the path towards the car. She got in, fastening her seat belt. 'Well, he was nice,' she said.

'They all are. In their own way.'

'Your tone implies that some of them might not be.'

He started the engine. 'It's not that. It's just...this is such a close community. People can be pushy when they want things. They make it seem like they're doing stuff out of the goodness of their hearts, when really they're...'

'What?'

He sighed, then shook his head, as if thinking better of something. 'Ignore me.' Owen smiled. 'I don't want to scare you off on your first day. They're all fine. They really are. They just find it hard to...to let people go, that's all.'

She thought about the secret send-off and bit her lip. She had no idea about Owen's life. How could she? Perhaps *he'd* had his fill of people being too close, too? Perhaps he needed space? She understood the need for that. She wouldn't want anyone invading her life either. She had to stand alone now. It had been made very clear to her that she had no other option.

A glimpse at Owen as he drove gave her the impression of a man keen to get away. Keen to be back in his own home. His furrowed brow showed his concentration as he drove along the dark streets, and he reacted quickly when a fox broke cover to run across the road.

'You need to be very aware of all the wildlife on night calls,' he said, turning to smile at her.

She liked his smile. Liked the way it brightened his sad eyes. What had made him sad? she wondered. She wasn't going to ask. It wasn't any of her business and, besides, he was leaving in a few weeks and it wouldn't matter anyway.

She would let him keep his privacy, as she would keep hers.

Lucy woke to the aroma of frying bacon wafting up the stairs and into her room. She sat up in bed and paused for a moment, looking around this strange new room and trying to tell herself that this was her new home.

Last night she'd lain in bed, listening to all the noises the old house made. Pipes rattling, floorboards creaking. She would get used to them in time.

Swinging her legs out of bed, she went into the en-suite bathroom and washed and brushed her teeth. Then she got dressed in a white blouse, a knee-length denim skirt and ankle boots, and headed downstairs.

Owen was busy in the kitchen and pouring two mugs of freshly percolated coffee. 'Ah! Good morning! I was just about to come and knock on your bedroom door to wake you.'

She gazed at the two plates of bacon and eggs and suddenly felt incredibly hungry. 'You must have got up early?'

'I always go for a run first thing. Five miles, roughly. Grab a plate. Tuck in.'

'You're very domesticated, Owen. Your parents must have trained you well.'

He laughed. 'My parents tried. I used to be helpless in the kitchen. I could burn a pan of boiling water.'

He sounded as if he'd once been like her. 'I'm something of a kitchen newbie myself. What fixed that?'

She was looking at him closely and saw his eyes darken. She'd touched a nerve about something.

'My wife.'

Her gaze dropped to his ring finger, but there was nothing there. 'You were married?'

He nodded, but said nothing more, and she knew the subject was closed. Fair enough.

'It's hard to lose someone you care about,' she said, thinking not only of Phillip, whom she'd thought she was in love with, but also her father. One day he'd been there, large as life, the next he'd been struck down in an instant and was gone. The shock of that still reverberated within her, and she had no doubt that it would never go away.

He sat down opposite her. 'You've lost someone, too?'

'Yes. And I don't like to talk about it, so don't feel bad.'

'About what?'

'About not wanting to talk about your wife.'

He smiled and gave a slight nod of thanks.

They ate in a pleasant silence for a while, until they were both finished, and then Lucy stood to gather their plates. 'I'll wash up.'

'Oh, I made the mess, so I should do it.'

'You cooked. Let me wash up.'

He held up both hands, giving in. 'Fair enough. You ready for your first full-on day?'

She began rinsing the plates before placing them in the dishwasher. 'I am.'

'Good. Start as you mean to go on.'

She was sure his words were meant to be positive. An encouragement. To show that he was pleased by her desire to get started. But somehow they had an opposite effect. They made her think about how her life here was going to be and, although she knew she'd be dedicated to her job, and making new friends and learning new skills, she remembered that she'd be doing it all alone.

That had never been her choice in life. She'd had the same dreams as anyone else—find someone. Settle down. Maybe get married. Have a family. She couldn't do that now. Her choices and her dreams needed to go in another direction.

And that made her feel incredibly alone.

He must have seen something in her demeanour, because Owen was standing close to her.

'Hey, you okay?'

She'd not been aware of him coming close, and now he stood too close. Those intense green eyes of his burning into her own.

Her heart pounded hard against her ribcage and she felt a rush of blood to her cheeks, inflaming them. He smelt so good, fresh from a shower after his jog, and he was so very attractive. And attractive men standing that close could cause things to happen she didn't want to happen.

So she took a step back, and then another, to get some space before wiping her hands on the dish towel. Looking down at the floor briefly, so that he didn't see the lie in her eyes, she said, 'I'm fine!'

It was clear in his face that he didn't believe her, but he didn't push. Didn't tell her that she could tell him anything in confidence. He simply nodded.

'Okay.'

Lucy was grateful. And startled by how her body had reacted to his proximity. It had been too much. Too soon.

Owen was a man she would need to keep at arm's length as much as she could until he left.

There'd only been four patients booked in for the morning clinic. A case of plantar fasciitis, a new hernia from trying to lift a wardrobe down some stairs, a child with asthma and now Mrs Janet Weaver, their last and final, who'd booked herself in with nausea, sweating and blood in her urine.

Owen had taken the lead on all the cases, introducing her to everyone and discussing patient histories with her so that she had the full background. Thankfully, Owen used a computer system that she was already familiar with, so she didn't need any training on how to find information about a patient on that.

Janet walked in looking most unwell. Pale, clearly in pain and slightly hunched over, as if she couldn't straighten up. There was a close sweat beading her brow, which she dabbed at with a handkerchief, as she sat opposite them both.

'Hello, Owen.'

'Hi, Janet. May I introduce Dr Lucy Childs? She's going to be taking over from me in February.'

Janet nodded. 'Oh, yes. I remember you said you were going. It's that soon, is it?'

'I'm afraid so. Now, then, why don't you tell us what's brought you in today?'

'I've not felt well for a day or so, then I noticed last night I had blood in my wee. I got like this the last time I had urinary stones. I wouldn't mind, but the pain is so bad, and what with sweating all the time and feeling sick with it… I'm finding it hard to get things done.'

It sounded like a clear-cut case of renal colic to Lucy.

'Would you mind if Dr Childs gave you a physical examination?' Owen asked.

'I don't mind.'

Lucy smiled. 'Let's get you up on the bed and I'll have a feel of your tummy.'

Lucy washed her hands whilst Janet got on the bed, and was drying them off with a paper towel as Janet lay down with some difficulty. She rubbed her hands together, to try and make them warm, and then gently began to palpate Mrs Weaver's abdomen.

'Ooh! That feels sore, there, Doctor.'

The pain was in her loins, exactly where Lucy would expect the pain to be if she had stones causing these issues.

'Let me help you up.' She helped the patient sit up and then helped her back to her chair. 'I don't suppose you could give us a urine sample?'

'I've brought one. I knew you'd need it. I only did it about half an hour ago, so it's not old.'

Lucy tested the urine with a testing strip and the result showed there was definitely haematuria. Blood in the urine.

Owen nodded as he gazed at the strip, too. 'Right, well, I think because you've had this problem before it might be best to get you scanned at the hospital. I'll do a referral for that, but in the meantime I've got some instructions for you.'

'All right. Same as last time?'

He nodded. 'You need to drink plenty, but not fizzy drinks. Water. Maybe add some fresh lemon juice to it. Limit salt, take painkillers—I'll do you a prescription—and I'll also write you up for some anti-sickness tablets and an alpha blocker to help the stones pass.'

'You think they'll pass on their own?'

'I hope so. But that's what the scan will help us determine.'

Janet smiled at them both. 'You're so kind. I am going to miss you, Dr Ledger. And I bet your parents will, too. I hope you'll be happy in your new post. I know your new patients are going to be very happy to have you.'

'I'm sure you'll all be just as happy with Dr Childs, here. She's very good. Very kind.' He turned and looked at her, smiled.

Lucy smiled back, grateful for his vote of confidence, even though he'd barely known her for a day.

'Well, I hope you'll be happy, Owen. It's been hard seeing you so sad since you lost Emily. You've not been the happy-go-lucky man we're used to.'

Emily. That had to have been his wife. She wondered how long it had been since he'd lost her.

Owen stood up, signalling the appointment was over. He reached out and shook Janet's hand. 'I'm all right. You take care of yourself, Janet, and any problems just make an appointment to see Dr Childs. She'll take care of you very well indeed.'

'I will. Thank you. You take care, too, Owen.' She came forward to give him a hug.

He didn't answer, and Lucy could see he felt awkward.

He waited for Janet to close the door behind her. When she did, Owen sank back into his chair with a heavy sigh and began to type his notes into Janet's patient record.

Lucy watched him. Clearly he did not want to talk about his personal life. She got that. She did. But she could see his pain now, at having had it brought up, and it was within her to want to ask him if he was all right. But would he see that as prying? She didn't want to upset him any further, because not only did they have to work together for the next few weeks, but they also had to live together, until Owen moved out at the end of January.

'Shall I make us a cup of tea?' she asked brightly, instead.

He nodded and smiled, his eyes brightening. 'That sounds great.'

As they wrapped up the morning clinic and packed everything away, they began to chat.

'So, did you always know you wanted to be a GP?' asked Lucy.

He smiled. 'Actually, no. When I was at medical school I thought I'd love my specialty to be emergency medicine. The idea of all those different cases walking through the door, having to think on my feet... I really thought I'd do that.'

'Why didn't you?'

'I nearly did. I had a placement. It was very frantic. There was never a moment to think, and I felt as if I'd not been able to spend enough time with my patients as I would have liked. It all seemed to be about the numbers. About getting people through as fast as you could. Triage and treat and on to the next. It wasn't for me. So I chose general practice. I thought that way I'd get the variety I wanted, but also the time to create a relationship with my patients.'

She nodded. 'I experienced the same thing.' She laughed. 'How odd. Though, I found myself unable to get to know all of my patients as much as I'd have liked in Wandsworth, so I wanted to find a smaller practice with a smaller patient list.'

'And so you came here?'

'Yes.'

Owen realised how much he was beginning to love

her smile. Her warmth. But the more he looked at her, the more he saw she was all woman, and all the things his body naturally responded to. The large doe eyes, the shape of her lips. Her smile. She seemed open and genuine, and in the few hours that he'd worked with her he'd seen how kind and empathetic she'd been with the patients.

Disturbingly, he hadn't been able to stop glancing at her throughout the morning's clinic, looking at her when she was busy examining a patient, taking in all the small details—like the way she'd tuck her short hair behind her ears when she was listening to someone speak. The way her right eyebrow would sometimes arch. The fact that she had a dimple in her left cheek when she laughed. The delicateness of her hands. The smoothness of her skin. The tiny diamond studs in her ears.

She was a woman who didn't need brash colours and idiosyncrasies to make herself stand out. She was demure and confident and quiet, and he liked that very much.

Stop.

He tried to take in a steadying breath as he leaned over his desk to turn off his computer and lock away the prescriptions that were in the printer.

He needed to remind himself that getting involved with someone here on the island was never going to work out and that he needed to maintain distance. She was his colleague. His roommate. And that was all. He was leaving this place behind and moving on.

He couldn't move on here.

And most certainly *not* with Dr Lucy Childs.

Owen had opened up the loft and slid out a ladder. He'd said he was going up there to sort out a few belongings.

Once the ladder was secure he went up, and she had to admit she took the opportunity to watch him go.

He had a very nice rear end.

She'd tried not to look, but what was a girl to do? She was single, a woman with needs if ever there was one, and Owen was right there. It couldn't just be his face that was attractive, right?

Heat flushed her cheeks, and once he was safely up there she went downstairs to make them both a drink, smiling to herself, slightly amused at her own behaviour.

Outside, the wind was whipping around the house, howling. It was still cold, and though she had no idea how warm or not the loft might be, she figured Owen would appreciate a hot drink.

She opened up cupboards, trying to find where everything was, and when she opened one that had mugs in it, she found the door had a photo tacked to the inside.

This must be Emily.

Emily had been everything that Lucy was not. Tall, with long blonde hair and blue eyes. In the picture, Emily was halfway up an indoor rock-climbing wall, smiling, with one hand held out making the peace sign.

She was very pretty, and Lucy tried to imagine this woman with Owen. They would have made a very lovely couple.

Lucy closed the door and made the tea, and then headed back upstairs with the drinks. 'I'm coming up,' she told him.

'Okay—hang on.'

She heard scuffling and movement and then Owen was in the hatch, waiting for her, his hand outstretched to take the drinks. Once she'd passed them, he put them inside the loft and then helped her up the ladder safely. He indicated a small stool she could sit on.

'Wow. This is a big space,' she said.

'Plenty of room to store stuff.'

There were certainly lots of boxes. 'Is all this yours?'

'Mine and Emily's.'

'Oh.'

She didn't feel she should offer to help him sort through stuff that had belonged to his wife. He might not like that. She remembered how much he hadn't wanted to talk about Emily at work with his patient.

'Thanks for the tea. You know, this is the first time I've come up here since...well, you know.'

'It must be hard.'

'You've no idea.'

'Do you know what you're looking for?'

Owen looked lost. 'Not really. I just know I put a lot of stuff up here, thinking I'd sort it out later, and it wouldn't be fair to leave you with it. I'd like to sort it before I go. Give stuff to family...charity, maybe.'

He began opening boxes labelled 'Emily' and at first found books, then clothes. She watched him pick up a yellow T-shirt and smile.

'There must be a lot of memories up here,' she said. 'I'll leave you to them.'

'Oh, you don't have to go. You can stay.'

'You're sure?'

He smiled. 'I think I'd like the company and...' He smiled at her. 'Having someone with me might make this feel a little less heartbreaking than if I was up here all alone.'

'Okay.' She smiled back, feeling something stir in her belly. It was a wonderful feeling. A warm feeling.

Lucy clutched her tea and watched as he opened another box of books, reached in, pulled a couple out and smiled. No doubt he was remembering his wife reading them. Had they been in bed together when she read? Or had Emily read on the couch downstairs?

'Do you read?' he asked.

'I like to when I can.'

'Maybe you should take a look through these, then? See if there's anything you fancy? Otherwise they'll just go to the charity shop.'

'It must be hard to think about giving away her things.'

She remembered how her mother had struggled with packing up Lucy's dad's things. She'd wanted to hold on to the silliest items—a train ticket, a receipt, an old birthday card.

'It's got to be done.'

'Maybe not all today, though. Do it bit by bit. That might be easier. Perhaps decide to only sort through a couple of boxes at a time?'

He smiled at her. 'That sounds like a great idea. I must admit I felt a little overwhelmed at seeing how much stuff was up here. I'd forgotten. It was all too easy to just box it and shove it away in a corner. Thank you, Lucy.'

She smiled. 'For what?'

'For helping make this easier.'

She blushed at the compliment and began looking through the books. It felt weird to think that the books she was touching had been held by his wife, maybe for hours at a time. That she had sat reading engrossed somewhere and now Lucy might read them. There were some good titles here. Books that she hadn't read yet and wanted to, but had never found the time. She should put them to one side, like he'd suggested.

'This feels a bit odd.'

He gazed at her. 'How so?'

'Reading your wife's books.'

'She used to love reading. She was a bit of a bookworm…

always in the local library. I'm sure she'd love it if you enjoyed them, too.'

'Really?'

'Of course! If you didn't know who they'd come from you'd read them, right?'

She nodded.

'So we're cutting out the middle man. Saving you a trip to the charity shop.'

'I guess… Okay. Thanks.'

'My pleasure.'

She smiled at him, but he'd already turned away to open another box.

He was such a nice guy. He didn't deserve to be on his own. A man like him—he needed someone. Someone to love. She could tell he was a keeper.

Just not hers, though.

That made her feel sad. Once upon a time she'd considered herself to be a person with a huge amount to offer someone. Now she'd had to close herself off from life. Remain open to friendships and working hard, but not having someone to love. Not unless she could find someone who didn't want kids, had no chance of changing their minds and didn't care that their partner could collapse at any time?

It probably narrowed the field quite a bit. But she couldn't bear the idea of being rejected the way she had been by Phillip. Couldn't bear how she'd had to take such drastic steps to move away from everyone she knew just so she felt as if she could breathe.

We humans are a fragile lot.

She placed a pile of books she liked the sound of to one side, then stood to grab another box. But her foot caught on the stool and before she knew it she was falling—straight towards the loft hatch.

As the opening loomed closer she cried out, spreading her arms to grab something to stop her fall. Then she felt a strong set of arms grab her around the waist and haul her back, almost winding her in the process.

'I've got you! You okay?'

His gaze met hers. Close. Too close.

She had been pulled in tight to his body, against his long, hard, lean form, and then she'd turned in his arms to look at him, shocked, surprised, stunned...

Grateful.

The loft light was behind him, so most of his face was in shadow, but his eyes gleamed an intense green as he gazed at her, waiting for her to tell him she was okay.

It had been months since a man had held her this close, and she was acutely aware that her hands were on his chest. She could feel him breathing. Feel the warmth of him through his shirt. And their faces were inches apart.

Owen had barely known her a day, and he was looking at her as if he really cared. As if he were concerned for her welfare. Of course, it could just be he didn't want to take the risk of his replacement getting injured, preventing him from leaving...but she doubted it.

There was something else there that she couldn't decipher. An awareness? Was that what it was? He was an attractive man. And single. Like her. Of course there were going to be...*feelings.* But he was leaving, and he knew there could be nothing between them.

But Owen looking at her like this was doing strange things to her insides. Owen being this close was causing strange physiological reactions that she hadn't felt for a long time. His arms were around her waist, his face so close, so full of concern, so...

Her gaze dropped to his mouth. She didn't mean it to. She couldn't help it. But one glance at his lips, at his sensuous mouth, unnerved her so much she was finally able to nod and say she was okay.

She broke free from his grasp, reluctantly pushing herself away. 'I'm fine,' she repeated.

He took a step back from her, too. 'Maybe you should stay on the ground from now on? I'll bring all this down.'

She smiled nervously. 'You're sure?'

'Absolutely.'

Lucy nodded and began to climb down the ladder—and became aware of just how shaky and trembly her legs were.

The Owen Effect.

CHAPTER THREE

OF COURSE HE couldn't sleep. How could he? All he could think about was how it had felt to hold Lucy in his arms. How it had felt to hold a woman so close again after all this time. A woman he'd felt his body respond to. A woman who had not been Emily.

That was the crux of the matter—she hadn't been Emily. And despite that he had felt moved by her, when he'd never thought a woman would make him feel that way ever again.

He'd made a start on sorting Emily's things in the loft—a job he'd been dreading. And having Lucy with him had been…soothing. Like balm on an open wound. She'd made it better just by being with him. Somehow he'd been able to sort through a couple of boxes and make firm decisions about stuff. Stuff that maybe Emily's family would want. Stuff he could give to charity. Stuff he could throw away.

At first he'd been glad to offer Lucy some of Emily's books, but later…

Guilt was insidious. And disruptive. Maybe the quicker he could get out of here, the easier it would be. Because Lucy confused him. She jumbled his senses and made him feel things he'd not thought it was possible to feel. Not here on the island.

Stopping her from falling through the loft hatch had been a natural reaction. He'd seen her trip and he'd reached out instinctively to save her. But the pulling her close part... What had *that* been about?

Up close, her eyes had been a dark melted chocolate colour, with flecks of gold. Her cheeks had flushed a soft pink and her lips... *Dear God, her lips...*

He'd not wanted to focus on them, but he had. Her lips had been parted in surprise, her bottom lip had quivered and she'd bit it as she'd looked at him. And that one action had practically turned him inside out with a lust and desire so strong he'd almost kissed her.

He'd told himself he was glad when she'd pushed herself away, when she'd created some distance between them once again. Because his body had been behaving so dangerously he'd not been sure he would be able to stop himself if she'd stayed in his arms, gazing into his eyes...

The loft space was small. Intimate. He'd decided he'd do better with her downstairs. And so he'd suggested it, glad when she'd descended the ladder safely and he'd been able to let out a long, low, steady breath and gather his senses.

The rest of that night he'd kept his distance, watching her read a book, trying not to look at her so closely, trying not to notice the shapeliness of her body, the concentration in her eyes, the way her fingers slid across the page as she turned it.

Emily had loved to read, too. But he didn't want to compare Lucy to Emily! That was what everyone else here would do, and he didn't want to be like them.

He missed his wife. Of course he did. But now he found his thoughts focusing on Lucy, and sleep eluded him as he puzzled over this startling new presence in his life.

He got up the next morning, weary and sleep-deprived, determined to keep Dr Lucy Childs at arm's length.

The morning clinic began at nine, allowing them both time to have a leisurely breakfast.

Lucy had heard Owen get up early and leave the house, and from her bedroom window she'd watched him jog down the lane in a long-sleeved top and shorts, until he'd disappeared from view.

How was he out there when it was so cold? Everywhere she could see was frosted with ice, after most of the snow had disappeared overnight, and a low mist hung over the land. And Owen was out there in shorts!

She told herself she was concerned for his health, not just for the fact that he had very nice legs and she couldn't stop thinking about them. Couldn't stop thinking about *him*—which was weird. Nothing had happened between them and nothing *would* happen between them. She was staying. He was leaving. Simple. Nothing complicated about that.

And it wasn't as if anything had happened last night. All he'd done was stop her from falling, and her confused mind and body had been so starved of human affection and touch for months on end they had gone a little gaga— that was all it was. Right? It had nothing to do with the fact that she found him incredibly attractive.

She headed downstairs and made herself some breakfast of strawberry jam on toast, and put on a couple of boiled eggs for Owen, in case he wanted something when he got back.

She was just perusing the books on his bookshelves when she heard the front door open and felt cold air filter in. And there he was. A little sweaty. A little tousled. His bare legs covered in dirt from where he must have run through some muddy puddles. She tried not to think of rubbing those legs under hot water to get the mud off. Tried not to think of trailing her fingers up his calves, past his knees and over those wonderfully shaped thighs, and instead concentrated on trying to smile and act natural.

'Good run?'

He pulled out his earbuds and grinned. 'Great. I'm just going to grab a hot shower.'

'Great,' she echoed, closing her eyes in dismay as he ran up the stairs and she began to imagine what he would look like standing naked under the showerhead.

What am I doing to myself?

Maybe she should take a leaf out of his book? Go running. Do some exercise. Work off the physical frustrations she could feel in her body. She'd always been a physical person, but over the last few years concerns over her health had stopped that. Or rather, her family had.

'You shouldn't run so much.'

'Do you really need to go to a spin class?'

'Maybe you should take up exercise that's more gentle. Like yoga?'

Being held by Owen had woken something inside her, long hidden, long repressed. And now a strong, handsome man was just upstairs, naked in a shower, and she was downstairs, pacing the floor, trying not to think about how it had felt to be pressed up close against his long, hard, lean body and the way he had looked at her.

He would no doubt come downstairs with wet, ruffled hair, smelling delicious and male and looking stunning, and she would have to pretend that he didn't exist and that she wasn't attracted to him.

Brilliant. Just brilliant.

At least work would begin soon. At work, she would

be able to focus on the patients and not on Owen. That was the plan anyway.

Lucy began cleaning the kitchen counters, scrubbing hard at imaginary stains, before she tackled the dishwasher and then decided the microwave needed a clean.

'You don't have to do that. I cleaned it last week.' Owen was coming down the stairs, ruffling his dark hair with a towel and looking delicious.

She tried not to notice how wonderful he looked and she just turned away and shrugged. 'Oh, I spilled some porridge in it when I made my breakfast.'

He came over, looked at it, and with him came the lovely aroma of male bathroom products—shower gel, shaving cream, soap. It washed over her like a tsunami and she tried her best not to let it affect her.

'Looks clean to me,' he said.

She smiled. 'Cup of tea?'

'Great, thanks.'

'Do we know how many patients we have this morning?' she asked, grabbing the kettle and filling it with water.

'Not until we get there. Helen will have the list.'

Helen was their receptionist. She sat in a small office space next to the clinician's room and took phone calls and answered any messages that had been left on the answering machine. She also booked the home visits. She was a nice lady. Calm. Affable. Liked to sit and read one of her romances when it was quiet.

Lucy nodded and made them both tea, passing him his cup and wishing he would put a comb through his hair, or something. Because right now, all ruffled like that... It made her want to run her fingers through it. And if she did that, she'd want to look him in the eyes and hold him close and...

Get. A. Grip.

She took a determined sip from her own mug and turned away. This was ridiculous. All these thoughts. All these *feelings*. She needed to remember why she was here. The *reason* she was here. She was here because she needed to get away from the complications that other people had created in her life. Her family. Her ex.

The first had smothered her, made her feel as if she couldn't breathe, and the second... Well, he'd just cut her loose. All because of her condition. Smothered or let go? Which was worse? Being told she couldn't be like other people, or being told she had nothing to offer a man?

She'd lost everything because of this syndrome. Her previously sane family, her father—whom it had killed—and Phillip, the man she'd thought she would settle down with and start a family.

Even that had been taken from her, and she'd so badly wanted to be a mother. It *could* be done, the doctors had said. She *could* get pregnant. But she'd have to be carefully monitored throughout and, worse, there was a 50 per cent chance of passing on her condition. A chance she was not prepared to take.

The stark reminder of who she truly was, was a large bucket of cold water on her fantasies. And she no longer wanted the tea, and no longer wanted to think about how attractive Owen was. Or what she wanted to do to him.

'I think I'll head on down,' she said. 'Say hello to Helen. See if there's anything I can help her with.'

'Okay. I'll grab a quick bite and join you in a few minutes.'

She nodded, grabbed her jacket and left, savouring the blast of cold air on her exposed face as she took the outdoors way to the clinic, rather than going through the house.

She could still smell the snow...

She smiled as she heard her dad's voice in her head, remonstrating with her that it wasn't possible to *smell* snow. She wished she could see him right now. Speak to him. Fling her arms around him and hold him tight. But she couldn't. She would never do that again. The familiar thought saddened her. It had been years since she'd lost him. Did the bite of grief ever get easier?

When she stepped into the clinic Helen was already there, just booting up the computer.

'Morning.'

'Morning, Dr Childs! You've got rosy cheeks. Isn't it cold?'

'It certainly is.'

Lucy entered her room and switched on the computer, then noticed the photo frame at the side of the desk that yesterday she'd not been able to see properly. She turned it round and saw a picture of Owen and his wife.

They looked very happy together. Heads together as the photo was taken. Smiling. Perfect. Where had it been taken? Behind them the sky was a clear blue, and the building was modern and stylish. Expensive... A hotel? Somewhere abroad?

He'd had his happiness and his future taken from him, too, and she felt that raw connection between them quite sharply. Loss. The taking away of hopes and dreams. The future. What were they meant to take from that?

As if her thoughts had summoned him, he suddenly walked in—hair now combed, though still damp—and gave her a smile.

She got out of his seat and moved over to her own, at the side, watching him as he sat down and noticed that she'd turned the picture round.

'My wife,' he said.

'She's beautiful.'

'Yes. She was.'

Lucy didn't know what to do next. Ask him more about her? Ask about how they'd met? He might not want to say anything—and besides, if she started asking him personal questions, he might feel that he was just as entitled to ask her about her own past. But if she didn't ask, wouldn't that seem rude? Most people would ask *some* sort of a question.

'How long has it been?'

Owen sighed. 'Two years.'

'It's hard, losing those you love.'

There must have been a tone to her voice that caused him to turn and look at her, and she realised that she'd unintentionally told him that she'd lost people, too. Her father, her partner, her dream future and, it seemed, her family. But she couldn't tell him any of that. Not yet. Maybe she never would.

'Yes.'

At that moment, Helen buzzed through from Reception. 'Your first patient is here.'

Owen pressed a button on the phone. 'Thanks, Helen.'

With relief, they began to see patients. It was the usual sort of complaints. Bad backs. Querying lumps. An asthma review. A COPD review... They were rattling through, and Owen was introducing her to everyone and allowing her to take the lead in asking the patients questions and doing examinations, and then chatting with her about each case after each patient had left.

They were working well together. Had developed a rhythm together—all of which came to a grinding halt when the next patient was announced.

Gemma Aickman had arrived for a thirty-six-week check-up in her first pregnancy. Lucy felt as well as saw

Owen tense when he heard who was coming into the clinic next.

'Problem?' she asked.

'No, it's just… It doesn't matter. I'm sure it will be fine.'

He called Gemma through and she came in, smiling, and sat down on the chair in front of them.

'Hey, Owen.' She smiled at him, then looked at Lucy. 'Hi, I'm Gemma. You must be the new doctor?'

'Gemma, this is Dr Lucy Childs,' Owen said.

'Pleased to meet you.' Lucy shook her hand.

'How have you been feeling?' Owen's tone was very businesslike.

Gemma nodded happily. 'I've been doing great. Baby's kicking a lot.'

'Good. No problems at all?'

'No. Not as far as I know.'

'As Dr Childs is going to be taking over from me when I leave, I thought I'd let her go through your examination and appointment—is that okay?' Owen stood up as if to go.

Gemma looked back and forth between them. 'Sure, but… I kind of wanted to talk to you, actually.'

'Dr Childs is perfectly qualified—'

'Not about the pregnancy. About something else.'

Lucy wasn't sure why she could feel so much tension in the room. She'd seen Owen actually stiffen when Gemma had asked to speak to him. Clearly he didn't want to stay in the room with this patient, but she didn't know why. He was trying to be polite about it, but he was obviously ill at ease.

Owen stared at Gemma. 'What is it?'

'I know you're leaving, but…but you were Emily's

husband, and I was her best friend, and we always talked about what would happen when we had our first babies.'

Lucy saw Owen swallow, the muscle in his jaw twitching.

'I always said that I'd want you and her to be godparents, and it's getting close now, and I know you're leaving and she's not here any more, but I meant what I said and I'd be honoured if you'd consider being this little one's godfather.'

Owen smiled and shook his head. 'I won't be around, Gemma.'

'That doesn't matter! You could come to the christening. Godparents hardly ever end up actually having to raise someone else's kids because of some tragic accident, do they? And the likelihood of both me and Darren dying—'

'I'll think about it. Now I'll leave you to Dr Child's ministrations.'

And he walked out of the room, the door closing slowly behind him with a gentle click.

Gemma turned to Lucy, frowning. 'Did I say something wrong?'

'No, no. Not at all.'

'I know he doesn't like to be reminded of Emily, and I think I'm a big reminder.' She looked down at her swollen abdomen. 'And getting bigger every day. We always wanted to be pregnant together,' she said sadly.

Lucy desperately wanted to know what had happened to Emily and knew this woman had the answers. But if Owen had wanted her to know then he would have told her, and at work was not the place to start talking about your colleague's personal life.

'If she were here, I'm sure she'd be happy for you.

So! Let's get you up on this bed and have a feel of your tummy, shall we?'

Gemma climbed on to the bed and pulled up her top so that Lucy could palpate her abdomen. It felt as if the baby was head-down.

'The last time I saw her was at the hospital. The one on the mainland... We both worked there. I'm a radiographer.'

'Are you? Do you enjoy it?'

'I do. It's how Emily and I met, actually. She brought a patient down with a suspected broken wrist. We got chatting and became friends. She was just so easy to talk to, you know?'

Lucy nodded.

'One day I was at work, and she'd come in for an appointment. She told me it was routine, but I suspected it wasn't. She'd been having these headaches...' Gemma bit her lip.

Lucy had a tape measure over Gemma's abdomen. She was measuring correctly for thirty-six weeks. 'I'm just going to listen to the heartbeat.' She grabbed the small handheld Doppler.

'You think you'll know when a conversation is important, don't you...? But you don't.'

No. The last time she'd spoken to her father he'd just been sitting in a chair watching television. It had been normal. Boring. Mundane. There had been nothing in the day to mark it as an important one. Nothing to indicate to her that anything was about to go wrong. He'd stood up. Said he was going to go and do some gardening. That there was a bed that needed digging over.

How were Lucy and her family to know? How were they to know that that small event would be enough to cause her dad to have a massive cardiac arrest? He'd seemed healthy until then. A normal middle-aged guy. They weren't to know that he had a heart condition. One that they later suspected had killed his own mother, too.

The baby's heartbeat played loudly in the room. Regular and perfect. Fast as it should be.

Gemma smiled.

'Do you know what you're having?'

'A girl.'

'Have you picked a name, yet?'

'Her middle name will be Emily, but we haven't decided on a first name.'

'Well, you still have a few weeks to decide.' She smiled and indicated that Gemma could sit up now. She was finished with her examination.

'Yeah…'

She filled in Gemma's pregnancy record and handed it to her, then told her she'd look forward to seeing her at thirty-eight weeks. She watched Gemma go, and when she was gone Owen came back into the room.

'Sorry about that.'

'It's okay.'

'Did she say anything?'

'About Emily?'

He nodded.

'Just that she missed her. That she wished she'd had the chance to say goodbye.'

He sat down in his chair and didn't say anything.

Lucy gazed at his profile, wondering what he was thinking. Here was a man clearly trying to avoid his past, whilst she was trying her hardest to do the same—only in a completely different way. She wished she could talk to him about it. She felt that he would have some wise words for her. Some calming words. He might even make her feel better about her situation.

They had so much in common when it came to losing those they'd cared about. But loss was such a difficult thing to bring up, and she didn't want to sadden him any more than he already was. Nor did she want to open up herself.

Their next patient was Harvey Price, there for an earwax removal. Lucy got the equipment ready and waited for him to arrive.

When he walked in, he gave Owen a hug, clapping his hands on his back in greeting. 'My going-away present to you, Owen. A bunch of earwax. Don't tell me I don't get you nice gifts.'

Owen laughed. 'They're unique. I'll give you that.'

'Maybe you could frame it? Have it coated in gold so that you don't forget me?'

'I think I'll stick to memories, if that's okay?' He smiled. 'Dr Childs will do the procedure. She's going to be your new doctor.'

Harvey looked at her and reached out his hand for her to shake. 'Nice to meet you.'

'You, too.'

'You didn't tell us your replacement was going to be a lovely young woman. I would have tried to make a better impression. Put on a tie.' He rubbed at his teeth with a finger. 'Maybe flossed...'

'You're fine, Mr Price.'

'Call me Harvey.' He sat down on the examination bed and waited whilst Lucy draped him in a blue paper towel, to protect his clothes from any water spillage, then positioned a cardboard cup under his ear.

'Could you hold this for me?'

She began to use the machine, squirting in water to wash out the wax, and as she did so Harvey seemed intent on talking to Owen.

'You coming to Emily's Evening next week?' he asked.

Lucy glanced at Owen, knowing he didn't like any conversations about his dead wife.

'I don't think so. I've got a lot of stuff to sort out before I leave, so…'

'I think Emily's parents are expecting you to be there, and you've not missed one yet.'

'I've been to the others. I think it's time to let go.' His voice sounded terse, and he began fidgeting with the paperwork on his desk.

Lucy chose to stay silent.

'You know it's for her birthday?' said Harvey.

'Of course I do!' Owen's voice rose a few octaves. 'It's just…' He sighed.

Harvey conceded. 'It's okay. I understand. You're leaving, you're starting your life anew, getting a fresh perspective. You're letting go of her.'

Lucy had managed to get the wax out of Harvey's ear, and now she dried it with the paper towel and began to proceed with his other ear.

'I need to,' Owen answered quietly.

'Good for you.' Harvey smiled.

But Lucy could see Owen was not happy. The conversation had clearly made him uncomfortable.

When she'd finished both Harvey's ears they waved him goodbye, and Lucy cleaned the equipment before putting it away again.

Owen got up and began to pace. 'You see what I'm facing here? The people of this island…they never let you forget!'

She turned to face him, considering him. Hoping that his assessment of the islanders wasn't true. Because what if they found out about her? If she'd thought her family chiding her for her activities was bad, what if a whole island did it?

'It sounds like they all loved Emily very much. Perhaps they're finding it hard to let go of her, so they're trying to keep her memory alive?'

'They can do that without dragging me into it. She's gone. She died. There's nothing we can do about that, so why won't they let her go?'

She sat down next to him, tried to get him to look her in the eye. 'They've lost her. And it sounds like she was loved. And they don't want to lose you, too. Perhaps you shouldn't be angry with them? They're only doing what they feel is right. Trying to show you how much they care.'

'But their caring only hurts me.'

She gazed softly at him. 'I don't think you're angry with them.'

He turned to her quizzically. Raised a singular perfect brow. 'Oh? Just who *am* I angry with?'

'I think you want to be angry with Emily. For leaving you to deal with all this. But you don't think you can be angry with a dead woman, so you're angry with yourself.'

'Why would I be angry with myself?'

She smiled. 'I don't know. That's for you to work out.'

CHAPTER FOUR

ANOTHER NIGHT SPENT staring at the ceiling of his bedroom did not a happy Owen make.

Lucy had planted some questions in his head and they'd made a nest there, got comfy and demanded to be fed. He kept mulling them over and over in his mind, and eventually he got up and stood outside Lucy's door, pondering on whether to knock.

It was late. She was probably asleep. Maybe it would be best if he just went back to his own room?

But then he heard noises downstairs in the kitchen. Was she down there? Getting herself a drink?

He padded softly down the stairs and saw she'd switched the light on in the kitchen and seemed to be making herself some cocoa.

'Hey. Couldn't sleep?' he asked.

'No. I tried counting sheep, but... What's up? Can't you sleep either?' Then she frowned. 'Oh, God, did I wake you? I'm so sorry!'

'No, you didn't wake me.'

She nodded, reassured, and turned back to her pan of milk. And that was when he fully noticed that she was wearing a fitted grey T-shirt and a little pair of pyjama shorts that clung to her lovely figure. He lifted his gaze back upwards, where it was more appropriate.

'I keep thinking about what you said today,' he said.

'About Emily? Look, if I stepped over the line I apologise. I don't know anything about what happened. I didn't know her—or the pair of you as a couple. Who am I to comment?' she smiled.

'It was fine. You'll hear eventually, anyway. The island grapevine is an unstoppable force.'

She smiled. 'Small communities, eh?'

Lucy was really easy to talk to, and he liked having someone he could talk to again. He and Emily had often had conversations going on into the night.

He headed over to the table and pulled out a chair. 'I've been thinking about why I might be angry.'

'Okay...'

'I've been telling myself that I'm blaming them—for not letting her go, for not letting me move on—and I've realised that maybe it's not them at all.'

She smiled. 'No?'

He smiled back, a little ashamed. 'No. I guess I should tell you about how Emily died...'

'Only if you want to.'

'She was a community midwife. She worked out of the hospital on the mainland. We met through work, fell in love, decided to get married. She'd been having some headaches, which we put down to stress—you know... organising the wedding... She went to see a doctor about them and eventually they referred her for an MRI, just to rule some stuff out.'

Lucy nodded.

'She had the MRI, then we got married and went on our honeymoon to Dubai. She still had the headaches, but they weren't getting worse or anything, and when we got home again she made an appointment to see her consultant. We were going to go together, but I had a weekend-long stag party to go to. I told her I'd cancel. Go with her instead. But she told me to go and be with my friend. Said that he was about to embark on the journey of marriage, same as us, and that as I'd known him since junior school I ought to go with him.'

'So she went on her own?'

He nodded. 'Yeah. And the scan showed a brain aneurysm. Quite a sizeable one. They told her they couldn't operate…that it was too dangerous. She…er…didn't know how to tell me. She told Gemma, who you saw today in clinic—the pregnant lady?'

Lucy nodded again.

'Emily decided she'd wait for me to get home from the stag weekend. I'd gone to Barcelona, and the flight back was delayed, so I was away an extra day—which, as it turned out, was one day too late.'

'It ruptured?' Lucy whispered in shock.

He nodded.

'Oh, Owen…'

Lucy reached out and grabbed his hand, and he was so surprised by the gesture, so taken by the feel of her hand on his, that it took him a moment before he could continue.

'I realised today that my anger stems from the fact that I wasn't with her. That she had to shoulder that news, that burden, alone. That maybe all the worrying she did, all the crying, might have made it—'

He cut himself off as he looked down and away, gathering himself.

'I think I'm angry because I wasn't there. I'm angry that she only told Gemma. That Gemma knew and I didn't. And that my love, my future, was taken away from me. That I lounged about in an airport reading a stupid spy novel, watching my friends suffering from hangovers, when my wife was… I want there to be closure, and there isn't any. So when everyone here keeps reminding me of Emily, they're simply reminding me of my failure. I, as Emily's husband and as a doctor, should have been able to protect her. And I couldn't. So I'm angry at myself for going away. And every reminder, every celebration of Emily, every place on this godforsaken island, simply serves to remind me of her and all that I did wrong.'

'It wasn't your fault! You didn't know about it, and you could never have known that the aneurysm was going to blow when it did. If you had been at home, instead of in Barcelona, the end result would have been the same.'

He shook his head. 'But she wouldn't have been alone.'

'Maybe not. But she will have known how much you loved her anyway. How much you would have wished you could be there. She was protecting you. She wanted you to enjoy your weekend. A day or so of having fun before she had to tell you devastating news. She wanted that for you. A couple of carefree days before you got bogged down with worry. She didn't want to ring you and have you panic hundreds of miles away until you got home.'

'I guess…'

'When you love someone, and you lose them, it's one of the hardest things to get over. In fact, I'm not sure we *do* get over it. We just learn to live with the pain until it becomes bearable.'

She sounded as if she'd had personal experience of that. He was intrigued. But she was clearly upset, and he could see the threat of tears in her eyes. Who was she upset for? Him? If so, she must be very empathetic. They hadn't known each other long and he realised he was being blessed by her friendship. By her caring about him that much already?

'Thank you,' he said.

'For what?'

'For caring.'

'Well, of course I'm going to care!' She tried to laugh off the evidence of those tears and wiped at her eyes. 'You still have people who love you and who wouldn't want to lose you.'

She meant his family, right? Or was she talking about someone else?

'Who have *you* lost, Lucy?'

She stared at him, then waved away his concern. 'No one! I'm fine. Nothing's happened to me!' And she pulled her hand free.

But Owen suspected differently. There was someone most definitely. He decided to leave it. It was late, and clearly she didn't want to talk about it.

Not yet anyway.

He felt better for having told her about Emily. He'd known she must have questions—especially after meeting Gemma today and talking to her. And it had felt good to open up. He'd thought he'd processed all of this, but maybe he hadn't?

Either way, he felt tremendously fortunate to have met someone as wonderful as Lucy.

The first week had gone well. Lucy was settling in, and Owen was finding time, now that she was here, to sort out the last few things before he left for good. Just that morning he'd been at his parents' house, sorting through some of his old belongings to see what he wanted to take with him, and now he'd brought some boxes home to go through.

Currently his life seemed to be permanently resident in boxes.

It was a freezing afternoon. The whole of the island

was blanketed in an icy frost, though signs of life were already springing up. Snowdrops. Crocuses. Outside, he could see his breath billowing around his face and could feel his nose going numb.

Hefting one of the boxes, he headed towards the house he was sharing with Lucy, and as he got closer he could hear loud pop music playing. Fumbling with the door, he managed to get the door open, and as he entered he stopped and smiled.

Lucy was unaware that he had come in. Her back towards him, she was dancing around the living room as she pushed the vacuum cleaner, shaking her hips and waving her free arm as she bopped to the beat.

He put the box down and silently closed the door, then leaned against the wall as he continued to watch.

She was happy. Free. Unencumbered. And he had to say that those tight jeans she was wearing fabulously showed off her rear.

Lucy began to sing as the chorus of the song began, and his grin widened as she hit note after note perfectly. Who knew Dr Lucy Childs was such a songbird?

As she turned to manoeuvre the vacuum around a particularly small coffee table she jumped, realising he was there. Her cheeks flushed and she stooped to switch it off.

'How long have you been standing there?'

'Long enough to know that you've got some moves.'

She turned off the vacuum. 'Oh.'

'And some pipes.'

'Ah.' She blushed even harder, if that were possible.

He laughed. 'Don't be embarrassed. It was…entertaining.'

She smiled. 'I'm just getting used to the idea that this place will soon be mine. Settling in. Kind of…'

Owen picked up his box. 'You settle in as much as you want.'

'You got what you wanted from your parents?'

'I think so.' He carried the box upstairs, intending to take it to his bedroom.

Lucy stood at the foot of the stairs, watching him go. She had stopped vacuuming. Once she'd got over the embarrassment of having been caught out singing and dancing, she went to sit by the breakfast bar in the kitchen, thinking about all she'd lost.

Owen was a clear reminder of all that she couldn't have, and she hadn't realised how much she was missing intimacy. Not just physical intimacy, but the ability to just sit and talk to someone who knew you through and through. No pretending. No having to hold back.

She felt she had to hold back with Owen, knowing what she did of what had happened to his wife. A brain aneurysm! Taken in an instant. Just like that. It served to remind her of her own condition and how dangerous that was. How the same thing could happen to her.

That was why she couldn't allow anything to happen between her and Owen. Hadn't he been through enough with one woman who had a life-threatening condition? The woman he'd lost?

Their talk the other night had made her feel low. Sad. Today, in a bid to cheer herself up, she'd done what she always did. Put on some loud music and danced whilst cleaning up. Housework was such a chore, but so much more fun when you could rock out to some music whilst you did it.

Owen catching her like that had been embarrassing. And now she felt lost again. Alone.

She picked up her mobile and dialled home.

'Lucy?' her mum answered.

'Hi. Yes, it's me.'

She heard her mother's relief down the phone. 'How are you doing? Are you settling in?'

'Yes. It's really nice here. Strange. Cold.'

'Well, it's winter, darling—but spring will be on its way soon! Tell me, what's everyone like? Is Dr Ledger easy to get along with?'

Lucy thought of Owen's smile. About the way he made her blush. About their late-night chat in the kitchen, when she'd held his hand as he talked about what had happened to his wife. How it had felt to be caught in his arms when they'd been up in the loft...

'Very,' she said. 'He's younger than I expected.'

'Oh...?' Her mother's teasing tone suggested the possibility of romance.

Lucy laughed. 'Nothing like that, Mum. You don't need to go buying a hat. Besides, I'm off the market, remember?'

'Don't let what Phillip did ruin your chances with anyone else.'

Lucy rolled her eyes. Her mum didn't understand. She'd not been there. Had not heard Phillip say all those horrible things. Her mum probably still liked Phillip.

'How are you feeling?' her mother asked now. 'All okay? You're taking your meds regularly?'

'Yes, Mum. I'm feeling fine.'

'You're not running?'

'I've been busy working. And you don't have to mother me like this. I'm a grown woman...perfectly capable of knowing my own limitations.'

'It's difficult for me, Lucy. With you so far away. I worry about you. You know what losing your father did to me. I couldn't bear it if I lost you, too.'

'You aren't going to lose me.'

There was a pause, and Lucy heard a little sniff. Had her mother begun to cry?

'I'd better let you go,' she said.

'You'll ring me soon?'

'Sure.'

'All right, darling. You take care. I love you.'

'Love you, too, Mum.'

Lucy rang off and stared at the phone. Had the chat with her mother made her feel any better?

When she turned around, Owen was there. She'd not heard him come down.

'Family?' he asked.

'What? Oh. Yes.'

'Is everything okay?'

She stared back at him, wishing almost everything was different.

'Everything's fine,' she said, slipping her mobile into her back pocket.

He felt guilty. Had he been so wrapped up in himself that he had failed to make Lucy feel welcome? All he'd talked about was *his* past, *his* problems, and all he'd done was dream of getting away. Maybe he should be doing more to make her feel that this island was a place to fall in love with—after all, she'd be here for some time. This place he was rushing away from was going to be her new home, and she would be staying, and he knew he had to do more to make her feel comfortable here.

Clearly she had some personal baggage of her own. Was she escaping from something, the way he was? If so, then it was within his power to make her feel that this was a safe place to fall.

Once he'd put all his boxes in his bedroom, to sort

through later, he stood and looked out of the window at the frost-covered land. It was the weekend. Technically they didn't have patients—not unless any emergency calls came through, and they didn't very often. In an emergency most island residents drove themselves over the bridge to the hospital on the mainland.

Owen went downstairs to the kitchen and smiled at Lucy. She seemed a little deflated after her phone call and needed cheering up. 'Get your coat on.'

'Why?'

'It's a lovely afternoon. Let's go for a walk.'

'Oh. Okay.'

She seemed to brighten and he smiled, liking having put such a sparkle in her eyes.

He waited for her to wrap up in a thick coat, that long scarf she loved so much, a woolly hat and some boots, and then they set off.

He walked them down the lane to the main road and then crossed it, taking her over a stile indicating a public footpath. Owen went over first, then offered his hand to help her over.

'Where are we going?' she asked, as she jumped to the ground.

'To see something beautiful.'

There was a low white mist hanging over the land. Beneath their boots the ground crunched as they walked, and the puddles were frozen over.

He watched in amusement as Lucy carefully walked on one, seeing her delighted face as she made it over without cracking the surface. She really was beautiful, and he hated to think that she was troubled in any way.

He knew what it was like to carry a heavy emotional burden. It did no one any good, and if you were to be strong enough to shoulder it you needed to have lighthearted moments, too. He hoped today he could show her what there was to love about this place, because there was plenty to see. It was just that he'd been so wrapped up in himself lately that he'd not taken the time to enjoy it either. And if he was leaving soon, then it made sense to take it all in one last time.

They crested a hill and passed a field filled with sheep that stared and baaed at them as they passed, and then they were walking down quite a steep incline towards Beacon's Peak. It was a small outcrop that jutted out and revealed a huge sweeping bay below, shaped like an arc and covered in sand, pebbles and rocks. And beyond that was the sea, so still and blue, the layer of mist making it look ethereal as further out a ship sounded its foghorn.

'Wow!' Lucy breathed, staring out at it. 'It's amazing.'

'It is, isn't it?'

'I never realised the coast was this close to the house.'

He nodded, pleased that she was happy. 'You wait till you see it in the summer. And over there by that post is a set of steps that take you down to a small private bay that only the islanders know about.'

'Really? Can we take a look?'

He nodded and began to lead the way. He was enjoying himself, he realised. When had he last gone out for something as simple as a walk? When had he last enjoyed the company of a woman who wasn't asking him medical questions in his surgery? He couldn't remember. Which meant it had been too long, and was something he was glad he was beginning to rectify.

They descended through the mist, the clifftop steps twisting and turning as they took them ever further down. As they got closer to the secluded beach they began to hear the soft, gentle lapping of the water at the shoreline. When they got to the bottom a stretch of flat sand arced out and away from them, revealing the still blue sea in all its glory.

'Wow! This is amazing, Owen!'

He was pleased that she liked it. The wonder on her face as she took in the beach, the rocks, and the arch of a cave entrance over to their left, made him feel warm inside. 'This is Carrigan's Cove. Named after quite a sad story, to be honest.'

'Oh?'

He indicated the cave. 'And that's Carrigan's Cave.'

'Who was he?'

He smiled. '*She*. Carrigan Clovelly. She used to work on the oyster beds, and the legend goes that she fell in love with a fisherman. One day his boat headed out to sea and a freak storm blew in out of nowhere. They say the sea was never angrier than it was that day and into the night, and those who had loved ones on the boat waited on this beach, day after day, night after night, torches burning, for the ship to come home. One by one they gave up, accepting the fact that the ship had been lost at sea—especially when bits of wreckage began to wash up. They all went home except for Carrigan, who sat in that cave and looked out to sea for months. The islanders would bring her food and water, but day by day she withered away to nothing, until she died of a broken heart, waiting for her love to return.'

Lucy was staring at him, her eyes forlorn. 'Did he? Did he ever make it back?'

Owen shook his head. 'No.'

'That's so sad.'

'It is. But perhaps the story tells us that we should know when to move on. When to accept the truth and live our lives, so that we don't wither away like that poor girl.'

'At least the islanders looked after her. They didn't

leave her alone down there. They rallied round. Tried to support her. Even in their own grief.'

Now it was his turn to nod. 'Want to head back up?' he asked.

'Just a minute.' Lucy walked towards the shoreline and stopped, staring out to sea.

In the distance, boats slowly passed, and the weak winter sun glinted down upon the shimmering waves.

Owen wondered what she was thinking and went over to her. 'You okay?'

'Thinking about lost love and what it can do to you.'

His thoughts turned to Emily. To what her loss had done to him. How it had changed him. How the island had rallied around to take care of *him*. And he thought of who Lucy had lost. Maybe she'd tell him one day?

He picked up a flat stone and threw it, skimming it across the surface of the water. Once, twice, three times it bounced, before it sank into the depths.

Lucy turned to him. Smiled. 'I've never been able to do that.'

'Here. Let me teach you…'

They spent a pleasant few hours at Carrigan's Cove. Lucy had initially felt saddened by the painful love story, but had then felt a weird connection to the place.

Sadness, loss, heartbreak… They weren't issues unique to her, or to Owen. They had been around for hundreds of years and had happened to people in worse situations than her.

She tried to imagine Carrigan Clovelly and what kind of woman she'd been, sitting there waiting for her love to return. And, strangely she hoped the story was true. It made her feel less alone.

She smiled as she stared out to sea and heard her dad's voice in her head, saying, *'Misery loves company.'*

And then Owen taught her how to skim stones.

It all started innocently enough, as these things do. He helped her find flat stones that were the right size and shape for skimming, and then he showed her how to throw them. How to hold the stone, how to stand at the right angle so that you just kissed the surface of the water.

Her stones just sank when she tried, so he stood behind her, wrapped his hand over hers and helped her throw.

Feeling him behind her like that, his warm body against hers, made her hyper-aware of him. The air was cold, but he was warm and solid and strong, and his hand upon hers made her heart beat faster, pounding in her chest.

She laughed. Because normally if she felt like that her mum would be panicking, thinking something terrible was about to befall her daughter. Only that was different.

She felt his warm breath on the side of her face as he gave her instructions or laughed alongside her. And then suddenly he let her go, and stepped away, and though she was disappointed she skimmed her stone.

It bounced four times across the sea's surface and she screamed in delight and raised her hands. Owen high-fived her. They were laughing and smiling and looking into each other's eyes. And then…it all came to a grinding halt.

It was as if the ghost of Carrigan Clovelly walked between them, reminding them that they were meant to be sad, that this was not a place for love to begin, but a place where love ended, and that they were getting too close.

Lucy felt guilt swarm over her. She'd been enjoying Owen's company too much, when she'd told herself to not get involved with the man. She'd seen something similar in his eyes, too. As if he'd suddenly reminded himself that he was a widower, and that he ought to be remembering his wife, not having fun with someone new.

And now they'd both gone silent and were simply staring out to sea for a moment.

'We should head back,' Owen suggested in a low voice.

'Yes, I guess we should.'

Lucy walked up the cliffside steps, cursing her foolishness. What had she been *doing*? Having fun with Owen, knowing that she had nothing to offer this man and that he had nothing to offer her? He was moving away! He was going to be leaving! And she'd heard him talk about his dreams of having a future and a family. This man wanted something she could never give him, and it had already been drilled into her that any life with her would be an empty one. Phillip had told her straight.

'It's like being with a walking time bomb! I can't live like this, Luce. I need to know I'm going to have a future. A family. I want to be able to relax, but I can't relax with you.'

'You're walking away from me because you won't be able to relax?'

'No, I'm walking away because you can't give me what I need. I want to have children, but any I have with you run the risk of being like you. Broken and fragile. And I can't live my life like that.'

Phillip had hurt her so much with his words, and at first she'd been so terribly sad at the ending of their relationship. It had only been much later that she'd got angry at Phillip and realised what a jerk he was.

But his words haunted her. Because, technically, they were true. She *was* a walking time bomb. Her heart could decide enough was enough at any moment in her life. Pregnancy would be risky, and any children she might have would run the risk of inheriting her genetic condition. Children, family, both were completely off the table now.

When they got to the top of the cliffside steps she felt as if she'd climbed a mountain—and there was still the long walk home.

'We're going out.'

Lucy looked up at him from the sofa. 'Where?'

'The Boar and Bloodhound.'

'We're going to the pub?'

'Sure. Why not? They've got a quiz tonight. It'll be fun to gang up on everyone and astound them with our amazing knowledge. Plus, it'll give me a chance to see a few people before I leave.'

She smiled and laughed. 'As long as all the questions are about human biology, we should rock it.'

He drove them down to the village and parked in the pub car park. He escorted Lucy out of the car, feeling good and happy as he walked them towards the entrance.

When had he last taken a woman out? Owen wasn't normally a pub guy, but he'd gone, on occasion, with Emily, because she'd enjoyed it. Playing darts or pool. Just taking a chance to let off steam. And then, when the quiz nights had begun, they'd gone regularly.

Since his wife's death he hadn't been at all, and it had seemed right that he should go one last time before he left. Though he did expect a few raised eyebrows. Everyone was so used to associating him with Emily... For him to walk in with someone else...a *female* someone else... He just hoped that they'd take it in their stride, acknowledge the fact that Lucy was his colleague and nothing more.

He wouldn't blame them for looking at them or giving them the side-eye. He felt strange about it, too. But Lucy was going to be an integral part of their community. This was a fun way to help her get to know them—and, damn it, a small part of him wanted to rebel by turning up with her at his side.

When they walked in he saw a few people turn to look. One or two raised a hand in greeting, many more smiled, but all of them looked at Lucy and raised an eyebrow.

'Just keep walking,' he said through a fixed smile as he placed his fingers in the small of her back to guide her towards the bar.

The landlord, Terry, met them, polishing a pint glass before putting it on to the shelf above his head. 'Doc! Glad to see you in. What can I get you?'

Owen glanced at Lucy.

'A small white wine, please.'

'And I'll have a lemonade. On duty and driving. Quiz on tonight?'

Terry nodded. 'Starts in a minute or two. You playing?'

'I thought Dr Childs and I could make a team.'

Terry served their drinks with a smile. 'Good to have you back, Doc. Dr Childs? Pleasure to meet you. I hope we see you on a regular basis—even if it is to kick everyone's asses.'

Lucy laughed. 'I'll try.'

'Make sure that you do.' He winked and smiled at her.

They made their way over to a free table and sat down. Owen tried not to pay too much attention to the glances he knew they were garnering, and instead focused on trying to see if he had a pen on him by searching in his jacket pockets. He didn't.

'What are you looking for?'

'Something to write with.'

'Oh, I might have something.' She reached into her bag and brought out a pen, placing it on the table with a smile.

'Great.' He smiled back at her, wondering what everyone was thinking. For years it had been Owen and Emily... Owen and Emily. Now it was Owen and... someone else.

This was the whole point about him needing to leave. He could feel their judgement already. Their prying eyes. Most of them would have heard about Lucy being the new doctor, but what about those who hadn't? Did they think she was his new girlfriend?

Terry's jovial voice came over the speakers. 'We'll be distributing answer sheets in just one moment, folks, so make sure your glasses are full, and we'll start as soon as we can.'

'I'm excited!' Lucy said, leaning her elbows on the table.

'Do you get competitive?' he asked, also leaning in— almost as if to spite the people who were watching and wondering. Might as well give them something to talk about.

'In quizzes? Absolutely! You play to win, right?'

He laughed. 'Yeah.'

'I wonder what the prizes are?'

'Oh, it's usually some business on the island giving away a gift certificate. A free meal for two at a restaurant, or a free haircut, or a hamper of some kind from one of the farms.'

'Great.'

One of the bar staff brought them an answer sheet, and Owen let Lucy fill it in with their names, smiling to himself as she simply listed them as *Lucy and Owen*.

Lucy and Owen... He liked that. *Owen and Lucy. Lucy and Owen.* It fitted. Sounded good.

He raised his glass to hers. 'A toast. To our quizzing success.'

'Our quizzing success!' She clinked glasses with his and laughed, clearly enjoying herself, and this time all he noticed was her.

He no longer thought about what anyone else thought. Quite frankly, he felt he'd spent enough of his life thinking about everyone else on this island and how they felt. Now it was his turn. Time to think about how *he* felt. And spending this time with Lucy made him feel good. To be with an attractive woman, who was kind and funny and intelligent... Well, that was something special.

She warmed his cockles, as his old dad would say—and the thought of his old man saying that made him smile even more.

'Question number one! What is the height of Everest in feet?'

Owen looked at Lucy blankly, but she simply smiled and began scribbling.

'You *know* that?' he asked.

She looked up at him after writing down *Twenty-nine thousand feet*. 'You don't? I'm rounding down, by the way.'

She gave him a cheeky grin, then turned to look at Terry for the next question.

Lucy was a marvel! And she'd certainly got them off to a good start.

'What is a group of otters called?'

They looked at each other blankly.

'It's something that floats, I think...' said Lucy, chewing on the end of the pen.

He tried not to focus on her lips, but it was difficult. 'A boat of otters?' he suggested.

'No, it's something else... A raft? I think it's a raft.'

He leaned in, whispering, 'How do you know all this?'

'My dad and I loved to play Trivial Pursuit. And we always used to watch quiz shows. I'm a mine of useless facts. Shall I put raft?'

'We don't have any other answer.' He sipped from his drink.

'Which is the only vowel not used as a first letter for an American state?'

He knew that one. He leaned in to whisper it. 'E...'

They were making a good team.

The questions seemed to come thick and fast. And they either knew the answer or could at least make an educated guess.

When the quiz was done, and the answer sheets were switched and marked, Terry went back to his microphone to announce the winners.

'In third place we have Kevin and Eric, with thirty points! Our runners-up, in second place, are Jules and the Gang, with thirty-five points! But our winners, ladies and gentlemen, with a total of thirty-eight points, and in receipt of our grand prize of a boat tour around the island and dinner for two at Jasper's, are... Lucy and Owen!'

Everyone clapped and cheered and they both stood to accept the applause. Lucy turned at the last moment, throwing her arms around him and planting a kiss on his cheek.

It was excitement, he told himself. The joy of the win. It didn't mean anything else.

But that didn't stop him from thinking about it *all night long.*

* * *

Their first patient in the clinic the next morning was Maisie Russell. She was fifty-seven years old, and had just been told that her lung cancer had metastasised to her lymph nodes, stomach and spine. There was a recent letter on the system from her consultant, whom she had seen last week and from whom she had received the devastating news.

'Prior to this we thought the cancer was restricted to her lungs only, but it looks like we're losing the battle on this one,' Owen said to Lucy, before calling Maisie into the room.

When she came in Lucy saw a well-put-together woman. Someone who clearly took a lot of time and care with her appearance.

'Morning, Maisie.' Owen shook her hand as she came in, then sat down with a sigh. 'I see the consultant gave you some big news last week?'

Maisie grimaced. 'You could say that.'

'How are you feeling about it?'

'I won't lie. It's knocked me for six. I thought we'd got a handle on this damned disease. We'd kept it under control for years. And then to have that scan and discover this…that it's spread… Well, that doesn't really seem very fair.'

'No. I agree, it doesn't.'

Maisie picked at a non-existent speck on her trousers. 'I still want to fight, Owen. I'm not going to give up.'

'Good for you. If you need anything—even if it's just to talk—I want you to feel you can call at any time. I won't be here, but Dr Childs will be, and I've filled her in on your case.'

'I'm all right. My consultant gave me some extra meds, but I wondered if you could give me a short course of sleeping tablets? This past weekend it's been difficult to get any decent rest, and if I'm to fight then I need to have my strength.'

'Of course.' Owen began tapping on the computer to bring up a prescription to be printed.

Maisie looked at Lucy. 'I used to be an actress, you know.'

'Oh, really?'

'Oh, yes. Nothing major—bit parts, walk-on roles. I got into the local theatre group when I moved here. Joined the choir.'

'Maisie has a magnificent singing voice,' Owen added.

'Well, I hope you'll keep on singing,' said Lucy.

'I will. I've got a role in our musical production of *Grimms' Fairy Tales*. You should come and see it. It opens this weekend.'

'I will. Thank you.'

When Maisie had gone, Lucy thought about the vibrant woman who had just walked out of the room. She had a terrible health condition, but was choosing to still enjoy life, still do the things that she loved. The things that gave her life. Gave her joy. Made her happy. Knowing that all the time the clock was ticking away.

It made her feel that she and Maisie were kindred spirits, in a way. Both determined not to let their health hold them back. It was definitely the way to be, rather than to have stayed where she was, feeling low, feeling as if she couldn't breathe, as if she was brittle and that the slightest knock could break her.

Both she and Maisie were reclaiming their lives—but was Maisie braver than her? Maisie was doing everything, yet Lucy still felt she was holding back. Yes, she'd walked away from her family, and come here to start a new life, but she was stopping herself from building any intimate relationships. Friendships were fine, but romantic entanglements…

She'd put the idea of those firmly in the *Do Not Trespass* area of her life.

It was the right thing to do.

'She's impressive, isn't she?' Owen asked.

Lucy nodded. 'She is.'

'We all only have one life, don't we? It's up to us to make the best of it that we can.'

'That's why you're moving?'

He looked at her. 'Yes. I can't let the past hold me back any more. I want to move forward. Like you've done.'

She blushed. 'I'm not as impressive as Maisie. I'll definitely catch her show, though. Something tells me I'm going to be impressed.' She looked at him. 'You should go, too.'

'Me? Why?'

'She's your patient, and you know her future isn't great. Why not choose to go and see her and remember her as an all-singing, all-dancing, amazing person, with a broad smile across her face, rather than remember her as you saw her here today? Sleep-deprived. Upset. Dying. I think she'd want you to remember her as she lived.'

He smiled. 'You're an amazing person, Lucy.'

His compliment did strange things to her insides. Things she didn't want to think too closely about. Because she knew that once she did start analysing those feelings she'd start reading things into them. She'd end up going down a road that would only bring heartache and pain. And not just for herself.

Owen had already been through so much. Losing his wife so traumatically… She couldn't run the risk of developing feelings for this man at her side. Though if she was honest with herself she knew it might already be a little bit too late for that.

She liked him. Very much. It wasn't just the physical attraction—though that was very nice indeed!—it was Owen as a person. As the man who'd met her in the kitchen for a midnight chat. The man who'd taught her how to skim stones. Who'd made her breakfast. The man who made her smile. Who went running in the mornings and came back with flushed cheeks and a broad smile every single time. The man who told her she was amazing. Whose touch made her nerve endings sing. Whose laugh made her want to laugh with him. Whose tragic past made her empathise with him and feel for him and want to make him feel better. The man who had stood in a blizzard waiting to bring her home.

He was wonderful, and she couldn't deny it, and if she'd known Owen before finding out she had a heart condition that might end her life at any moment, then she would have made more of an effort to flirt with him by now—because he was just her type.

Tall, dark, handsome.

The perfect trifecta.

The kind of man to tick all her boxes.

Kind, caring, intelligent.

He's edible.

She wanted to respond to his compliment—wanted to say, *You're an amazing person, too.* But fear and doubt stopped her. Fear that he would drop her like a hot potato the way Phillip had, when he realised she couldn't give him a family. Fear that she would have to break his heart.

Fear that she wasn't enough for him.

That she was never going to be enough for anybody.

Owen had already lost the love of his life and she couldn't imagine how that must have felt. What he must have gone through to come out the other side and be the man she saw today. She knew her own limitations. Knew she could not put him through something like that again. To even ask him to, to expect him to, was just unimaginable.

He only deserved happiness now—not more heartache.

To allow anything to happen between them would be totally irresponsible on her part.

CHAPTER FIVE

AFTER THE MORNING CLINIC, Lucy very much felt that she needed some fresh air. It was a beautiful day outside. Crisp. Bright and shiny. With the sun beaming down from a clear blue sky and no wind at all, it felt quite good to be out. For mid-January, it wasn't that bad at all.

'I've heard there's a market in Southney. I thought I'd go and take a stroll around. Maybe pick up something nice for dinner,' she said.

'Want me to come with you?' asked Owen.

Of course she did. She enjoyed spending time with Owen, and how hard would it be to resist him in public? Easy, right?

'Sure.'

He drove them across the island to its southern point, and as they crested a hill and began to head downwards she saw the village of Southney, spread out in the valley below. It was quite picturesque.

The cottages they passed looked like the kinds of homes you saw on postcards and greetings cards, with thatched roofs and perfectly presented gardens. There were old-fashioned streetlamps and even a village green, with replica stocks in the centre.

'My mum used to threaten to put me in those every time I was naughty as a child,' Owen told her.

She turned to look at him, shocked. 'Naughty? You?'

'Apparently I used to be a tearaway. I don't remember it that way, of course.' He smiled as he pulled into a nice little parking spot, underneath a tree that was beginning to show signs of new life.

'Oh, I'm sure you were the best little angel.'

He laughed as they got out of the vehicle. 'Market's this way.'

They began to walk down the small street and she took a moment to acknowledge how comfortable she felt with Owen. If she ignored the raging attraction she felt…put that to one side…this felt…*good*.

Why did he have to be leaving? Why did she have to suffer the knowledge that it was best if she remained single? Not just for herself, but for him? How could she imagine the pain he would go through if they got together and he lost *her*, having lost his wife?

They passed a corner house that had a wrap-around garden. In it, ten or twelve young children were playing. It looked as if it was a private nursery, or something, as there was a sandpit and a small slide, and lots of pedal cars and bikes and balls. Three adults stood watching, wearing pink tabards and name tags.

Lucy smiled at the children enjoying this rare bit of winter sunshine and found her gaze taken by a particular young girl with golden hair, who was using her plastic spade to pat down the top of the bucket she was using in the sandpit. The little girl was intent on what she was doing, so she didn't notice Lucy watching her, trying not to think about how this was the way her own imaginary daughter might look. The daughter she'd hoped to have with Phillip.

How they'd talked that day—before her dad had died, so before they'd known she was sick—about how they'd both like to have a daughter first. But that dream was gone now. Only to be found in memories.

'You okay?'

She'd stopped walking and Owen was a few paces ahead. He must have realised she was missing. She nodded. 'Yes.'

She caught up with him, and she could see the market stalls ahead.

'You like kids?' Owen asked.

'I do.'

'Maybe one day you'll have plenty of your own.'

She smiled, hiding her feelings, knowing he was wrong. 'What about you? You said you were going to have a family with Emily.'

'Kids would be great one day. But I'm in no rush. I'll get myself settled first. Do it when the time is right. When I find the right person.'

'Is there ever a right time? Don't you think that we can waste time, waiting for the right moment? That we should just do what we want, whilst we can? We can never know what the future might bring to spoil everything.'

'You're in an optimistic mood today.'

'I'm in an optimistic mood every day.'

She moved forward to take a look at the first stall. It was filled with carved wooden figures. Some big enough to sit in the garden, or in a grand house, but also smaller items, too. Mostly animals, but there was also a beautiful man and woman entwined at their base, curling up and away from each other, as if caught in a whirlwind, carved out of a single piece of driftwood. The couple were reaching for each other, needing each other, but doomed to be apart for ever.

Lucy picked it up. It was very clever. Very poignant. 'I like this.'

'You think so? It makes me feel sad.'

'But it makes you feel *something* when you look at it.'

'I feel plenty of things. Too much, sometimes. I don't need a figurine to make me feel worse.'

She put it down and walked on to the next stall, which was filled with all kinds of leather products. The aroma was amazing, and she saw a nice little purse that she liked. The next stall was fruit and veg, and she picked up a whole bag full that would keep them going for the next week. Oranges, bananas, potatoes, avocados, grapes, cauliflower and carrots.

'Are we on a health kick?' Owen asked.

She smiled at him. 'You should be the change you want to see in the world. And besides, you're the one who goes out running every morning.'

'I shall miss running by the coast when I move away.'

She looked at his profile. 'I'm sure you'll find a nice park, or something.'

'It won't be the same. There's something to be said for living on an island. The beaches... The sea air... It gets into your heart.'

'You're going to miss it?'

He nodded. Smiled. 'I am. I do love this island.'

'Have you had any thoughts about tomorrow night?'

He stopped, turned to look at her. 'You mean Emily's Evening.'

'I do. Are you going to miss that?'

Owen seemed to think hard about it.

'It might be your last chance to go,' she said 'Maybe you should take it? You might miss it when you're gone.'

Now he looked at her. 'Is there something you miss? From home?'

She thought of her father. Her overcaring family. Phillip. She missed some things. Some things she'd lost for ever. Loss hurt. 'Plenty. You know, if you don't want to go alone I'd be happy to accompany you.'

'You would?'

She nodded. 'I'll stay out of the way, give you some privacy, but I'll be there if you suddenly need someone to bail you out—I could say we've got a patient emergency.'

Owen smiled, squinting in the sun. His green eyes gleamed like the finest emeralds. 'All right. You're on. Thank you.'

She nodded. She was happy to go. Happy to spend as much time as she could with him before he left her behind, too.

Stefan Knight wheeled himself into the morning clinic to receive his B12 injection. He'd recently been diagnosed with pernicious anaemia and was currently receiving his loading doses.

Lucy printed out the prescription for the injection and put it on the clipboard to be dealt with later.

'How are you doing, Mr Knight?'

'I'm all right. How are you doing, Doc? Settled in?'

'I'm good. Now, which arm did we put the injection in last time?'

'My right.'

'And any problems?'

'Just an achy arm afterwards, which can be a bit of a pain with the wheelchair.'

'How long have you been in it?'

'Six months. I was in a car accident.'

'I'm sorry. Was it just you in the car?'

'Thankfully, yes.'

'So no one else was hurt?'

Stefan sighed as she injected the red liquid into his arm. 'No. I was texting. Didn't pay attention, and before

I knew it, I'd drifted across the lanes. I swerved to get back, but ended up hitting a tree. My own fault, really.'

She wasn't sure what to say. He was right, after all. It *was* his fault. Texting whilst driving was dangerous. He could have not only killed himself, but someone else. His reckless actions might have caused irreparable loss. Whole lives changed. All because he hadn't been able to wait to answer a text message.

Why did people do that sort of thing? Put themselves at risk when they had their whole lives ahead of them? Why introduce unnecessary danger? It was the sort of thing that angered her, but she couldn't show it. She had to remain impartial.

'There you go. You're done.'

'Thanks, Doc.'

He wheeled himself out just as Owen came into the room with two mugs of tea. 'Here you go.'

'Thanks.' She moved the mug to one side, so she could fill in the patient's record without knocking it over.

'Everything all right?' he asked. 'You seem tense.'

'Just…some people amaze me, that's all. Their lives are perfect. There's nothing wrong, their whole future is ahead of them, and then they—' She stopped speaking, feeling herself getting angrier with every word. This was not the place or the time to feel exasperated. Stefan Knight had received his punishment and now the poor man was confined to a wheelchair until the end of his days. He didn't need her fury, too.

'Stefan upset you?'

'His situation upset me.'

'His anaemia?' Owen seemed confused.

'No. The circumstances around his accident.'

'Ah. Yes… Did you say something to him? Because he seemed fine when he left.'

'I didn't say a thing. I *am* a professional, you know.'

'I know that.'

'It's just people like him madden me. Taking risks like that. They don't know what they're doing. What if he'd killed someone? What if he'd paralysed someone other than himself? How would that make him feel? Ruining someone's life through his own selfish actions.'

'Is there something you want to talk about?'

He settled down into the chair opposite her and looked intently into her eyes. He was doing that doctor thing. Creating silence so that you felt impelled to talk.

'I used to be engaged.'

'Okay…'

'His name was Phillip and I thought he was a great guy.'

'I'm sensing he wasn't?'

She laughed cynically. 'No, he wasn't. He was a catch in the beginning, though. Handsome, charming, clever… And he said that he loved me. Wanted to spend his life with me. Have children with me.'

'What did he do wrong?'

There were so many ways she could answer. But Lucy didn't want to come off as a scorned and bitter woman. Not now. Not when it was so many months ago.

She sighed. 'He promised me the world. He promised me a bright future. Marriage. Children. Happiness. And then he took it all back and walked away, without so much as a backward glance. All my dreams—gone in an instant because of him. He broke my heart.'

'Did he ever explain why?'

She knew why. But to tell Owen about her Brugada syndrome… She didn't want him looking at her with concern in his eyes, the way her family did. She didn't want him looking at her as if she was faulty, the way Phillip had. She wanted Owen to look at her as the woman she was and nothing else. Maybe even now she had told him too much.

'He said I wasn't the woman he'd thought I was.' It was as near to the truth as she could put it, because she didn't want to lie to Owen.

Owen looked at her carefully, then reached out and put his hand upon hers. 'Then he was mistaken. Because you're a wonderful person, Lucy. Don't let what he did define who you are or how you think of yourself.'

She gazed down at his hand upon hers, fighting the urge to turn her hand so she could take his hand in her own and squeeze it. Trying not to think about the feelings that were currently swirling around in her gut, her head and her heart.

Oh, how she wished to be held!

But she couldn't ask that of him. He didn't understand how deeply her pain ran; he didn't know how lonely she felt. How she missed the physical contact you got when you were in a relationship with someone. And she didn't just mean sexual touch. She meant the way you could touch that person as you passed them in a room. The casual drape of a hand on a hip or the small of the back. The way you could snuggle into them for a cuddle. The way you could be close, watching a film, feeling that intimacy that came with being in a romantic relationship. A kiss on the lips, or the cheek, or the neck. A caress that spoke volumes even in the deepest silence.

She was a grown woman with needs, and Owen made her want them to be fulfilled.

'Thank you.' It was all she could manage to say. 'I don't even know where all that came from.'

'Life affects us in strange ways.'

She looked back at his smiling face. At his kind, caring and empathetic face. She wanted to reach out and brush her thumb over his lips, even knowing that she couldn't. Owen was forbidden to her, and that made her want him even more. But she could not have this man. At all. And yet life had thrown him into her path unexpectedly and made her want him.

'It certainly does.'

It was time to go to Emily's Evening. Owen kept checking his watch and then checking his reflection in the mirror. It wasn't a formal evening, but then again, it wasn't casual either. It was in that strange category in between, where it would be so easy to overdress or underdress, so he'd chosen a pair of dark jeans, a white shirt and a dark crew-neck jumper.

He checked his watch again. It started at seven and it was nearly ten to. They'd have to get a move on if they were going to arrive on time. He'd had so many qualms about going, but now the night was here he was grateful that Lucy had offered to go with him, so that he might get through it. As she'd said, she could offer him a way out, if he needed it, by faking a medical call. But he was glad to be going now. This would be his last time, going to one of these. If he'd chosen not to go, how would he have felt about that later?

'Lucy? You ready?' he called from his bedroom.

She appeared in his doorway and it took him a moment to get past how beautiful she looked, and how that was affecting him internally. She was wearing a wrap-around navy dress with a pair of small kitten heels, and it was the first time he'd seen her wear make-up and earrings that weren't small studs.

She looked *stunning*.

She frowned. 'It's too much? I'll go and change.'

'No! It's…' He smiled. 'It's perfect. You look…' He
wanted to say *amazing…gorgeous…beautiful*, but none
of those words got permission to leave his mouth. 'Perfect.'

She bit her lip and smoothed down the dress. 'I wasn't
sure what to wear… I mean it's not really a *party.*'

'It kind of is. Emily never liked people to be maudlin.
Everyone has agreed that she'd want music and food and
laughter and good conversation. She'd want everyone to
have a good time.'

'Oh… Okay, then. What time do we have to be there?'

'Seven.'

'Then we'd best be off.' She smiled at him. 'You look
very nice, Owen.'

Her compliment pleased him more than it should. But
he tried to ignore it and let her take the lead downstairs,
where they grabbed their coats and went out to get into
the car.

'So…shall we have a safe word?' Lucy asked with a
smile.

'A safe word?'

'One that tells me I need to come up with an immedi-
ate call that requires our attention?'

'Oh. Right. I don't know…dolphin?'

Lucy laughed. 'Owen! How on earth are you going
to get "dolphin" into normal conversation? It's got to be
an everyday word.'

'Like what?'

'I don't know… Coffee? Book? Help?'

He smiled. 'What about wine? I could say something
along the lines of, *Can I get anybody some more wine?*
and you'll know that's the point where I want to go.'

'But what if you are actually getting someone a re-
fill of wine?'

'Okay. What do *you* suggest?'

'What about cheese?'

'Cheese?'

'Yes. You could say, *You know what would go nicely with this wine? Cheese!*'

He thought about it. It sounded good. 'Okay. Cheese it is.'

They drove through the dark streets until Owen pulled up outside a large house. Even from their vehicle, they could hear music playing.

Lucy unfastened her seat belt. 'Are you ready?'

'As ready as I'll ever be.'

'What do you want me to do? Just mingle?'

'Just stay close.'

'I can do that.'

She smiled, but then immediately got out of the car, leaving him sitting there for a moment, pondering on the way she'd said it—and not only that, the way she had looked at him as she'd said it, her voice softening.

He got out of the car.

It wasn't so cold that evening, and he escorted her up the path with his hand in the small of her back, stopping at the front door to rap the knocker.

After a few moments Emily's mother answered the door. 'Owen! What have we told you? You don't need to knock here.' And she stepped forward to embrace him, hugging him tight.

He squeezed her back, then took a step backwards. 'This is Dr Lucy Childs, who will be taking my position at the surgery.'

'Hello, Dr Childs.'

'Call me Lucy.'

'Come on in, the pair of you. The party's started. Lucy, let me introduce you to everyone!'

And with that Lucy was whisked away into the crowds of family and friends who had all known and loved Emily.

Which were a lot.

He felt oddly bereft without Lucy at his side. She was meant to be his means of escape, but if she wasn't around to hear him mutter the safe word then he guessed he had nothing to do but grin and bear it.

Above the fireplace in the living room was the huge portrait of Emily that David and Laura had had done after their daughter's death, and it was as if his wife was looking down on them all with her broad smile as she looked out from the canvas.

It was one of his favourite pictures, and he realised that he'd reached the stage where he could look at it and not feel pain any more. The picture served only to make him remember the fond memories they had.

His sister, Bridget, suddenly appeared at his side, with a glass of wine in her hand. 'Hey, you're here! I didn't think you were going to come.'

'I had my arm twisted.'

'Well, I'm glad you're here. Come on! Let's head to the kitchen. Josie has brought a wide selection of amazing cakes and I'm starving!'

He allowed himself to be pulled through the assembled throng. People stopped to acknowledge him with a raise of a glass, a quick hello, a touch to his arm or back. And then Bridget had got him in the kitchen and was asking him what drink he wanted.

'A small white wine will be fine.'

'How's everything going with the new doctor? Lucy, is it?'

He nodded. 'Everything's good.'

'I've heard she's very pretty.' His sister smiled, teasing him. 'And you're alone together...in that house.'

'That's right. We're both in the same lodgings.'

'And *is* she pretty?'

'*Bridget!*'

'What? Can't I ask my brother simple questions about his roommate?'

He sighed and took a sip of the wine that she'd handed him. She'd certainly not given him a small measure. 'You can ask. You just can't *imply*. Lucy is here to do my job, plain and simple. Anything else is—'

'Ooh, so there *is* an "anything else"!'

'No!' he answered, exasperated, because Bridget was pushing her questioning in a direction that he wasn't ready to tread.

His feelings for Lucy were complicated. He liked her very much. And, yes, if he was honest, he was very much attracted to her. But that was all it could be. She had clearly come here with some baggage and was looking for some sort of fresh start. He had to let her have that. And that did *not* involve having any sort of fling with her! Besides, he was leaving and there wasn't much point. Why complicate matters? Why act on that attraction when it wasn't going to lead anywhere?

And it didn't feel right thinking about his feelings for another woman when he was at his dead wife's birthday evening.

'Can we change the subject, please?' He looked around the table, at all the food piled high. Bridget was right. Josie had made some delicious-looking cakes. 'These look great.'

'Thanks,' Josie said with a smile.

'And this is Owen's sister, Bridget. And that's Josie Atkins.' Owen's mother was speaking as she escorted Lucy into the kitchen. 'This is Lucy, everyone.'

Bridget stepped forward, her hand extended. 'Hello, Lucy. Owen has been telling us all about you!'

Lucy blushed. 'All good, I hope?'

'Oh, absolutely.' Bridget smiled.

Owen didn't like the predatory look on his sister's face. He knew what she could be like. Once Emily had been gone for a year and all those awkward firsts had passed—first birthday without Emily, first wedding anniversary without Emily, first Christmas without Emily—Bridget had started trying to fix him up with a variety of women she thought suitable for him. And she had that same calculating look on her face now. He wondered how much wine she'd had to drink.

'Lucy, can I get you a drink?' he asked.

'I'm driving, remember? Just a fruit juice. Maybe orange? With some lemonade in it?'

'Ice?'

'Yes, please.'

He made her a drink and passed it over, smiling at her, glad that she was now back at his side. For a moment there he'd thought that his family had organised a divide and conquer strategy, but now she was with him again he felt better.

Lucy nudged him on the arm and indicated to where she could see Gemma Aickman, Emily's best friend. 'You should go and talk to her.'

'Do you think so?'

She nodded. 'I do. I think you two have got some unresolved issues. It'd be good for you to clear the slate. So you can leave Morrow Island without any regrets. It wasn't her fault that she knew about Emily's condition.'

He let out a sigh and took a fortifying drink of wine. 'I'm not very good at apologising.'

'How will you learn if you don't practise? I think she'd love it if you went and spoke to her.'

'You think so?'

'I know so. You may have lost your wife, Owen, but she's lost her best friend.'

'Okay.' He passed Lucy his drink and squared his shoulders, before making his way through the crowd to stand by Gemma. 'Can I speak to you for a moment?'

She turned and smiled when she saw it was him. 'Sure.'

'Somewhere private?'

'Okay.'

He led her into the back garden. It was lit by some garden lights and there was a small bench by Emily's mother's favourite water feature. He waited for Gemma to sit down, and then he sat next to her. 'I thought we should talk.'

'Okay,' she said again.

'About what happened. I just wanted to...to apologise if you feel that I've been blunt with you...or rude to you. I didn't mean to be.'

'Thank you. But I know it's been difficult for you.'

'You knew about Emily. About her aneurysm. She told you because I wasn't there, like I should have been. If I'm honest, I was always a little jealous of the bond the two of you shared, and in that moment—in her final hours—you were the one to be there for her.'

'I didn't mind.'

'I know you didn't. It sounds stupid, but I *did* mind. I was her husband. I felt she should have told me. But she waited, and then it was too late. And instead of having me at her bedside she had you, and I was angry about that. I shouldn't have been. I should have been grateful to you for being there. For holding her hand. For not letting her be on her own.'

Gemma's eyes were filling up. 'I wished it were you instead of me.'

'You did?'

'Of course! Watching her go like that... It was terrifying. I didn't know what to do! You would have known. You're a doctor. I didn't know if what I was doing was right. I tried to give her CPR, but I'd not done it before and...' Gemma dabbed at her eyes with a tissue. 'I should have been stronger for her. I was her best friend and I was a wreck.'

'You did everything you could.' He took hold of her hand, squeezed it. 'And I'm so grateful to you. I thought you ought to know that. Before I go.'

'Thank you.'

'And there's something else.'

'Oh?'

'I'd be honoured to be this little one's godfather. You just let me know the happy news and a date and time and I'll be there at the church.'

Her face lit up. 'Really? You will?'

He smiled. 'I will.'

'Oh, Owen!'

She flung her arms around him and he felt good as he hugged her back. It had been the right thing to do, and he felt so much better for getting his feelings out in public, instead of all the angry internalising he'd done over the last couple of years. And it would never have happened if Lucy hadn't suggested it. He needed to thank her. Once again.

'Let's go back in. It's getting cold.'

He escorted Gemma inside and went to find Lucy. She was in the lounge with Bridget, who seemed to be regaling Lucy with some sort of childhood tale. They were both laughing, and then he heard the words *spider* and *bucket* and knew exactly what his sister was talking about.

At that moment Emily's father started trying to gather people together for photos beneath Emily's portrait.

'Owen? Come on, let's have you in there with Bridget.'

People shifted and moved out of the way to create space, and then they were both standing there.

'Say cheese,' said David.

Owen smiled and met Lucy's gaze with a little shake of his head. 'Cheese!'

Next thing, he was organising all Emily's friends for more photos, and Owen drifted over to Lucy.

'Need an escape yet?' she whispered.

'Strangely, no.'

'You're enjoying yourself?'

'Odd, but I am.'

She smiled. 'Good. How did it go with Gemma?'

'It went great. And I have you to thank for that.'

'Me? No, I didn't do anything.'

'You got me here. You suggested I speak to her. And I'm really glad that I did.'

'Cleared the air, then?'

'Cleared and freshened like a summer's day.'

'Good. I'm glad for you.'

He looked at her, taking quick glances whilst pretending to watch Emily's father shepherd groups into poses for photos. Lucy really was a remarkable woman. Caring and kind. Clearly she thought about others a lot, and tonight he really owed her. He wished he could do something for her to show her how much she meant to him. He wished this was a different kind of party. One with loud music. Dancing.

And that was when he suddenly realised he was ready to go home. To be alone with her. Maybe talk.

He leaned in. 'Cheese.'

She turned to look at him quizzically. 'Really?'

'Yeah. I've said everything I came to say.'

'Okay. I'll send a bleep to your phone.'

Lucy was surprised that he wanted to leave so early. She'd thought he was doing so well, and she'd actually been enjoying herself. She'd spoken to Josie Atkins, who ran the baking courses, and signed herself up for some classes. As Owen had been taking steps forward with Gemma, and mending fences, she'd taken the time to take some steps forward, too. Towards building her life on this island. Towards making new friends.

Because that was what she would have to fill her life with. Work and friendships. And sometimes friendships could be worth so much. Sometimes they were even better than family, and she and Josie had been getting on well.

So when Owen had said the safe word she'd been surprised.

As they said goodbye to all the guests, she could see how much Owen was loved. So many people here tonight were sad about saying goodbye to Owen for the last time, and it showed.

She drove them home, and when they got inside Owen let out a huge sigh as he pulled off his shoes.

'Tired?' she asked.

'Yes. I feel bad about lying about a patient emergency, though.'

'Let's just pretend that you're the patient.' She laughed. 'What can I get you? Tea? Coffee? Biscuit?'

'I'd like to dance with you.'

Her heart thudded so hard she almost felt it hit her ribs. 'I'm sorry?'

'I wanted to dance with you at the party. But it would have been strange to dance with another woman at my dead wife's birthday party. So I thought we could do it here.'

She suddenly felt shy. 'There's no music.'

Owen picked up a remote and pointed it at the music system. Some slow jazz began to play. He held out his hand. 'Would you do me the honour?'

Lucy felt her mouth go dry at the prospect. A dance with Owen? Up close and personal? Body against body? She wanted it more than anything, but knew it was going to be dangerous. Did he see it as an innocent dance between colleagues...or something else?

She couldn't deny that she had already thought about what it might be like. To be pressed against him again. For their faces to be inches apart. To be gazing into each other's eyes. But those images had always become much racier than she imagined Owen would want things to go.

He just wanted to dance with her.

That was all.

Or could she dare hope that he wanted more?

But if he did want more, then...

Her brain kept whizzing about with *what ifs* and *maybes*. But hadn't she spent the last few months of her life playing safe? What if this was her one chance to do something she actually wanted to do?

She stepped forward to take his hand and he smiled as he pulled her slowly into position, as if they were going to waltz.

Lucy felt uncertain. Could feel her heart pounding. But that was from excitement, right? Nothing else. She met his gaze. Allowed herself a glimpse into those intense green eyes and saw them smiling back at her. A hesitant smile curved her mouth and she hoped she was blushing nicely, rather than becoming blotchy and looking as if she was having an allergic reaction.

The music led their movement and Owen led her about the living room…slowly, gently. This way, then that. His hand in hers felt right. He was strong and in control, and she had to admit he was a really good dancer.

Lucy enjoyed dancing. But mostly when she was on her own and no one was watching. She hoped she didn't have two left feet and made only tiny movements, in the hope that she wouldn't tread on his toes. She'd done it in the past. She'd danced with Phillip once and he'd sworn never to dance with her again. Had said she was like an elephant.

But, then again, Phillip had said a lot of things.

Do I want to be thinking of Phillip whilst I'm in Owen's arms?

'You're good at this,' she said.

'I haven't done it for a long time.'

'Me neither.'

The music broke from a lone trumpet into a gentle piano and she felt him adjust his hand in the small of her back. Felt him press her closer. Their proximity to each other was thrilling. She almost couldn't breathe. And the sensations she was feeling in her rapidly pounding heart were making her feel a little light-headed. Her chest hurt with palpitations—

Oh-oh.

'I think I need to sit down.'

'What's wrong?'

She let go of his hands and sank down on to the couch, one hand pressed against her chest, feeling her heart thrum like a racing car engine. She knew she was having one of her attacks. She hadn't had one in such a long time, and she felt devastated that she was having it in front of Owen.

'Lucy? What's happening?' He reached for her wrist, felt for her pulse. His eyes widened.

'Call for an ambulance...' she managed to whisper, her eyes full of apology.

CHAPTER SIX

HE DIDN'T KNOW what was happening, but he did know he was scared. One minute he'd been dancing with Lucy... The next...

He was having flashbacks. His life had been perfect, everything going well, and then there'd been panic. A race to the hospital to find out what was going on.

His mind was racing.

What had happened to Lucy?

They'd just been dancing. And it wasn't as if they'd been doing anything over the top. It had been a slow dance—and what a slow dance it had been! Being that close to her, looking into her eyes, watching that perfect smile creep across her face, feeling her tiny hand in his, feeling that he was wrapped around her, protecting her, keeping her safe, making him feel...*what?*

There'd been so many thoughts. So many feelings. And his prime thought had been, *Should I kiss her?*

He'd wanted to kiss her. Very much. But he'd been so terribly afraid, so fearful that if he did so, he would be sending them both down a road that would only lead to sadness and disappointment.

He was going to be leaving in a couple of weeks! Now was not the time to start kissing a woman!

She would have been the first woman he'd kissed since his wife had died two years ago.

If he had leaned in to kiss her then, yes, it would have fulfilled his physical desire in that moment—but what then? What would have come after? They would still have had to live together for a short time, and if she'd kissed him back the likelihood was that their relationship would have advanced to something physical...

But it wasn't just about the physical, was it?

And that was what his logical mind had been screaming at him. First it had begun to tell him what a fool he was, having asked her to dance in the first place, and then it had really gone to town when she'd been in his arms.

Not that she was unsuitable, or anything. Lucy was amazing. It was just the timing...

And now, as he watched the paramedics assessing her, attaching electrodes to her chest, he was glad that he hadn't taken that step.

'I have Brugada syndrome.'

He frowned. 'What?'

She lifted the oxygen mask away from her face so that she could speak to both him and the two paramedics who had shown up. 'It's a rare condition. It affects the way electrical signals pass through the heart.' She breathed in oxygen for a moment. 'I only had one glass of wine. It shouldn't have caused this.'

Brugada... He tried to rack his brains to see what he knew about the condition but, as Lucy had said, it was rare, and he didn't know enough to be sure.

'How long have you known?' he asked.

She looked at him, her eyes filled with fear. 'Long enough.'

He couldn't quite believe this. First Emily... Now Lucy had a condition she hadn't told him about...

'I'm on...'

But she didn't get to finish. Suddenly her eyes rolled back and she went limp in the chair, and then the paramedics were leaping into action as her trace on the ECG machine showed a ventricular fibrillation.

'She's having a cardiac arrest.'

Owen was stunned and didn't know what he should be doing. The paramedics were working fast, providing oxygen and CPR. He simply could not believe he'd gone from such a wonderfully pleasant evening to an absolute nightmare.

Was this how everyone had felt when Emily had collapsed on them? One minute having a perfectly fine conversation...the next watching the world fall apart?

'She's back! Let's get her into the ambulance ASAP.'

Owen let out a breath when he saw a regular heart rhythm return to the monitor, and he hurried after the paramedics and clambered into the back of the ambulance. He sat beside her, holding on to her hand and talking gently to her, whilst one of the paramedics, Al, observed her and monitored her output.

The drive to the hospital seemed to take an interminably long time. The traffic on the island was busy, and cars had to get out of their way on the bridge that connected it to the mainland, but then it was only about five minutes at full speed before they got to the hospital.

Eventually he was aware of the ambulance reversing into position, the back doors were opened, and Lucy's trolley was lowered to the floor and wheeled into Resuscitation.

He followed, feeling like a lost sheep—which was odd. Because normally in a hospital setting or a clinic he felt right at home. But this feeling he had right now was familiar. It was the same one he'd felt on entering this hospital to find out his wife had suffered a fatal aneurysm. That lost feeling…that hopeless and impotent feeling… cushioned him slightly. Almost as if his brain had taken a rain check for a moment, so that he didn't feel the full brunt of his fear.

Owen stood to one side as medical staff swarmed around Lucy. Her eyes had opened again and the doctors were introducing themselves and asking her questions. He heard the word 'quinidine' and his brain helpfully provided an explanation. Quinidine was used as an anti-arrythmia agent. Had they given it to her, or was she saying that was what she took? He'd not been aware of her taking any tablets, but then again why would he be? She would keep any medication in her room.

Now a doctor was asking Owen some questions. How long since she had been diagnosed with Brugada? What sort of symptoms had she been experiencing? What could he tell them about her condition?

'I'm sorry, I don't know. I didn't even know she was sick.'

She must have heard about Emily and felt she couldn't tell him about her own condition. Poor Lucy! How must she have felt? Not wanting to burden him with such news?

'Any family members we could ask?'

He realised he didn't have any details. They would be somewhere. The local trust would have them, wouldn't they? They'd interviewed her for the post—they must have done the paperwork.

Anger surged through him at being so helpless once again. Was this his fault? How had he not known? How had he made her feel as if she couldn't tell him? And she'd done so much to help him! Look at tonight. He'd gone to Emily's Evening, met with friends and family, talked to Gemma, apologised, offered to be godfather. Tonight he had taken huge steps forward, all thanks to Lucy, and now she lay there on a hospital trolley, fighting for her life?

The lead doctor stood beside him. 'It looks like we'll need to take her to surgery, install an implantable cardioverter defibrillator to monitor her heart rhythm and deliver shocks if her rhythm goes crazy again.'

'Right. Okay.'

'We've given her some pain meds, and she seems to be stable right now, but we'll monitor her and get her into surgery as quickly as we can.'

Owen nodded. 'Can I talk to her?'

'Sure.'

He stepped towards her bed, came alongside it and reached out for her hand. 'Hey, you.'

She smiled at him. 'Hey... Sorry if I scared you.'

'Me? Nah. I was fine.'

She chuckled. 'Liar.'

He bent to kiss her on the forehead, then looked deep into her eyes. 'You should have told me.'

'I didn't want to worry you.'

'I would have preferred to know.'

'I'm sorry.'

He smiled. 'Yeah, well, no more dancing for you.'

A nurse strolled into the cubicle. 'We're ready to take her up to Theatre now.'

Owen nodded, turned to look at Lucy and kissed the back of her hand. 'Don't you go pulling any crazy stunts in there, okay? I want to see you in Recovery.'

'I'll do my best.'

He very reluctantly let go of her hand and watched as they wheeled her away.

* * *

The procedure had gone well, and the surgeon had been able to implant the device under sedative and local anaesthetic.

'You'll need to take it easy for a few days,' he told her as he discharged her two days later. 'We'll send you an appointment with a cardiologist to help monitor and regulate the device, okay?'

'Thank you for everything,' Lucy said as a nurse wheeled her out to the main entrance.

Owen stood waiting for her with the car and a huge smile on his face.

It felt good to see him. She'd been so worried about him. About how he'd cope with all this. But he had been an absolute star. Never complaining...never pessimistic. If he'd had those moments, then he'd certainly never showed them to her.

'Ready for home?'

'You bet.'

'Looks like you're in good hands,' said the nurse. 'If you're going to go home to rest, might as well go home with a doctor.'

Lucy thanked the nurse and stood up, taking Owen's hand in hers as she took steady steps over to the car.

Generally, she felt great. Just a little sore from the incision and device placement, and also feeling the pain from the rib that had been broken during CPR. She wasn't going to complain about that, though. That pain showed her that someone had fought for her life. She was still standing, thanks to them. And thanks to Owen, who had been here every minute that he could over the last two days, whilst she recovered.

He'd managed the island's morning clinics, then come over to the hospital each afternoon unless he had a home

visit. And now it was Friday morning, and a long weekend of doing nothing loomed ahead of them.

She was looking forward to getting home. To a proper
bed. A proper cup of tea. Home luxuries and no constant
ringing of telephones, no nurses waking her at odd times
to take her blood pressure.

Owen held the car door open. 'In you get. Watch your
head.' He helped her fasten her seat belt and then walked
around the vehicle to get into his side and start the engine.

It was an easy drive home. Only ten minutes, and they
didn't hit any traffic. Back at the farmhouse, he walked
her in and sat her down on the couch, then made her a
hot cup of tea. 'Here you go.'

'Thanks, Owen. You've been really good to me...
considering.'

'Considering?'

'That I kind of sprung this on you. That it took me
having a major episode before you found out the truth.'

'Yeah, well... I know now, and that's what counts. Are
you sure you don't want me to invite any of your family
to stay? We have the room.'

Lucy looked at him and laughed. 'Are you kidding me?
This is the whole point about my moving away. They'd
be great, no doubt, but I wouldn't be able to breathe with
them here. I've told them what's happened. They know.
That's enough.'

'I'm surprised they didn't come running. If my daughter had had a cardiac arrest I'd be there.'

'I told them not to.'

'And they listened?'

Now she felt a little uncomfortable. 'I might have said
something along the lines of if they came to Morrow Island I'd never speak to them again.'

He looked at her from across the room. 'Can I say something?' he asked.

'Of course. You can tell me anything.'

'You know how you looked at my situation and taught me that maybe I wasn't angry with everyone else but mad at myself?'

'Yes…'

'Well, I see a family that's terrified of losing you. They just want to know that you're okay. That you're safe. And it's because they love you.'

'But what if that caring for someone smothers them? So much so that they have to take huge steps—like move away entirely?'

'So talk to them. Tell them it's too much. But you've got to let them care for you, Lucy. They love you so much. Why won't you let them?'

Why? She didn't know why. And thinking about it made her head hurt.

His last patient of the morning had arrived—for which he was grateful. He wanted to get back to Lucy, make sure she was following doctor's orders and taking it easy for a few days. He'd got up that morning and found her cleaning the kitchen surfaces, so he'd ordered her to sit down and then taken over himself.

Heaven only knew what she was getting up to without him there, watching over her.

There was a soft knock on his door and then Samira Ranjit was wheeling in her buggy and getting out baby Indira.

He saw the problem almost straight away.

'She's had a high temperature since last night and I don't think she's feeling very well.'

Owen ran through a series of diagnostic questions with

Samira and then proceeded to do a physical examination on Indira. He got her mother to lay her on the examination bed and remove her clothes.

Indira's cheeks were bright red, though the rest of her seemed okay. 'Is she having plenty of wet nappies?' he asked.

'Yes.'

'Eating okay?'

'She takes her bottle, no problem.'

'Bowel movements seem normal and regular?'

'She had a little bit of diarrhoea, but not much.'

'Okay, you can dress her now.'

He busied himself at the computer, typing in the patient report until Samira sat back down with Indira on her lap. 'I think Indira has what we call fifth disease—or slapped cheek syndrome.'

Samira gasped.

'Oh, don't worry—I know you haven't actually slapped her cheeks. It's just a name because that's the appearance of it. It could look like this for a couple of weeks, but it'll pass. Keep her hydrated, give her infant paracetamol if you think she needs it, and I'll write you a prescription for a skin emollient, in case she develops an itchy rash.'

He passed her the prescription. 'It can be contagious, so make sure you wash your hands properly and often. Don't share Indira's towels with other children, for example. And if you're worried about anything, or unsure about any rash that might develop on her body, bring her in and I'll check her out again. Any questions?'

'No, Doctor. Thank you.'

'Good to see you, Samira. Take care.'

When she'd gone, he finished writing his notes and then switched off the computer. He was feeling hungry and hoping to get home so he could make some lunch for himself and Lucy.

He was rather enjoying having her to look after. It made him feel useful, following those first few hours after her attack, when he'd felt as useless as a chocolate teapot. And he liked the intensity of their hours together. He really thought that he'd found a new friend, and he wanted to spend as much time as he possibly could with her before he left.

He had to admit he was rather worried about doing so. He knew the patients of Morrow would be in good hands with her—she was a fantastic doctor, she worked the same way he did and she had a great rapport with her patients. It was just... She'd suffered a major medical event, and although she had the defibrillator now, and should be fine, he was still concerned.

He had feelings for her. Strong feelings. And he couldn't forget that he'd wanted to kiss her just before her heart had jumped into an abnormal rhythm.

But she had issues with letting people help her. Even this morning, when he'd admonished her for wiping down the kitchen surfaces, she'd huffed and puffed and told him that she was fine, and that she was more than capable, and he'd wondered if he was making her feel the way her family made her feel.

He didn't want her to be annoyed by him.

As he stepped into the main house she was in the kitchen again, making a sandwich.

'Want one?' she asked.

'Sure—that'd be great. What kind of morning have you had?'

'Uneventful. You?'

'A case of slapped cheek, rheumatoid arthritis, a dodgy knee and a whiplash injury.'

She smiled. 'Not all the same patient, I hope?'

He laughed. 'Thankfully, no. How are you feeling?'

'Are you going to ask me that every day?'

'Absolutely. You can bet on it.'

'Then I'm fine.'

'Really fine? Or just saying you're fine to get me off your back?'

'You're not on my back, Owen.'

'Good.'

'My mother is. She called again.'

'Let her come and stay, Lucy. At least until I have to go. And then you can kick us both out at the same time.' He winked at her.

She laughed. 'We spoke for a bit. And I did some thinking afterwards.'

'What conclusions did you come to?'

Lucy sighed and sat down opposite him. 'I thought about what you said the other day. About why I won't let them care for me.'

'And?'

'And... I realised it was guilt.'

'Guilt?' He didn't follow.

'My father died. We knew he'd had episodes. He'd end up in hospital, with everyone worried, then he'd come home and the cycle would begin again. After the attack that killed him it was suggested that he might have had Brugada, and if he had then we should all get tested for it. My sisters got tested and they were in the clear. Then my brother. He was clear, too. We were just waiting for my result. I assumed I'd be fine. Mum and everyone else were so relieved, we just thought my result would be negative, too. Until it wasn't. I watched my mother crumble, Owen. She'd been dealt one blow, losing Dad, and now she was terrified of losing me, too. Every day she looked at me, and I saw her being worn away just a little bit more. I felt responsible. And guilty. And I thought if I could take that away it would help her. She wouldn't have to see me every day and worry…she could pretend that everything was normal.'

'You don't think that she worries even more because she *can't* see you?'

'I didn't think about that. Plus, there was all that rubbish with Phillip…' She trailed off, trying to think of the best way to explain fully. 'We broke up when he discovered there was something wrong with me and I told him we couldn't have kids as I didn't want to pass it on to any child. He just walked away.'

'I'm so sorry.'

'Not your fault—he's a jerk.'

'No, but on top of everything else…'

'Yeah… I felt like I was causing complications in everyone else's life. All because of me and my dicky heart. So I made a plan to leave. Determined to look after me, myself and I. To throw myself into work, make new friends, take up new hobbies, find things to make me smile again.'

'So you came here?'

'I came here. Because it's quiet, and part-time, and gives me back a life that I can enjoy.' She met his gaze. 'I never meant to upset you, Owen. The fact that it happened… The fact that I put you through that… I—'

'Hey, it's okay.'

'No, it's not. Now I've got *you* looking after me. Watching me like a hawk. You shouldn't be worrying about me. You should be preparing for your own fresh start. Getting away from here, forgetting about me.'

He could never forget about her. It wouldn't be that

easy. 'You're not the kind of person that people forget.' He meant it.

'Thanks. Neither are you.'

For a moment the situation was tense. Awkward. He was glad she'd reached some insight into her own situation, and glad that he had helped her get there. And though there was a growing rage and disbelief in him over the actions of Phillip, he knew he had to stay calm and be the friend she needed right now.

'Well, the option is there to invite her if you change your mind. Perhaps after I'm gone? So you're not left on your own?'

She nodded. 'Maybe. I'll think about it.'

'Good.' He got up, wandered over to the fridge and opened cupboards. 'Baked potatoes and chilli for dinner?'

'Sounds great.'

He stabbed the potatoes and put them in the oven, then started chopping onions and tomatoes for the chilli. For some reason he kept thinking about that kiss. The one they'd never had. The one he'd wanted to enjoy so very much.

If he had known back then about the Brugada would he have kissed her?

He didn't know. He hoped the answer wasn't no. Because that would make him exactly like this Phillip.

But if he had kissed her—if he had taken their relationship to the next level—what would it mean for them now? He had under two weeks to go and then he was meant to be leaving. But instead of preparing to go and start a new life, he was getting more and more embroiled in hers.

And he couldn't work out if that was a good thing.

Or a bad one.

* * *

'I thought we could go out for dinner?' Owen said as soon as he came in from work the next day.

'Really?'

'Yes. We should celebrate your new-found health. You're doing great, and you can start back at the clinic with me tomorrow—we should celebrate that.'

'Did you start to feel like you were never going to get to leave?' she joked.

He smiled. 'Course not. Anyway, how are you doing?'

'I'm feeling good. It'll be a nice change to get out of the house.'

'That's what I thought. Alfie's does a nice little evening menu. Fancy that?'

'What sort of food is it?'

'Typical stuff, nothing too fancy.'

'You really know how to sell it.'

'Well, how about if I tell you that Josie provides a lot of their cakes and desserts?'

'Sold! Let's go.'

Lucy loved Josie's cakes. They were so yummy, and she was looking forward to starting her classes with her. But one step at a time… She'd recovered well from her health crisis, and her work began again tomorrow. But her workload was light, and she'd be sitting down most of the time. Life was beginning to get back on track and she knew she had Owen to thank for that. He'd really been attentive and kind.

Alfie's was set off the main village high street, down a lane, and once they'd parked she was able to see it for the first time. It looked like an old Elizabethan building, with white outer walls and black beams, lights set in flower beds shining up from the ground. It was really quite small and quaint, and she was looking forward to going inside.

Inside, the walls were covered with old farming equipment and black-and-white pictures framed in expensive frames, showing people from the 1800s working on farms. When they were seated at their table Lucy read on the menu that Alfie had been a real person and was, in fact, the man in some of the photos, who'd begun his years as a farmer and then become a cook when a health crisis had stopped him from working the land.

She liked Alfie's immediately, and felt a kinship with the original owner.

They ordered crab cakes and lasagne for Lucy, and surf and turf for Owen.

'So, you've not got long left before you leave,' she said. 'How are you feeling about that? Excited?'

He nodded. 'Yeah. I am. It's something that's been a long time coming, but now that it's about to happen I think there's a part of me that doesn't quite believe it. I've always come back here, you know?'

'Home has a strong pull.'

'It does. Have you thought any more about inviting your family over?'

She nodded. 'I spoke to Mum today. Told her that I'd love her to come and visit, but it would be best to wait until spring. Maybe summer. So that she sees the island in all its glory.'

He smiled. 'I'm pleased—and I'm sure she was thrilled, too.'

'She was. She was so surprised when I suggested it, and I told her she had you to thank.'

'Oh, you would have got there eventually without me.'

'I'm not sure that I would have. Take your credit where it's due.'

A waiter arrived with their drinks and her crab cakes.

'So what will your hours be like in the new place?' she asked.

'It's normal surgery hours. So I'll have plenty of time to write that book I've always wanted to write.'

'Excellent. What else will you do?'

'I don't know. It's going to be strange, being in a place where people don't know anything about me. I guess I'll socialise with the partners, get to know them and their families, make new friends.'

'Do you think you'll settle down again? Find someone? Is that on the agenda?'

He sighed. 'One day. If it's right. I'd like to think I'll have kids one day.' He looked up at her. 'Sorry, I shouldn't have said—'

'Don't be silly. You're allowed to talk about wanting to have kids.'

But suddenly the crab cakes felt dry in her mouth. She knew how it felt to want to have children. She'd wanted them herself, and thought she would have them with Phillip. But finding out about the Brugada had seriously made her put her foot on the brakes where that issue was concerned. And it wasn't just the risk of passing on her condition to her child—it was the guilt she'd have to live with if she did. She'd be like her own mother. Constantly worrying, constantly fretting, and that wouldn't do her own health any good.

No. Having children was something that she couldn't do. Not biologically, anyway. Adoption? If she were going to adopt children she'd want to be in a secure, committed, loving relationship, and she didn't feel she could hope to find one of those.

The man sitting across from her would be the type of candidate she'd have hoped for. He was amazing. Handsome. Kind. Funny. Caring. Intelligent. But he was leaving. His life was not going to be here, was it? Not on this island. He'd said he felt as if he couldn't breathe here, and she knew how that felt. His pain was her freedom. And vice versa.

'How many would you want to have?' she asked.

He smiled. 'I always thought two would be nice.'

'One of each?'

'I guess… What about you? I know you thought you'd have kids one day. What did you dream of having?'

'I used to think I'd have loads of kids. A house filled with laughter and joy. A little girl first… I don't know why.'

Just talking about her old dreams made her feel incredibly wistful. Talking about them with Owen felt good, though. A little sad, but he made it easy to talk, without it being the incredibly painful topic that it once had been.

'I guess we've both got to find someone we can feel comfortable with first.'

I feel comfortable with you.

'I don't think I'll be looking for anyone, Owen. I want my work and I want some friends—that'll be enough for me.'

'Will it?' He stared at her.

She opened her mouth to say, *Yes, of course it will.* But the words didn't come out. They got stuck in her throat and she struggled to think of how to answer him.

'I long ago came to the decision that my life would be a solitary one.'

'But why? You have so much to offer! You're sweet, you're kind, you make people laugh, you care about them, you're *genuine*. You deserve to have someone special in your life.'

'I had someone special and he broke my heart. Not

the way Brugada has, but…' She laughed, but inside she was hurting.

He reached a hand across the table and took her hand in his. 'Promise me you won't remain alone. That you'll find someone.'

'What if I've already found that person and they've left me already?'

'You're talking about Phillip? Trust me. He wasn't your person.'

'I thought he was.'

'But life tricks us, Lucy. It plays cruel games. Perhaps Phillip was just the warm-up act.'

'To what?'

'To true love with someone else!'

She laughed and looked away. 'You still believe in true love? After what happened to you?'

'I don't believe we only have one person we can fall in love with. Who can be our soulmate. I believe there are many of them out there. We just have to keep our eyes and our hearts open to the possibility.'

'So that's why you're moving away? You know everyone on the island and you know your true love isn't here?'

He sipped his wine and looked down at his plate. 'I'm moving away because anyone I choose to settle down with on this island will be judged and measured against Emily, and that's not fair on that person or us.'

She leaned in. 'So there is someone on the island?'

He shook his head. 'I never said that.'

She didn't believe him. Could it be there was someone on the island *right now* that Owen could see himself falling in love with? And yet he was trying to imply that he was somehow falling on his sword and uprooting his life to find love elsewhere…to give any future relationship a chance?

Who could it be?

She tried to think of all the young women she'd met so far. Gemma was married, so it wasn't her. And everyone else she knew didn't seem right. He couldn't possibly be talking about her because—*let's face it*—he was not going to fall for a woman with a condition that could kill her at any time. Why put himself through that sort of pain a second time?

The waiter came and took away their plates. The crab cakes had actually been delicious. It was just the topic of conversation that had been difficult...

'I'm sorry. I didn't mean to push.'

'No, it's okay. We've both been through it with our respective partners.'

'We deserve medals.' She laughed, trying to lighten the tension.

'Don't we just?'

'You'll keep in touch, Owen. Won't you?'

'Of course I will. And I'll be back for the christening of Gemma's baby. I'm going to be godfather, remember?'

'I do!' She smiled, trying not to think of how hard it would be to watch Owen leave. 'I'll miss you, that's all. It'll be good to keep in contact.'

'I'll miss you, too.' His tone was heartfelt.

At that moment their main courses were served. Lucy's came in a dish, with a side of steamed vegetables, and Owen's arrived on a large oval plate, brimming with trimmings.

The moment was gone. Lucy was glad that they'd talked, but she still felt sad. The date for Owen's leaving was getting incredibly close now, and tonight was the first real time she'd imagined herself standing on the doorstep of that house, watching Owen pack his bags into a taxi and be driven away.

The idea was painful, and it had caused a lump in her

throat. Maybe what she was feeling was more to do with the fact that Owen had looked after her so well after she'd got sick? Maybe it was to do with the fact that, despite not wanting her family here to smother her, she was glad someone had been taking care of her?

It couldn't possibly be anything else—because anything else was doomed.

They both wanted different things, and Owen deserved a kind of happiness that she could not give him.

He deserved to walk into his new future and find a wonderful woman who could love him, who didn't have a health crisis and who could give him the two children he dreamed of. Along with the house, the white picket fence, the many years of happy marriage. He deserved to feel free. His new relationships deserved the chance to flourish, without being in the spotlight of this island's grapevine. Without being judged alongside his former marriage. Without the women being assessed as better or worse than Emily. He deserved that clean slate.

It was what she had come to Morrow to do, too, after all. Find a clean slate. She'd been given that chance—why shouldn't he have that, too?

Because he'll be taken from me, and I'm not sure I want to lose such a good friend. Such a good man.

She refused to think that her feelings ran any deeper than that. But it was hard. Because the more she sat there, eating her meal opposite the most perfect man she could ever hope to meet, she realised that her feelings for him were more than friendship and probably always had been. That if she were going to set him free she was going to have to take a step away from him. Broaden the gap. Create distance.

Would she be able to do that?

Looking into his gorgeous green eyes, she wasn't sure she stood a chance at all.

CHAPTER SEVEN

'So, I've booked myself in for one of Josie's baking classes. I'm determined to learn how to cook,' she said, as they walked in through the front door after their dinner at Alfie's.

Lucy had begun babbling after her realisation about how she felt about Owen. Talking to him about personal things would just draw her in, so her brain had told her it was best to keep things simple. Talk about work or hobbies. Talk about what she planned to do after he'd gone.

'That sounds great. I'm sure you'll do brilliantly.'

He helped her off with her jacket and then she kicked off her shoes and settled down on one of the single chairs.

Distance. Always distance.

'What else are you planning on learning?'

'Oh, I don't know...' Her gaze swept the room and fell upon an item in the corner. She pointed at it. 'I might learn to play the guitar.'

'Have you ever tried it?'

'No. I played the recorder at school, and then made a disastrous attempt to learn the clarinet, but the guitar intrigues me. Plus, it's good for manual dexterity,' she added, thinking about doing sutures or other minor surgeries. 'Do you play? Or is that just an ornament to make people think you do?' She smiled to show she was joking.

'I play.' He reached for the acoustic guitar and placed it on his lap. 'What do you want to hear?'

'I don't know… Play something you enjoy.'

He looked a little self-conscious. 'Okay, let me think.' He frowned a little, and then smiled, and slowly he began to play.

Lucy recognised the tune immediately. It was one she'd known for many years, but she couldn't think of its name. It was quite haunting, mournful, and it pulled at her heartstrings under Owen's expert playing. She allowed herself to be mesmerised by the way his fingers manipulated the strings and the sounds he was able to create, and then she closed her eyes as she swayed with the music and just allowed the feelings to flow through her.

It took a moment for her to realise he'd stopped playing, and when she opened her eyes her cheeks were wet. 'Oh!' She laughed, wiping them clear. 'Sorry. That piece of music always gets me. What's it called?'

'"Greensleeves."'

'Yes! That's it! I *knew* I knew it. I just couldn't think what it was called.' She paused. 'You play beautifully, Owen. You should play more often.'

'I played a lot after Emily died, but recently I haven't really picked the guitar up.'

'Well, you're excellent.'

He met her gaze and smiled. 'Thank you. Every musician hopes to achieve an emotional response.'

'Well, that's me. Emotional.' She laughed, a little embarrassed. She stood up, feeling awkward. 'Well, I guess it's time I ought to go to bed. Thank you for dinner. It was lovely.'

He put the guitar down and stood up, too. 'My pleasure. Goodnight, Lucy.' And he leaned forward to kiss her on the cheek.

It should have been a quick moment. Over and done with in a flash. A quick peck, a smile, a goodnight, and she would have been on her way up the stairs.

But something else happened entirely.

Owen leaned in to place a kiss on her cheek and his hand touched her upper arm.

Lucy closed her eyes to savour this brief moment of his lips on her skin, expecting it to be over as soon as it began, hoping she could bottle the moment to examine later.

Only Owen's lips lingered by her cheek, as if he wasn't quite ready to pull away from her just yet.

She opened her eyes and met his gaze.

There was a question in his eyes. A wariness. A want. A desire. A need. A hope for something more. But the question showed that he wasn't sure. Whether he wasn't sure what he wanted, or whether he wasn't sure she'd allow him to kiss her, she didn't know.

But she did know she wanted that kiss.

And even though deep down she knew, logically, that kissing Owen was the wrong thing to do, the painful thing to do, she couldn't help herself. She wanted to feel his lips on hers…wanted to feel his body pressed against her…wanted to feel his hands upon her skin.

They were stuck at a perfect crossroads.

To move forward on a path together, or to bring a halt to these proceedings and go their separate ways.

Lucy gave in to *together*.

She turned her head, just ever so slightly, giving him permission to kiss her. Meeting his gaze, she stared deeply into his now dark green eyes and told him with a look that she wanted the kiss. That even though it might be the most ridiculous decision she would make that day, she wanted him to do it. She needed him to do it.

He leaned in, slowly, bringing his mouth closer to hers. He stopped when their lips were only millimetres apart, hesitant for one last moment, and she knew if this kiss was going to happen she was going to have to make the final move.

She closed her eyes and pressed her lips to his.

And her whole body sprang into life.

It was like being a flower. As if she'd been wintering for so long, she'd remained in the dark and withered, waiting for sunlight, waiting for warmth. Meeting Owen had caused her to become a small bud. Cared for, watered, fed. Spending time with him had given her hope that there would be life. And now... Now that he was kissing her she was blooming. All her colours were on show, and she was basking in his sunlight, in his warmth, in his caress. And, like a hungry flower, she wanted more.

Her hands cupped his face, felt that stubble beneath her fingers, and she moaned softly as she felt the length of him press against her. His long, lean body was exactly as she'd imagined it would be and he felt glorious.

His hands were in the small of her back, sweeping down over her hips, brushing over the fabric of her dress, and she knew that she wanted to feel his hands upon her bare skin.

All her reservations, all her logic—all were gone.

All that mattered in that moment was Owen. Experiencing him. Having him. Exploring him.

She reached for his shirt and began to undo the buttons, and then his hands were on hers, halting her progress, and she opened her eyes to look into his.

'Is this a good idea?' he asked. 'Shouldn't we be taking this steady? Your heart—'

'Has its own defib machine now, and the consultant said there was no reason why I can't have sex or exercise or live my life normally.'

'I don't want to be responsible for hurting you.'

She heard his words. Knew that he was protecting her. Looking out for her the way he had ever since she'd come here. But that didn't stop her from feeling irrevocably frustrated and annoyed.

'No. I guess you're right. Maybe it's too soon. Though by the time it's *not* too soon you'll have left anyway, so…' Now she just felt embarrassed. 'Goodnight, Owen.'

And she headed up to bed, slamming the bedroom door behind her.

He heard her door slam and he winced, before sinking down on to the sofa, his head in his hands.

What had he done? How had it come to this? Why couldn't he have just kissed her on the cheek and been done with it? Why had his body not wanted to move away from her? It had seemingly stayed put all on its own! Because in his head he'd simply wanted to kiss her goodnight.

Well, maybe that wasn't all…

He'd had thoughts about kissing Lucy before. Of course he had! But a kiss had started this whole problem the first time!

They were such simple things…kisses. When you really thought about them they could mean so many different things. *Hello. Goodbye. Thank you. I want you. Stay. I'm sorry. Please don't go. I need you. I want you.*

I wanted Lucy.

That was for sure. It was strange how quickly this had

happened, but she'd just got under his skin. Was it her vulnerability? Was it knowing that he could look out for her? Help her? Care for her and keep her safe? The way he hadn't been able to with Emily?

Was he using Lucy as some sort of easing of all the guilt he'd felt over his wife? Because if he was, then that wasn't fair to Lucy. Maybe that was why he'd stopped her from unbuttoning his shirt? He'd thought he was being fair.

No, that wasn't it.

He knew the real reason. It was because he'd been scared. Scared that if he'd let her proceed then many things would happen.

He'd fall ever deeper for Lucy.

He'd put her heart at risk because having a passionate encounter might give her an unstable rhythm.

He wouldn't want to leave the island.

For so long his plan for the future had been to leave this place. To get away. To start afresh.

What was his plan right now?

Upstairs, Lucy was no doubt upset. Maybe angry. Crying? Embarrassed? Would she be afraid to look him in the eye in the morning? He had to take responsibility for that. He didn't want her to feel awkward. He didn't want things to be awkward *between them*.

He looked at the stairs. Should he go to her room and apologise? Would she even let him in to talk?

He knew he had to try. There was no way he could leave it like this.

Owen made his way up the stairs and halted outside Lucy's room. It was quiet inside. He raised his hand, paused, then knocked gently. 'Lucy, can we talk? I don't want things to be bad between us. I'm sorry.'

He waited for a response. Hating this door that was between them.

'Lucy?'

He hoped she was okay. What if her heart was giving her another attack? What if she was collapsed on the floor inside?

Fear rushed through him, faster than adrenaline, and he was about to open the door when she opened it instead.

He met her gaze, relieved to see she was okay. 'Hi.'

'Hi.'

'I didn't want to upset you. I stopped you because I was worried about what would happen if we carried on.'

'What did you think would happen?'

'I was worried about your heart. Worried that you'd have another attack. I was worried about—'

She flung herself around him and pressed her lips to his in a sudden passionate kiss.

Once he was over the surprise he sank into it, fully enjoying every moment, feeling his body respond immediately.

Lucy pulled back to look at him directly in the eyes. 'I get to make my own decision about this, and I want this to happen—all right?'

He smiled. 'Okay.'

'We can take it nice and slow. In fact, that sounds like incredible fun. What do you think?'

Oh, yes.

'Sounds great to me.'

'Good. Now, shut up and kiss me.'

And she pulled him into her bedroom towards her bed.

She woke expecting to find herself in bed alone. Expecting Owen to have crept out at some point during the night or to have got up early to do his usual five-mile run.

But when she opened her eyes she realised he was still naked and wrapped around her, breathing softly, still asleep, spooning her.

She smiled and bit her lip. This felt so good! Last night had been... Well, it was hard to describe accurately, but she'd happily apply the title Best Night of My Life to it. To lie here, to bathe in the warmth and the comfort and the feeling of being *wanted* was just too delicious. She didn't want it to end.

They'd taken things slowly. Owen had been wary of raising her heart rate, so he had touched her and kissed her and *treasured* her in infinitely inventive ways, paying attention to parts of her body that she'd had no idea could be erogenous zones.

The inner wrist, anyone?

She'd always thought her wrists were just wrists. They were what she used to rest on her desk so she could type on the computer. Occasionally they held a watch, or a bracelet. But for them to be delicately tickled and kissed and licked had been an illuminating experience, and she'd thought to herself, *If he can do this to my inner wrist, then what the hell is he going to achieve with my inner thighs?*

Never mind all the other wonderful things he had done to the rest of her body. Every inch of her had come alive under Owen's expert attention.

She'd certainly not been disappointed. She could only hope that he had enjoyed what she had done to him in return. The fact that he was still in her bed was good news—but what would happen when he woke up and reality set in?

This man was going to be leaving.

He had a new home waiting for him. A new job. New patients. He'd come back here—what? Once...maybe twice a year? To visit his family? His godchild? Would she even figure on that visiting list?

She hoped so. It would be nice to know that he was all right. That life, for him, was going swimmingly, and that fate was finally treating him kindly and giving him everything he wanted from life. He'd been through enough torment. Surely there wasn't any more left in store for him?

Lucy stroked his forearm as she thought about getting up, and eventually felt him stir.

He sighed and pressed his lips into her neck. 'Good morning.'

'Morning.'

'Do you feel okay?'

She smiled. Would anything be able to scrub the smile off her face today? 'I feel great. You?'

'Starving.'

'I'm not surprised, after last night.' She turned to face him and, God, the man was even more stunning when he was all rumpled, with his hair tousled and his face extra stubbly.

Those wicked green eyes of his glinted at her and she leaned in for a morning kiss, one hand on his muscular chest, the other trailing down beneath the covers and finding him eager for her.

He smiled. 'I should be going for my run.'

'There's another workout we could do instead,' she whispered, nuzzling his lips with her own.

'Are you trying to seduce me?'

She laughed. 'Very much so.'

'It's working.'

After a shower together, which might have taken slightly longer than it should have, they both headed into the clinic and said good morning to Helen.

Owen was feeling great, and he couldn't remember the last time he'd felt so relaxed and refreshed and as if everything was right with the world. He'd truly thought he'd messed everything up with Lucy, but after going to her room to apologise, she'd accepted his apology... with gusto!

Last night he'd made love to Lucy. There were no doubts about that. It hadn't been just sex, and it hadn't been about scratching a physical itch. It had been meaningful and caring and the most amazing thing he had experienced with a woman.

Taking it slow, taking it easy, being aware of her heart, not wanting to hurt her, had made the whole thing exist on another level—and, God, he had wanted her so badly. He'd almost been tempted to rush it, to give himself the release he'd so craved, only he hadn't. He'd wanted Lucy to have an experience that would blow her mind, and he thought—hoped—that he had given her that.

She certainly seemed happy this morning. She didn't seem to be having any doubts about what had happened, or feeling any awkwardness, or having second thoughts about what they'd done, or fearing it had been a huge mistake. She'd embraced it as much as he had, and that had been life-changing for him.

He didn't know what it meant for him regarding his future, but he knew he couldn't make any rash decisions. Right now he just very much wanted to enjoy what they had. Time was fleeting. You never knew how much of it you truly had. So it was important, in moments of intense connection with another person, to fully embrace that. Doubts, questions, logic, reality—all that could come later.

Their first patient of the day was Georgia Spencer. She walked in, and he thought she was not looking her usual self. No make-up. Just jeans and a T-shirt with a jacket, her hair scraped back into a harsh ponytail.

'Morning! How can we help you today?' he asked rather too brightly.

'I'm not dealing with things very well, Doctor.'

'Tell me about that.'

Georgia went into a monologue about how she was struggling to cope with her aging mother, who had dementia. 'My brother is with her right now,' she concluded. 'He has to be, so I can come here to this appointment, and he even begrudges that. He turned up last night, stayed on the couch and wanted to be off first thing. But I asked him to stay so I didn't have to bring Mum with me.'

'Are things getting worse with Joy, or are they the same?'

'A little worse. She's always known who I am. *Always.* But the last month or so... She tells me I remind her of her daughter.'

Dementia was hard. Not just on the patient, but on their families, too—and especially their carers, who were often with them twenty-four seven. It was a disease that Owen fervently wished there was a cure for, but there'd been little progress in that direction. There was medication to try and halt the disease, but...

'Are you getting enough sleep?' he asked.

'Not really. Mum wakes up in the night, and the dark frightens her, so we keep the lights on, as it's easier. But she wakes so much, and wanders around. I have to stay up with her until I can get her back into bed.'

'And you don't have anyone to provide you with some respite, do you?'

'No, we're on our own. I don't resent looking after my own mum, Doctor, but sometimes I just wish that things were...different.'

'Of course—that's perfectly understandable. If you'd like, I could put in a few calls. See if I can get a care team in? Maybe someone to help you during the day and at night?'

'I do think it's time. Though I feel guilty for admitting it.'

'You have to look after yourself, too. If you got sick, who would look after your mum then?'

'I know…' Georgia sniffed and dabbed at her eyes.

'Do you feel you need to talk to someone? You can refer yourself for talking therapy. Or if you feel that you need some antidepressants?'

'I don't want pills. Maybe chatting to someone could be good? But I'm not sure how I'd be able to make the appointments.'

'Well, there are many options these days. You can do phone consultations, or chat via email, and of course there's video consultations online.'

'Really? That sounds good.'

'And what about getting some help for you? Do you want me to refer your mum for that?'

'I think so, yes.'

'All right. I'll get an assessment sorted for you. If you have any concerns, or if you want to talk to us again, phone Helen and get booked in to see Dr Childs, here. She'll be taking over from me soon.'

Georgia looked at Lucy and smiled. 'We'll be seeing a lot of each other, I think.'

'That's what we're here for, Georgia. To help,' Lucy said.

When she'd gone, Owen let out a big sigh. 'She's stronger than she realises.'

'It's hard to see that in yourself when you feel worn out and done in every day. You think you're failing and you can't see the effort you're putting in to keep your head above water. It's debilitating.'

'I'm glad she's asked for help. Some people don't.'

Lucy looked at him sharply.

He raised his hands, palms outwards. 'I didn't mean you.'

'I didn't think I was drowning. I thought I was treading water. I was doing okay. Until *you* got involved, anyway.'

'What does that mean?' He wasn't sure if he was being blamed here, or not.

'You've...confused me! Made me doubt my decisions—made me rethink my choices in life.'

'I'm sorry.'

'No.' She smiled and reached for his hand, brought it to her lips. 'Don't apologise. You've helped clarify many things for me and I am so glad that I met you. That we... got close.' She blushed.

He liked seeing her blush. It did wonderful things to her face. Her eyes twinkled, and that dimple showed itself. That rosy glow was just delightful in itself.

'You and me—we've both made choices in life because of things that have happened to us. We've both been given a tough time of it. I'd like to think that life has thrown us this time together to enjoy before we have to go our separate ways.'

He'd liked what she was saying up until the part about them going their separate ways. The idea of leaving Lucy...of walking away from what they had... It felt incredibly special. But did it feel that way because they both knew it would be cut short? Or did it feel that way because they were meant for something more?

Doubt caused him to look away, to begin typing Georgia's consultation notes into the computer.

If he walked away from Lucy, would he be making the worst mistake of his entire life? Or the right decision?

Her Brugada syndrome complicated matters. It was a relief that she now had an internal defibrillator, but she'd told him that she didn't want kids. Not biological ones, at least, because of the risk of passing on her disease. And kids were something that he very much wanted in his future. His own children. It was what he'd always dreamed of, and if he stayed with this beautiful, wonderful and yet somehow fragile woman, he would be closing the lid on those dreams of a family.

If he stuck to his plan—took the chance that he'd meet someone else, find a woman he could be with the way he had with Emily and now Lucy, then he'd have everything he'd ever wanted.

But what was the likelihood of his finding another person who was this special? Who made him feel the way Lucy did? Lucy made him feel as if he were a superhero. As if he were invincible. As if he could do anything he wanted.

He fervently believed that everyone had more than one soulmate, but what if he'd met both of his already? What if his soulmate was this broken, fragile woman who sat to his right? What if his soulmate was already right here and he had to think about changing his life expectations? His future? His choices?

It was all too much to think about right now.

They had patients waiting.

'Do you want to call in Abe?' he said.

'Abe?'

'Abraham Blake. He's a hundred years old but looks like a man in his sixties. If I look half as good as him when I make it to his age…'

She turned at the door. 'You look bloody amazing already.'

And she blew him a kiss.

Abraham Blake came walking into the consultation room under his own steam. No stick. No frame. He had a full head of silver hair and the cheekiest blue eyes she'd ever seen on a man of his age.

He doffed his hat at her as he passed. 'Good morning, Doctor.'

'Morning, Mr Blake.'

Abe sat down in front of Owen's desk.

'How are you doing, Abe?'

'Not bad, Owen, not bad. Bit of an ache in my dicky hip, but apart from that I'm firing on all cylinders.'

'What's brought you here today?'

'Well…er…bit personal.' Abe turned and looked at Lucy. 'Would you mind if I had a chat with Owen by myself?'

'Sure. No problem.' She got up to go.

'Abe's our last patient on the list,' said Owen. 'You might as well finish for the day. I'll close up.'

'Okay.'

She gave him a smile and left them on their own. She said goodbye to Helen and headed out, taking the short walk to the front of the house to get some fresh air. The sun was shining and it was unseasonably warm.

When she got to the front of the farmhouse she saw a woman peering through the glass of one of the windows.

'Can I help you?'

The woman turned around.

'Mum! What are you doing here?'

'Lucy! I'm so sorry… I couldn't wait. I know you said to stay away for a bit, but I just couldn't. I had to come and see how you were. I thought I'd stay for a few days, is that all right?'

'O-of course,' she stammered, thinking quickly. They had plenty of room—that wasn't the problem—but she'd been hoping to be able to enjoy the rest of the time she had with Owen before he left. Now her mum was here…

She helped her mum in with her suitcase and gave her a short tour of the house.

'Oh, so you work around the back? Nice short commute.'

'Yeah. It'll be perfect in winter.'

'It *is* winter.'

'Yeah, but you know what I mean.'

Her mum nodded. 'So, how are you? Really? When we got that call from Dr Ledger we were terrified!'

'I'm good. Honestly. All recovered.'

'Show me.'

Show her what? Oh, the implanted defibrillator. Lucy pulled her shirt to one side, so her mum could see the incision.

'Does it hurt?'

'No, not at all.'

'And that should shock your heart if it goes into a fast rhythm?'

'That's right.'

'Do you know what caused the last attack?'

'No. I'd not been for a run, and I'd not done any exercise. I was just…talking.'

'With this Owen chap? When do I get to meet him?'

'He's just finishing off with a patient. He'll be in soon.'

She wanted to ask her mum what she meant by 'stay for a few days'? How long did she actually mean? Three days? Four? A week? As much as she loved her mother, she wasn't sure she wanted her hanging around when she wanted to spend precious time with Owen. He made her feel good. She'd found something really special with him and she didn't want to waste it. But if she was going to have to chauffeur her mother all over the place and spend time with her... Lucy didn't want to seem ungrateful, but this was hard.

'How long, exactly, are you staying for?' she asked.

'Until I feel that I know you're absolutely all right.'

'But I am! You can see that by looking at me.'

'You know as well as I do that that can change in an instant.' Her mother's face was severe.

'Not since the implant, Mum. I'm much safer now.'

'But didn't that consultant say to you before you left home that having an implant would make you a high-risk patient?'

Well, yes, he had. But...

'Yes, but now I've had the surgery, there's no reason why I can't live a normal life. I could go running now. I could train for an Ironman Triathlon, if I wanted.'

Her mum looked horrified.

'I'm not going to. But I thought I might take up swimming again. That's quite gentle exercise, as long as I take it easy.'

'I just get so worried with you being so far away...'

'But that was the whole point, wasn't it? Me getting away. So I didn't have to see the worry on your face every single day. Look at how you're looking at me right now.'

'You're blaming me for caring?'

'No, of course not. I love it that you care so much. But I'm not a child any more, and having you watch me the way you do makes me feel like I'm ten years old. I'm a grown woman and I've started this new life and it's going well! I'm happy, and I'm settled, and I don't want to take a step backwards.'

'You want me to go?'

Lucy shook her head. 'I'm saying there's no reason to come. Not unless you're here just to visit. I don't need a mother hen.'

Her mother nodded. 'Understood. Can I at least meet the man who saved your life? This Owen?'

'Of course you can. I'm not saying you've got to leave straight away.'

'Good. Because that would be quite rude, dear, and I didn't bring you up to be rude.'

Lucy smiled. 'Let's make you a cup of tea. You can meet Owen…stay tonight.'

'All right. I'm looking forward to it.' Her mum leaned forward on the kitchen counter, resting on her elbows. She winked. 'Now, honestly, how handsome *is* he?'

'So why did you want Dr Childs to leave the room, Abe?'

Abe chuckled. 'Well, it's private stuff. The kind of thing I thought I was well past, to be honest. You know my Mabel died ten years ago?'

Owen nodded. Mabel had been Abe's wife for nearly sixty years.

'Well, I've been on my own all this time since. Thought my days were going to be lonely, but I've made a good group of friends on those organised coach trips you told me about.'

'That's great. I'm glad you're enjoying them.'

'I've met a lot of new people. A few of the same faces. Widowers, like me.' He smiled. 'One or two hotties from the mainland.'

Owen raised an eyebrow. 'Okay…'

'I never thought I'd fall in love again, Owen. Not at my time of life. I'd resigned myself to never finding any-one as wonderful as my Mabel. Only I have. Her name's

Ava. She's a young slip of a thing, compared to me—
only eighty-two—but she got that twinkle in her eye... I
think she's expecting things that I haven't thought about
in years, and I'd like to think the old engine is still running, if you catch my drift?'

'I think I do.' Owen smiled.

'I know that in medicine these days they've got those
little blue pills... I'm not saying I'll need to use them,
but it might be handy to have some around—just in case,
you know?'

'Sure. I understand. But unfortunately, Abe, due to
your angina you're not eligible. Any sexual activity will
increase your risk of experiencing chest pain, and if
you've taken a little blue pill, then you can't take your angina medication. I'm sorry, but it's not an option for you.'

'There's nothing else I could use?'

Owen sighed. 'There are operations for penile im-
plants, but at your age I'm not sure any surgeon would
want to do it.'

Abe looked shocked. 'Slice and dice me down there?
I don't think so.'

Owen leaned forward on his desk. 'You know, there's
a lot to be said for keeping Ava happy in other ways.'

'You mean like cuddling?'

'That, and being together, sharing good times, making each other laugh...'

'I could do that if she ever sees me naked.'

Owen laughed. 'Are you sure Ava even wants to take
things in that direction? She might just be happy with
having someone in her life who cares for her. You don't
need to do all those physical things, and you certainly
don't need to put your own good health at risk to do them.'

'All right. I'll talk to her. Explain my limitations and
give her the damned best cuddle she's ever had in her

life!' Abe got to his feet. 'Well, good talk, Doc! You're leaving soon, I'm guessing? I'm going to have to talk to that young lady who left earlier from now on?'

'Dr Childs. She's a very good doctor.'

'Pretty, too. You're on your own...you lost your wife. You ever think about settling down again?'

'Sometimes.'

'You should try it! Though at your age you'll probably get to do more than cuddle!' Abe chuckled and waved and turned to go.

Owen watched him leave with a smile, and then started writing up Abe's patient notes.

It had been an eye-opening moment. Abe, even at his time of life, was still open to the possibility of creating a relationship with a woman. Someone who had become special to him.

It made Owen feel good about what he and Lucy had found. It was a relationship that had been unexpected. Did that make it more enjoyable? All he knew was that he couldn't wait to get back to her and see what the rest of the day held for them. Though, if he remembered correctly, hadn't Lucy said she had a baking lesson with Josie? He would have to find a way of filling the time until she got back. Hopefully she wouldn't be too long.

He finished off his notes, filled out a few repeat prescriptions he had to catch up on and then switched everything off. He turned off the lights, locked up and headed through to the main house.

As he approached, he heard voices. Was Lucy on the phone?

He stepped into the kitchen and saw Lucy sitting at the breakfast bar, chatting with a woman who looked remarkably similar to her.

'Owen! My mother's here! Mum, this is Owen. Owen—Mum.' She made the introductions.

'Call me Deborah.' Lucy's mum smiled, before turning back to her daughter. 'You were right! He *is* an absolute dish!'

Owen smiled and shook her hand.

Josie's house was a neat little cottage about ten minutes away from the farmhouse. Lucy was glad she had the opportunity to get away from her mother and the shock of her arrival, to spend some time on her own, but she'd felt quite reluctant to leave her mother alone in the house with Owen.

No doubt he would get grilled about *everything*. About whether Lucy had told him about the Brugada, and every detail of the attack, her stay in hospital, what the doctors had said, the procedure, how she'd been since…

Hopefully he wouldn't give her any details of their physical activities!

Yes, right now the baking class was very welcome. A chance to forget all that and clear her head, so that maybe she could go home with some baked goods and steer the conversation on to safer territory.

Josie met her at the door with a hug and invited her in, and immediately draped her in a cute little white apron with a bluebird appliquéd on the chest.

'We're going to make a Victoria sponge and a lemon meringue pie. Now, have you made either of those before?'

'No.'

'Good! We'll start with the basics, then, and preheat our oven.'

Josie led her through some of the rules of kitchen safety and hygiene, explained the importance of organising her workspace and keeping the area neat and tidy at all times, and then they began to measure out flour.

'How long have you been baking, Josie?' Lucy asked her.

'Ever since I was a child. My mum baked every day and she was always in the kitchen, up to her elbows in flour and butter and sugar. She used to make the most amazing jam tarts you have ever tasted in your entire life.'

'She's no longer with us?'

'No. She died when I was fourteen.'

'She must have been young?'

'Late forties. The doctors said it was pneumonia...but I think it was a broken heart.'

Lucy frowned. 'I'm sorry... You don't have to talk about it if you don't want to. I'm just trained to ask questions, and sometimes I forget that I'm not at work.'

'No, it's okay. I can talk about it.' Josie showed her how to sift the flour and then went on. 'I...er...had a baby really young. I met someone, thought he was special, and I thought he liked me, too. But then I found out I was pregnant and his parents moved him away. Mum and Dad were shocked. I'd only just turned thirteen. They didn't want me to keep the baby, and sent me away when I began to show. I went to live with my aunt.'

'You must have been so scared...'

'Oh, yeah. They told me I couldn't keep the baby and yet I wanted it so bad. Here—use this.' Josie passed over the sugar. 'I had a little girl, but they took her away from me. I came home to the island and my mother was a shadow of her former self. We lost her six months after that.'

'I'm so sorry.' Lucy stirred the sugar into the flour and

then grabbed the eggs, cracking them into a small dish. 'What was your baby's name?'

'I called her Diana, but her new family called her Sarah.'

'That must have been so hard…giving up the baby you loved. Someone you wanted to keep by your side.'

'It was the hardest thing I ever did. But now, with hindsight, I see I gave Diana a gift. The gift of freedom— of having a better life than the one I could have given her.'

Lucy thought about the day she'd have to say goodbye to Owen. How hard it would be to say goodbye to someone as wonderful as him. How did you say goodbye to someone you wanted to keep in your life? Could letting them go be an act of love, the way Josie had let Diana go?

'But how did you cope back then?'

'I'm not sure I did. Not at first. I cried a lot—especially when my milk came in. It was almost like my body was taunting me, you know?'

Lucy nodded. 'Did you ever try to find her?'

Josie smiled sadly. 'I did find her. I had this dream in my head of the wonderful reunion we'd have. I expected it to be a little awkward, maybe, but I thought she'd hear my side of the story, my reasons for giving her up, and I expected that she'd understand.'

'And how did it go?'

'It was awful. She didn't want to know me. She told me I was from her past. A past she wanted to forget. That she had a family—a mother and a father and people who loved her—and that she didn't need me. That she had everything she wanted.'

'That must have been hard to hear.'

'It broke my heart—but she was right. Me turning up on her doorstep like that must have been a terrible shock. She'd had a whole new life. Closed the chapter on me and thrown away the book. My pain had happened because I couldn't forget her. Because I couldn't let go. So I did.'

Lucy laid a hand on Josie's arm. Just a gesture of comfort. But then she realised she'd had flour all over her and had left a ghostly imprint on her new friend's sleeve.

'Oh, my goodness! I'm so sorry.'

'It's fine. It'll brush right off.'

As they prepared the mixture for the cakes, buttered cake tins and poured cake batter into them, Lucy thought about Owen. And then she thought about her mother, who had just turned up out of the blue. Her mother hadn't been able to let go of her, but she had arrived on her doorstep for a different reason. Lucy hadn't been adopted at birth. Her childhood was not a chapter she had closed the book on. But she had tried to, and now the people who loved her, her mother and her family, were only trying to keep in touch. To be allowed to love her and make sure she was all right.

She suddenly felt awful for trying to shoo her mother away. This was her *mother*! She loved her. And she was so lucky that she'd had such a wonderful childhood.

And Owen? When he left she would make sure that she let him go properly, no matter how difficult it was or how much it hurt her. There would be no point in hoping she would always remain someone special to him. She had to expect that he would move on. She knew he wanted very much to close the chapter of his life that had been on Morrow Island.

I need to let him do that. There's no point to holding on and trying to drag him back into a painful past.

Lucy placed her cake in the oven and turned to Josie. 'Okay. Now what?'

'Now we clean up our mess and start again!'

'I can do that.'

* * *

Deborah had expressed an interest in seeing some of the island so Owen had offered, after Lucy had left for her baking class, to drive her around and show her some of the sights before they had to pick Lucy up.

'Sounds wonderful. Thank you, Owen.'

He took her along what was locally called the Morrow Forty. It was a coastal road that took in the entire perimeter of the island, giving them wonderful views across the sea towards the mainland, and also sea views that stretched for miles into the blue horizon.

He pointed out Mariner's Way, where the remains of an old lighthouse still stood, and the sweeping beaches that in the summer were filled with many desperate mainlanders, stretched out on the sand, trying to get summer tans.

Deborah seemed to like what she saw. 'This is beautiful. And you're leaving all of this? You must be mad. I'd give anything to live in a place like this.'

'It's just time for me to move on.'

'And your family is here, I understand from Lucy? What do they think to your moving away? I can tell you from personal experience that although you're proud of your little birds when they flee the nest, you still like to know that you can keep an eye on them.'

'Yes, my mum and dad are here. My sister, too. They… er…took some time to get used to the idea. I think they worry about me.'

'Of course they do!'

'I think they kind of thought I'd be the GP here until I retired.'

'What's making you leave? Career prospects?'

Clearly Lucy hadn't told her mother everything, of which he was glad. He knew he could trust her, and it was easier to explain to someone who was technically a stranger.

'Life prospects. I love my job, but emotionally I'm stalled if I stay here. I want a family. I want someone to settle down with. And that can't happen here.'

'Why on earth not? I'm sure there are plenty of lovely girls on this island who'd be only too pleased to settle down with a handsome doctor.' Deborah smiled.

He returned the smile. 'It would be difficult. They're all my patients, for a start, and there are lines you just don't cross.'

'Oh, I hadn't thought about that. My Lucy isn't your patient. You two would make a fine couple!'

He tried not to let anything show on his face. How could he tell this woman that he'd spent the entire night in the loving arms of her daughter? And not just the night, but this morning, too? And then in the shower...

'Lucy's great. You must be very proud of her.'

Luckily, Deborah was redirected by his compliment of her daughter. 'Oh, I am. And her father was, too, God rest his soul. We were so frightened when we heard what had happened. You must have stayed so calm.'

Calm? No, he hadn't been calm. His adrenaline had been pumping like crazy and he'd tried desperately to claw for the calm exterior he normally used when there was a medical crisis happening in front of him. But it had been different with Lucy. He'd already been emotionally involved. So he understood a little of what Lucy's family must have gone through.

'I did tell her she needed to call you. Have you visit.'

'You did? Bless you, Owen. I can tell you're a very kind man. And a good friend to my daughter.'

'I always will be.'

'Well, I hope you get what you want when you go. My

daughter left to find a new life. To find a place she could be herself. I hope you're able to find that, too.'

'Thank you.'

But he couldn't help but wonder if he would. He'd have the job he loved. He'd have a brand-new place to live. But would he find someone else to love?

He'd had one great love and lost it way too soon. Now he had this thing with Lucy that was growing exponentially, and he didn't know how to control his feelings, how to tell himself that he needed to rein himself in. So he might be able to take those steps and walk away…but what if he was walking away from the next great love he would ever find?

Being with Lucy felt so right.

It was hard to argue with that. Hard to reason against it. Hard to convince himself that leaving was still the right thing. Why would anyone walk away from something so wonderful? *Someone* so wonderful?

But Lucy was a huge risk. Not because of her health thing. He really believed that now she had the internal defibrillator they didn't have to worry so much about that any more. It was still an issue, but there was no reason she couldn't live as normal a life as anyone else. No, it was the fact that she didn't want what he wanted. She had come here to get away from all the pressures that other people were putting on her. They'd been smothering her with what *they* wanted. And he wanted a family.

Didn't he?

Wasn't that what he'd dreamed of almost his entire life? The day he'd finally become a father and hold his very own baby in his arms?

Lucy didn't want kids. She'd even told him she didn't want a relationship once. *'I'm here to concentrate on my work and friends.'* That was what she'd said.

He frowned as he drove, forgetting that he was meant to be pointing things out. It was only when Deborah pointed at the old theatre that he suddenly remembered and forced himself into the present.

For twenty more minutes, he was the consummate tour guide, and then they returned to pick up Lucy, who came out of Josie's with two plastic tubs, bearing them before her as pleased as Punch.

'Hey, you two. Hope you're both hungry!'

'Absolutely!' answered Deborah. 'Smells delicious.'

Owen smiled and nodded.

You okay? Lucy mouthed to him.

I'm good, he mouthed back, feeling anything but.

Owen went out in the evening and brought back fish and chips. As they sat eating them out of long polystyrene trays, Lucy decided to tell her mother she could stay for as long as she liked. She was thinking that with her mother here it would help her have that distance from Owen that she needed. Rather than have more time to enjoy him, she needed to accept the fact that the man was going soon and she had no right to hold on to him. Having her mother here would help with that.

She'd expected her mother to grab on to the invitation with both hands, but…

'Oh, you're very kind, sweetheart, but you know what? You were right. I can see that you're fine, and that you don't need me here, getting in the way of your new life. You need time!' she said, brandishing a chunk of cod on the end of her wooden fork. 'Time to establish yourself here. Get settled in properly. Let people get to know you. You don't need me hanging around your neck like a millstone.'

'Honestly, Mum, it's fine! I'd love it if you stayed.'

'Next time I visit I'll stay for a week. I just needed to know you were okay, and I can see that you're more than that. I can go home and tell your sisters and your brother that you're thriving and that you're happy and that we don't need to interfere.'

Lucy smiled and nodded, almost feeling emotional.

Now, where the heck are all these feelings coming from?

Was it because she felt as if her mother was seeing her for the very first time? Understanding her needs? Accepting this new twist in her life? Or was it because if her mother was leaving, then it meant she would have to deal with keeping her distance from Owen all by herself? And that was terrifying—because she wasn't sure she'd have the strength.

Owen was…everything.

Already she missed the feeling of his body against hers, and she had no doubt that he was feeling the same!

I am in so much trouble.

CHAPTER EIGHT

It was strange to wave her mother goodbye. For so long now she'd spent the majority of her time thinking that she needed to get away from her family, and now her mother was leaving her. Now that they'd reconciled the way they both felt it was odd. And she couldn't help but think about how it would feel when the day came that she had to wave Owen goodbye at the train station.

She tried not to focus on that as she arrived back to join him in the clinic, but when they were in the consulting room together he came around the desk and gazed into her eyes.

'You okay? How was it?'

She smiled. 'It was okay.'

'You need a hug?'

Oh, yes!

But should she have one from him?

It would be rude if she said no, she thought, so she nodded and allowed herself to sink into his arms, to lay her head against his chest and just breath him in.

He felt so good!

She couldn't quite believe that she would be losing this soon. This thing with Owen. Had she been a fool to allow it to develop in the first place?

But now he was lifting her chin, smiling at her and

pressing his lips against hers, and all the questions just disappeared. For a few seconds all that mattered was his lips and his kiss and *him*.

'We need to call in our next patient,' he said at last. 'I was thinking that you should take the lead on everything now. I'm confident you know what you're doing, and it'll be good for the patients to start relying on you whilst I'm still in the background.'

She nodded. 'Are you staying to observe?'

'There are a few things I need to do. But you can call me on my mobile if you need me. I'll just be in the house. A few paperwork basics for the new job,' he explained.

'Oh, right. Well, you go, then. I'll be fine.'

He smiled. 'See you later. I've planned a treat for us this afternoon.'

Her heart raced a little. 'A treat?'

'It's a secret. No guessing.'

He kissed her once again, grabbed his bag, and then he was gone, leaving her standing there, touching her fingers to her lips.

What was it about Owen that made her feel so… *complete*? It was a strange sensation, because when she wasn't with him she felt as if a part of her was missing— and that was strange, because when she hadn't known Owen she'd not felt that way…

And yet now…?

She sat down in front of the computer and looked to see who was next.

With clinic over, Lucy headed back into the house. As she always did when she got home, she kicked off her shoes, washed her hands and went to change into something comfy.

Owen was in the kitchen, on the phone.

'I'm on hold with HR.'

'Fun. How long have you been on hold?'

'About fifteen minutes.'

She winced. 'Want a cup of tea?'

'I'd love one. Thanks.'

She began to make them both a drink, taking the time to look in the fridge for possible dinner ideas for later when she went to get the milk. Then her phone beeped. She looked at it, read the message and then got Owen's attention.

'We've got a home call-out. I think we should go together.'

'What is it?'

She turned her phone to show him. 'Gemma.'

Emily's pregnant best friend.

'HR will have to wait. Come on.'

They grabbed their go-bag, which was kept by the front door, and got into the vehicle. Lucy drove, with Owen directing her. She was beginning to recognise the roads and the layout of the island much more easily now, and had a fair idea of where they were going.

The message on the phone had said that Gemma was at home, unable to get out to the car so she could get to the hospital. Gemma's partner, Darren, had panicked after being told that an ambulance might take an hour or two to get to them.

'This baby will be early,' said Lucy.

'But not too early. She was thirty-six weeks when we last saw her, so everything should be fine in that respect.'

They pulled up outside the house and Lucy grabbed the bag as Owen headed towards the door.

Darren met them. 'Thanks for coming, Owen. She says she can't move, and she's kind of stuck on the floor in the hall. I can see the head when she pushes.'

'You've done the right thing in calling. Show us where she is.'

'Down here.'

He led them through the living room and up the stairs. At the top, on the landing, they found Gemma breathing heavily, her face red from exertion, on her hands and knees.

'The baby's coming, Owen!'

'It's okay, Gemma. Lucy? You got gloves?'

'Here.' She passed him gloves and put some on herself, and then she knelt by Gemma's face and smiled at her. 'You can do this, okay?'

'Can you pass me the portable ultrasound?' asked Owen.

'Sure.'

Equipment was passed back and forth, and Owen listened in to the baby's heartbeat. It was going strong, and Gemma smiled when she heard it.

'The contractions... I thought they were Braxton Hicks, so I ignored them! And then suddenly I'm pushing and I can't move!'

Lucy tucked a piece of Gemma's hair behind her ear. 'You did the right thing. You're about to become a mama. You ready?'

'No! I kind of wanted all the drugs. Tell me you brought drugs?'

Lucy smiled. 'I think you're a bit late for that, Gemma.'

'The baby is right there, Gemma,' said Owen. 'A couple of really strong pushes and she'll be here, okay? So when you get that next contraction I want you to take a big, deep breath in and push until I tell you to stop.'

'Here's one now.' Gemma sucked in a breath and began to bear down.

Lucy coached her, counting, stroking her back, until

she got to ten. 'And again—big breath for me. That's it—and *push*!'

'You're going to feel some stinging, Gemma, but that's normal. I need you to push through it for me.'

Gemma cried out. 'I can't!'

'Yes, you can. You're strong. Now push again!' Owen said.

'I can't! It hurts too much!'

Owen moved round to look Gemma in the eye. 'Gemma? I want you to reach down and touch your daughter's head.'

She nodded and lifted one hand off the floor to reach back. There was a pause, and then Gemma gasped and gave a happy cry. 'That's her?'

'That's her. She's *so* close. You can do this, okay?'

Gemma nodded. 'Just tell me when and how.'

'Okay, you're getting another contraction. Deep breath—and *push*!'

'You can do it, Gemma!' Lucy cried. 'That's it. Keep pushing.'

'That's brilliant, Gemma! That's fantastic. Okay, now pant for me…'

Gemma huffed out air, strands of her long hair dancing in front of her face. Lucy tucked it back.

'Okay, the head's out!'

Lucy beamed and leaned in again. 'One more contraction, Gemma…'

Gemma pushed with all her might, crying out with one last gasp as behind them there was a gushing sound, and suddenly the lusty cry of a newborn baby.

Lucy watched as Owen clamped the cord and wrapped the baby before Gemma turned around and leant back against the stair rail to cradle her newborn daughter. Darren was at her side, his eyes filled with tears.

Lucy smiled at Owen. What a joyous moment it had been to see him cradling that newborn baby and handing it over to Gemma. There was nothing quite like it. The thrill of new life. Of seeing someone come into the world. And as she stared at him she knew that she could never deny him the chance to hold his own baby like that.

'Thank you so much! I could never have done it if you two hadn't turned up.'

'Of course you could. You did all the work—we just assisted,' said Lucy.

'She's gorgeous!' Gemma cried. 'Don't you think she's gorgeous? Emily would have loved her, wouldn't she, Owen?'

He nodded. 'She would.'

Outside, they heard the rumble of an engine and then the sound of a hefty knock at the front door.

Lucy stood up. 'Probably the paramedics. I'll go and let them in and then I'll make everyone a much-needed cup of tea.'

The paramedics bundled up the stairs and Lucy stood at the bottom, hearing all the good-natured chat and laughter and congratulations and feeling very much on the outside of it all.

Seeing that baby born had made her realise two things. One, that Owen deserved a child of his own, and two, that she was desperately sad she would never get to experience herself what she had just observed.

She hadn't thought it would have the power to make her cry, but as she stood over the kettle, waiting for it to boil, she wiped away a few silent tears.

And then suddenly someone was touching her shoulder, and she turned around, and it was Owen.

He saw her tears and pulled her into his arms. 'Hey, it's okay...'

She laughed. 'I know it is. It's silly. It's a happy thing. I'm happy for them.'

'I know.'

'It just makes you realise a few things, this kind of thing. Makes you look at your own life…makes you re-think the things that you want.'

He stopped to look at her. 'You want to have a baby? I thought you didn't want that?'

'I know, it's just…' The sting of tears burned her eyes as they filled again, and she had to turn away.

Owen pressed her damp face against his chest and she let him soothe her, accepting his comfort. So much had happened in the last few days—it was no wonder she was all over the place! And now this…

She was finally grieving for the child she would never have.

It was quiet in the car on the way back home. Owen drove, his mind churning with a thousand thoughts, a thousand possibilities, not knowing which way he wanted to go. But what he did know was that he didn't want to go straight home, so instead of turning left to take them to the cottage, he decided to turn right and take them to the place he'd planned to take her earlier.

Lucy dabbed at her nose with a tissue. 'House is back that way.'

'I know. I'm taking you for that treat, remember?' He frowned. 'Unless you don't feel like being out and about?'

She smiled. 'Out and about is good. Better than being at home, allowing myself to ruminate on things.'

'Good. It's a happy day, today. We've seen something wonderful, so let's celebrate that.'

'Are we going to the pub?'

'No. Somewhere better.'

'Better than the pub?' She laughed.

He smiled. 'Much better.' And he pulled up outside of Ye Olde Scone Shoppe.

'Scones?'

'A proper Cornish cream tea.'

She brightened, and he liked seeing the joy and delight glimmer in her eyes even more than he'd liked seeing them before.

'So, tell me which way you fall?'

'With what?'

'Cream first? Or jam?'

She smiled. 'I don't know. I guess...jam first? It's easier to spread on the scone, and then you can dollop the cream on top.'

'You've just made all of Cornwall very happy. You can stay.'

'I'm very glad to hear it.'

They went inside and found a table by the window. The tables were covered in red-and-white gingham, and the furniture was all painted white. Around the walls were decorated teapots in all shapes and sizes, and each table had a glass jar holding a wooden spoon, painted with a number.

It was cutesy, and perfect, and best of all it was making Lucy smile. He'd hated seeing her break down and get upset in Gemma's kitchen.

He ordered them both tea with scones, jam and cream, and when the waitress brought over their teapot he saw it looked like a ceramic watering can, filled with flowers on the top and around the spout. Their cups were mismatched china, and there was a little bowl filled with a mix of brown and white sugar cubes.

'How are you feeling now?' he asked, as he gave the teabags inside the pot a stir.

'Better. I'm sorry about before. That was unprofessional.'

'No apology needed. And you're allowed to get emotional at births. Everyone does.'

'Yes, but usually they're happy tears.'

'Moments like those…they affect everyone in different ways.'

'They certainly do.'

He poured them both tea and offered her the little pot of milk. Then the waitress arrived with their scones, jam and cream, and it all looked so delicious they tucked right in.

Owen hadn't realised how hungry he was. He'd not had any lunch, having finished clinic and then been on the phone to his new place of work, trying to sort out the paperwork, and then getting called out to Gemma. Maybe it was all the adrenaline, but he was starving.

The scones were perfect. Soft and melt-in-the-mouth. The jam was rich, and home-made on the premises. The cream smooth and sweet. It was an idyllic combination. They worked so well together. Rather like he and Lucy…

He'd not expected this month to go so well. It seemed such a long time ago that he'd been standing in that blizzard on that freezing platform, waiting for her train to come in, and now here she was, well acclimatised to her new post, sitting in a sunny window, eating scones and drinking tea.

'You have a spot of jam…' He reached out to wipe the corner of her mouth and she blushed and looked around them.

He'd almost forgotten they were in public. That someone might notice such an intimate gesture.

He'd missed touching her. It had only been a few hours, but already he was hungry for more, and that both thrilled him and scared him. She was so beautiful, and he knew he already had strong feelings for her... His head was a mess. And his heart was...torn.

Just a few hours ago he'd been on the phone to his new place of work, but even as he'd been making his calls and talking to HR his heart had been making him doubt his decision to leave. He and Lucy were brand-new, and there was no way of knowing if they'd work long-term, but right now it felt so good.

And at Gemma's Lucy had said she wanted a baby. Well, she'd implied it. And he'd always thought that was off the table for her as an option for the future.

He wanted a family one day, too. And medicine came on in leaps and bounds every day. What if something came along to help those with Brugada so that their lives weren't at such risk? So that their condition wasn't unstable, but perfectly controlled and barely thought of? It *could* happen. It was possible. And if he stayed, and they wanted a family together, then by the time it happened there could be something like that. There *could* be!

It felt so right, being with Lucy, and yet here he was thinking of walking away from that! His life was set up for him to walk away. A new flat had had his deposit put down on it for rental. His new job was waiting. Technically, he would be on a three-month probationary period, so it wasn't exactly permanent just yet, and he wasn't tied into it—though he hated the idea of letting them down when they thought they'd filled the post.

He really didn't want to let them down.

But he really didn't want to leave Lucy either.

To walk away from...*love*.

This felt like love. He knew what real love was—he'd

felt it before, and he'd had to say goodbye to it before, and he certainly did not like how that had made him feel.

Was he being a fool, walking away from a chance at happiness here?

'What did you think of the baby's name? It's cute, isn't it?' asked Lucy.

He nodded. It was.

'Darcy Marie Emily Aickman...'

'Lucy?'

She looked up at him, dabbing at her mouth with a napkin. 'Yes?'

He swallowed hard, nerves thrumming nervously throughout his body. He'd not meant to say anything yet, but there were so many thoughts and feelings in his body it was as if he had to say something, to get some of them out.

'I've been having second thoughts.'

She looked worried. Frowned. 'What about?'

'About leaving.'

The air whooshed from her body and she felt herself grow hot. He didn't want to leave? Why? And then all the images of their night together came crashing in and her cheeks flushed. She hoped he wasn't staying because of her.

'But you've made all those plans. Of course you're going to go.'

He shook his head. 'I may. Perhaps for the probationary term, because I promised them they'd have a doctor and I don't want to let them down, but... I've been thinking about coming back.'

No. No, no, *no*! He couldn't! He *had* to go! This was his chance to get away and start his new life!

'Owen…'

'We have something, Lucy. Something special. And I don't think we should lose it because I've made some other arrangements.'

She sat there, hoping she wasn't gaping at him open-mouthed.

'I know what it's like to lose someone special, and you've become very special to me. I don't want to walk away from you.'

She felt sick. *No.* This couldn't be happening! All the words he was saying were wonderful, and perfect, and her traitorous little heart was filled with rapture at hearing them, but her brain and her logic were screaming. Part of her wanted to stay—wanted to lean in and hear him whisper all these wonderful things and a declaration of undying love—but her fear and her fright made her suddenly get to her feet, her chair scraping loudly across the floor behind her.

'No. No, you're going.'

And she pushed past him to make her way outside, the bell above the door tinkling happily as she strode out, tears coming for a second time that day.

He had the keys to the car, so she turned away from the vehicle and headed towards the harbour. She couldn't think of where to go—she just knew that she needed to get away before he said something so wonderful that she'd grab him by both hands and accept.

Only she knew she couldn't have the happiness with Owen that she wanted. He wanted a family. A future. She couldn't give him the child, or children, that he wanted.

And, actually, this was cruel of him. To taunt her with happiness when he knew—*he knew!*—just how heart-broken she was at wanting to have a child of her own.

They'd—what?—slept together once! And, yes, it had

been the most amazing night she'd ever had, and she hadn't realised sex could be so wonderful and mind-expanding, nor that she could ever feel that close to any-one ever again. But was it enough for him to want to change all his life plans, derail them, for someone who couldn't give him his one aspiration in life?

It all came down to having a child.

Owen wanted a family of his own. He'd told her this many times.

Lucy couldn't have a child of her own. Well, techni-cally she could. Pregnancy with Brugada was possible, but she could not run the risk of passing the condition on to her child.

Imagine that! Knowing her darling daughter or darling son as a baby, as a toddler, and being terrified that at any moment the child could go into an abnormal heart rhythm and die? She knew what her mother felt like. Had seen what it had done to her. And she could not live her life like that. In absolute fear. Day after day. For months. For years. What would that do to a person? And what about the guilt she would feel for passing on her condition?

No.

'Lucy!'

She heard Owen calling her name but she didn't want to be found by him. Didn't want to hear him try to explain things. Didn't want to hear him try and plead his case. Didn't he know how much that would hurt her? Having him offer her his heart? A life by his side?

She wanted that *so much*! But she could not take his dreams away from him. Being together might be fine to start with, but after a few years the resentment would creep in and destroy them, and she'd rather her time with Owen be unblemished by hatred.

She slipped down to a small jetty that took her away

from the harbour and among the boats. They bobbed about in the water and seagulls flew overhead, their cry haunting. When she got to the end of the short pier she stopped and looked out at the water.

'Lucy?'

Owen was right behind her.

She closed her eyes in pain and tried to fight back the tears. Why was he making her do this? Why was he forcing her to push him away? She didn't want to do it this way. She'd wanted simply to drive him to the train station, give him a hug and wish him well, waving him away and crying *after* he'd gone. Not like this. Not before it was time.

She turned and gazed at him. 'We can't be together, Owen. You know that.'

'Do I?'

'Yes! We both want different things in life.'

He stepped forward, imploring her. 'No! We want the same things! You said so. You want to have a baby—'

She held up her hand to stop him, anger flaring inside her. 'Yes, I want a baby—but I know that I *cannot have one*. I may have had a brief moment in which I was weak, and it might have forced me to look at what I was going to lose, but that is all! I will not have a biological child and you want one more than anything—along with a future with a wife you can love. I *need* you to leave for Tavistock, Owen. I need you to. You cannot stay for me. I will not have you resent me for the rest of my life.'

'I could never resent you.'

'That's so easy to say now. In the heat of the moment. But, please, if my happiness means anything to you then you'll go. You will walk away from this place and you will take the future that just a month ago you wanted more than anything.'

She saw the pain and hurt on his face and it broke her inside, but she knew she had to hold firm and not let him break her.

'I thought… I thought we were creating something between us. Building something. I thought we had something special.'

'We do. But we both knew at the beginning that it would only be brief.'

'You really see no future for us?'

Did he know he was tearing her in two?

'None.'

It killed her to say it when she herself had hoped that maybe, if circumstances had been different, there might have been a future for them. But even though they both wanted the same thing, the difference was that Lucy knew she couldn't have her dream. Not at the expense of his.

He stood there, nodding. Were there tears in his eyes? She wanted to run to him, fling herself into his arms and say she was sorry, never let him go. But she held herself back. Kept herself restrained, even though it was the hardest thing she had ever done in her life—and she had been through a few things.

It came to her that she was now in a kind of role reversal. With Phillip, she'd been the one trying to convince him that they could still be together, and he had been the one standing firm and telling her there was no future. Now she was doing the same thing to Owen.

Had Phillip hurt as much as she herself was hurting in this moment? She didn't think so. Phillip had seemed cold and aloof, and there'd been no emotion in his face.

Lucy felt drained of all energy, and when she saw the slump of Owen's shoulders she knew that he felt the same. The fight was gone. It was over. She'd convinced him of her truth. And although she should have felt triumphant at finally severing their connection, so that he could fly free and find happiness, she felt nothing but sorrow and grief.

'I guess we ought to go home, then. Nothing for me to do but pack my things.'

He turned away and began walking back to the car. At first, she wasn't sure whether she should follow him or catch the bus home, but she decided she didn't want to take either of those options.

He turned to look at her. 'You coming?'

'I think I'll walk.'

He frowned, then nodded and walked away from her.

Every step that he took cleaved her heart in two, and she lifted a hand to where the internal defibrillator was and thanked heaven for it—because she wasn't sure she'd have been able to get through this break-up without the security of it being there.

The pain she felt right now was unbearable. This emotional pain was more intense than the chest pains she'd felt when she'd had her heart attack.

She waited until he was out of sight and then she turned back to look at the water. It looked so dark and secretive. What was in its depths? Did it hold danger and threats to life? Water was meant to be good for you, but too much of it could kill you.

Was love the same?

It felt good at the beginning, when you floated on a cloud of euphoria and joy, but inevitably it changed, and then love could cause you the worst pain in the world. People you loved died. People you loved left you. People you loved *hurt* you, and those were the worst wounds that you had to bear in life. You had to learn to recover, and bounce back, and try to carry on. And then what? Hope to find love again?

She turned and began walking. Thankfully it wasn't raining. The sun was out. Daffodils danced in people's front gardens. Trees were beginning to sprout green buds. Spring was trying to get here early, it seemed.

She tried to find joy in these signs of new life. She tried to think about how a cold winter inevitably gave way to spring and how every year brought new opportunity for growth.

She'd made a terrible mistake, allowing her feelings to get involved where Owen was concerned. She should never have slept with him. She should never have allowed their relationship to go as far as it had.

And now she was paying for it.

Back at the house, Owen had packed his final few things into a case. He had until the end of the week before he had to leave for Tavistock—but, really, what was stopping him from leaving now?

Lucy.

He didn't want to leave without saying goodbye. It didn't feel right.

He sighed, wondering just how the hell it had gone so wrong. Everything had been going so well for them. They worked together well. He loved spending time with her. And physically they'd been the perfect match. But...

He'd really made a mistake in thinking she'd changed her mind about having a child. He should have known. Should have realised. She'd told him before that she couldn't risk giving a child her condition, and to be perfectly honest he'd been worried by that, too. But he'd been blinded, misguided, by her tears—had felt her sadness at what she felt she couldn't have and somehow leapt to giant stupid conclusions. He'd taken it as a sign that it meant that she was considering the possibility of having a baby of her own. With him.

Having a child with Lucy? That had seemed to him like heaven, right there. The two of them parenting a child together... He hadn't been able to see how that could go wrong. Maybe they would have genetic counselling, IVF, select embryos. But they'd be wonderful parents. Both of them. He'd had no doubts.

Only her fear of Brugada had been stronger than he'd realised, and he'd stumbled into an awkward, ridiculous situation with Lucy, forcing her to push him away because he'd not understood her.

He'd been wrong. He thought he'd been making a future with Lucy, but all he'd been doing was making castles in the clouds. It wasn't real. It was only temporary. And to her he had only been—what? A bit of fun? Something to while away the month that he was here?

He couldn't believe that he'd read her so wrong! He'd truly believed they were building something.

Maybe because he'd had a committed relationship before, that was all he saw. Commitment. But Lucy must have been serious when she'd more or less spelled out that after her diagnosis and her betrayal by Phillip she was only looking for casual relationships going forward.

He'd pushed her too hard. Demanded too much of her. And what hurt the most was the loss of hope. The loss of the possibility that he had found another woman to love. Because he had no doubt that he *had* fallen in love with her.

Should I have told her that?

On the pier. Should he have told her that? Would it have made any difference if she had known the depth of his feelings?

Probably not. Lucy clearly hasn't changed her mind.

He couldn't kid himself. What would be the point of that, except to cause himself more pain?

Owen dragged his cases towards the front door and then sat and waited for Lucy to return. Hopefully she wouldn't be too long, because he wanted to call a taxi and get out of here.

A clean break was what they both needed.

She saw the cases as soon as she got inside, and looked up and met his gaze. 'You've packed.'

'I'm ready to go. There's no point in stretching this out.'

She felt tired and sick. As she'd walked up the lane towards the house she had wondered if he would still be there and, if so, how it would be to live around each other for the next few days.

Now she didn't have to wonder.

'Have you called a taxi?' she asked.

'Not yet. I wanted to say goodbye to you first. It didn't feel right to just walk away.'

She nodded. 'Right.'

It was hard not to cry, but she truly thought she was all cried out. Instead, she just crossed her arms and told herself that she had to remain strong to get through this final part.

'You'd better call one, then.'

He stared at her for a moment, as if not quite believing she'd said that. But hadn't he packed his bags a few days early and told her he was leaving? She had a right to feel cheated out of the final few days she'd hoped to spend with him. Days in which they wouldn't have had a fight. Days in which they might have snuggled together on the couch, her head resting on his shoulders. Maybe one more night together? He'd stolen all that away.

He pulled his mobile from his pocket and made a call. When it was over, he looked at her and said, 'It'll be here in ten minutes.'

She was still standing by the front door, feeling awkward, so she decided to head for the kitchen. Make a cup of tea, or something, so that she had something to do with her hands.

'The islanders have arranged a leaving party for you. On the thirty-first. You're going to miss it.'

He nodded. 'They'll understand.'

Behind her, she could almost feel him standing in the lounge, silent, probably full of things he wanted to say but couldn't.

How had it come to this?

How had it all gone so terribly wrong?

When the toot of a car horn sounded outside, her heart sank even more.

Owen appeared in the doorway. 'I…er…need to go now.'

She nodded, not trusting herself to speak, biting the inside of her lip, trying to concentrate on that pain rather than break down and cry in front of him. Because she felt that if she did he wouldn't go, and she *needed* him to go.

'I hope you're happy here. I hope…' He sighed. 'Goodbye, Lucy.'

And he stepped forward and dropped a brief, too-short kiss on her cheek, and then turned away before she could respond to that and walked towards the front door.

She watched him go. Watched the taxi driver load Owen's cases and bags into the boot. Watched Owen as he got into the car and gave one last look at the house.

She opened her mouth to say something, but the words got stuck.

What could she say that would make him feel better? Nothing.

So she simply gave him a sad smile and a wave and tried not to sink to her knees as the taxi took him away.

She watched as the taxi moved down the lane, keeping her focus on Owen's head, wondering if he would turn around and look for her one final time. Hoping that he would.

What would she do if he did?

But she didn't get the chance to find out. Because he didn't turn around. Didn't wave. Didn't look for her.

And then he was gone.

And it was over.

CHAPTER NINE

THE SPRUCE PRACTICE, in a village a few miles from Tavistock, was decorated for upcoming Valentine's Day. Everywhere Owen looked when he was at work he saw red hearts, pink hearts. Bunting. Roses. There had even been red heart-shaped cupcakes when he'd come in today, baked by one of the receptionists.

It was a great practice. Fantastic colleagues, amazing admin staff, and the team of receptionists always had a smile and a joke or two.

Everyone was doing their best to help him fit in.

But he couldn't help but feel that his heart had been left on Morrow Island.

Why had he ever thought that he could only be happy by leaving?

He'd been doing an awful lot of thinking in the days since he'd left Lucy. An awful lot of planning. And today was the day he would finally put that plan into place.

He rapped his knuckles on the door to the office of the senior partner of the practice, Dr James Rogers, and he heard James call him in.

'Owen! Come in, come in—take a seat.'

'Thank you.'

'Have you tried one of these? They're amazing,' James said, biting into a cupcake.

He smiled. 'Yes, I have. Sue's a great baker.'

'She'll make us all fat—and then what kind of role models will we be?' He laughed, putting the cake down and brushing his fingertips together to get rid of the crumbs. 'How can I help you today?'

'It's about my probation time of three months...'

James narrowed his eyes. 'And you're wondering if you can make it shorter?'

Owen blinked. How did James know? 'Er...yes, actually. How did you...?'

James leant forward, smiling. 'Starting a new job is always difficult, Owen. We all know that. But it's been very clear to me since you've been here that even though you're a marvellous doctor, and the patients, staff and myself believe you to be an amazing addition to our team, clearly something has been bothering you.'

'It has. I think I've...er...made a mistake. Not in choosing this place—the Spruce has been and is fantastic. I can't fault it.'

'It's just that your heart isn't in it?'

'I think I've left my heart back home.'

'Want to talk about it? Is there any way we can help? I'm very keen to keep you here.'

'Thanks, James. That's good to hear, and I wish I could say yes, but things were...complicated when I left home. Unresolved. And I need to sort that out.'

James nodded. 'I understand. Could you give us a few more days? Give us time to find a locum?'

Owen let out a tense breath. He'd hated the idea of having to have this conversation with James. He didn't like letting people down. 'Of course. I'll stay till the end of the week.'

'Fantastic. Okay. But you know, once you get everything sorted, if there's a chance of you coming back, we'd love to have you.'

Owen stood and shook James's hand. 'Thanks.'

But he knew there wouldn't be any chance. There was a lot to sort out, and staying on the mainland was not part of his plans. The mainland might have to play *some* part, but he still needed to sort that out. See if it was possible. Agreeing to stay till the end of the week would give him time to do that.

Lucy stared out across the sea. She'd come to Carrigan's Cove again, her legs carrying her there because she felt some sort of bond with the young woman who had spent months in those caves, staring out to sea, waiting for her loved one to return.

She knew how Carrigan had felt.

The yearning hope. The terrible despair that she had lost the man she loved for ever. And although Owen wasn't lost at sea, she felt as if he might as well be.

Though in her heart she knew she had done the right thing by letting him go, the torment she felt was not eased by the knowledge. They'd had such a short time together, and she knew she should cherish it and allow those memories of Owen to cause her happiness, not pain, but it was hard when she was hurting so much.

She worked, she saw patients, she baked muffins and brownies with Josie, and she had even gone for a walk with Gemma and her new baby. But no matter what she did to fill her day, at the end of it she had to come home. Where the large farmhouse was empty. Where his room was vacant and yet still smelt like him. He'd left behind a can of his antiperspirant and she'd been spraying it into the room and standing there inhaling it, as if she was sniffing a flower, trying to recall how it had felt to be so close to him. To hold him in her arms.

And now it was especially hard, because everywhere she looked there were Valentine's decorations. Two days until Valentine's Day and every shop, every cafe, every hairdresser—every business, it seemed—had filled their windows with hearts, selling the fourteenth of the second month as the day for those who loved each other to be together.

The thought of the day taunted her. Almost made her feel as if it was laughing in her face.

At least down here in the cove there were no hearts except her own.

And, although it was a very lonely place to be, she at least felt that Carrigan would have understood.

His interview with the hospital had gone well, and he'd been offered a locum post to work in the minor injuries department of Accident and Emergency. It was one step closer to achieving his goals.

No matter what happened, he would stick with this plan—because this one felt right. It was something he had to do. Return home to Morrow Island and commute to the hospital on the mainland for work—because Lucy had his old job. He couldn't expect to move back into the farmhouse. That was Lucy's, too. But his parents had offered to have him back with open arms. In fact, they'd been over the moon at the thought of having him back, once they'd heard everything regarding his decision to change his mind.

'This will always be your home, Owen,' his mother had said over the phone.

He'd kept his promise to James. He'd stayed at the clinic until the end of the week and then he'd packed everything up and travelled home to Morrow, dropping off his cases with his parents before racing straight out again. He had things to collect before he could go and see Lucy.

He hoped that surprising her on Valentine's Day wouldn't be too presumptive...that there'd be a happy ending... He couldn't think of a more romantic day to declare his love for her.

Armed with flowers, and a little something extra special, he ordered a taxi to drive him to the farmhouse. Morning clinic would be over. Lucy would be at home—unless she was out living her life, as she'd said she wanted to when she'd first come to the island.

He had assumed there wouldn't be someone else yet. Lucy didn't seem the type to quickly rush from one relationship to another, and he'd seen the pain in her face at their break-up and separation, no matter how hard she'd tried to hide it. He would obviously step back if there *was* someone else, but he didn't think it was a real possibility.

Not that she wouldn't be able to find anyone if she chose. Lucy was amazing. Any man would be lucky to have her by his side.

The way he had been lucky. And hoped to be again.

As the taxi pulled into the long lane leading down to the farmhouse he felt adrenaline course through his veins. The sight of the place made him really feel he was coming home, and he discovered he hadn't realised just how much he'd missed this place, even though it had only been a couple of weeks since he'd left.

Had it only been two weeks?

It felt like much longer, and he couldn't wait to stand in front of her and explain why he was back.

He hoped it would go well...

The taxi stopped and he got out and paid the driver, and then, when the car was on its way back up the lane, he turned, sucked in a deep breath to steady his nerves and rapped his knuckles on the front door.

When Lucy opened it, her eyes widening in surprise and shock, he smiled and thrust the roses towards her. 'Happy Valentine's Day.'

She gaped, took the roses and touched them to her nose to inhale their scent. 'Owen! What are you *doing* here?'

'I'm here to speak to you. May I come in?'

'Of course! Of course you can!'

She stepped back and he passed her by, resisting the urge to peck her on the cheek. They needed to talk first, and he had a lot to say.

'Would you like a hot drink?' she asked.

'Whatever you're making will be fine.'

Lucy couldn't quite believe her eyes! Owen! Back home! Why on earth was he here? Had her dreams and wishes and the pleas she had made in Carrigan's Cove brought her love back to her, if only for one day? It was going to be torturous if he had to leave again, but right now she was so happy he was here, so that she could look at him once more, bathe in the sound of his voice and his smile and his focus.

As she made the tea she realised her hands were trembling, so she put the mugs on a tray, with some biscuits that she'd made in Josie's kitchen—white chocolate chip and cranberry—and carried it through to the lounge.

He was standing by the fireplace, looking around. 'I see you've been making some changes.'

'Just one or two. I'm so happy to see you. Are you just here for the day?' She passed him his mug of tea and offered him the biscuits.

'No, not for the day. Did you make these?'

She nodded. 'I've been doing a lot of baking since you left. It's been quite therapeutic. Although I may have put on a few pounds…'

He wasn't only here for the day? Where was he staying? At his parents' place? A B&B? So many questions!

He settled down beside her on the sofa.

'How's the new clinic?' she asked.

'Good. It's been good. A great group of people. But that's not what I'm here to talk about.'

'Oh. Okay.'

She would let him speak, then. Clearly he had something he wanted to say, and she would hear it. Anything to keep him here a little longer. She'd missed him so much! To have him here, sitting next to her on the couch…it was like a dream come true, even though her inner voice kept telling her to be sensible, not to get carried away, that nothing had changed.

'I'm here to talk about us.'

She swallowed. Hadn't they already been through this? Was he here to rake over old ground?

'Us?'

'Yes. I've had time to think about us since I've been away, and I've come to a few conclusions.'

'Okay…'

'We both want the same thing. A family. A happy future.'

'Owen, we—'

'Please, Lucy. Let me finish.'

She nodded.

'Everybody has dreams for the future—and, yes, my dream was to build a family and hold my own children in my arms. That's been a dream I've had since I was small, really. I wanted to build my career first, which I did, and then to find love. Which I also did. Twice.' He smiled.

She couldn't help but smile back. He hadn't expressly said *I love you*, but it was close. It meant the same thing and it was good to hear. Good to hear that things hadn't just been one-sided.

'I met you. And you're wonderful, and complicated, and caring, and all I could ever want. I thought about that when I was gone. The *all I could ever want* part. I needed to examine that. I needed to look at it carefully and see if that was true—because if it was, then I had some decisions to make.'

She could feel tears burning behind her eyes. Happy tears. Confused tears.

'And you *are* all I could ever want. You make me so happy, Lucy. The love I feel for you is…something that I can't adequately describe! Simple words don't do it justice. The time I spent away from you was the most painful time in my life. I couldn't understand why I was doing it, and I kept coming back to those words that you said about me wanting to have a child of my own. Yes, that was my dream. But sometimes, Lucy, dreams have to change. Life isn't perfect. It throws spanners in the works. Yes, a child of my own would be wonderful—but it's not the be all and end all for me. Being with you is what matters to me. And if we choose to have a child or children in other ways, or not at all, then that's perfect. That's my new dream. Being with you. Anything else is icing on the cake.'

He smiled and reached into his trouser pocket, pulled out a small velvet-lined box.

Lucy sucked in a breath at seeing it. Was this really happening? Was he about to propose? Was he offering her everything? A future? Happiness? Was being with her really enough for him? He'd said that it was!

'Owen…' She was in tears now. Happy tears. He was

saying all the right things. All the wonderful things. 'Are you sure? Because that's a big change to your dreams.'

'I'm incredibly sure. I love you, Lucy. More than you could ever know. I love you, and I'll never leave you, and whatever kind of future we build will be perfect—because it will have been created by us. We can build a family, if we want one, and it will be *our* family, chosen by *us*, no matter how it's made. No matter how it comes to our door and into our hearts, it will be ours. And if that means babies, or dogs, or cats, or rabbits...' He laughed as he flipped open the box, revealing a beautiful diamond ring. 'Then it will be ours. And perfect. So, Lucy Childs. Would you do me the honour of agreeing to marry me? And making me the happiest man in the whole wide world?'

She was crying with joy. With happiness. With overflowing ecstasy and delight. She wanted Owen more than anything. Loved him more than anything. And that was the key. She loved him more than anything else. And he was right. They could create a family in many different ways.

'Yes! Yes, I will!'

She threw herself into his arms, squeezing him tight, and then they both pulled back to look at each other with such happiness and love in their hearts it was flowing out of their eyes. And then they were kissing. Kissing each other with every ounce of their being. Kissing like lovers long separated. Kissing as if they'd never been apart.

The world had been put right again.

The ache in their hearts was gone.

EPILOGUE

Lucy and Owen had been sitting in the hospital waiting room for some time. In reality, it had probably only been fifteen minutes or so, but their nerves, their excitement, their hope and the endless minutes of no one coming back into the room, made it seem triple that.

'Do you think there's a problem?' Lucy asked.

Owen held her hand. 'I hope not. Do you want me to go and check?'

She shook her head. 'No. Let's give it another five minutes.'

It seemed silly, but in her mind she felt that if Owen did go out there, then somehow this day would come crumbling down around them—that only by staying in this room, where they'd been told to wait, would everything go right.

Her gaze went to the clock for the umpteenth time. 'You'd think they wouldn't have such a loud clock in such a small room.'

Owen smiled and squeezed her fingers tight.

And then they heard the clack of the woman's heels. The woman called Amber, who had told them to wait there.

She was coming back.

They both stood up, hearts pounding, stomachs churning. This was it. They'd waited such a long time for this. Had looked into all their options and decided which way they wanted to go. Whether to go for surrogacy with a donor egg, or fostering, or adoption.

They'd decided on adoption.

The paperwork had been complicated. Endless. The questions and assessments they'd gone through had seemed they would never finish—until one day they'd been approved.

That day had been a red-letter day. A day of celebration. And then another wait had begun. The wait for someone they would match with.

And then the call had come through. A young girl who wanted her child to have a better life than the one she could provide. A young girl who wanted to do right by her baby…who knew her own limitations, who loved her child enough to give her the chance of a better start elsewhere.

Lucy and Owen had been over the moon at the news that they were to get a newborn. The mother didn't want to meet them, but she knew all about them. Knew that they were both doctors. It was enough reassurance for her. The agency knew what they were doing, and she knew they would only give her precious child to people who could be trusted to put her child first and raise her as their own.

The door opened.

Lucy sucked in a breath.

Amber came in with a baby wrapped in a pink blanket, wearing a soft white knitted hat. 'Say hello to your daughter.'

Lucy stepped forward to take her, her arms hungry for the feel of a newborn baby, her heart expanding with love in that instant as she took in her daughter's features.

She was sleeping. Her eyes were closed. And she was the most beautiful thing that Lucy had ever seen.

'Owen, look! Isn't she wonderful?'

Owen pulled the blanket back a little, to see her face more clearly. 'She is.'

She heard the tears in his voice. The emotion. And she looked up and cradled his cheek in her hand as she began to cry herself.

'I'll give you some time to bond. If you need me, I'll be outside.'

Amber quietly left the room and they sank down on to the couch and just gazed in adoration at their new baby daughter.

'She's just so perfect. Look at her tiny fingers!' Lucy touched her daughter's fingers and was blessed when the baby gripped her index finger tightly.

'Can I hold her?'

'Of course you can… Daddy.'

Lucy smiled and wiped her eyes after passing the baby to Owen. He looked so wonderful, cradling his daughter in his arms. All the angst, all the pain, all the waiting, was worth it for this moment in time.

'I know we said we'd call her Daisy… Do you think it suits her? I do.'

'She's a Daisy, all right.'

Lucy leaned into Owen, her head resting on his shoulder as they both beamed in delight at their little girl.

They would give her a wonderful life.

She would be loved so much.

This was a family they had created together.

* * * * *

COMING SOON!

MILLS & BOON

THE HEART OF ROMANCE

A ROMANCE FOR EVERY READER

MODERN

Prepare to be swept off your feet by sophisticated, sexy and seductive heroes, in some of the world's most glamourous and romantic locations, where power and passion collide.

ISTORICAL

Escape with historical heroes from time gone by. Whether your passion is for wicked Regency Rakes, muscled Vikings or rugged Highlanders, awaken the romance of the past.

MEDICAL

Set your pulse racing with dedicated, delectable doctors in the high-pressure world of medicine, where emotions run high and passion, comfort and love are the best medicine.

True Love

Celebrate true love with tender stories of heartfelt romance, from the rush of falling in love to the joy a new baby can bring, and a focus on the emotional heart of a relationship.

Desire

Indulge in secrets and scandal, intense drama and plenty of sizzling hot action with powerful and passionate heroes who have it all: wealth, status, good looks…everything but the right woman.

EROES

Experience all the excitement of a gripping thriller, with an intense romance at its heart. Resourceful, true-to-life women and strong, fearless men face danger and desire - a killer combination!

To see which titles are coming soon, please visit

millsandboon.co.uk/nextmonth

MILLS & BOON

Coming next month

SECRET FROM THEIR LA NIGHT
Julie Danvers

Last night was just a fluke. It doesn't have to mean anything. It doesn't have to be a slippery slope back into old patterns. She'd simply had a moment of weakness, brought on by loneliness and old memories, and she'd given in to temptation. With time, she could forgive herself for that. But first, she needed to find her shoes.

Ah. She spied the pointed toe of one ballet flat poking out from beneath the bed. She gathered up her shoes, not bothering to put them on. Her own room was only a few floors away, and it was early enough that the halls were still empty. She turned the doorknob; the door creaked as she opened it, and she slowed so it would open quietly. At least she hadn't lost her silent creeping skills.

As she stepped out, Daniel turned over in his sleep, and her heart rose in her throat. His snores paused, and for a moment she was certain he'd woken up. But then she relaxed as his breathing returned to a slow, even pace. He really was very attractive, with his dark, tousled hair and his barely shaven stubble. But great hair or not, she needed to put last night behind her. Daniel, fun as he had been, represented a past she had tried her best to forget, and the past was where he needed to stay.

One brisk shower later, Emily was back in professional mode. She took a cab to the convention center and found the right conference room a few moments before orientation was scheduled to begin. She was the last one into the meeting, but only just; a few other stragglers were still hanging their jackets when she arrived. She took the last seat available, next to a dark-haired physician who turned to greet her.

Her stomach dropped.

His brown eyes widened.

Emily was completely tongue-tied, but somehow, he was able to speak.

"Dr. Daniel Labarr," he said, holding out one hand. "I do believe we've met."

Continue reading
SECRET FROM THEIR LA NIGHT
Julie Danvers

Available next month
www.millsandboon.co.uk